AFTER 5

A JENNIFER CLOUD NOVEL

JANET LEIGH

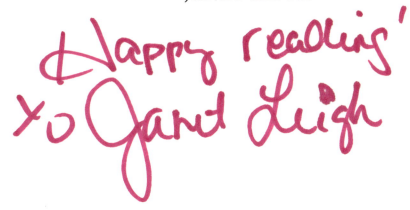

Happy reading!
xo Janet Leigh

JANET LEIGH BOOKS

After 5
A Jennifer Cloud Novel

Janet Leigh

This is a work of fiction, names, characters, businesses, places, events, locales, and incidents are either the products of the author's imagination or used in a fictitious manner. Any resemblance to actual persons, living or dead, or actual events is purely coincidental.

~

Edited by: Penni Askew

Cover by: Lindsey Lewellen

For my great great Grandfather
PVT. Samuel M. Raney
34 Tennessee Infantry CSA
&
Matt Bryant
Every family should have a historian.
My family is one of the lucky ones.

CHAPTER 1

Forrest Gump said, "Life is like a box of chocolates, you never know what you're gonna get." Lately, my life choices have mirrored my chocolate selections—full of god-awful molasses. Whoever thought chocolate-covered molasses would be a good thing to put in the box ought to be shot.

I'm Jennifer Cloud. I love chocolate, shoes, and a man who can make my toes curl. My current boyfriend, scratch that, EX-boyfriend, Caiyan—pronounced like the hot pepper and is analogous to his rockin' hot body—dumped me and quit his job as my defender for the World Travel Federation. He went on to plot dastardly deeds with the Mafusos, an evil family of time travelers who make my skin crawl and keep me busy making sure the past stays the way it's printed in my history books.

Normally, I wouldn't be so upset about the dumping. He asked me for time to sort out some issue he had with the bad guys. I can respect his wish to get his ducks in a row before committing to me. I have a few ducks I need to tend as well.

I consider myself to be a female version of Clark Kent. During the day, I'm a mild-mannered chiropractic assistant working at my brother's chiropractic office, and at night, under the light of the full moon, I report to the World Travel Federation, where I work as a time traveling transporter.

My defender travels to the past to prevent brigands from stealing, plundering, and wrecking the lives of those living in that time. Transporters are normally female, except for my good friend Ace. He's a transporter like me.

We must wait on base until summoned by our defenders to pick up the trash, aka brigands, and bring them to justice. Hence the reason I want to work with my defender instead of waiting around like a good girl to do his bidding. For crying out loud, this is the twenty-first century.

Before the restriction, I helped my defender with the takedown. Okay, maybe I didn't transform into a superhero to catch my mark, but somehow, I landed Superman results. My boss, Agent Jake McCoy, stamped me as lucky. He considered my skills to be less Superhero and more along the lines of Daphne from Scooby-Doo.

Jake is one of the ducks I need to tend. We had history. He was my best friend in high school, and later he showed me what the words friends with benefits meant. He left me to find his way in criminal justice, ended up working for the CIA and giving orders to the World Travel Federation, or WTF. The common acronym for the derogatory expression of disbelief is considered dual purpose for our top secret organization. And was the first word Jake uttered when he found out I inherited the gift of time travel. I didn't know myself until I experienced an unexpected escapade to the past.

The WTF deemed it unsafe for transporters to travel with their defenders. Ace was fine with the change. He preferred to wait for his defender to summon him—but not at headquarters. It encroached on his play time, and he wanted the order to remain on base during the moon cycle lifted.

Ace's defender, Brodie, preferred Ace stay as far away as possible, so he was in favor of the current rule.

I act as the lobbyist. Honestly, trying to make everyone happy caused my bottle-blond roots to darken early and the tension in my neck to limit my range of motion.

Jake offered me a test drive. I could go on a mission with my current defender, but if anything went awry, the restrictions would remain in place. In other words, if I wasn't a good girl, the WTF prohibition of the transporters stayed, and I wouldn't get the thrill of adventure I craved. If I was too awesome at my job, the transporters would be sent alongside the defenders, and Ace wouldn't go shopping with me anymore.

The WTF headquarters is hidden at Guantanamo Bay, Cuba. Not a place I would call home, but its isolation and perpetual military guard offers maximum security to keep the travelers hidden from the outside world à la Hogwarts style. Only the top of the top levels of the government know we exist. The CIA manages us, and the military keeps us in line.

Catching the brigands is always the hard part. Jake recognized having a transporter to assist the defender is more efficient, even if the transporter may find herself in a few awkward situations. At least he was supporting my cause.

The fringe benefit to my job is being able to lateral travel when the moon cycle is phased out of the full moon. I can pop over to Milan during fashion week in the blink of an eye.

Currently, my situation involves traveling with my defender, a gorgeous blond god named Marco, and the reason I found my gift in the first place. He secretly delivered my key-which gives me the power to time travel-and my vessel to me after my sweet, great-aunt Elma Cloud died. My vessel is a rusty old outhouse with two seats, one for me and one for my passenger. On a busy day, I can make room for two passengers.

Traveling with Marco is difficult, particularly when it's been months since I've had any sexy time. My cousin, Gertie, tells me I've been a royal pain in the ass. I'm trying to deal with the reason Caiyan ditched me, not hump the first guy who comes along—even if Marco and I have a sexual tension that sparks a fire from a distance equivalent to a football field.

Bringing me full circle to capture a brigand and figure out why my boyfriend, pardon, ex-boyfriend needed to join the bad guys and leave our relationship on the cooling rack.

I rubbed the back of my neck and surveyed the people around me. Dressed in basic pilgrim attire, the women covered their heads with a cap or bonnet and clothed their bodies from wrist to toe as they went about their daily chores. The men seemed to be lingering in the pubs.

Marco and I took a break from hunting our mark to find food. We searched for one of the few places offering a meal in the Puritan town of Salem, Massachusetts.

Our seer, a retired time traveler with the gift of second sight, can locate a traveler who has crossed the time portal. He informed us the Mafuso transporter jumped to this location. We were ordered to follow her.

Odd she jumped without a defender, but the Mafusos weren't doing things like normal lately. A few months ago, Marco and I had followed the oldest of the time traveling Mafuso grandchildren, Mortas, to 1927. He attended game three of the World Series and the only thing stolen were bases by the Yankees. I was downright giddy to watch the all-star lineup known as "Murderer's Row" which included the Sultan of Swat, Babe Ruth. He hit a home run in the bottom of the seventh and Marco was beside himself, cheering like a crazed fan. We both agreed, rooting for the legends in the original Yankee stadium was worth the risk.

Gian-Carlo Mafuso has three time traveling grandchildren I refer to as the three m's. They consist of Mortas, Mahlia, his younger sister and their only transporter, and their youngest brother, Mitchell. Mahlia looks like Megan Fox and shoots a pistol like John Wayne. Mitchell's been on the outs with the family ever since he screwed up a time travel and hasn't seen much action.

Marco stopped outside Beadles Tavern. "I'm thirsty, let's go inside and grab a drink."

We had money left over from living on salted cod and goats' milk for the last two days.

"Good morrow," a sturdy woman greeted as we entered. The

patrons were a mix of Puritans, farmers, and fishermen from the port. A few heads turned in our direction. We sat down at one of the tables.

The woman who greeted us came to our table and asked if we wanted a mug of ale. I pegged her to be late fifties, but in this time, people didn't age well, if at all.

"Two," Marco said.

"Let us see your coin." Her reference of "us" had me glancing over my shoulder expecting to see her burley husband, or maybe a bouncer, behind me. When I figured out she meant only herself, I relaxed.

She eyed Marco as he removed the coin from his pocket.

"Are ye from another village?" She awarded us a view of her rotten teeth when Marco produced enough coin to buy the place.

"Yes." I answered. Marco handed her the money.

"Pray thee, tell me the one from whence you come?"

Marco hesitated, and I answered, "Boston."

"Are ye here to see the witches turned out?"

Marco gave an uncommitted shrug and shook his head slowly.

"We're traveling to visit relatives in Newberry's town," I added, and felt an uneasiness to her barrage of questions.

Her gaze drifted between us.

"We've been recently married," Marco said. He grabbed my hand and stared at me like a lovesick puppy. "A man's heart is endeared to the woman he loves, he dreams of her in the night, hath her in his eye and apprehension when he awakes."

He raised my hand and brushed a kiss across my knuckles.

The woman's eyes shined. "Yes, my Mr. Beadle felt that way before he met our heavenly father. He left me the tavern." She waved her hand, indicating all of this was hers to manage, and retreated to get our ale.

"Geesh. What's with her? She asked more questions than my cousin Hildy." I removed my hand from Marco's. The heat generated between us made my palm sweaty.

"I don't think the Puritans approve of an unmarried couple traveling together." He reached for my hand again.

"What's with the fancy language?" I asked him, drawing my hand away.

"It's a quote from Thomas Hooker."

When I gave him a blank stare, he sighed. "Jen, you really need to study before you travel. Thomas Hooker was a prominent Puritan colonial leader. He founded the town of Hartford."

"In Connecticut, where the University of Hartford is?"

"Yeah, they have a parade. Haven't you ever heard the saying 'Hartford was founded by a Hooker'?"

"Uhm, no."

Marco tsked me, then flashed his gorgeous smile at the tavern owner as she brought us two mugs of a brown liquid. She blushed slightly, plopped them down on the table, and left to help other customers.

I took one sip and spit the foul liquid back into the mug.

"You don't like it?" Marco chuckled and upended his mug.

"It tastes like pancake syrup and Christmas trees."

"It's a form of mead combined with molasses."

I made a sour face, and he grinned at me. The deep dimple cut into his chin winked back at me. I licked the sickening sweet off my lips and cursed myself for wanting to run my tongue down the rugged line of his square jaw and kiss the indention.

His grin changed to a firm line. He tipped his head and I followed his gaze toward the door. A man entered and glanced around the room. Marco bowed his head down and I mirrored his move, adjusting my bonnet to hide my face as the man took a seat at the counter behind me.

"Who's that man?"

"I believe it's Toches."

I spun around to get a better look at the brigand I'd almost single-handedly taken down in Berlin. His back was to me as he ordered a mug of ale.

"It doesn't look like Toecheese." I said turning back around to face Marco.

A smile pulled at Marco's mouth. My mispronunciation the first time I heard Toches's name became my nickname for the evil brigand and gave my fellow defenders a chuckle. "He's good at changing his appearance."

Kishin Toches was a nasty brigand I had encountered during a trip back to the Second World War. He had the special gift of personifying others. He took a key that didn't belong to him and I had to take it back. He wasn't happy about the outcome, and I'd been on his shit list ever since.

"Are you sure? I thought Mahlia made the jump, how come he didn't register?"

Marco shrugged. "I know as much as you do. Maybe Mahlia is transporting for him."

"I'm surprised they let him travel. I mean, he doesn't have a key, and I doubt Gian-Carlo would give him one. Maybe she dumped him here. Are you positive it's him?" I didn't want to harass a local.

"Yeah, beady eyes, slouched gait, and he didn't acknowledge a single soul. Besides, he's imitating Rasputin—his beard's too nineteenth century for this time."

I did a double take, and sure enough the doppelgänger of the Russian religious charlatan sat at the counter sipping sludge.

"Should we wait and follow him?" I asked Marco.

"No, the moon cycle is closing. I'm hungry, and I need a taco."

"And grouchy."

"I'm not grouchy, traveling with you makes me uhm…irritable."

"Why is that?"

"You know what I mean." *He meant horny.*

"What would you like to do?" I asked.

"Let's go ask him why he's here?"

"Ask him?" Allowing a mark to make us wasn't on the smartest things for a WTF agent to-do list.

"Yep, unless you can think of a faster way to get to the bottom of this."

I shrugged, agreeing with his plan. Tacos sounded good to me, too.

Marco reflected my nod. He rose, taking his mug with him. I left mine on the table. We bookended the sneaky brigand. His thin frame and squirrelly attitude made him a little less scary than Mortas, but he was unstable. Toches might pull out a gun and shoot us, regardless that when a time traveler kills another time traveler they also die.

"Hey Kishin, fancy meeting you here," Marco said to Toches as he took the stool next to him.

Toches's head jerked up from his ale, and he started to bolt out the opposite side of his chair, but I blocked him.

"You can't leave without paying the barkeep, that would be very rude of you." I wagged a finger at him.

Marco placed a hand on Toches's shoulder. He sat down with a thud and pulled his mug of ale closer.

"I'm here on vacation," he said, an evil grinch grin turning up the corners of his mouth.

"What kind of vacation?" Marco asked him.

"The kind you take when a guy wants to go somewhere for the hell of it."

Marco pondered this idea for a minute, and I wondered how long it had been since Marco had been on vacation. Then I remembered I hadn't been on a vacation in a long time. Jake owed us some down time.

"Why would you take a vacation to Salem in 1692?" I asked him.

"I want to see one of them witches burned at the stake." He took a sip from his mug, and his previously underdeveloped bicep strained against his shirt sleeve.

The last time I saw Toches, he was trapped in 1945 pretending to be Adolf Hitler with slick hair, arrogant attitude, and identical evil 'stache, since the vessel determined the clothes and hair. There were times when my defenders would have a full beard or hair down to their waist. This trip, the mustache had been traded for a scraggly beard and there was a little more buff to his wiry frame. Since the vessel didn't turn a traveler into Captain America, I assumed the rat had seen time at the gym.

"Toecheese—" I began.

"Stop calling me that. My name is Toches, and that's Mr. Toches to you."

Marco smiled and took a long pull from his mug.

"What are you really doing here?" I asked.

"I told you. I'm on a fun trip."

"A fun trip?" Marco questioned, looking around the sparse room and the peasantry style clothing of the customers.

"Yep, Gian-Carlo ordered us to have a good time. Those were his exact words. I want to see a witch. It's on my bucket list."

"You know witches don't exist, right?" I arched an eyebrow, and he huffed at me.

"Besides," Marco said. "They don't burn witches at the stake in Salem."

He eyed Marco then turned his attention toward me. "It seems your Scottish lover boy has been replaced with tall, blond, and stupid."

A low growl rumbled from Marco's throat, and I shook my head to deter him from tossing Toches across the room.

"He's right. They don't burn the people accused of witchcraft here, they hang them."

Toches wrinkled his nose in disgust. "Really...damn."

"And don't let these Puritans hear you cuss, or you'll find a noose around your neck," Marco warned.

"Why don't the two of you toddle on back to your secret lair and save your advice for someone who gives a shit." Toches took a drink of the ale and made a face.

I agreed. It gave craft beer a whole new meaning.

"Speaking of Caiyan," I referred back to his mention of my Scottish ex-boyfriend. "Where's Gian-Carlo sending him and how is he getting there?"

"That guy needs to go back and fight for the good guys. He doesn't have the balls to work for the Mafusos," Toches snickered.

"I'm surprised you feel that way. Since he's a talented grifter, you'd figure he'd be valuable to Gian-Carlo."

"Oh, Gian-Carlo's all stoked about him joining up, even wants to make him a full-fledged member, but there's not enough keys. I don't have one, thanks to you by the way. I had the Sleigh key in my grasp, then you took it from me."

Not exactly what happened, but he was brooding and spilling his candy, so I let him speak.

"Whose key are you wearing?" I asked.

"That's a secret." He laid his hand over the top collar of his shirt.

A few moments later, a man and two young girls came inside the tavern. They took a table toward the back. As I glanced around the room, people were whispering and staring in our direction. Not good. My inner voice made the let's get going signal. I ignored her for the moment. I needed more information about Caiyan.

"What does Gian-Carlo want with McGregor?" Marco asked.

Toches was silent. He drank his ale, and a bowl of pottage was placed in front of him by a tavern worker. He took a bite and nodded kindly at the server.

My stomach growled when the aroma of the stew-like dish hit my nostrils, but I was determined to find out where Caiyan was traveling. Marco wasn't so determined.

"If you tell us why Gian-Carlo wants McGregor, then we'll leave you in peace to enjoy your vacation."

"We will?" I questioned.

Toches took another bite and chewed the request along with his meal. "The Scot knows of a key Gian-Carlo's been after for some time. Gian-Carlo's offered him a deal. If he takes Mortas to find the key and satisfies the remaining details of the contract, Gian-Carlo will return his key."

"Why do they want McGregor to get the key? Why don't they go get it themselves?" Marco asked.

"He's the only one who knows the location, and he's not telling, only showing." Toches took another spoonful of the stew.

"What happens after they get the key?" I asked.

"Gian-Carlo has a plan, not one I agree with. He's going to induct your Scot into the Mafusos and give him his key back, if he does exactly what Gian-Carlo's ordered."

"What are the orders?" Marco asked.

Toches face dropped. "I'm not going to tell you the details. Now shoo. You promised."

Huh. I wondered what these details involved.

A group of three men entered the tavern and were led upstairs by the woman who had waited on us earlier.

Toches pushed his empty mug away from him as the men brought a young woman down the flight of stairs. She couldn't have been more than seventeen. Her hands were bound behind her back. Her amber eyes went wide as the patrons accused her of being a witch, and the men led her toward the exit.

Someone yelled, "Take her to the gallows!

The crowd emptied out of the tavern into the cobblestone streets.

A church bell tolled in the distance, and Toches slipped off his stool. "Showtime. Catch you two troublemakers on the flip side."

We walked outside. The frightened young woman was in the clutches of a stout man who reminded me of a whiskey barrel.

Another man held a bible open in his long, slim hands and his mouth danced the doorknocker beard he sported as he ranted on about witches and sins.

The townspeople gathered around the bible man, cheering and showing their support. I categorized him under evil-eyed authoritative figure, right next to David Koresh.

"Take her to Proctor's," the people chorused. "The hanging tree!"

The young woman was loaded into a haycart and a mess of townspeople followed behind her as the cart rolled away.

Toches gave a crooked smile. "Think I'll get a front row seat."

He was a sick dude.

"Should we follow him?" I asked Marco. "We did promise to leave, but..." I glanced toward the unruly crowd.

He shrugged. "I guess."

Marco and I followed Toches and the group of rabble-rousers toward the edge of town. Bits of hay floated off the cart as it rattled down the cobblestone road.

The entourage stopped at the edge of a hill. The people clustered together in front of a sturdy tree. A rope hung from one of its thick branches and swung gently in the summer breeze.

Proctor's Ledge. I remembered reading about the area believed to be the site of the hangings of the famous witch trials. In my time, the small knoll stood uphill from a CVS and wasn't anything spectacular. It was hard to imagine the scene before me, and now that I was here, my stomach turned.

The crowd watched as the young woman was unloaded from the cart. Straws of hay clung to her hair and clothes. The men pulled the stumbling woman toward the makeshift ladder she would stand on to end her life. Toches was, as promised, front and center. Marco and I stood watching the mob.

"We should help her," I said.

"No," Marco said firmly. "You know the rules. We watch from a distance. Toches hasn't done anything to arrest him for, yet."

The crowd's jeers heightened, and I fought off a roil of nausea.

"Marco, we have to do something. We can't let that innocent woman hang."

"If you screw up the past, Jake won't let you travel again."

I fidgeted and racked my brain for the names and dates of the people accused of witchcraft and hung in Salem. "I don't recall this one. I thought the first hanging was on June 10th?"

"Jen, it happened. The history books don't always have a correct accounting of the past. You have to get over the fact that things occurred in history that weren't fair or humane."

"I know but..."

"We're here to watch our mark, arrest him if he steals or kills, period."

The whiskey barrel hauled the young woman to the tree. The people threw rotten food at her and called her names. *Sinner...Devil worshiper...witch.*

The man with the bible stood on a fallen log, elevating him like the preacher at Sunday service. He shouted a passage to the crowd. The crescendo of his voice rose above the people, creating a frenzy of excitement throughout the crowd.

"I'll risk it," I said to him and pleaded with my baby blues. A girl's gotta use what a girl's got to use.

He rolled his eyes heavenward, huffed, and relented. His shoulders sagged and he mumbled. "OK, I'll see what I can do, but you'd better be ready to leave as soon as I free the girl. These people are going to be upset they didn't see a good show."

"Thanks." I leaned up and gave him a peck on the cheek.

We scanned the area, searching for the best possible place to cause a diversion so Marco could free the young woman.

She stepped up onto a short platform built directly under the tree. The crowd grew quiet, waiting for the last words from the woman found guilty of witchcraft.

"I am not a witch," she shouted to the crowd.

The people cried out at her. "Speak thy Lord's Prayer." And "The devil has possessed her."

I hoped Marco made his decision quickly. The crowd was growing intense.

"I'm going to take the right side and grab her before he pushes her off the platform. You stay close so we can get out of Dodge immediately after," Marco said.

As we made our way closer to the stage, I bumped into a stooped, cloaked woman. She turned toward me, her wise blue eyes peering at me from under her hood.

"Pray thee, pardon," I said to her.

She smiled and her eyes twinkled. A feeling of déjà vu struck me. I shrugged it off and the old woman made her way through the crowd. Everyone wanted a front row seat.

Marco and I moved closer. We had to hurry for Marco to reach her in time.

Whiskey Barrel served as the executioner. He reached for the rope.

Marco moved, ready to spring into action.

Before Marco could make his move, and before Whiskey Barrel could slide the noose around her neck, Toches tackled the man.

Toches, Whiskey Barrel, and the young woman fell off the platform and tumbled head over tail into a roll down the short hill, ending at the haycart.

Marco and I stood slack-jawed along with the angry onlookers.

A uniform gasp sounded from the crowd, followed by whispers of the devil. I added my gasp as Toches had regained his footing and held up a Bic lighter.

The crowd took a step back at the sight of the small fire flickering from his fist.

He proceeded to set the hay in the cart on fire.

The fire caught quickly and spread to the cart, creating a billow of smoke. Through the smoke, I saw the young woman retreat into the woods alongside the cloaked figure I bumped into earlier. Maybe the old woman was a relative of the girl. Good for her.

Toches vanished behind the veil of smoke, and I assumed he'd made a break for wherever he'd come from.

The fire raged, and I wondered if Proctor's tree would become the famous witch hanging tree after all.

The townspeople were in a chaotic frenzy trying to douse the fire. Men were shouting, teenage girls were falling on the ground like the young woman had bewitched them upon her escape.

The bible man preached the good word from his log.

"What are the chances Toches's conscious got the best of him, and he saved that girl without any hidden agenda?" I asked Marco.

"Doubtful, but it's safe for us to go," Marco said. "Toches will be heading for his vessel. We can piece together the intel at base."

I turned to walk toward the opposite end of town. There was an old homestead site in the middle of the woods we used for landing. The log home had fallen into disrepair but offered us a thick grove of trees that allowed us to safely call our vessels.

As we walked toward the woods, a frantic shout came from behind us.

"Run you idiots!"

Toches flew past us, followed by a mob of angry Puritans.

"There, those people were speaking with the witch!" A young girl, who couldn't have been more than thirteen, pointed her finger at us. I recognized her from the tavern.

"Get them!" a voice from the mob shouted.

I stood mouth gaping, not believing what I was seeing.

Marco grabbed my hand and pulled me along, one hand on his key and the other dragging me beside him. He mumbled as he ran.

The landscape blurred around me, and a warped sensation passed through my body like I was running inside a bubble. His gift slowed time and the mob seemed to drift off into the background as I stumbled along behind him.

When the time warp returned to normal, Toches hightailed it into the woods and I lost sight of him. Marco released my hand.

The few minutes he was able to stall time allowed us to cut through the woods and double back toward our clearing. We ran hard, cutting through the thick underbrush.

Marco was steps in front of me. We were almost to the clearing when I tripped over something large and fell face down in the muck of the forest floor. I lifted my head and looked behind me to see Toches lying face up in a mangle of vines.

"What the hell?" Marco asked as he returned to help me. He leaned over Toches, panting hard, his hands on his knees.

I moved over the brigand's lifeless body and felt for a pulse in his neck.

"He's got a pulse." I saw the slow rhythm of his chest. "And he's breathing."

A giant welt bloomed on the pale skin of his forehead.

Marco urged me on, the faint sound of people shouting in the distance alerted me. *Hurry.*

"Let's go," Marco commanded.

"We'll have to take him with us."

"Why?"

"We can't leave him here. They'll hang him."

Marco huffed.

I untied the collar of Toches's shirt.

"What are you doing? We need to get out of here!"

"I have to see if he's wearing Caiyan's key."

"Jen," Marco urged.

"I have to take it from him before he comes to," I said. I knew I'd be breaking a WTF rule, but Caiyan's key was at stake. I opened his shirt and exposed the shiny key gleaming around his thin neck.

"It's Mahlia's key," I said, dumbfounded. "I can't believe she'd give her key to this scumbag."

Just as I said the words, Marco grunted and flew forward, landing on his hands and knees a few inches from me.

"What the fu...?" he cried out, rolling around on his back in pain.

I didn't hear a gunshot, but scooted over to him, keeping my body low to the ground. I ran my hands over his back, searching. "Hold still. Where are you hit?"

Marco sat up. I didn't see any blood seeping through his shirt.

"Am I shot?" he asked, trying to look at his back.

"Fare thee well, witches!" A voice sounded from up in the trees. I followed the voice to two young boys armed with slingshots.

"Marco, you were hit by a stone," I said as another flew inches from my face.

He turned and saw the boys. Dodging flying stones, he stood and marched toward the tree.

The boys scampered down the trunk to flee. He grabbed them by the collars of their shirts as they reached the bottom and jerked them away from the tree.

"What should we do with them?" I asked, joining Marco and adding a witch cackle for good measure.

"I'm going to feed them to my dragon." Marco released them and put his hand to his key. In seconds his vessel, a shiny red racecar, materialized in the clearing.

"'Tis a dragon," the taller of the two boys said. They stared as if in a hypnotic trance, no longer struggling or calling for their parents.

I summoned my vessel, and the boys stood slack-jawed.

"The witch lives in a privy." They frowned with disappointment.

"Not everyone gets a dragon," I said to them.

"Pray thee, do not turn us to toads," the shorter one said.

"Don't tell anyone you saw us, or I'll find you, and my dragon will burn down your houses..." Marco paused, "and kill your mothers!"

The boys began to cry, nodding their heads as snot and tears wet their dirty faces.

"Away with you boys!" Marco shouted. They turned tail and ran.

"Did you have to threaten to kill their mothers?" I asked Marco as he helped me tie up Toches and load him into my vessel.

"It's a good threat. No boy wants to lose his mother at ten. That comes much later...like fifteen."

I cocked a brow at him.

"Oh, we want them back again around twenty-one, so it's all good." He stepped back from my outhouse. "Take him to Gitmo, and I'll meet you there."

I climbed in next to Toches. "We need to cover his face if I'm going to take him back to headquarters."

Marco's gaze ran the length of my dress.

"What do you suggest? I arrive at headquarters naked?"

"I don't know, be creative." He slammed the door.

I tried to figure out what to use to blindfold my unconscious brigand. Normally, women of this time didn't wear panties, but I had persuaded my vessel to provide me with the type of breeches worn by men. What can I say, traipsing around in the seventeenth century without any underwear made me nervous.

I slipped off the pair of linen breeches and wrapped them over his head. If he woke up, at least he'd have trouble seeing through the fabric until Jake could provide a hood.

CHAPTER 2

My outhouse landed with a thunk. I sighed with relief at the familiar sound of wood on cement. Thankfully, the landing grid in the hangar of the WTF consisted of twelve by twelve concrete squares embedded with special wiring and neodymium magnets to attract our vessels to the correct spot. The advanced technology prevented me from plopping down in the middle of Camp Delta and causing a national security alert.

The door to my vessel was yanked open. I blinked rapidly as the bright fluorescent lights from the hangar beamed in through the open door.

Jake stood front and center dressed in his normal WTF work uniform of black suit, white dress shirt, and black tie. Two WTF employees lurked behind him, also clad in black suits. The three of them—all sporting short-cropped hair, muscle, and alpha male attitude—looked like the next act in Magic Mike.

Marco joined Jake, and the foursome stared up at me. How did he always beat me back to base?

A wide smile broke out on Marco's face.

Jake's shoulders shook as he bit into his bottom lip, trying to contain the laughter he held inside.

The men in black smiled, something I had never seen them do. I glanced over at Toches, then did a double take. The outhouse had changed me back into present day clothes. My Yumi Kim floral summer sundress and Jimmy Choo espadrille cork wedges I'd bought at Nordstrom Rack for seventy percent off were back in place, along with my VS red lacy thong currently strapped across my passenger's forehead. One eye was covered with the lace and blocked nothing.

Jake stepped up on the platform and moved to stand on the threshold of my outhouse. He slit the door, blocking the view of head-quarters with his body, and called for a hood.

Marco's laughter bellowed from the outer sanctions of the hangar.

"They were much bigger in 1692." I shrugged.

"What the Sam Hill happened to you two?" Jake's amusement was replaced with the intense tone of a stern CIA agent. "The rest of your team has returned."

"Toecheese happened," I said. Toches groaned at the mention of his name but remained obliviously unconscious.

A smile returned to Jake's lips at the mention of my nickname for Toches. "Go on."

"We found him in a tavern, and next thing you know he's running for his life with fifty angry folks behind him carrying pitchforks. It was right off the pages of Frankenstein. I understand why the monster felt the need to flee."

"Did he steal something?"

"No."

Jake hesitated. "Kill someone?"

"No."

"Why did you capture him?"

"We didn't exactly capture him. He was hit by a rock, fell, and hit his head on another rock, which knocked him out, so we saved him."

Jake huffed. "The general isn't going to like this."

"If we left him in Salem, another dead witch would be added to the history books."

"Any other infractions?"

"Not created by me," I said, mentally thanking Toches. I made it through an entire mission without changing history. If something went askew, it wasn't my doing.

Jake raised an eyebrow but didn't interrogate me any further. Knowing Jake, he was saving the good stuff for later. He reached across me and pulled my thong off the brigand's head. "I liked this one. It was my favorite."

I jerked it out of his grasp. From his demeanor, I presumed something had him fired up, and it wasn't that Marco and I came back with a brigand. There was more to his agitated tone.

"Damn, that's some goose egg." Jake motioned toward the bright red bump swelling above Toches's left eyebrow. "He'll have a humdinger of a headache when he wakes up."

"Marco has a similar one on his back," I said.

"Are you injured?" Jake asked, suddenly aware he hadn't considered my well-being.

"I'm fine. Not even a scratch."

Someone spoke to Jake. He reached behind him and produced a head cover. Securing it on the unconscious brigand, he opened my door and allowed me to exit my vessel.

I stepped down off the platform and we watched the medics load Toches on a stretcher.

"That's going to leave an ugly mark. The rock was the size of my fist and the kid had a slingshot that would make David envious and Goliath run for cover," I said to one of the medics as she gave Toches a sedative.

The drug would keep Toches floating happily in la-la land for a few hours. Enough time to doctor his wound and secure him in a cell. He'd wake up with no idea where he was or how he'd arrived.

If Jake had to release him, Toches would receive another round of the magic cocktail, and one of the transporters would be summoned to deposit him in an undisclosed location.

A beefy security guy followed behind the stretcher as it was wheeled out of the hangar, in case the magic cocktail wasn't enough to keep Toches down for the count. Marco walked with the medics, giving me a sour look as he exited the hangar.

"Where's Marco going?" I asked Jake.

"I sent him to the infirmary to have his back examined. He insisted he was all right, but I ordered him to get checked out, anyway."

Marco hated doctors, medicine, and people prodding him. I knew Jake would insist he see the doctor. Marco might say he was fine, but I imagined the welt on his back told a different story. Telling the boss he'd taken a hit explained Marco's irritation at me. He'd pay me back later for being a tattletale.

"What was Toches doing in Salem?" Jake asked me after the entourage left the area, minus one expressionless security officer who loomed at the entrance.

"He wanted to see a witch burn," I answered.

"They didn't burn witches in Salem."

"That's what I told him."

"You spoke to him?" Jake asked me, an undercurrent of irritation lacing the tone of his question.

"It was more of an interrogation."

"That's it?"

"As far as I could tell. He saved a woman accused of witchcraft, but there wasn't any sign of a key, and I didn't get any sensations of another traveler among the mob of angry peasants chasing us into the woods."

Jake paused and arched an eyebrow at me. "Why were they chasing you?"

Oops. I wasn't going to mention we were seen speaking with Toches in the tavern. "Guilt by association. A girl who couldn't have been more than twelve accused Toecheese of being a witch, and she might have seen us together at the tavern."

"Do I even need to ask why you were having a beer with a dangerous brigand?" Jake sighed.

"Um, convenience?" I bit my lower lip. *Did I say we had a beer?*

"I can't hold him for saving the woman unless we can prove she's a brigand. But I'll have to confirm the changes, if any, he caused to the present.

Jake turned toward me. "Meet me in the blue room. You can

21

debrief after our meeting. The other members of your team are already there."

I saluted and received one of Jake's dark-brown puppy-dog eye rolls. Over his shoulder, Marco's Indy racecar reflected the fluorescent light. The beautiful car stretched catty-corner on the landing pad, its front end inches from the edge.

Each traveler landed on one of the pads directed in by the magnetic force. Jake and his men in black always stood toward the back wall in case the magnetic force failed and the vessel did a skid. This never happened, but it was good to take precautions.

I exited the hangar. The moon cycle began earlier in the countries to the east, allowing Jake to manage several teams in the same moon cycle.

There was a time when the British secret service controlled the travelers outside of the United States, but due to budget cuts or whatever, MI6 handed the reins off to the CIA.

We have an Eastern European unit. Most of the travelers in this unit are assigned to China, Japan, both Koreas, and parts of Vietnam. I can't be on that team because I flunked Mandarin 101. There were too many symbols for me to wrap my head around and trying to speak Chinese with my Texas drawl gave Jake permanent lines between his eyebrows.

There are no travelers from the Middle East. At least that we know of. If the insurgent, territory-controlling, religious fanatic terrorists from these countries knew we had time travelers…the world would be a different place.

There's the European unit, which Caiyan used to be a part of after my great-aint Elma died and left him without a transporter. It was the reason the obnoxious Russian criminal, Rogue, was the main brigand he followed.

Most of the travelers were combined now. We still had different teams, but a person could be assigned to any team depending on the languages they mastered and their heritage.

The Russians, as the WTF called them because two of the five travelers were from Russia, were made up of the two Russians, a beautiful Polish girl, and our newest traveler, Campy.

I walked to the blue room, stopping off at the ladies' room to pee. Using a toilet instead of urinating in the woods was top priority. I searched my locker for an extra pair of panties. It icked me out to return my thong to its original location since the red lace had contacted Kishin's drool, but going commando didn't seem appropriate.

Our conference room at the WTF, aka the blue room, had trippy eighties wallpaper met in the middle by a chair rail. The penny-pinching hand of the government didn't reach out to the secret agency located in the basement of Gitmo. Interior décor wasn't top priority. Instead, the funds were spent on soccer fields, satellite TV, and razor wire.

Thanks to Lyndon B. Johnson, the WTF was a super covert agency. The former president founded the top secret organization to help the travelers become an alliance. It also clearly divided the brigands from the righteous.

The camps of Gitmo were worn, and expensive for the government to maintain. The oblivious politicians and their lawyers tried to close the maximum security prison on a consistent basis. Only the top military officials knew of the WTF, because if the politicians knew they had time travelers who could change history, they'd piss themselves trying to overturn election results in their favor.

I entered the blue room. My team was seated around the conference table, inhaling the complimentary donuts. Everyone was present except for Ace, who was routinely late, and Marco. Casual greetings welcomed me as I poured myself a steaming cup of government-grade coffee and sat at my usual place.

"Yo, Jen," came a mouth-filled hello from Brodie. My cousin Gertie, who also happens to be my roommate, considers Brodie her boyfriend. Thanks to me, the pair has been happily hooking up.

Brodie had powdered sugar on the front of his Bob Marley t-shirt, giving Bob a Christmas feel.

I gave Brodie a finger wave and joined the group at the conference table.

"Hey cookie, you mind passing me one of those chocolate covered donut holes? The ones with the sprinkles."

I snagged a glazed donut hole and popped it in my mouth, then pushed the tray closer to Gerry. He was an irritating defender. At a little over four feet tall, the dwarf had a giant attitude. He specialized in sneaky.

Tina, his transporter, sat beside him. Her dark hair was cut in a cute bob with the right side shaved over her ear. One headphone dangled on her shoulder, the other secured firmly in her ear as her fingers moved with rapid pace over her phone.

With her Asian skin and youthful appearance, sans makeup she could pass for a boy and used this talent to persuade brigands to lower their guard. Once, I asked her why she transported for the obnoxious Gerry instead of being assigned to the Eastern European team, and she told me if she was caught in her homeland she would be executed. Good reason.

"Where's Marco?" Tina asked, and heads turned in my direction. Apprehensive eyes waited for my reply.

"We picked up Toecheese in Salem and brought him into custody," I said, and explained Marco's predicament.

When one of our team members didn't show up for the meeting, there was concern, but rarely for Marco. It was nice for someone to be concerned about him. The other defenders were a bit miffed he had joined the WTF after years of refusing to be part of the team.

Brodie and Caiyan were tight, and Brodie took Marco with an uneasy lack of trust. Gerry didn't have an opinion on the matter, and Ace slobbered uncontrollable infatuation when Marco was near.

"Poor guy," Gerry said. This caught me off guard, because Gerry never had a nice word to say about anyone. "Salem's a tough time. The guns are shit, and those people can do more damage with words and pitchforks than most outlaws with a fully loaded shotgun."

24

"Good job. Toches was due for some cell time," Brodie said, still somewhat bitter about losing the Thunder key to the brigand in a prior tussle.

A round of congrats followed for our capture. I didn't want to spoil the goodwill by explaining we had saved Toches.

"Ace and Campy caught a brigand, too. One of the Cracky boys." Gerry popped another donut hole.

"Campy?" I asked.

"Ace transported for Campy because Fredericka's on vacation." Tina answered, not taking her eyes off her phone. "They caught one of the Cracky Clan lifting the original recording of the iconic rock group Queen. The Cracky Clan were trying to steal Bohemian Rhapsody before it made its famous debut and pass it off as their own. Campy and Ace are in a debriefing with General Potts."

"Wow, Campy's first capture, impressive." I washed another donut hole down with a sip of the strong coffee.

"Totally set them up, I did," Brodie said. "If I didn't have ta chase Caiyan's mark, I'd a had them Crackys last travel."

Brodie and Caiyan were buddies. They were like Butch Cassidy and the Sundance Kid. However, Butch Cassidy took a leave of absence and left the kid a mess of brigands to clean up.

Caiyan's normal mark, Rogue, had been a thorn in my side from day one of my time travel adventure. We chased him, almost caught him once, but he was devious and slippery.

Brodie normally chased the Cracky Clan, three Irish brothers and a couple of female cousins. The Crackys never did much damage. They liked to steal things. I had a sneaky suspicion Brodie and the Crackys drank beer together at the pub during the off cycle.

Jake entered, sat down next to me, and started clicking around on his laptop. He paused and waved a hand in the air. "Give me a second. I need to get some information in the system."

"Is Campy OK?" I asked him.

"Be here in a minute." Jake focused on his screen as he answered.

A few minutes later, Ace entered, followed by Campy. A round of fist bumps congratulated Campy on his capture. Ace sat down next to me as Campy circled the room, accepting praise from his peers.

Campy was Caiyan's nephew, and the resemblance made my heart ache. He had his uncle's sly grin and quick wit but lacked the manipulation and con skills in which Caiyan excelled. I hoped Campy never found the twisted talents Caiyan perfected, but a seasoned defender needed a few lifesaving skills.

I held my fist up for a bump of congratulations, but Campy leaned down and wrapped his arms around me from behind—despite the rule of no contact between travelers or staff while on base. He squeezed me in one of his warm hugs, and I inhaled his fresh, earthy scent.

"Congrats," I said. He released me from his bear hug and snagged one of my donut holes. He sat down on the other side of Ace. His green eyes lit up as he leaned in and spoke to me.

"Can ye believe I got him on the first try?" His accent held a blend of Scottish and British. Campy grew up in England with his Scottish mother, Caiyan's sister. His father was in the wind. He spent some time with their aunt Itty in Florida, but in the last few years, the teen had turned into a handsome man.

I sent him a warm smile.

"You should have seen him," Ace babbled. "He jumped the brigand like a pro, caught him red-handed, and then took him to the ground." Ace dabbed at his eyes with the donut napkin.

"Who are you, his mother?" Gerry asked Ace.

"I can be proud of him."

"Don't forget who gave you the intel on that one," Brodie said to Campy.

"I appreciate it, dude," Campy said.

"Yes, and don't forget who gave YOU the tip," Tina said to Brodie, her eyes lifting from her phone for a brief second to make her point.

"Did you hear the news?" Ace paused for attention. "Campy has been moved to our team. The little devil." Ace gave six foot two Campy a tweak on his dimpled cheek.

I raised an eyebrow at Jake. He stopped typing and huffed. "That was classified, Ace."

"Oopsy," Ace said, placing his fingers against his lips. "My bad."

"What gives? When Caiyan returns we'll have a large team." I glanced at Campy, "Not that I don't want you on our team, but we only have three transporters." I envisioned having to wait at the WTF until a defender summoned me. Transporting for more than one defender was always a challenge. My goal of being the wingman to my defender was hindered by a transportation issue.

"When are you going to get a clue, cupcake?" Gerry frowned at me. "Your Scottish backstabber has left us high and dry to go work for the bad guys. He's probably stolen more booty in a moon cycle than I'll have in a lifetime. He's rolling in the dough."

"No, he's undercover." I glared at Gerry. "He left for our safety."

"Yeah, Uncle Cai would never sell us out," Campy added, and I welcomed the support.

Gerry huffed. "He's probably told the Mafusos of our secret location and they're waiting for the right time to infiltrate us."

"Gerry, put a sock in it, ya wee nit," Brodie shouted from down the table.

"Are you making fun of my size? I'd like to file a form 436s for discrimination against the vertically challenged."

Ace huffed. "If anyone's going to make a report of discrimination, it should be Jen and me." Ace gestured to me and then to himself. "The way you speak to us…it's disgusting."

The brawl escalated from name calling to gestures across the table.

Jake stopped typing. "Enough."

Gerry shrugged, and Ace stuck his tongue out at the dwarf. Yep, we were one step up from a preschool.

I waited for Jake to say something, anything, to support Caiyan's decision to leave the WTF.

"Agent McGregor has turned in his badge, and as far as the WTF is concerned is considered a brigand."

OK, not the words of comfort I wanted. I crossed my arms over my chest.

Jake sighed, "He gave me his word, he would not disclose our location."

The room grew quiet. Campy dropped his chin to his chest, the celebration of his victory forgotten. Caiyan hadn't contacted Campy either. The loss took its toll. Caiyan was more of a big brother to Campy than an uncle, and the only male role model he'd ever had in his young life.

Caiyan was the first WTF agent to ever work both sides of the fence. If Jake trusted him to keep his word, so would I. My inner voice began ticking off, on her fingers, all the times he lied to me. When she took off her shoes, I cut our connection.

Jake stood and relayed his laptop to the projection screen via a handheld remote. A world map appeared on the screen with each location of our recent travels marked with a red X.

"As you know, McGregor doesn't have a key, so if he's traveling it must be with Mahlia, or the Mafusos are loaning him a key. We've been trying to follow him, but so far, we haven't had any luck."

I swallowed hard. The sticky situation Caiyan had his fingers in stuck in my throat along with the glazed donut hole.

"Those wanker brigands have us on a wild goose chase," Brodie said. "We've been following the Mafusos, but there's been no sign of McGregor."

"I agree," I said. "We thought we were searching Salem for Mahlia but found Toecheese instead. He told us he wanted to see a witch burn at the stake."

Campy's eyes widened like he might also find that cool. I frowned at him and he schooled his face. Shameful.

"They didn't burn witches—" Gerry started.

"Yep, that's what we told him." I ended the sentence for him.

Gerry leaned forward and interlocked his fingers on the table. "Same for us." He tilted his head Tina's direction. "We chased that tall, drink of water, Mahlia, to Paris. Thought we were chasing Mortas, but we found her at the Moulin Rouge."

"You should have seen it, Montmartre in all its glory. Cancan dancers, champagne, and music. Ever since I saw the movie Moulin Rouge, I've wanted to see the elephant," Tina said.

"Girl, I loved that one. I didn't know Nicole Kidman could sing," Ace said, and Tina agreed.

"Can't say I minded the trip, but Mahlia didn't do anything illegal. Didn't even seem like she was scouting the place. Just enjoying herself. She had her little brother with her," Gerry said.

"How is that possible?" I asked Jake. "Toecheese was wearing Mahlia's key."

"How do you know?" Gerry arched a suspicious eyebrow at me.

My inner voice held up a flash card of rule # 216b. If you are not arresting a brigand, you cannot violate them by identifying their key.

"Uhm…"

"He lost his cravat in the fall," Marco's reply came as he entered the room. "I saw it, too."

He sat down next to Campy and helped himself to a nutritious bar with lots of good, healthy grains.

"Do you think one of them is wearing the Thunder?" Brodie asked.

We only knew of four keys the Mafusos owned—Mortas's, Mahlia's, Caiyan's, and the Thunder key, which originally belonged to Toches but he refused to wear it because he claimed the key was cursed.

"Knowing Gian-Carlo's superstitious ways, I doubt he would allow any of his grandchildren to wear it," Marco said.

"Since Mortas didn't jump this cycle, my guess would be Mitchell wore the key that belongs to Mortas, and," Jake paused and turned to meet my curious gaze, "Mahlia was wearing Caiyan's key."

My jaw went slack, and Jake continued. "His key showed up on the travel screen after Gerry and Tina jumped. I thought Gian-Carlo was finally allowing him to use his key, but now I believe differently."

"With the addition of the new grandson who has power, the Mafusos are short a few keys," Brodie said.

One of Gian-Carlo's other grandsons came into his power last year. With Toches and Caiyan joining the Mafusos, they were short

29

two keys unless Gian-Carlo was continuing to travel—then they needed three.

Caiyan had traded his key and his vessel to Mitchell in order to save my life; however, Gian-Carlo was quick to confiscate it from Mitchell.

If it was true and Mortas was calling the shots, the WTF might have their hands full trying to figure out who is where. Mortas didn't exactly play fair.

"Switching keys makes it difficult for us to find them in the past," Jake said. "We can't match the travelers with what Pickles sees."

Pickles was the federation's only seer, a time traveler with the gift to foresee the travelers' decisions where they will jump when the portal opens. It was a rare gift and not one I envied.

"We're not going to know which brigand to scout. It could be any of them," Marco said.

"Yeah, a live shell game. You can't tell which shell the pea, or in this case Caiyan, is under," Tina added.

Gerry gave a snide chuckle, and I mentally flipped him the bird.

I agreed with Tina—if the Mafusos switched keys, they could give Caiyan any of the keys to travel with instead of his own, and we wouldn't know where to find him. Since Mahlia was the Mafusos only transporter, if they transported him back without a key, it would have to be with Mahlia.

Brodie stroked his small beard. "Rogue doesn't work with the Mafusos, but he went to the premiere of a Broadway musical. Damn wanker, I had to sit through an entire musical about a bunch of cats. Most disappointing trip of my life."

Tina and Ace snickered. I tried to contain a laugh, but it escaped through my lips like a motorboat. The image of Brodie watching a musical was priceless. The guy literally turned green when we suggested any outings that included the arts, especially if singing was involved. Unless it included a guitar and a bar.

"I'm betting if they offered Rogue payment in exchange for a random travel, he'd take it," Marco said. "I'm surprised they were able to track him down."

If the payment were big enough, Rogue would oblige. A permanent end to Caiyan's travels would make the stealthy brigand come out of hiding, I assumed, but didn't share my thoughts. Caiyan was disliked enough at the moment.

"Why do you think they're doing this?" I asked instead.

"My guess would be to throw us off track." Jake rubbed his chin as he glanced up at the map displaying the places the brigands went this cycle. "There was no rhyme or reason for the choices they made, and there weren't any violations to the code."

"Wasn't Toches arrested?" Gerry asked.

Jake explained the circumstances surrounding Toches's ride to the WTF. He was still checking out the girl Toches saved, but he was coming up empty-handed.

I felt Gerry's criticizing eyes on me for allowing them to think Toches was in custody.

"Where did Mortas go?" Tina asked.

"As far as we know, he didn't jump this cycle," Jake responded.

"He would have to wear the Thunder key if he jumped," Gerry said. "No moron in his right mind would wear that key."

Caiyan wore that key when he asked me to marry him.

"I'm more concerned about them dumping McGregor in the past and leaving him there." Jake reflected what I held inside.

"How are we going to find out what Caiyan is trying to steal?" Tina asked. "It has to be something big."

All eyes looked at me.

"I haven't seen him."

"You mean he's gone all this time without getting any booty?" Gerry asked.

I narrowed my eyes at Gerry. "I told you. I haven't seen him."

"Maybe he's unsatisfied, and he's getting his tail somewhere else," Gerry snickered.

I leapt over the table and lashed out at the dwarf, missing him by inches. Marco and Campy were both on their feet.

"Run, run, run, as fast as you can, you can't catch me, I'm the sneaky little man." He sang out as he leaned back out of my grasp.

Jake put two fingers in his mouth and whistled. "Everyone, take your seats!"

"I'm going to get you—you twerp." I folded myself back into my chair and realized I had donut holes smashed down the front of my sundress. Perfect.

Ace, who had been unusually silent during the scuffle, crossed a knee and sat back filing a hangnail. "If Caiyan wanted us to know, we'd know."

"What do you mean?" I asked him.

"The Scot never does anything without a reason. We need to wait for his plan to come to fruition, and then we'll see what he's up to."

"What if it's too late, and the damage has been done. He could ruin all of us." Gerry's contemptuous words cut deep.

"Do you think it's a conspiracy theory?" Brodie asked.

Jake clicked off the projector. "I don't know what to think. I doubt the Mafusos have plans for world domination, but whatever it is, it's big."

"More like traveler domination." Tina stopped pecking at her phone and gave everyone a fearful stare. "If Caiyan has information on the King's key, Gerry's right, we could all be in trouble."

The King's key was rumored to be the start of the time travelers. The first key worn by the chief of an ancient tribe.

Silence filled the room. Only Jake's shuffling through files in his briefcase broke the deadly quiet.

"I have intel on the sword Caiyan took from the museum a few months ago." Jake plucked a file from his briefcase.

My ears perked up. While Caiyan was under the influence of the Thunder key, he had stolen a Confederate sword from the American Civil War Museum in Appomattox. He told me he was going to trade it to the Mafusos for his key, but then changed his mind. Instead he offered to join them.

Jake placed a yellowed newspaper clipping secured in laminate in front of me. The article was from 1950. The story highlighted the last Civil War veteran in Texas. A man by the name of Sam W. Raney, who had recently passed away at the age of one hundred and three.

"Was this man a traveler?" I asked.

"No," Jake said.

I read the article further. There was a big to-do in the man's small hometown following his death. His sword was anonymously donated to the Museum of the Confederacy in Appomattox, Virginia.

Reporters interviewed the man's seventy-five-year-old son, who reported his pa had given the sword to a friend before his death.

"He was from Franklin county. That's in Texas, not too far from Aint Elma's house."

"I researched the location, but we have no connections to any travelers outside of Elma's family in the area."

"Do you think there's a link to a key?" Tina peered across the table at the clipping, and I scooted it toward her to read.

"There's something worth looking into here, or McGregor wouldn't have gone to the trouble to steal it," Marco said.

"And the Mafusos wouldn't want it," Brodie added.

"I can search his apartment." I felt my face heat as I offered to help. "I've—um—got a key." Technically, it wasn't breaking and entering if I had a key. "Maybe there's a clue as to what he did with the sword?"

"It's possible," Jake said. "We've had eyes on his place, but no sign of him for the last three months coming or going from the building."

"The bloke probably hid it in his office. I mean, any collector would give their eye teeth to have an actual Civil War sword," Brodie said.

"Fine. Jen, after Brodie does his recon, I'll clear you to check the apartment." Jake stacked his files. "Brodie, search McGregor's office and his home in Scotland. You three," he pointed to Marco, Tina, and Gerry, "Keep an eye on the Mafusos. And...everyone, get some rest. I think our next moon cycle might be a busy one. This meeting is adjourned."

"I'll arrange a meeting next week with his partner. Maybe he left it in his protection." Brodie gobbled down the last of the smashed donuts before he stood to leave.

I doubted Caiyan would leave an important clue for the Mafusos to find easily. Knowing Caiyan, it was probably stashed away in an obscure crypt or buried in a graveyard.

When Caiyan was under the influence of the Thunder key, he had given me the key to his apartment and asked me to marry him. The proposal went belly up, but he showed me a side of him I had never seen. One that might want a wife.

I wanted those things eventually, and I thought I wanted them with Caiyan. The possibility of never seeing him again made my heart constrict. We had to find him soon.

Marco fiddled with the leather bracelets on his wrist. I knew he had feelings for me, and I tried not to lead him on. It had been difficult transporting for him and working side by side without any physical contact. The touch that used to spark hot between us died down to a simple simmer. I wanted to be Marco's friend, not his lover, but a small part of me wondered how it would have been to be with him.

CHAPTER 3

*a*fter we were dismissed from the meeting, I cornered Jake while he was logging out of his computer. "I'd like to speak with Toecheese."

Jake paused. "I can't hold him much longer. I'm going over to question him, now. You can watch from the two-way mirror in the interrogation room."

"No. I want to talk to him alone, in his cell. He knows others will be watching, listening, in the interrogation room. I want to speak to him in private. Since I saved his life, he might give me a clue to the Mafusos' plans."

"Jen, it's not safe."

"He's in a padded cell. How dangerous could he be? I can protect myself from him. Besides, he won't have anything but his hands, and you can cuff him if you think it's necessary."

"OK, but I'm securing his hands and feet, and I'll watch through the window."

"Hands only, and you won't watch."

Jake sighed. "Why is everything a battle with you?"

I shrugged.

"Hands and feet, I won't watch, but you'll tell me everything."

"Deal," I held out my hand to seal the deal, and he ignored it. Instead, he made a call to alert the guards on duty of my impending visit.

I turned to leave, and he grabbed my wrist.

"Don't think that because you saved his life, he's indebted to you. Keep your distance, he's still dangerous."

"I will," I said.

He released my wrist, stood and picked up his laptop. "And after you speak to him, I need to debrief you. Meet me in my office. General Potts is in with Marco now, so you get me."

General Potts wasn't always on base, but when he was, he demanded to debrief the defenders. He liked receiving his intel from the horse's mouth. He'd embellish the details and report to Washington. It was fine by me, because the snooty secretary who followed Jake around like a lost puppy had to serve the general's needs when he was on base.

Jake and I parted ways. I turned left toward the stark white area used to detain the prisoners. The WTF annexed holding cells from Gitmo for the captured brigands. They couldn't be combined with the prisoners at Gitmo for fear they would figure out the location.

If we were lucky enough to force them to remove their keys, they were given a nice, comfy, padded cell, but not much human contact. Currently, all cells were empty except the one occupied by Toches and the one containing the Cracky brother.

The WTF normally exchanged the brigands for something important, like the crown jewels, but so far, we haven't caught anyone important enough to exchange for Caiyan's key. I assumed the WTF was trying to barter Toches for the key. I doubted Gian-Carlo would bite. He didn't like Toches for reasons beyond my paygrade.

If he knew I'd rescued Toches, he'd know we didn't have probable cause to hold him. Giving up a valuable possession like Caiyan's key would be in vain, and Jake knew he didn't have much time until the Mafusos would demand his release. The shifty brigand would be free in a matter of days.

I peeked through the tiny, round window. Toches stretched out along the bunk in his cell. A taller man would have to bend at the knees to fit on the bed. His wrists and ankles were cuffed like Jake promised.

Toches in present day clothing appeared different from the man I dealt with in my travels. Gone were his scraggy locks from Salem, and in their place were a tidy beard, dark hair, and beady eyes that stared at the cracked plaster ceiling. He reminded me of the Head Gamemaker, Seneca Crane, from the first Hunger Games Movie.

Since I didn't apprehend Toches, he retained the key he wore, and he wasn't shy about hiding it.

I motioned for the officer to open the door. According to Jake, the staff wasn't in the loop. They rotated every twenty-four hours, so having a new guest was not always a concern for them.

When I entered, the chains clanged as Toches sat up and swung his legs around to sit on the side of the bed. He leaned forward, elbows on knees, and interlocked his fingers.

"I wondered who was coming to call after they shackled me like a terrorist."

His forehead sported a large bandage. I leaned against the wall opposite him. The holding cell was small in comparison to the living arrangements of the normal Gitmo prisoners. The WTF worried a brigand might summon a vessel, so they safeguarded by providing tight quarters, making it impossible to call for a ride home.

In the past, a brigand had his key until the WTF could torture it off. Proper torture took time and planning. Since the WTF discovered I had the ability to remove keys, the torture took a back seat, but we still took care when snatching keys to avoid the repercussions from the brigand's posse.

"How's your head?" I asked Toches.

"Hurts like a son of a bitch. But they gave me good drugs. I imagine it would hurt ten times worse if I didn't take the meds."

I nodded.

"I hate this place."

"Most do."

He bit his lower lip then looked up at me. "Why didn't you leave me in Salem?"

"I couldn't let you die at the hands of the hangman's noose—that would be too poetic."

"Those people were nuts." A nervous laugh escaped, and he lowered his gaze to his bound hands.

"Why were you really there?" I asked.

"I told you before, I wanted to see a witch burn."

"Who was the girl?"

"Just a girl."

"Was she a traveler?"

Silence.

"Why did you save her?"

"I can't tell you. Mortas would have my balls for breakfast." He sighed. "He's going to go berserk when he finds out I've been captured."

"Toecheese, you weren't captured. I saved your life."

"Stop calling me that. It's disgusting." He stared at me in defiance, then dropped his head. By the way his shoulders slumped, I almost felt bad for the guy. "You don't understand."

I pushed away from the wall and squatted in front of him. "Help me understand."

He raised his eyes to mine. "The old man thinks I'm a loser. Not good enough to be in his family." Toches air quoted the word family with his fingers. "He considers me on the same level as the Cracky Clan. I might as well be pond scum."

The Cracky Clan were the bottom feeders of the time travel world; however, they rarely caused damage to the past.

"Why do you care what Gian-Carlo thinks?" I placed my hand over Toches's clasped hands, and a wave of jealousy and frustration washed over me. Toches yanked his hands out from under mine. The force knocked me back on my ass, and he laughed at me.

The ache in my backside reminded me of Jake's warning not to touch Toches.

I stood and crossed my arms over my chest. I wasn't giving up that easy. "If you give me something, I'll try to get you out of here."

"They can't hold me. I didn't do anything." He fidgeted. "Besides, it's personal."

"You saved a girl from hanging. They can keep you until they find the girl."

"For real?"

"Yes. Could be months, years before they locate her." I knew this wasn't entirely true, but hey, what's one more little white lie in my book of tall tales? I crossed my fingers for good measure.

Toches huffed, confirming my notion he didn't know all the rules of the pact made with the Mafusos, and I played it to my advantage.

"I'll put in a good word for you. Saving the girl and all. I'll also tell them you saved Marco and me by alerting us of the angry mob."

"That was nice of me, wasn't it?"

I turned and headed for the door. "Have it your way."

He spoke before I raised my fist to knock and alert the guard. "I'm surprised your Scot has really switched sides. I didn't believe it at first. I even warned Mahlia not to trust him, but now…"

"Now what?" I turned toward him.

He cocked his head in my direction.

"If he was keeping your sheets warm, you wouldn't be here asking all these annoying questions."

"What are the Mafusos doing with Caiyan?"

"Your Scottish boyfriend is in danger."

"What kind of danger?" My heart skipped a beat.

"I'm not at liberty to say, but I can tell you, I don't mind if he gets dumped in the past and forgotten."

"They're going to leave him in the past?" My voice raised an octave. "Don't you care he's going to be left without a key?"

"No."

"Toecheese, I saw you rescue that girl. I know you have a heart in there somewhere, and you know how miserable it is to be stuck in the past."

When I first met Kishin Toches, he was stranded in 1945 at the height of World War II. His key had been stolen from his ancestor, and it was as if he never received it, leaving him with no way to get home.

He grimaced. Either because he recalled the horror of remaining in the past, or because I used the nickname he hated.

"Let's just say he's going to get something I want, and I don't want him to have it. If he gets lost in the past well…" he shrugged, "makes it easier for me."

"I thought Gian-Carlo wanted Caiyan to join the Mafusos? You told me in Salem he was going to induct him into the family."

"Yeah, Gian-Carlo wants your boy in the gang, but Mortas doesn't, and he's calling the shots. Oh, the old man has the upper hand, but Mortas has seen to it that once Caiyan finds the key, the Scot will be lost forever, and the Mafusos won't have to worry about him changing sides again."

"What key?"

"Oops, now I've gone and given the game away." A devious smile pulled at his upper lip.

His chains clinked as he scooted back on his bunk. Leaning against the wall, he stared at me. "You still care about him even though he's going to…" he paused leaving his words dangling in the air.

"Even though he's going to what?" Toches was probing me. I was familiar with the technique of leaving a question dangling to see if the other party knew the answer.

When he was certain I was in the dark, he continued "I can't say, but I have the only transporter key, and if you don't release me, Mortas will probably have McGregor killed. His mission is based on dropping him in the past, and only a transporter can carry him there."

A confident smile crossed his lips.

"Did you plan this with Mahlia?" When I said her name, his face softened. "Is that why you have her key?"

"I have her key because Mortas wanted to mix things up. Lead you fools on a wild goose chase. When the time comes you won't know where the Scot is or who is with him."

"Don't you think Mortas will give him a key to get whatever Gian-

Carlo wants?" I asked, knowing Mortas wanted to please his grandfather more than life itself.

"They're not that crazy. Even the old man knows the crafty Scot can use his gift to get away. If McGregor gets the key, then he can exchange it for his own key. If not...then he can live out his days singing Dixie."

"Why would they leave Caiyan in the past? Isn't he more valuable working with them?"

"Only if he's really switched sides. He has to prove his loyalty."

"How? He's left the WTF. He left me. He came to Gian-Carlo of his own free will, to make a deal with the Mafusos."

"He came naked. Without a key, he doesn't have any power, only the gift. The Mafusos have plenty of gifted talent. What they need is another key."

I had seen Caiyan tumble locks, and make other travelers drop in pain. But did he have other gifts I didn't know about?

Toches huffed. "I've said too much. I can't tell you any more. If I do, I'll never be allowed inside the family."

I saw the wall go up behind his eyes and thought a small plea for help shouted at me before the last brick was set in place.

"I'll see what I can do to get you out of here." I knocked three times on the door.

"Much obliged. And by the way," he paused. "Thanks for saving me."

"You're welcome, Toches."

Ace met me on my way back from speaking to Toches. "There's been another jump." His voice taking that aggravated tone that meant our shopping trip was about to be put on hold.

"What? The moon cycle is closing. Who'd be so stupid to travel this late?"

"Looks like we are the stupid ones, because Agent Sexy Buns has ordered us to the lab. I was on my way to get you."

The other travelers left for home following the meeting. Ace was waiting on me for some post-travel shopping.

Jake's shoes clipped down the hallway. "Good, you found her.

Since you two are the only travelers left on base, you get to make a late jump." He barked orders as he passed us and motioned for us to follow him.

Ace and I tried to keep up.

"Christ, I can't waste another minute summoning someone else back to base. Mortas has jumped to Purley, Texas, and I need y'all to track him."

The last time I traveled with Ace, our mission was not approved by the WTF. We attracted trouble like ants to a summer picnic.

"Tell me quick, what did Toches say?" Jake made a right turn, and I hustled by his side.

"He didn't reveal anything about the girl, but he told me Caiyan's in danger."

"What kind of danger?"

"He hinted the Mafusos might leave Caiyan in the past, and when I touched him…"

"You touched him?" Jake stopped in his tracks and Ace almost bumped into him.

"Um—" I said. Warning bells went off in my head, forcing me to choose my next words carefully. "I read him. Anger and jealousy over something Caiyan's going to receive from Gian-Carlo that Toecheese wants."

"Probably the old man's unrequited praise," Ace said. "Kishin has self-esteem issues."

"Jen," Jake's agitated stare bore trouble. "I ordered you not to touch him, but I don't have time to argue with you now. I'll meet you in the travel lab. I need to secure funds and intel." He left in a flurry of angst.

"That one needs some serious spa time," Ace said as Jake disappeared around the corner.

Al stood at the threshold of the door to the travel lab. His blue eyes danced with delight from under gray, bushy eyebrows when he saw us approach. He wore a wrinkled white lab coat over his button-down shirt and brown slacks. The array of colored pens, pencils, and gizmos lining the breast pocket of his lab coat clattered as he hugged me.

"Seems like you're going on another adventure," he said, smiling and greeting us as we entered the travel lab. The computers hummed and buzzed. Lights flashed on flat screens located in various positions throughout the room. The travel lab had come to life with the aftermath of the events of the recent travels.

"Brilliant," Ace mumbled, the syrupy sarcasm thickening the tone of his voice.

Pickles sat behind his semicircular workstation, hands flying over keyboards, dreads cut short Wiz Khalifa style. He glanced up and gave us a wide smile.

I sent him a finger wave.

Al shuffled us over to the giant screen that held center court in the room. A map displayed on the screen that normally flashed with multi-colored dots now only held a trail of red. Remnants of the travelers' paths, and the people they connected with in the past, were indicated by red dots moving like ants across the map. All the teams had returned from fighting the brigands and saving the past from corruption.

He pushed a few buttons on a remote-control contraption he held in his palm. The map spun and focused on my home state and a location not too far from my Aint Elma's farmhouse. A black dot blinked at me, indicating a brigand on the move.

I swallowed hard. "Is Mortas after my family?"

"I don't think so," Al said, choosing a pointer from the pocket on his lab coat. Al tapped at a place on the map. "There's a clearing here."

I studied a picture of my landing spot. When I traveled, my vessel needed about ten feet of secure area for landings and takeoffs. I had landed in tighter spots, but it wasn't safe. The chance I could end up in a wall, or in a body of water, scared me to my core.

I preferred not to drown in the past. The town was about five hundred yards away from a secluded wooded area. I agreed it was the closest secure area.

"Jennifer, if you land here, the walk to the town will be close to half a mile." Al tapped on the route to the town.

"Hold the front door," Ace said, hands on hips. "I'm driving."

43

"Jennifer should drive," Al said to Ace. "Her outhouse is less likely to cause concern if seen."

Ace huffed. He never liked traveling without his cozy vessel, but his photo booth wasn't exactly something found in the middle of the woods; then again, most of the vessels weren't, but when we had the option to blend in with our surroundings, we took it.

Pickles came over and added some insight to our mission. "Dis is a sleepy town. Not much going on here, so I've no idea why Mortas is d'ere." The lyrical cadence of his Jamaican accent had a calming effect on me.

He squeezed the bridge of his nose. "I'm sensing another traveler has broken da time portal, but I believe it's from a jump in da past."

"What do you mean?" I asked.

"He means," Ace said. "There's activity from a past traveler who has jumped to this time mucking his vision."

"There's always the chance another traveler has been to this time," Al added.

"Can you see the other traveler?" I asked.

"Sometimes I can, but it's difficult for me ta see who it is until I've gone into da deep meditation. There's no time for dat now, da portal is closing."

"Is it hard to have so many visions?" I asked Pickles.

"If I remove my key, my mind has a vacation." He tapped a finger against his temple, and the stack of leather bracelets he wore slid down his smooth, mocha skin.

"This is where the man in the newspaper clipping lives. The man who owns the sword." I chewed my bottom lip. "I'm curious why Mortas wants the sword."

"With the switcheroo games these Mafusos are playing, it bloody well could be any one of them." Ace moved forward, examining the black blinking dot designated to Mortas.

"No. Dats Mortas. I see him clear as da bell."

I considered the way Pickles envisioned the decisions of the destinations made by the travelers. "Can you see the time portal if you wear a different key?" I asked him.

"Das a good question. I've never worn another, but unless da key belonged to a seer, I do not believe I could see da portal." He shook his dark curls. When he met my eyes, a glint of understanding for the reason behind my questions sparkled in his eyes. "It's important to wear da key given to you by your ancestors. It holds energy from da wearers of da past. It's da best key."

"So, if someone didn't have their key, they wouldn't be able to use their extra gifts."

"Most often, that is the case," Al said.

And the reason Caiyan seeks his key. In my opinion, Caiyan's gifts of tumbling locks and causing pain in another traveler wasn't reason enough to quit our relationship and leave the WTF.

"It's possible all has not been revealed, but maybe the answers you seek will present themselves." Al gave me a grandfatherly pat on the back and motioned toward the exit. "Time to go."

I committed the landing coordinates to memory, and Ace and I left the travel lab.

"That guy creeps me out sometimes," Ace said, referring to Al. "He's starting to sound like Yoda. What did he mean by all has not been revealed?" he asked, imitating the legendary Jedi Master from *Star Wars*.

"I'm not sure," I answered, but I had my suspicions there was more to Caiyan than he allowed me to see.

Jake met us in the landing area. "Be careful. You don't have much time until the portal closes. In fact, it's quite risky to make the jump so late in the moon cycle. The time continuum is acting strange, but since Mortas hasn't traveled in months, I want to know what he's up to. This is an in and out mission."

When I first began traveling, I would return a few hours after I left. Easy to call in to work and disappear for a short time. My family didn't question where I'd been.

Now, the time has stretched. We are missing days, sometimes the entire five days of the travel cycle. Pinocchio's nose would've extended three New York City blocks if he told the lies I've told my family. Having Gertie in the know helped; she covered for me most of the time, but Eli had blown up Jake's cell more than once trying to locate me.

Life became easier when we found out Eli had the gift. The WTF doesn't know Mamma Bea gave him the key and vessel that belonged to her husband, my papa Cloud. Another truth I withheld from Jake. I was really racking them up, but Eli refused to travel. If the WTF knew about his recent acquisitions, they'd be all up in his business trying to recruit him. Or even worse, take his key.

Eli's more understanding about me being absent from work for a few days, now. We had to come up with a reason for me to miss work, and I now have a condition called CFS, or Chronic Fatigue Syndrome, brought on by the Epstein-Barr virus responsible for mononucleosis. It's a good cover, and the office manager bakes me cupcakes when I return.

I focused on the orders Jake was dishing out. "Only observe. You should have about five hours, then you need to return, regardless of whether you found Mortas. Do you understand?" He was looking directly at me.

"Roger that, Captain," I said with an air of bravado while I held my knees from knocking together. Chasing Mortas with only a smidge of time left before the moon cycle closed made me not only nervous but scared. Without Marco to lend his support, I went from Wingwoman to Wonder Woman. I hoped I could muster up her courage if things went south.

Jake moved to speak to one of his agents, leaving Ace and me preparing for travel.

"I'll be with you, doll. No worries," Ace offered, as if my thoughts were transcribed across my forehead like the ticker tape for the New York Stock exchange.

"I'm not worried."

"Why do you look like you just shat your knickers?"

"I'll be fine," I confirmed, but my inner voice pulled the cord on her life preserver as Ace and I boarded my outhouse to jump to Franklin County, the year 1949.

CHAPTER 4

I managed to land my vessel without any problems in a group of hundred-year-old oak trees on the outskirts of Purley. The short walk to the small town deemed unreportable.

The small country town in 1949 wasn't much different than the small country towns in the present.

Ace and I stood outside a five and dime surveying the scene. There wasn't any sign of Mortas. People milled about doing their daily errands. No one seemed ruffled by a recent chaos that disrupted their everyday lives.

"Why in the world would Mortas choose to come 'ere?" Ace huffed. "The man has no sense of fun. There's nothing going on in this hick town and it's hot. I've got sweat beads under me mustache. It's going to ruin me dermal filler treatment I had done last week."

I rolled my eyes at Ace. The vessel had dressed him in faded blue jeans, a tan button down, and a mustache that would have made Yosemite Sam jealous. In my book, he fit the slow-paced East Texas town, but Ace's preferences were less Sam Elliott and more Rhinestone Cowboy.

"Honey, don't roll those baby blues at me, you could use a few injections of Botox around the eyes. This job is taking a toll on you."

I rubbed the corner of my eye. "My eyes are fine! Laugh lines show character."

"Huh, this job will give you more than laugh lines. One day you'll wake up to crow's feet and forehead wrinkles. It's the stress that does it by releasing harmful toxins into your body. For example, take your U.S. president."

"The current president?"

"Any of them." Ace wafted a hand at me. "He's sworn into office looking all suave and debonair."

I raised an eyebrow at him.

"Hear me out, hon. When his four years are done, there's an old man in his shoes. God forbid he gets reelected."

"You don't look so bad, and you've been doing this longer than me."

"I take care of meself. Weekly facials, and I exercise every morning on the treadmill, followed by an hour of hot yoga twice a week."

"I think I'll pass. The training Jake imposes on me is enough." I did my time at the gym. Not every day, but I managed to turn my spaghetti arms into toned, tanned flesh.

Jake saw to it I had the proper skills to measure up to the WTF standards and reduced my body fat to twenty-four percent. At least the last time I checked. I might have indulged in a pint of Ben and Jerry's Chunky Monkey, so I could have some extra.

"Let's try and focus," I said. "We don't have much time. Something is going on, because Mortas is here and he wouldn't risk his life getting stuck in the past for an entire travel cycle if it wasn't important."

"Where should we start, doll?" he asked, taking in the town. A Victorian style courthouse sat at the north end of the square. A hardware store, feed store, and the dime store we currently stood in front of ran the length of the buildings to the right of the courthouse. A second row of buildings stood perpendicular to us. A bar flanked by the library and a grocer, then ended with a barber. We stood on the northwest corner catty corner from the library. A Studebaker pickup and a Buick were parked at the dime store, but a handful filled the spaces in front of the bar.

"We should go across the street to the bar," I said to Ace. I learned from past travels if you wanted information, the bartender and the barber knew everything. I had more bad haircuts than I could count trying to get the lay of the land from the barber.

The bartenders were inclined to be less chatty, equating their information to the confessions given to the local priest. I might have to throw back a few drinks to encourage the bartenders to loosen their lips about the secrets in this town, but I wanted to try them first and avoid a bad haircut.

Ace tweaked his mustache. "I like having the little 'stache—makes me feel mysterious."

"I hardly recognize you," I told him. "Is the mustache fake?"

"No, it's the real deal."

"I'm always amazed when you grow facial hair. The vessel did a great job making you fit in with the time." I glanced down, admiring his alligator cowboy boots.

"You too, doll. That hat is to die for."

My blond hair was done up in a bun at the nape of my neck and topped off with a straw hat adorned with plastic flowers. The blue floral cotton dress had cute capped sleeves and hit me mid-calf. I liked the dress; however, the padded shoulders made me feel like a line-backer. The ensemble was finished off with a pair of sturdy pumps. I couldn't complain, because at least this outfit enabled me to move freely. Much better than the pencil skirts of the fifties or the eighteenth-century petticoats.

Ace and I stepped off the curb to walk the block to the bar. A man exited the bar and headed in our direction. His gray pinstriped suit and fedora felt out of place in the farming town. The Clark Gable mustache threw me off, but the casual lean to his stride sent off warning bells as he walked toward us.

"It's Caiyan," I said to Ace.

As he got closer, the frown that normally accompanied his discovery of me intruding on one of his missions didn't appear. He tipped his hat in my direction, but we weren't close enough to speak. I had a few things I'd like to tell him.

Ace stopped short, grabbed my arm, and steered me away from my approaching ex-boyfriend.

I glanced at Caiyan as he passed. He practically ignored me. My breath caught as I smelled the familiar scent of cinnamon and fresh earth.

Caiyan turned and walked toward the Buick parked in front of the dime store.

I stood dumbfounded and took a deep breath to shout out a few deserving words I had stored up for him.

Ace clapped a hand over my mouth. "It's not him."

"It is him," I said prying the hand from my mouth.

"No, hon. It was him, but a younger Caiyan. He's the traveler in Pickles's vision from another time. If he remembers you when it's time for your little meet cute in Scotland, it could screw up your past tryst."

Ace was right. There wasn't a glint of recognition from Caiyan when our eyes met. His face lacked the hard lines Ace believed were acquired by years of time traveling. Was he older than when I first met him in Scotland? The time he took me for a roll in the hay and left me stranded.

Watching him walk away, he was leaner, and his stride boasted the arrogance of a younger man. Younger, I guessed, but couldn't tell which man strode away from me. His scent hung in the air and my boy howdy tingled.

"Don't stand gawking doll, he doesn't forget much." Ace pulled me across the street and into an alcove next to the bar. "Let's hope his mind is preoccupied with other things."

Caiyan's playboy attitude preceded meeting me. A random woman on a side street in a town where he was obviously on a mission wouldn't be exceptionally memorable. Besides, the hat shadowed my face and I was dressed like a woman in the nineteen forties.

When Caiyan first met me, I had an ugly brown toboggan over my then dishwater blond hair, sans a few highlights, and the inhibitions of a young female. I barely recognized the woman I had become.

"I can't tell how old he is, or if he's already met me."

"Bloody 'ell. Based on that tight butt, I'd say it's definitely the time he wasn't working for the WTF."

"Good, that's before he met me," I said. Glad I didn't mess up my "meet cute" with the man of my dreams.

Caiyan started the Buick and passed us on the way out of town. "We need to follow him."

"Hunting the pirate may not be a good thing. If he discovers us, we could cause problems back home."

"My gut feeling tells me Mortas is looking for him, too."

"It's your call, doll, but let's hurry 'cuz I don't want to be stuck here wearing these knickers longer than necessary."

I decided not to ask what he meant by that and searched for keys left in the ignition of the few cars in front of the bar. We came up empty. These farmers locked their cars. They weren't taking any chances with the money they'd invested on their transportation.

"What happened to leaving the key in the ignition?" I tugged on the last door handle with no luck.

"That's the fifties. These cowboys saved their pennies to buy these cars, and they're not parting with them easily," Ace said. "We could check out the hardware store and see if they have something to jimmy the lock."

At the end of the row of buildings, a tall, chestnut mare was tied up to a hitching post located at the side of the barbershop.

"I've got a better idea," I said and walked toward the horse. Ace followed.

"Oh no, I don't do horses." Ace stood hands on hips.

"What you mean you don't do horses?" I asked. "I thought horse-back riding was part of our training requirement?" I had spent three weeks at horse camp learning how to ride.

"I skipped that lesson," he said.

"Ace, we're in a hurry. We need to follow Caiyan before he gets too far ahead."

"I'm not riding that beast."

I put my foot in the stirrup and asked for a boost. Ace rolled his eyes and pushed my behind up onto the large horse. It wasn't easy straddling the horse in my dress, but a girl's got to make do.

"We need to find Mortas. I have a feeling Caiyan is the common thread here. We're going to follow him. So, alley oop."

He frowned up at me.

"Ace come on, this is not debatable."

Ace stood his ground. "Everything's debatable, hon."

"What's it going to take?" I asked, trying to keep the horse steady.

He paused. "Full day at the Shibui Spa with a facial, mani-pedi, and an aromatherapy massage by one of the hot guys, not one of the wimpy females with the small hands."

"Done." I held out a hand to Ace.

He put his foot in the stirrup, grabbed my hand, and I boosted him aboard.

The horse gave a snort at its new passenger.

Ace leaned into my back and huffed into my ear. "I should have held out for a microderm abrasion."

After a few minutes, I became acquainted with the horse. As we trotted down the street, a man, most likely the owner of the horse, ran out of the barber shop, shaving cream on his beard, shaking his fist, and shouting profanities my way.

"Hold on!" I shouted at Ace, and he wrapped his arms around my midsection. I gave the horse a good thrust with the heel of my shoe, and he galloped off down the road.

I headed the direction Caiyan took in the Buick and slowed the horse to a steady gait after I confirmed the angry owner wasn't in full pursuit. Ace maintained a steady bitching about being saddle sore.

"How can you be sore already? We've been riding less than ten minutes."

"My parts are sensitive."

The horse slowed to a walk and tried to nibble at the grass alongside the road. Clenching my teeth, I did my best to keep him on the asphalt. Between the two of them, I wasn't sure which one was more belligerent, Ace or the horse. Ace might be right. This job could definitely cause wrinkles.

A few miles up the road, I spied the Buick parked in the rutted dirt driveway of an old farmhouse. The small frame farmhouse sat a good distance from the road and had an orchard of wise pecan trees posing across the front pasture.

The Texas dogtrot style house had two identical sides with a breezeway that split it up the middle, the kitchen and main living area on one side and bedrooms on the other. My aint Ozona had one similar. The breezeway allowed a cross current of air to keep the bedrooms cooler and away from the heat of the kitchen. A wooden swing hung across the right end of the porch and swayed in the occasional breeze as if a ghost relaxed in the lazy summer evening.

We dismounted, and I tied the horse's reins to a tree. I couldn't have him running out into traffic. Checking up and down the road, there wasn't another soul to be seen. The road stretched for a few miles in either direction.

When I was positive the horse was safely secured, we walked toward the house, keeping cover behind the rows of mature corn planted in the field adjacent to the house.

Caiyan's car was parked at the far end of the driveway in front of the barn. He struggled with a bulky machine he lifted from the back seat of the Buick. I'd never seen one the size he carried, but I was positive it was some type of tape recording device.

He paused and cocked his head in my direction. We froze and waited while he scanned the area. When he decided we were mere cornstalks shushing in the breeze, he walked toward the house.

We hung back a bit and gave him time to put some distance between us. He approached the house from the rear.

The barn provided cover for us from the eyes of the old man sitting on the back porch, his rocking chair centered in the breezeway. When Caiyan focused on the man, we moved closer, allowing us to hear the conversation without being seen.

The man had a long white beard and held a pipe in his hand. Although it was ninety degrees, he wore a red sweater and cap. White hair stuck out from under the cap, reminding me of a wiry Santa Clause.

Caiyan approached the man. "You Samuel Raney?" he asked.

I gasped. It was the man from the newspaper clipping Jake had shown me at headquarters.

"Who're you?" the man asked Caiyan.

Caiyan explained he was a reporter for the Dallas Morning News.

"I haven't been to Dallas in sixty years," the man said. "Last time I was there, I helped pave the streets with bois d'arc blocks. I suppose it's growed some."

"Yes sir," Caiyan said.

"Nothin' but a bunch of carpetbaggers in Dallas. Hear it still is."

Caiyan gave the man an appreciative smile.

"You seem mighty familiar, have we met before?" the man asked.

"No sir. I never forget a face."

Oh boy!

Movement caught my eye off to the right of the house. A man leapt over the fence separating the yard from the pasture. His height and athletic build disguised his age. As he approached, his weathered features placed him not as old as the man on the porch, but late sixties, possibly early seventies. The man on the porch introduced him as his youngest son, George.

"This here's some feller from Dallas." He pointed to Caiyan. "What'd you say your name was?"

"I didn't, but my name's John Smith." Caiyan balanced the machine on his knee and extended a hand to George.

I snorted. Could he pick a more common name?

Ace shushed me. Caiyan explained he was doing a story on the Civil War. He was told Mr. Raney could still perform the rebel yell and owned an actual sword from the Civil War.

"Papa can, but it's probably best if he don't. The last time he done it, I believe, was seven years ago," George said, scratching his chin. "It's best if he don't. He went to a coughing fit afterward, and he best not."

Mr. Raney waved a hand at his son, and George grew silent. He offered Caiyan a chair. Caiyan set the recording machine down on the porch and joined the men.

Sweat trickled down from my temples as I strained to hear the conversation.

"We need to move closer," I said.

Ace pointed toward the side of the house. It jutted out from the breezeway and we could see them through a cross window. If Caiyan didn't return to his car, we were golden. We snuck around the barn and came up next to the weathered clapboard. Ace and I leaned against the house and listened to the story the old man told of the Civil War.

"An angel swooped down from the heavens and saved me from a hero's death," Mr. Raney said.

"An angel?" Caiyan asked.

"She was a beauty. Her white hair blew in the wind. Pink flowers scattered in it, and she wore my colors. I remember her as clear as it was yesterday." His gaze looked far beyond the pasture behind the house. "She told me it wasn't my time to go yet, I had lots of living to do. I have six children, twelve grandchildren and fourteen great-grandchildren, thanks to my angel. My first great, great will be born this August".

"That's a lot of kids."

"You have any young'uns?" George asked.

I craned my neck to see Caiyan's response.

He shook his head. "No sir. I'm not cut out to have kids."

My heart sank. Caiyan and I never talked about kids, but I was pretty sure I wanted some…eventually.

"You gonna be missing a lifetime of happiness. My wife, God rest her soul, was the firm hand, and I was the easy goer. Was the most blessed time of my life, raising those young'uns."

"Tell me about the angel," Caiyan said.

"I was in the middle of a fierce battle. Most of my regiment had been used as cannon fodder. Bullets and guns blazed around me. I was hit in the abdomen and knew my time would be over soon. Them damn Yankees shooting at us from behind the stone wall would be upon me. I'd be taken prisoner, or, worse, my life would be ended by one of the angry ones. We heard tale of them. They robbed your belongings and shot the soul dead out of you. I called out for help, but it was no use, everyone around me was dead."

I swallowed hard at the man's story.

"Then a bright light and the beautiful face of an angel lit my soul. She swooped down and helped me toward the safe place."

He ended the story with the fact he'd turned one hundred and three this year.

Ace's eyebrows lifted, and he lowered his voice. "I need to know the man's secret. He looks fabulous!"

"No Botox or spa treatments around here," I said, causing Ace to frown at me.

"How old were you when you entered the military?" Caiyan asked.

I didn't know if Caiyan was asking questions to substantiate his cover, because he seemed legitimately interested in the man's story.

"I was sixteen when I joined up. My first action was in the battle of Murfreesboro. I lived in Tennessee back then. The older boys was joinin', thought I'd go along with them. It was a fight in fire. The cannons set the cedar trees afire. The band played, and we charged."

The old man threw his head back, cupped both hands around his mouth, and let out a guttural opera-singer quality high note followed by an angry elephant scream. There was a deep, throaty holler, then a falsetto echo back as if a mountain lion, coyote, and a screech owl sang in chorus.

The yell ended in a bout of convulsive coughs and the sound of Caiyan patting the old man on the back while his son ran to the well to fetch his father a dipper of water.

"Sorry about that," Mr. Raney said after he regained his voice. "Gets harder every time I give it a go."

"I'd like to record the rebel yell." Caiyan said, his phony drawl sending a sexy sensation skipping down my spine. "Do you think you could do it again for me?"

"I can try," he said.

"Where can I plug in this recorder?" Caiyan asked, holding up a two-pronged plug.

"Mr. Smith, we ain't got no power," George said. "We never did tie onto the REA to get the electricity."

"You'll have to go buy some batteries." Mr. Raney motioned toward the town as he started another coughing fit.

"I think Papa best not try again." George held the dipper of water to the man's mouth.

"How about letting me take a look at the sword from the Civil War?"

"Sure," Mr. Raney said.

George helped his father stand, and they made a right inside the small farmhouse.

Ace and I looked at each other. "Go. Go!" He swished his fingers at me.

We scooted around to the front of the house and planted ourselves in a hedge of Red-tipped Photinia under an open window.

The sound of Mr. Raney's graveled voice floated outside with the floral curtains as they blew in the lazy breeze.

I snuck a peek between the curtains. The men were in the main room of the house. Mr. Raney sat in a patched fabric chair. Caiyan and George stood examining a shiny sword racked above the fireplace.

"Take 'er down gently now, son, no sense in losing a finger. She may be old, but she still has a bite."

"Don't worry, Papa, the sword's in its scabbard."

"Right. My eyesight ain't what it used to be."

George removed the sword hanging above the mantle of the stone fireplace and handed it to Caiyan.

Caiyan held the sheath out at arm's length and gave a long, low whistle. "May I?" he asked Mr. Raney.

The older man nodded. Caiyan unsheathed the sword.

"It's a beaut. Ain't it?" George beamed at Caiyan.

"Don't believe I've ever seen one in such fine condition."

I had. It was the same sword Caiyan had stolen from a museum in

57

New York and stashed in his treasure collection. I recognized the fancy handle.

I remembered there had been some engraving on the blade, but I couldn't recall reading the inscription. I was annoyed with Caiyan when he showed me his treasure room, and so I didn't pay attention to the minor details.

Mr. Raney started another coughing fit. "Let me get you another drink from the well, Papa," George said, leaving the room.

Caiyan pulled something from his pocket and palmed it in his right hand. When Mr. Raney started to cough again, he ran his hand across the blade several times. A rough sound of rock against metal added to the coughing. Caiyan slid the sword back into the scabbard.

The son returned from the well, and the man took a long drink from the dipper.

Ace cringed next to me. "Blimey." Germs were not his thing.

I put a finger to my lips, "Shush it."

If Caiyan caught us, we could jeopardize the entire mission. He had damaged the sword, and I had a good idea why. It was the information to a key.

"That's a mighty fine sword you have here, Mr. Raney," Caiyan said. "It should be in a museum."

Mr. Raney cleared his throat. "A good friend gave me that sword. He was a doctor."

"How about I purchase this sword from you and take it to a museum?" The urgency in Caiyan's voice had me worried.

"I don't know…" Mr. Raney said.

"We sure could use the extra money, Papa. Crops haven't been producing as well, and my granddaughter needs that operation for her feet," George said.

"I reckon it'd be better off hangin' in a museum than here."

"How about five hundred dollars?" Caiyan asked. "And I'll make sure it has a placard with your name as the donator underneath."

George's eyes grew wide at the amount Caiyan offered.

"I believe that's a fair price," Mr. Raney stroked his beard.

Caiyan pulled a wad of money from his pants pocket, peeled off the bills, and handed them to Mr. Raney. I was curious to know who he stole the money from. There was no way he could transport that amount between his cheek and gum. Of course, there were other ways one could use to bring small present-day items to the past, but not any I would participate in.

The roar of a car engine sounded in the distance, and I turned in time to catch a four-door sedan turning into the long driveway. I pulled Ace quickly back into our hidey hole.

Footsteps moved above us, and I caught the tip of a finger as it pulled the curtain aside to view the driveway.

"I trust you will do as you say, young man," Mr. Raney said.

"You have my word." Caiyan promised he'd return in a day with his tape recorder, batteries installed, to make a full recording of the rebel yell.

I heard movement above me like young Caiyan was gathering up his tape recorder. He thanked the men and made a hasty good-bye. The screen door slammed as he left out the back.

From my viewpoint between the Photinia bushes, the Cadillac came to a full stop in the driveway with Mortas behind the wheel.

"Uh oh," Ace said. "The bad guy's here."

We hunkered down to avoid our arch enemy's evil gaze.

I couldn't see Caiyan's car parked behind the house at the end of the drive, but I assumed, based on his speedy exit, he knew a brigand was arriving. I prayed they didn't have a meet cute. If something happened to the young Caiyan, our meet cute would never take place.

I let out the breath I was holding when Mortas cut the engine, exited the car, and took the steps up to the front porch.

His dark hair was slicked back and tucked under a cowboy hat. The corners of his eyes showed a few lines probably caused from his constant evil glares. He rapped on the door. This was the Mortas I knew and despised. The Mafuso from my time.

George opened the screen door and stood in the doorway.

"It's been a spell since we had this many out-of-town visitors," George said after Mortas introduced himself as a collector from New York City.

Mr. Raney shuffled to the doorway. "Who's this feller?"

"He's from New York, says he's a collector."

"Ain't never been to New York," Mr. Raney said.

George didn't invite Mortas into the house. Both men stepped out onto the porch, inches away from our hiding place.

"Can't say I ever have the notion to go up thataways," Mr. Raney gave Mortas the once over.

"It's quite spectacular," Mortas said.

"Not sure if I can do the rebel yell for ya, havin' been I just did it," he said.

"The rebel yell?" Mortas questioned.

"Why yes, Papa's the last man alive can do the yell. Isn't that why you're here?"

"Uhm, no." Mortas seemed confused, "I'd like to know if you have any Civil War relics?"

The sound of a car's motor engaging rumbled at the side of the house.

Mr. Raney shook his head. "Sorry son, just sold the only souvenir I had from them awful days. Proud to have served alongside my friends, but the reminder of the ones who died, I reckon, would be better displayed in a museum."

"You sold it? To who?" Mortas asked.

"A reporter from Dallas. He's going to give it to a museum and put my name underneath as the donator." The old man puffed his chest out. "Mighty proud to be donating to a museum."

As Mr. Raney finished his sentence, Caiyan zoomed past in his Buick, window down, flipping Mortas the bird, and crowing out his version of the rebel yell. The anonymous donator from the information in the yellowed newspaper clipping wasn't being very anonymous.

"Son of a bitch!" Mortas shook his fist at him and stood staring as Caiyan barreled down the driveway engulfed in a cloud of dust.

"There goes the big to-do," I whispered as Caiyan sped away.

"He did a pretty good job, if I do say so myself." Mr. Raney chuckled.

"Where did the sword come from?" Mortas asked.

"Found it in the salvage wagon after the war."

"Thank you for your time."

"Don't you want to hear the rebel yell?"

"No, I have a feeling I'm going to hear it plenty in the near future."

Mr. Raney huffed. "I thought I's the last one who knew how to do it?"

Mortas started to leave and then turned. "Did the sword have any words inscribed on the blade?"

"I can't say I recall," Mr. Raney said.

George piped up "I think…"

Mr. Raney began one of his coughing fits.

The brigand's face darkened and a displeased expression twisted his mouth.

"Sorry sir, Papa needs to sit a spell. When he's had one of his coughin' fits he best not speak to anyone for a while."

Mortas stomped off toward his car.

"I'm fine son, just let me rest here and enjoy the breeze." Mr. Raney sat down on a porch swing hung at the opposite end of the porch.

We watched Mortas enter his car, make a U-turn, and spit dust as he drove away.

George asked his father, "Papa why did you lie to that man about the sword?"

"He ain't nothin' but one of them damn Yankee treasure hunters. I can smell them a mile away. If'n he wants to know, he can go see it at the museum. Maybe in his search, he'll learn a thing or two about the war."

The porch swing squeaked with the weight of the man and his son as they rocked gently, talking about the nice young reporter from Dallas. Geesh.

Ace and I were stuck in the bushes until the men went inside. My stomach ached with a subtle cramp. A sign the moon cycle creeped to a close and we needed to hurry back to our landing point.

"Would they go back inside already?" Ace companied, "Me ass is sore from sitting here, and I can't be stuck in this hick town. I've got a date tonight."

"Your ass gets tired easily," I replied, keeping my voice low.

"I might have had some work done."

"What kind of work?"

"The surgical kind."

"You know the WTF doesn't allow cosmetic surgery, right?" I arched an eyebrow at him.

"I don't plan on getting shot in the ass."

"What did you have done?"

"I had a few implants to make me bum a little fuller, like Beyoncé."

I looked behind him and he huffed, "You can't see it when I'm sitting down. I need to stand for you to see its magnificence." I thought about the fact Ace had missed the last moon cycle. He told Jake his grandfather was ill.

Mr. Raney and his son finally retired to the house. "Coast is clear," Ace said.

We tiptoed to the end of the house and stood, stretching our legs.

"What do you think?" He lifted his shirttail.

I noticed his behind was a bit rounder at the top, but I didn't think it was enough to warrant surgery or risk Jake's wrath.

"I'm impressed, but what if you get fired?"

"They can't fire me, doll. We have so many brigands trying to muck up the past they need every available traveler. We don't have enough defenders to chase them all, and even fewer transporters."

I agreed. We did have the WTF by their short hairs. They needed us, which made negotiating some things simple. The last few travels, the transporters were restricted to base. We mutinied, and Jake relented, petitioning General Potts to make allowances for the trans- porters to travel with their defenders instead of being summoned.

Now, I was under the microscope to prove I can travel and not muck up things in the past. Bending the rule made watching Marco's back easier and my sleepless nights disappear. I had to ensure I didn't screw up.

The sun showed pinks and oranges as we made our way to the

middle of the pecan grove. The Raneys long inside, we didn't have time to return to the clearing we landed in originally.

With Mr. Raney's poor eyesight, I felt safe to call my vessel at a respectable distance from the house. As my vessel appeared, I turned for one last look.

"Let's go doll, I need to ice me buns," Ace said, stepping into my outhouse.

I followed him, but there was a gnawing feeling in my gut that this wasn't the last time I would meet Sam Raney.

CHAPTER 5

I opened the sliding glass door and entered my house. The fatigue that accompanied time travel was beginning to rear its ugly head. Food and sleep were first and second on my priority list.

"Gertie, I'm home," I hollered out in my best Ricky Ricardo impersonation. Gertie worked at the library on the SMU college campus. Sometimes she stayed late on Saturdays, but I expected she'd be home by now.

Gertie rounded the corner from the den. Her freckled face broke into a wide smile and she wrapped me in one of her full-on hugs. Gertie always hugged tight. It was one of the things I loved about her. There were no secrets with Gertie. She wasn't afraid to show everyone who she was or tell them what she thought. Her life was an open book and mine was written with disappearing ink. I trusted her completely.

"Hey, glad you're back safe and sound," she said as she released me.

"Yeah me too." I moved toward the fridge. My trip to Purley had been a little unnerving. Meeting the younger version of Caiyan called for a glass of wine.

Gertie wore a cute pair of Lululemon leggings and a flowing top that accentuated her blue eyes.

"Cute leggings," I said.

"Thanks, I hope Brodie feels the same. He's on his way over. We're going out to eat and then to a movie. Want to come?"

Brodie always stopped by his farm in Australia when he returned from a travel. His family thought he worked in sales and traveled with his job. He left the running of the farm to his brothers but helped out between moon cycles.

"No thanks. I'm beat, and I'm starving," I said and reached for the refrigerator door.

"About that..."

I opened the refrigerator and surveyed the contents. Empty, except for a sad head of lettuce, a six pack of Brodie's favorite beer, some questionable yogurt, a can of whipped cream, and a box from the Cheesecake factory.

"You didn't go to the grocery store?"

"I know it was my turn, but I met some girlfriends after work for drinks, and we ended up catching a concert at the House of Blues. There was so much pot passed around we got high off the secondhand smoke. Afterward, we came back here and had pizza and cheesecake." She motioned to the stack of dirty dishes on the counter. "I saved you the leftover cheesecake, and I picked up a can of that whipped cream you like when I stopped for beer and gas on my way home from work today."

Whipped cream from the gas station might be a little risky, but what the hell. I was a girl who looked danger in the face and told it to F-off. I uncapped the can, squirted a large dollop into my mouth, and devoured the delicious topping.

"For the love of all things sanitary, please don't suck that out of the can," Gertie said as she filled the sink up with hot, soapy water.

"What are you doing?" I asked, then replaced the top on the can of whipped cream and returned it to the fridge.

"The dishwasher is broken," she said as she submerged the first dish in the water.

"Did you call my dad?" My parents were our landlords, and my dad doubled as the handyman. He lived an hour away in a hoity toity over-fifty community, but he still worked at his feed store in Sunnyside during the week.

"No. I didn't want to bother him on the weekend."

I grabbed a can of vegetable soup from the pantry and dumped it into a bowl, then set the microwave for three minutes.

"I'll call him tomorrow," I said, taking a dish from her and drying it with a towel. I stacked each dish on the counter.

The microwave signaled my soup was done cooking. I left the dirty glasses for Gertie, retrieved my soup, and sat down at the table to eat.

A gurgle and a crack sounded outside, and Brodie's bathtub materialized in my backyard.

Gertie squealed a little noise of delight as she dried her hands and met him coming in the door. He pulled Gertie in for a giant hug followed by a deep kiss. When they came up for air, he noticed me.

"Hey Jen, I heard ya had a second travel."

News travels fast at the WTF. "Mortas took a late jump. Ace went with me." I scanned his face. "We saw Caiyan."

He paused. If Caiyan was communicating with Brodie it didn't show on his face. I corrected myself. "It wasn't Caiyan, but a younger version of him."

"Did he see ya?" Brodie asked me.

"No, he didn't make us."

"Good."

I filled Brodie in on the details of my travel, but he didn't know anything about Caiyan's trip or the sword.

"Are you sure you don't want to come with us?" Gertie asked, her arms securely wrapped around Brodie's waist.

"Yep. Positive," I said, envying the couple. "I'm going to take a shower and go to bed."

Gertie grabbed her Hobo bag and chose two bottles of beer from the fridge and two boxes of candy from the pantry to sneak into the movie.

"That's my girl," Brodie said as he watched her dump the items into the bag. "Always saving me coin."

"I'm not paying those high prices," Gertie said. "We're on a budget."

"Ooh, can we stop and get some of them lime chips?" Brodie asked. "They're bloody good with the chocolate covered raisins."

I smiled at the two of them. They were so cute. The couple left a few minutes later, leaving me in peace. I finished my soup, washed my bowl in the sink, and placed it on the dish cloth next to the plates to dry.

After watching an episode of *Outlander—ha time traveling through the stones, that girl had it easy*—I wandered into the kitchen.

A bottle of nighttime cold medicine promising a good night's sleep sat next to the dish rack. I could take some and be out for the count. A long, restful night's sleep sounded perfect.

I took the recommended dosage of the green cold medicine and added an extra capful for good measure. I wanted the stuff to knock me out and make me forget how much I missed Caiyan. The big *L* word hovered on the edge of my vocabulary.

As I set the bottle down, a fifth of whiskey next to the coffee pot beckoned me. Mamma Bea always told me two fingers of whiskey would do a body good. There were lots of promises coming from my kitchen. I took a shot from the bottle, enjoyed the burn, and followed it with a drink of water.

Attack cat meowed below me. I dumped a few treats onto the Corian countertop, and he jumped up next to me. I didn't stroke his fur because that normally resulted in a swat from him and blood drawn on my part. The gray tabby preferred to be touched by the select few.

He licked his paw while I put away the cold medicine, indifferent to my presence.

"Not even a thank you for the treats, you flea bag."

An angry hiss startled me. I glanced at him. His ears were back, and his tail bottle brushed as he bared his teeth at the ceiling.

The creak of footsteps echoed against the hardwood floors above me. Someone was upstairs. My nine-millimeter handgun was hidden in a Nine West shoe box in my shoe closet adjacent to my bed. If the intruder was in my bedroom, I'd have to find another means of protection.

I inched my way up the stairs, avoiding the third and eighth steps I knew from my childhood days of sneaking out of the house were the creaky ones. Another noise came from the direction of my bedroom.

My bedroom door hung ajar. If I leaned in and turned on the lights, I could surprise the unwanted guest, but first, I needed to arm myself.

I ducked into the nearest room and searched for a weapon. When I was younger, this room belonged to my sister. After she left for college, I converted it into my closet. Clothes hung from rollaway racks around the perimeter of the room.

I picked up a belt. What was I going to do, whip the intruder? A box of Manolo Blahniks four-inch stilettos sat in their box on the makeshift center island I had purchased from IKEA.

My shoes were housed in floor to ceiling shoe racks in my bedroom. My dad built them for me when, in fourth grade, I discovered shoes were my passion. And still are.

These new additions hadn't made it to their place with the rest of my precious footwear collection. I found the fun, gold pumps on clearance at Nordstrom's Anniversary Sale and needed to try them on with a dress I planned to wear to the next wedding I attended.

Many of my high school friends were either getting engaged or married. It was an age thing. The dreaded "if you don't get married by age thirty, your life as an old maid begins" syndrome.

I opened the box and pulled out the right shoe. The thin heel gleamed like a dagger in the moonlight streaming in through the window. I could gouge an eye out with it. I jabbed it in the air, practicing my gouge.

The sound of the slider on my closet door forced me to raise my weapon. Not only did someone break into my room, the thief was stealing my shoes!

I held the shoe at the level of my eye and slowly eased my way toward my room. Peeking inside, the familiar scent of cinnamon and pine crossed my bedroom along with the silhouette of a figure heading toward my balcony. I flipped on the light switch.

"What are you doing here?" I asked.

He stopped short and turned toward me. His eyes ran the length of my body and leveled at the shoe held in my hand.

"Death by shoe, I dinnae think ye'd do much damage, Sunshine."

His black t-shirt stretched across a well-toned chest.

I fought the urge to move toward him and lowered my shoe. "Why haven't you contacted me?"

"I couldnae. The Mafusos have a babysitter that follows me wherever I go. I finally ditched him, and here I am." He opened his arms, presenting himself.

He was being held prisoner. Well, almost. I cocked an eyebrow at him.

"I'm sorry, but I did warn ye, I'd be deep undercover."

"With the Mafusos." My words came out in an accusatory ire.

"Aye."

I huffed. "Why are you leaving?'

"I'm naugh leaving." He bit his bottom lip, then released it and moved toward me slowly. "Look, I need to speak to ye."

His dark, mussed hair and the way his emerald eyes held mine sent tingles to my nether regions. I couldn't control my desire to kiss the pouty lip he had released.

The shoe clattered to the floor as I jumped into his arms and wrapped my legs around his middle. My mouth pressed to his, and he enveloped me in the kiss that I'd been dreaming of for months. My lady parts wanted him naked. His tongue trailed over mine as his passion ignited a fire inside me. Zap, tingle. We hadn't missed a beat. The sensation went all the way to my toes.

"Ye missed me, yeah?"

"Yeah," I said. "Where have you traveled? And why haven't you sent any word?"

My inner voice screamed at me to stop being an inquisitive bitch. She wanted some action, and I had to admit I did, too. He avoided my question with a long, deep kiss.

"You missed me, too." I unhooked my legs from his waist. Leaning against him, wrapped in his arms, and pleased to feel his hardness pressed against my thigh, I ran my hand down to encourage.

"Jen, seriously." He pulled away from me, turned and ran a hand through his tousled hair.

"What's wrong?" I asked.

He opened his mouth to reply, then closed it, finally admitting, "I'm starving, have ye got any food?"

OK, not like Caiyan at all, putting food before sex.

"I havenae had a bite all day."

I eyed him. The Caiyan I knew never postponed naked for Newtons. "Uhm, I'm...not sure. Gertie didn't do the grocery shopping while I was...away." I turned, and he followed me downstairs.

He leaned against the counter and watched me ramble through the pantry. I surfaced with a box of macaroni and cheese.

"Sorry, it's all I've got. We could order out?"

"'Tis fine," he said.

I put a pot on to boil, but my instincts told me he had something on his mind. If I waited, maybe he would tell me why he was acting all kinds of strange. I opened the fridge and offered him one of Brodie's beers.

He opened it and took a long pull from the bottle. The way he looked at me through heavy-lidded eyes made me wonder why we were down here in the kitchen instead of upstairs satisfying my extreme urges.

My mind churned with reasons why he hesitated after so many months apart. I absentmindedly pulled the whipped cream can from the fridge and upended it into my mouth. I heard him mumble, "Shite!"

When I glanced over at him, his lips parted slightly as he watched me lower the can and swallow the mouthful of white cream.

He had me naked on the kitchen table faster than I could recap the can. He retrieved the whipped cream can from the floor where I had dropped it and sprayed a happy trail from my belly button down to my boy howdy. Much to my satisfaction, he proceeded to have a Jen sundae. When we came up for air, the can of whipped cream was empty, and the pot had boiled dry.

He ran a finger down my cheek. "I thought aboot ye often, Sunshine."

"Me too. I mean, I thought about you, too." I gathered my clothes and turned off the stove.

He beckoned me with his index finger to follow him upstairs to shower. I smiled. The old Caiyan had returned. We were back, the old us. My hunger satisfied by a can of Reddi-wip.

After a hot shower, more kisses, and more everything else, we headed back downstairs for real food. I made the mac and cheese and we stayed in the kitchen leaning against the kitchen cabinets, the table covered with the aftermath of whipped cream and love.

Caiyan wore his jeans low on his hips, his muscled torso covered by the soft cotton t-shirt. Curls of his hair, jet black from the wet of the shower, framed his face.

"Where have you been traveling?" I asked. With my guilty pleasure satisfied, I wanted answers.

"I cannae tell you." He placed his bowl in the sink and rinsed it out. "Yer in danger jest by me being here."

"How can I help you, if you don't confide in me?" I rinsed out my bowl and placed it on the countertop next to the dishes. Frustrated with his secrecy, I turned and caught him staring at me. I stifled a yawn. The cold medicine was kicking in, delayed by the adrenalin rush sparked by our sexcapades. I wanted to go upstairs, snuggle together under my down comforter, and fall asleep satisfied in his arms.

"Jen, I have to gain the Mafusos' trust in order to get my key back."

"But you don't trust me enough to tell me what's going on? What if they leave you stranded in another time? I could find you, if you would quit being a bullheaded ass and talk to me."

"Jen—" He stopped and raked a hand through his hair. The mussy, dark hair made my lower half tingle. I wanted to kiss the scar that cut through his top upper lip. I ignored the want and waited for answers.

He stared at me.

"Jake thinks the reason you're helping the Mafusos has something to do with the sword you swiped from the Appomattox museum."

"I dinnae steal it, I borrowed it. Besides, it belonged to a friend of mine." His eyes grew sad with the last words he spoke.

"You mean Mr. Raney?"

He paused, considered. "It was you in the town. The blonde in front of the five and dime." He smiled. "Seems like a long time ago for me, but only a few days for ye, yeah?"

"I hoped you wouldn't recognize me and mess up our meeting in Scotland."

"Aye, I dinnae until now, but I never forget a pretty face. The sword belonged to a friend who died a long time ago. He left me a message to help him, and I failed. If Mortas finds the sword, he could cause damage beyond repair."

"So, this quest you're on is tied to the sword?"

He didn't answer. Months ago, under the influence of the Thunder key, Caiyan was using the sword as a bargaining tool with the Mafusos to swap for his key.

"Didn't you tell me you stole the sword from the museum to sell to the Mafusos?" I arched an eyebrow at him. *Esplain, Lucy.*

"Jen, 'tis for yer own safety that I keep my reasons to myself, and ye need to tell yer boss to stay clear until I'm done."

"Jake is your boss. Why don't you tell him yourself?"

"Was my boss. Ye need to think of me as a brigand now."

"There's no reason for you to do this. We can find you another key."

"Jen," he began again. "I need my key to—"

"I know, so ye can protect me," I mocked. "I don't need you to protect me. I'm perfectly capable of protecting myself."

He huffed. "Gian-Carlo has made a deal with me. If I complete a mission, he weel return my key."

"That's it?" I placed my hands on my hips.

"Naugh entirely. I have to show my commitment to the family by —" he paused, then sighed. "I wanted to tell ye myself." He stalled, and my stomach clenched.

"Jen." He turned and walked a few paces away from me. He ran his hand through his hair in an agitated gesture. "I need to tell ye something."

"Tell me what?"

"Now, dinnae get mad."

"Why would I get mad?"

"Jest hear me oot." He backed the farthest he could away from me.

"Spill it."

"I have to marry Mahlia."

I'm not sure when the first plate left my hand, but the third one missed his face by mere inches. He backed out of the kitchen, dodging plates as I flung them like Frisbees.

"Jen, 'tis for the greater good," he yelled.

"The greater good?" I shrieked. "You couldn't tell me this before we had sex?"

He stood speechless.

I launched another dish, and he ducked. It shattered against the wall and fell like rain, meeting the other victims on the tile floor.

"Jest calm down," he said.

My face heated as my blood pressure rose to a level a normal person would have called the paramedics.

"Calm down?" My voice screeched. "I am calm!" I threw another dish, and it felt exhilarating. I continued to chunk the dishes until my arm ached and there weren't any dishes left on the counter. Sometime between me telling him to never come back and cursing at him, he fled.

White shards of ceramic sprinkled across the floor, and the back door stood open. I moved toward the open door and kicked something. The empty can of whipped cream rolled across the tile. I bent over and picked up the can, sat down at the table, and cried.

CHAPTER 6

"Jen! Jen! Wake up!" A frantic voice called out to me.

I blinked my eyes open. A fuzzy image blocked my line of vision. A face. Someone had her face in front of mine.

"Ma?" I asked.

"No, it's me, Gertie."

I blinked again, and Gertie's freckles became clearer. A look of relief crossed her face when I lifted my head off the table. She was kneeling next to me.

Brodie stood behind her staring down at me.

"What in the bejeesus happened to you?" she asked me.

"Thwat do you mean?" My heavy, fat tongue caused my words to slur.

Gertie snapped orders at Brodie. "Wet a cloth with cold water." Gertie helped me sit upright, then something wet and cold smacked me across the face.

"I thook medidine," I explained as she wiped the cold cloth over my face.

"And then what? Decided to face plant into the cheesecake?" Brodie asked.

I looked down. There was a perfect outline of my face in the center of the cheesecake. Sometime after Caiyan left, I opened the cake. Then I remembered what happened, and the tears stung my eyes.

"Caiyan thopped by."

"He did?" Gertie asked.

"That explains the whipped cream," Brodie chuckled.

Gertie gave him the stink eye, and he stopped laughing. Brodie thrust a glass of water at me, and after I took a long drink my tongue moved freely.

"He has to marry Mahlia," I said, and the waterworks turned on again.

Gertie shot Brodie a concerned glance.

Brodie shrugged. "He hasn't been communicating with me."

I set the water glass down on the table, sniffed, and blew my nose into the washrag. "Why does he have to marry the bitch from hell?"

"Yeah," Gertie said. "Why would he do that?"

We both looked at Brodie.

"Like I said, the bloke hasn't kept me in the loop on this one, but I do know one thing. If the dingoes are playing hardball, he'd agree, but wouldn't go through with it." He paused. "Unless it was important."

"That's what I'm afraid of." I dropped my face into the washrag and wished I could wash away the heartache.

"Your ma called," Gertie stuck her head in my bedroom. "She's coming over with a surprise."

The sun streamed in through the French door in my room.

"What time is it?"

"Eleven. I figured you needed to rest after the travel and…all."

I pushed aside the covers along with last night's events with Caiyan and lumbered out of bed.

"When is she coming?" I asked. My mom rarely came to the house. I grimaced. I'd missed a few Sunday dinners due to the moon cycles. Eli covered for me, but I'd still get the Catholic guilt speech.

"She said around noon. I'm cleaning the house, and I did the grocery shopping."

"Thanks. I owe you."

Gertie shrugged. "You needed to sleep, and I know how particular Cuzin Mary is about…well everything."

Gertie feared my mother more than carbs. My mom was Mary Poppins on the outside, but she'd give Cinderella's stepmother a run for her money when it came to a clean house. She'd open the fridge to check our supply of food and click her tongue if the contents were too bare or too unhealthy. We'd also get a tongue click if there was dust on the tables or clothes on the floor.

I tossed my clothes from last night in the hamper. Picked up the shoe I almost bludgeoned Caiyan with, and now wished I had. Returned it to the box. Made my bed, showered, and dressed.

What kind of surprise would my mom bring? Maybe a new pair of boots for fall. She liked fashion. Her taste was a bit straitlaced for me, but I'd roll with a new purse or pair of shoes.

I went downstairs. Gertie was sweeping up the last of the plate remnants.

"Sorry," I said, staring down at the pile of shattered porcelain.

"Don't worry about it. Your reasons were justified. Brodie cleaned up most of it last night. I was giving it a second sweep to make sure he didn't miss any, which he did." Her snub nose wrinkled into a frown.

"I'll replace the dishes."

"I saw a new pattern from the Pioneer Woman I liked." Gertie smiled at me.

I was thankful she didn't badger me with questions about Caiyan. I didn't want to talk about him this morning. I helped Gertie dispose of the broken pieces of my life and finished tidying up the den.

At precisely twelve o'clock, there was a tap, tapping on the front door, and my mom breezed in. Chanel No. 5 and self-confidence floated around her like the dust cloud that surrounds Pigpen in the Peanuts comic strip.

I stopped lint rolling the cat hair off the back of the sofa and hid the roller behind a throw pillow.

"Hi, Mom." I moved toward her, but she whisked by me, sending me an air kiss as she passed. Her hands were laden with a covered dish.

We resembled each other with the full bust line and slim hips. Her blond hair was cut in a short bob, her Kate Spade bag dangled from the crook of her elbow, and she wore a sensible lipstick.

"Hello, girls," she said as she sat the dish and her purse on the kitchen table.

I followed her to the breakfast nook to give her a hug.

"Howdy, Cuzin Mary." Gertie put aside the broom and came to inspect the contents of the dish.

"It's cousin, not cuzin, Gertie. Now that you're a librarian you need to watch your English p's and q's." Mom hugged Gertie. She lectured and embraced simultaneously. The woman had talent.

I grinned at the way my mom mimicked Gertie's pronunciation.

Gertie gave me an eyeroll. "Yes, Cousin Mary."

My mom smiled her approval. "Gertie, I see you were sweeping. So nice to keep a clean house. Don't you agree, Jennifer?"

"Is this our surprise?" I asked. Avoiding her sarcasm, I sneaked a peak under the foil. "It's a casserole." I said, my bottom lip jutting out in a teenage pout at her. I have an animosity for casseroles. My family demanded casseroles at all our functions, and I despised them.

"It's not for you."

"It's not our surprise?" Gertie asked.

"Heavens no, Jennifer hates casseroles."

I blew out a sigh of relief.

"I made you a ham and a chocolate cake. It's in the car." That piqued my interest. Mom made a delicious strawberry glazed ham, but chocolate cake, too? I raised an eyebrow at her while Gertie was performing a celebratory fist pump and giving Mom extra hugs.

"So, our surprise is ham?"

"Of course not, dear. Your surprise is," she paused. "Well...we bought the townhouse next door."

"And?" I knew there was more. Buying another investment property wouldn't warrant ham and chocolate cake.

77

"Your cousin Darryl is moving in."

"Cuzin Darryl!" Gertie and I erupted together. Mom arched an eyebrow at us. The food was a bribe.

Cousin Darryl was the kind of guy who said, "Hold my beer and watch this." He couldn't keep a steady job. He had warrants out for his arrest in three counties for disorderly conduct, and last I heard, he was living in a trailer with his grandmother.

Gertie chewed a nail while I stared slack-jawed at Mom.

"When is he moving in?" I asked.

"Today." Mom smiled and smoothed the pleat in her Nike golf skort.

Smart woman. She didn't warn us ahead of time. Our complaining would have meant weeks of fielding our objection with baked goods of guilt. "I thought I would bring a casserole over for you girls to give him. You know, to make him feel welcome. He's never been out on his own before. I thought it was perfect—you girls could keep an eye on him, help him get acquainted with living in the city."

She meant babysit him.

"Anyhoo, I also brought a plant as a housewarming gift. It's in the car."

"I'll get them," Gertie said, then headed outside to retrieve the bribe.

"That's nice of you, dear," Mom said to Gertie and gathered up her purse.

"Don't you want to stay until Darryl arrives?"

"Oh, no can do. I'm playing in a scramble with the girls this afternoon, and then your dad and I are going to the club for dinner."

"Darryl isn't wearing an ankle bracelet, is he?" I asked. "You know, the electronic kind monitored by the authorities."

"Heavens no, but your aunt Loretta has had enough of him, and your dad wanted to help out. He's harmless, just needs someone to show him the way."

"Does he have a job?"

Mom pursed her lips. She didn't approve. "He has a job bartending in Terrell. Be nice to your cousin. He doesn't have any friends in the city."

I didn't think my cousin would have trouble meeting anyone. He was born winking at the nurses.

"There's no family dinner tonight since you'll be helping Darryl get situated. Not that you've been to any lately. Tell your brother I'll see him next Sunday. You and Gertie should come too, invite Darryl."

"It's going to take a lot of chocolate cake to live next door to Darryl," I said to Mom.

"The chocolate cake is for you. I heard you broke up with your Scottish boyfriend." How did she learn these things?

"Eli told me you might like some chocolate cake. That's your comfort food dear, so I probed. Don't get mad at Eli for telling me. You should call occasionally. I'm sure the two of you will make up. Give the man time. Men need to sow their wild oats before they can settle down."

I knew Caiyan had been sowing a lot of oats lately; there couldn't be any more left in the field.

Gertie entered carrying two travel containers and balancing a potted palm on her hip. "The ham smells yummy, Cousin Mary." She strained to say the word cousin correctly.

Mom broke out in a wide smile at Gertie's perfect cousin. She sent us air kisses and waved as she exited the door.

"Tootles, girls! Put the ham in the oven on three fifty for an hour. I know I can count on you."

Gertie and I examined the spread on the table. Strawberry glazed ham cooked to perfection. Accompanied by green beans with the right amount of garlic to keep away the vampires, and chocolate cake, iced like a pro and topped with curly cue chocolate shavings. Gertie and I inhaled the aroma of home baked food.

"I love your ma," Gertie said, munching on a crispy green bean. "But sometimes she's a little intimidating."

"Just wait. We're going to pay for this meal. Darryl is a handful."

"Yep, but I heard he's trying to turn over a new leaf. He's got a new side business and he's a real good singer. He's trying to raise money to try out for one of them contests, like American Idol, or that other one with Blake Shelton."

I had a vision of Darryl on *The Bachelor*. A new mission to find a woman who will take him off my hands began to take shape. I filed it behind strangling Caiyan and buying Gertie new dishes.

I grabbed a bottle of wine from the fridge and poured Gertie and me a glass. "Drink up, we need to prepare for Darryl."

GERTIE SLID the ham and green beans in the oven to warm for dinner, then joined me on the couch to watch the next episode of *Big Little Lies*.

I had just poured myself a second glass of red wine when country music blared from a radio outside the house. Gertie paused the show, and as we made our way to the front door to locate the cause of the ruckus, a gunshot made us flinch and drop to the ground. I managed to keep all my wine inside of the glass.

"Someone's shootin' at us," Gertie yelled, covering her ears.

I peeked out through the front window. A rusted-out Ford F350 Dually, hooked up to a one-horse trailer, sat idle at the curb. The truck was raised six inches off the ground, had a stocked gun rack—and a Confederate flag flying from the antenna.

The truck let loose a window-rattling backfire, and I informed Gertie she could uncover her ears.

She joined me at the window.

"Is that Darryl?" I asked Gertie.

"It's either Darryl or the president of Willie Nelson's fan club."

The engine on the Ford gagged then died, Cousin Darryl jumped down from the cab and sauntered in our direction. Neighbors gawked at Darryl from their windows. His straw Stetson sat high on his head. His lean frame wore wranglers and a faded t-shirt that read *get high on life*.

He stopped and looked up at the townhouse next door.

"We should go out and say hi. See if he needs help unloading," Gertie said.

I upended the glass of wine and downed the contents. "OK, I'm ready."

Gertie opened the front door, and we went outside. The smell of corn dogs and cow shit met us as we stepped off the front porch.

"Hey Darryl," Gertie said as we approached him.

"Well I'll be, if it ain't Gertrude." He grabbed her by the waist and swung her around rag doll style. Placing Gertie back on her feet, he turned toward me. I held up a hand to fend him off.

"Cu-zin Jen."

My mom would have a field day with this one.

He ignored my hand and embraced me in a hug that lifted me off my feet. Darryl's grandma was my dad's sister, making him my second cousin and Gertie's third. He'd spent more time with Gertie when she lived in Mount Vernon because his grandma, my aint Loretta Lynn, lived in the same town. His mother had MIA, or what my family refers to as musician induced amnesia. She ran off with a musician and forgot she had a kid.

He released me, then stepped back and tipped his hat at me. "My, my, cuz, you sure filled out in all the right places."

Ick. I forced a smile. "Mom told me you were moving in today."

"Yep, it was awful nice of your parents to let me move into the brick house." He turned and admired the townhouse.

I raised my eyebrows at Gertie, and she interpreted softly, "As opposed to living in the house *on* bricks."

"Do ya need any help unloading your stuff?" Gertie asked.

Darryl eyed his horse trailer and shook his head.

"Is there someplace I can park my trailer?"

"There's a carport out back." Gertie gestured with her thumb over her right shoulder. "If you unhook it, it'd probably fit underneath."

"My mom sent you a casserole for dinner," I said.

"Um...that sure was nice of her. Let me get my stuff unpacked and I'll come by and pick it up later."

Alrighty then. He waited until we went back into the house before he turned toward his truck. Gertie and I peeked out the window as he unloaded a knapsack and a guitar.

"That's it?" Gertie whispered. "What's he going to sleep on, and where are his clothes?"

"We're inside, why are you whispering?"

"I don't know, seems when you're spying on someone you ought to whisper."

We watched Darryl carry his things inside. Mrs. Jones, the prior owner of the townhouse, moved to an assisted living apartment. She left her bed and a few sticks of furniture behind.

Darryl exited the house, started up his truck, and, with a loud bang, drove away. A few minutes later we heard him pull into the carport next door. Having Darryl as my neighbor would be a challenge. What if he saw my outhouse do its disappearing act?

A few hours later, there was a knock on the front door and Darryl entered without waiting for the door to be answered.

My inner voice padlocked the door.

He whistled as he walked into our house. "Nice digs you got here. Mine smells a little like mothballs and Bengay, but I'll have her ship-shape in no time at all."

"Here you go," I said and handed him the casserole.

Gertie boosted up the potted palm. "Welcome home."

"Cool. Hey how about I stay and y'all can eat supper with me? There's more than enough casserole, and I don't like eating by myself."

Gertie and I looked at each other, and the timer on the oven chimed, announcing the ham was ready to melt in our mouths.

"You know, Darryl. We have dinner cooking. Why don't I put your casserole in the fridge, and you can eat with us tonight?"

"Sounds like a mighty fine idea." He handed the casserole to me and removed his cowboy hat, hanging it on the newel of the stair railing.

Gertie took the ham out of the oven while I set the table.

Darryl peeked out the sliding glass door, and his voice caught. "What do we have here?" He threw open the slider and whistled as he stepped out into my backyard.

Gertie and I looked at each other, then followed hastily behind him.

"Is that what I think it is?" he asked.

"What?" I asked, hoping he was referring to the rusted-out grill and not my outhouse.

"That Aint Elma's outhouse?"

I sighed.

"Yes, it is," Gertie said. "She left it to Jen in her will."

"Well lucky duck, they don't make outhouses like this anymore."

Unless you live in the outskirts of Alaska, the need is not what it used to be.

He skipped through my soldiers of roses to the outhouse and opened the door.

"Darryl, I wouldn't do that if I were you," Gertie cautioned.

It was too late. He stood inside and ran his hand along the grain of the wood.

Gertie and I took a step back. "I reckon these handles are for —yeee!"

Before he could finish his sentence, my outhouse belched him into the air. He landed face to the sky in the hedge of Japanese Boxwood.

Gertie rushed over. "Are you all right?"

I casually followed behind her, suppressing a small, proud smile.

"That was awesome! Gosh, how much you want for it?"

"Um, it's not for sale," I said and offered him a hand.

"Why do you want an outhouse?" Gertie asked him.

He grasped my hand, and I pulled him to his feet. "I'm a picker."

"A whatter?" Gertie asked.

"A picker." He plucked the spiky leaves off his pants.

"I thought you were a singer?" I asked.

"And a bartender," Gertie added.

"I do those jobs after five during the week and on the weekends. During the day, I'm a picker. I take old things and make them cool, then I sell them on Etsy, eBay, and other Internet sites.

"Sorry, the outhouse isn't for sale," I said again.

His shoulders slumped. "Too bad. It'd make a nice potting shed."

We returned inside, and Gertie plated the ham. I offered him a choice of beer or wine. He took the beer, and I poured Gertie and me a glass of wine.

"Where do you find most of your things?" I asked as we sat down at the table.

"I go to estate sales, garage sales, and sometimes I drive around and see what people leave out at the curb. Once I found a hundred dollars someone left in an old dresser."

"Cool," Gertie said.

I wasn't sure I wanted to live next door to a Junker, but it was better than living next to a drug dealer.

"Y'all will have to come over once I get all moved in. I got some real good pieces you might want to buy."

We sat around my table eating the ham. Darryl shook his head and pinched his arm.

"I can't believe I have a whole house to myself."

"Is this the first time you've lived away from home?" I asked him.

"Yepper, I'm going to miss my mee-maw, but I have you gals to keep me company."

Hold the front door! "We're not home much," I said, and Gertie elbowed me.

"What Jen means is we go out, but if you need anything, just holler."

I didn't want Darryl hollering at me or peeping over the fence and seeing my outhouse vanish. He didn't seem like the type to spy on his neighbor, but then again, I had spied on him earlier.

He was a few years younger than me. A good-looking guy in a "I can hog tie a calf in under thirty seconds and have the body to do it," sort of way.

He told us how he grew up in the trailer park with his mee-maw and his six younger cousins. Apparently, Aint Loretta's son wasn't any prize either and dumped his six kids on her doorstep.

"My mee-maw's got her hands full with the young'uns. I'm going to send her money once I hit the big time."

He looked a little uncertain about his talents.

"Clyde's going to love the new place." He paused and grimaced.

"Who's Clyde?"

He slid his jaw around before he answered. "My potbelly pig."

"You have a pig?" I asked, a fork full of ham halfway to my mouth.

"Yeah, but he's real quiet, like a mouse, and clean, too. He only does his business in the litter box. I trained him." Darryl chewed a mouthful of ham and used his fork wand style as he spoke.

Oh boy.

"Now Daphne's another matter. She goes where she wants, but always comes back when she's tuckered out.

"Daphne?" I sent Gertie a concerned look.

"My hawk."

"Darryl, does my mom know you have a small farm living with you?"

My mom was the firm one growing up. No pets of any kind were allowed in the house. Eli brought home a bullfrog in his coat pocket once, and he was grounded for a week. The bullfrog was released to the wild.

Darryl's face dropped. "I might not have mentioned that I have a few pets, but I remembered you was an animal lover, so I thought you'd let me get by with a few friends."

I raised my eyebrows at him. "Animal lover?"

"You remember, don't ya? The way you loved to ride Buttercup. Couldn't get you off her to give anyone else a turn."

The last time I saw Darryl I was ten. He encouraged me to ride his Shetland pony. The pony sucked in its round belly and the saddle slipped to the side. I clung to its mane, afraid I'd fall to my death. My dad had to pry me off the beast.

We ate cake, and Darryl told us about his new job. He was bartending at a club in Terrell, a nearby town home to the local mental hospital. The club was a stone's throw from the DMV, so I was familiar with the small town, but I had never been to the club.

"I start next weekend."

After dinner, Darryl stood and stretched. He walked to the back door and peered out at the backyard. "If'n you ever decide to sell, I'd like to have first dibs."

"Sure," I told him.

"Thanks for the supper. I'd best be getting home. Daphne gets upset if I'm gone too long."

"Let me get your casserole out of the fridge," Gertie said.

"Um...Darryl what happens when Daphne gets upset?" I handed him the potted palm.

"Hey there, kitty." Darryl either ignored my question or was distracted by Gertie's gray tabby perched on the back of the sofa, the cat's normal sweater-snagging location.

Darryl balanced the plant on his hip, then scratched the cat under his chin. The cat purred and gave Darryl a nudge with his head.

Amazing.

"Daphne likes to show off by bringing me her roadkill," Darryl said then lowered his voice. "You might want to keep an eye on the kitty."

Gertie met us at the front door with the casserole. "I can carry this next door for you."

"Nope, you ladies have been kind enough. I've got it."

I opened the door for him, and he left, plant in one hand and Tuna Scroodle in the other.

"I think Darryl's got more than a few pets next door."

"At least he's family," Gertie said.

"Yep, there's that."

CHAPTER 7

The next morning, I walked into the chiropractic office with a box of donuts under one arm. I admitted to myself I was eating my feelings, but the sugar and saturated fat made me feel better, temporarily, and that's all I needed to get through the day.

"Hey," Eli said as I sat down in the chair across from his desk and chose a donut from the box. He stopped notating a chart, and his blue eyes glanced at my face, and then focused on the chocolate glazed donut I held in my hand.

"What gives?" He clicked his pen closed and leaned back in his chair.

"What do you mean?" I asked, but I knew. My hair was in a messy top bun, and I had dark circles under my eyes. I hadn't bothered with makeup this morning because by the time my insomnia relented at three a.m. I slept through my alarm. Leaving early to pick up donuts and get to work on time was more important than a Kardashian presentation.

"You look like crap. That donut you're eating is going to clog your arteries and make your ass big."

Just like a brother to tell it like it is.

"Thanks," I said. The sarcasm dripped like the chocolate off my donut. I licked my hand where the wayward icing landed. "It's nothing."

He clicked his pen a few times and cocked an eyebrow at me.

"I'm struggling with an upcoming event." I shrugged.

"And?"

"And remember when I told you Caiyan and I took a break because he had to go deep undercover?"

"Yeah." *Click, click, click.*

"Caiyan's fallen into the abyss. The Mafusos have asked—" I stuttered and tried again. "Gian-Carlo wants—" I huffed. "Caiyan is getting married to—" My shoulders slumped, and I took a big bite of courage. With my mouth full, I forced the name from my lips, "Mahlia."

Eli let out a long slow whistle. My brother had dated Mahlia. She was searching for a key and thought Eli would be a good avenue into my navigation system of family secrets. He thought he loved her, but in the end, he decided she was a little high maintenance.

I swallowed the glob of stress-coping, gluten-filled pastry. "I thought we were on a sort of hiatus, but he has a self-imposed mission. It involves him gaining the trust of the Mafusos."

"So, to prove he's legit, he has to marry Mahlia," Eli finished.

I wondered if he might be a tad jealous. "You don't still have feelings for her, do you?"

"No. She's a nutcase. The great sex blinded me for a moment, but there's not much else to fall in love with." *Click, click, click.*

I released the deep breath I was holding, while my inner voice smashed his pen with her stiletto.

"Is this some kind of ploy, or is he going through with it?" Eli asked.

"That's just it. He hasn't confided in anyone. Not even Brodie. We confirmed he's switched sides. The travel lab can't find him because he doesn't wear a key. He's become a brigand." My eyes filled at the last words despite my attempt to hold back the tears. I opened the box and pulled out another chocolate glazed donut.

"I'd give you a brotherly hug to console you, but I'm afraid my white dress shirt will be caught in the fusillade of chocolate retaliation."

"I'm fine." I bit into the donut and gave a troubled sigh.

Eli plucked a tissue from the box on his desk and passed it to me. He pointed to the area above his upper lip.

I swiped at the wayward chocolate icing on mine.

"Maybe he's got a plan." Eli thought for a moment. "Maybe he's keeping you safe."

Safe. Like the sword he's protecting. "He stole a Confederate sword that dates to the Civil War. Jake thinks there might be a connection."

"Jen, no way are you traveling back to the Civil War. Do you know how many people died? And not only from the war, but from the diseases that followed the soldiers around like a tick on a coonhound." *Click, click, click.* Eli waved the pen at me like a magic wand.

"I don't understand your reasoning. I went back to World War II. I've been in a shootout with Bonnie and Clyde and held captive by Pancho Villa. Why won't you trust me to use my brains and do my job?" I crammed the rest of the chocolate glazed donut into my mouth.

"Because I love you, and this thing you do makes me crazy."

"It's the thing I choose to do, so treat me the same way you would if I worked as a police officer."

"At least the police get to wear a Kevlar vest. With you, there's nothing to protect you. Do you know how inaccurate the guns were back then?"

I shrugged and moved on to the sprinkle-covered donut holes.

Click, click, click.

"You might get hit by a stray bullet, or worse, by cannon fire. The Union cannons killed an entire company of men in one shot. Dad took me to the reenactment in Pennsylvania. It's not pretty. Those cannons pop out canisters that explode grapeshot. It's like a shotgun on methamphetamines." Eli's voice elevated and his eyes were growing wide, Charles Manson style.

"I have my key."

He tossed his pen on the desk, yay! and stared blankly at me. There was no arguing with him. The men in my life went to extremes to keep me safe.

"I'm going to take the rest of these to the girls." I held up the donut box.

He grimaced at me, and I took my donut enhanced booty to the breakroom.

My coworkers, Paulina, Elvira, and Helga, fussed around the coffee machine and cheered when I slid the box of donuts onto the table.

They knew I had a relationship with a Scottish hunk, but their knowledge of him ended there. When I explained he dumped me for another woman, they agreed Caiyan was a slimeball.

Devouring the donuts, we made up names to call him. It was childish but satisfying. Elvira, the collections manager, told us about the time she ran over her ex-husband.

"Did he die?" Paulina, Eli's perky assistant, asked.

"No, but he broke both his legs when I hit him the second time."

"Did you get arrested?" Helga asked.

"Not that time. I claimed self-defense. He was mean as a black-tailed rattlesnake. The hospital put him in a half-body cast. Because I felt guilty, for three months I waited on him hand and foot."

"Did he get better?" I asked and imagined running over Caiyan in my Mustang.

"Did he ever. Nine months later his physical therapist gave birth to a bouncing baby boy. The kid had a knit of eyebrows like my guy. We got divorced."

"How did he manage to have sex in a body cast?" Paulina asked.

"Let's just say there was one thing that wasn't a disappointment."

A round of laughter drew Eli into the breakroom.

"Ladies, let's get to work."

Everyone popped a donut hole and exited the breakroom.

"Jennifer, I hope your man comes around," Paulina said to me as we headed toward the front office.

Me, too.

I worked the morning trying to forget about Caiyan. As I was fetching my purse to head out for lunch, Mary, the feisty widow who worked as Eli's office manager, paged me to the front. One donut hole sat alone in the box on the breakroom table. I ate the sole survivor and headed toward the front of the building.

When I entered the front office, the girls were standing at the window, mouths open slightly, drooling.

"What are y'all staring at?" I asked, trying to peek over them.

"Forget what I said about your man," Paulina said. "This one's got to be better."

Marco stood in the reception room thumbing through a back issue of *Men's Fitness*.

He looked up when he saw me, and the dimple in his chin winked and enhanced his chiseled good looks.

Paulina sighed.

I gave him a wave and motioned I'd be right out.

"What's wrong with him? Does he have a small penis?" Mary asked after she closed the sliding window.

Paulina placed her hands over her ears. "If he does, I don't want to know. It would ruin my dream tonight."

I ignored Mary's question and went to meet Marco.

"What are you doing here?" I asked him.

He leaned down and kissed me on each cheek. The murmur of the office girls from behind the window at the very Italian gesture caused me to roll my eyes.

"I heard about Caiyan, and I came to see if you were OK?"

"I'm fine."

"Are you sure, because you smell like a glazed donut." I gave him my best no idea what you're talking about look then changed the subject. "I'm on my lunch hour. Let's go somewhere we can talk."

We walked around the square to the Italian restaurant. Marco insisted on ordering a veggie pizza, and I agreed because the string on my scrub pants had to be loosened after the donuts.

I tapped my fingers on the plastic tablecloth while Marco gave the waitress our order.

"So, you want to talk about it?" he asked me.

I wasn't sure I could confide in Marco. He knew my feelings for Caiyan, but still tried to weasel into my underpants occasionally. He wanted to see what kind of carnal explosion would occur if we had sex. I agreed, when we touched, the heat between us could set an Eskimo on fire.

If things were different between me and Caiyan, I might consider his offer. My inner voice reminded me things were different between me and Caiyan as she held up a save-the-date postcard. Thankfully, the date was blurry. They're not married, yet.

Maybe there was more to Marco's visit than his concern over my reaction to Caiyan's bad choices.

"Did Caiyan ask you to keep an eye on me?"

"Not this time." He paused as the waitress brought our drinks.

"Do you know if they've set a date for the wedding?" I imagined it would be an extravagant affair. I sipped my sweet tea and waited for his answer.

"I haven't heard anything in the social circles." He held his gaze steady with mine. "Jen. I'm worried about you. McGregor's making you crazy with his irrational behavior. He's never going to make you happy."

"I'm guessing you can make me happy?"

A smile tugged at the corner of Marco's mouth. "I could make you happy for a few hours, if you needed someone to take your mind off the Scot."

Hours? It sounded promising, but I brushed him off. "Funny, but I'm not exactly sure why Caiyan's doing this. Doesn't it seem unusual to you that he's joined up with the Mafusos and he's agreed to marry Mahlia? I mean, what could be so damn important for him to do this?"

"You want my honest answer?"

"Yes, of course."

"You."

"Me?" I stared at him. "You remember he dumped me to marry Satan's bitch, right?"

"I mean he's protecting you somehow. Or he's protecting all of us. Still, it doesn't make him any less of an asshole."

I tossed the statement over in my mind. "It started with the Civil War sword. I think if we find the sword, we will have a few answers."

"Maybe."

The waitress brought over our pizza. She leaned down in front of Marco to place the pan of pizza on the table, offering him a perfect view down the front of her shirt.

"Here ya go, sugar," she said, batting her full, fake eyelashes at him. She turned to check on another table but gave Marco a glance over her shoulder on the way.

Oblivious to the woman's flirtations, Marco frowned at the pizza. Obviously, not up to New York standards. He folded a slice and took a bite. "The sword was Confederate, right?"

"Yes, I'm sure Caiyan told me it was a Confederate sword. Do you think the Mafusos are going to drop him into the Civil War?"

"Mortas wants the sword, and he's forcing Caiyan's hand. My guess would be that Caiyan is going to lead him on a wild goose chase. I don't know what to think about the marriage."

"If Mortas gets the key, then Caiyan is supposed to get his key back." I selected a slice of pizza and contemplated Caiyan's possible logic for his actions.

"I've never known the Mafusos to be forthright. Caiyan knows this also. He's probably going to bag the wedding." Marco chose another slice.

I picked the green olives off my pizza and felt hopeful for the first time in a long while.

"The next full moon cycle begins at the end of the month. What's the next major event in the Civil War?"

"You're joking, right?" His dark eyebrows shot upwards.

When my blank stare told him I wasn't, he finished chewing his pizza and took a long drink of the tea. "The Battle of Gettysburg begins on July first."

"That was a pretty bad one, right?"

"The worst battle of the Civil War."

He gave me the look like I shouldn't have slept through my American history class.

"I hope they don't drop him there," I said.

"Me, too. The guns are shit."

We ate in silence until I moved the last slice onto my plate, and he finished his pizza.

I leaned back in my chair, the string on my scrub pants threatening expansion once again.

"Have you heard from Agent McCoy?" Marco asked.

"I'm waiting on Jake to approve the search for the sword at Caiyan's house. He wanted Brodie to check the other potential locations before I went rummaging through his personal space."

"Be careful. If the Mafusos catch you in the area, they'll hang you off the Empire State Building."

The visual made me shudder. When I visited Caiyan, I tried to avoid the Mafusos' area of New York City. They kept close to the docks in the import/export areas in the Bronx. There were rumors Gian-Carlo kept a bank of offices close to the harbor, but he wasn't getting any younger and frequently stayed at the house in the Hamptons.

"I can't believe Mahlia is going along with Gian-Carlo's demands," Marco said.

"Mahlia wouldn't like anything better than to have a Caiyan sandwich and rub my nose in it."

"What did he say when you asked him what he was doing?"

"He told me to be patient, and he said something about smoke and mirrors."

"Hmm sounds like he's got a plan. You should sit back and see what happens."

"I'm afraid it might end up with me eating wedding cake alone."

"I'll postpone being a shoulder for you to cry on until we figure out what the Scot's got up his sleeve."

"Maybe afterward, if he says I do, you can bail me out of jail."

"I'll comfort you in ways you can't imagine."

I smiled. "Thanks. You know how to make me feel better."

"You think I'm joking, but in reality, I'm rooting for the other team."

I attacked my last slice of pizza. Marco was a good friend. I didn't feel the same connection as I did with Caiyan. I was attracted to him, but what breathing woman wasn't?

"Friends can have benefits, you know?"

My mouth dropped open at his spot-on accuracy of my thoughts.

"You just tore at that slice of pizza with your teeth. I saw a bobcat do that at the zoo once." He added a fake shiver.

"Sometimes I worry you can read my thoughts. You don't have ESP, do you?"

"Jen, I'd love to be inside that head of yours, but sadly I have to base my findings on observation alone. I am interested in the benefits part of that statement."

"Is getting me in the sack all you ever think about?"

Before he could answer, the waitress sidled up to our table.

"Can I get you two lovebirds anything else?" she asked.

"Um, we're not a couple." I said, unraveling any notions of fringe benefits.

A little whoop of delight left her lips. "In that case, I'll just leave the check right here. You can pay anytime." She slid the check face down toward Marco and left with a longing gaze.

"I bet money she left her number on the ticket," I said.

Marco flipped over the bill, and a wide smile spread across his face. When I reached for my wallet, he waved me off.

I ignored the fact he put the number in his wallet after he paid the check.

Marco kissed me on the cheek and left me standing in front of the office. A slight tingle remained where his lips brushed my skin.

The girls were standing at the plate glass window watching Marco walk across the street when I entered the office.

"Where's he going?" Elvira asked me. The three of them were staring out the window nodding approvingly.

"He parked down the block." Marco was headed to the wooded area of the park to call his transportation.

"Seems outta the way to me. He coulda parked in front of the office," Elvira harrumphed. Exercise to Elvira meant making an extra pass down the frozen food aisle at the supermarket.

"He's dreamy," Paulina said.

"He's a friend."

"Can I have him?" Helga asked.

"Only if you live in New York. He's not from around here."

"Obviously, they don't make men like that in these parts."

"I resent that remark." Eli entered the room.

"Dr. Cloud, you're dreamy but in an unavailable way," Paulina piped in.

"Good to know." Eli sent a curious glance my direction.

"Marco came for a visit," I added. "To take me to lunch."

"Ah, that explains why all of my employees are staring out the window instead of preparing the charts for the afternoon patients."

AFTER WORK ELI walked me out to my car. He had changed into his shorts and workout shirt. "I'm going to the gym, want to come?"

"Jake forces me to exercise two days a week, and I'm not adding to my plan."

"Suit yourself. I thought with all your Lara Croft adventures you might want to buff up a little."

"I'm fine. I have a date with Gertie. We're watching a Civil War documentary."

"Just make sure you don't go back there."

"Aye, aye captain."

He frowned, then entered his car and drove away to build a better body. I, on the other hand, was going home to watch thousands of men die, followed by a glass of wine and a bubble bath.

CHAPTER 8

When I arrived home, Gertie was on the couch thumbing through one of the Civil War books I'd asked her to bring home from the library. A photo of a few wounded or dead soldiers were on the cover. It was hard to tell.

Mr. Raney had told Caiyan the sword came from the Civil War. I thought maybe watching a couple of documentaries and perusing a book of photographs might be useful. I sat next to her and we took turns making shocked remarks upon each turn of the page.

"It's incredibly gory. Why did they take so many pictures of the dead and none of the battles?" I asked, turning my head away from a particularly gruesome still.

"Would you want to be in the middle of a battle?" Gertie asked. "The photographers stayed behind after the battle. I read they would move the bodies to stage the pictures. See, this guy's in two different photos."

I dismissed the mental image of nineteenth century photographers dragging dead bodies to locations of better lighting and ordered takeout on my phone. While I waited for the food, I Googled a few things on the Internet about the battles of the Civil War.

"Is this true about Gettysburg? The Confederate soldiers went to town looking for shoes and it started a battle?" I asked Gertie.

"I think that's a fabrication, but the Rebels did meet a Union regiment and ran them back into the town."

"Marco told me the next big battle of the Civil War is at Gettysburg."

"When did you see Marco?"

"He came to the office today and took me out to lunch."

Gertie smirked. "He's moving in to claim his territory."

"Don't be ridiculous. He heard about Caiyan and was concerned."

"Concerned you might need a big, muscular shoulder to cry on."

"Gertie, about the battle…"

"That's true. The battle of Gettysburg began on July 1, 1863."

I chewed on a jagged cuticle as I thumbed through the information on my phone. "Gert, there's battles all around the town of Gettysburg, I'm not sure there will be a safe place to land if the Mafusos jump there next moon cycle."

Gertie flipped open a page of her book and showed me an illustration of the area around Gettysburg.

"Since the commanders didn't have good forms of communication, the troops were directed by signal flags and scouts. It was like a huge game of telephone, and not one I'd want to get in the middle of." She paused and a whimsical look came over her face. "But what I wouldn't give to see General Lee in all his glory." She shook off the fangirl moment. "Let's hope the Mafusos aren't stupid enough to jump in the middle of that heap of trouble."

It wasn't the Mafusos who concerned me. If Caiyan got his hands on a key, he'd be crazy enough to jump to Gettysburg and take whatever they sought there.

After we watched a documentary about the famous battle focused in the small Pennsylvania town, accompanied by a generous portion of Chicken Chow Mein and glasses of wine, Gertie clicked off the TV.

"That was intense," I said.

"I agree. I hope you're not going there."

"I need to find the sword. I'm supposed to wait until I hear from Jake before I search Caiyan's apartment."

Gertie stopped opening her fortune cookie. "I know that look, and the answer is no. You're not dragging me to New York to rummage through Caiyan's belongings."

She knew me well. "C'mon Gertie. I need someone to watch my back in case the Mafusos have the place watched."

Jake had eyes on the apartment as well, but it would be too late by the time he found out.

"What if Mahlia's at his apartment? Or worse, Caiyan's home? You know how he hates you sticking your nose in his business."

"I believe the sword has a clue to where Caiyan needs to go."

"I'll make you a deal. Brodie's heading to Scotland to search Caiyan's house and his European and New York offices. Give Brodie two weeks to do his job. If he comes up empty, you'll contact Jake and get approval, then I'll go to the Big Apple with you."

"OK," I said. My shoulders drooped as I chose a fortune cookie. My patience was running thin, but I knew Gertie was right.

She ripped off the plastic from her cookie and broke it in half, peeling the white strip of paper from its insides.

"What does it say?" I asked.

"Your true love will show himself to you under the full moonlight." Gertie frowned. "I guess I'll have to drag Brodie outside next cycle."

"It's supposed to happen naturally, like you see a guy and realize he's standing under the moonlight."

"Sounds kind of corny to me. What's yours say?"

I pulled out the white paper. "No distance is too far, if two hearts are tied together."

"Huh," Gertie said. "Let's hope those tangled up hearts don't lead you to Gettysburg."

A WEEK AND A HALF LATER, I drove home from my morning shift at the chiropractic office. I loved Fridays because we only worked half the day, leaving me the afternoon to scour the gossip sites for tales of Caiyan. My cell dinged, and I put Jake on speaker phone.

He informed me Brodie had turned up empty at Caiyan's offices and at his home in Scotland. Jake gave me the thumbs up to check the apartment.

"My surveillance team hasn't seen Caiyan in months, but he could be in disguise. There hasn't been anyone in the apartment all week. I'm clearing you to search it because you have a key and prior knowledge of the interior contents. If there's any sign of a Mafuso, you get the hell out of there."

"Sure thing, boss." I disconnected and smiled as I pulled into my driveway. I couldn't wait to tell Gertie she was taking a little trip.

WE LANDED in Central Park at my normal hidey hole amongst the Ramble. My summer mini-shift dress stuck to my skin as we walked toward Caiyan's apartment. The June afternoon lent itself to humid and hot, the breeze off the Hudson blocked by the jungle of concrete surrounding the park. I tapped my flip-flop as we waited for the cars to clear Central Park West. After we jaywalked across the street, the sturdy doorman stopped us at the entrance.

"Miss Cloud." He bobbed his head in my direction.

It always surprised me the doorman knew my name. I guess it was their job to know the comings and goings of their tenants, but it still caught me off guard. His dark brown eyes assessed me as I spoke.

"Hi, I'm going up to 10A." I nonchalantly started to pass him.

He held an arm out, halting my advance. "Sorry, ma'am, Mr. McGregor left strict orders. No one allowed upstairs. Only the missus and her assistant."

Gertie looked sideways at me. I paused then explained I was the missus.

"No ma'am, you're the ex-missus."

The heat flushed my face as Gertie dragged me away from the door.

"What did he mean by the missus?" I asked Gertie. My voice cracked as I spoke. "You don't think Caiyan has her living here, do you?"

Gertie shrugged. "Wouldn't surprise me, the rat bastard."

"We need to get up there." I leaned back and counted the floors to ten, identifying the windows belonging to Caiyan.

"How are we gonna do that, when he's got it guarded by stubby Mike Tyson? They know you by sight."

"There has to be another entrance," I said.

The large, white building stretched the entire block from 86th to 87th street. As the doorman greeted another resident, we skirted around the west side of the building.

A delivery driver unloaded boxes onto a dolly. Gertie and I stood next to the subway stop pretending to check my phone for routes. As he pushed the boxes through the iron gate leading to the back of the building, we followed him.

He knocked twice on a door and it opened. As he let the door shut behind him, I stuck my flip-flop in the jam. Gertie and I waited. No one returned to find the door ajar. We tiptoed inside to find the hallway empty. My guess would be whoever let him inside returned to his post. I replaced my flip-flop, and we took the service elevator to the tenth floor.

Gertie knocked on Caiyan's apartment door.

I released a breath when no one answered and palmed the key Caiyan had given me. It was his way of establishing a sense of trust between us and to prove he had surrendered his womanizing ways.

"I don't think anyone's home," Gertie said.

"Caiyan gave me the key, but I think he meant for me to use it in case of an emergency."

Gertie harrumphed at me. "He's engaged to Satan's bitch. If you don't figure out why, he's going to marry her. Think of it as an emergency for your biological clock and time's a tickin'."

I inserted the key into the lock, and turned it open. We entered the apartment, and I stopped short in the hallway. Gertie bumped into me.

"What's wrong? Is he here?" she asked, looking frantically around the foyer.

"No, it smells like him." The apartment smelled of cinnamon and leather. My knees felt weak, and I stood paralyzed in the entry.

Gertie pushed past me. "Toughen up, soldier. There's no time to get gooey, we need answers."

She was right. I needed to get a grip.

"Yoo-hoo!" She called out. No answer.

I pocketed the key and shut the door behind me. The Scottish coat of arms hung on the wall opposite me. My Scot hadn't moved out of his digs. I eased into the main room to join Gertie.

The apartment seemed tidy. There were no coffee cups in the sink, unopened mail on the breakfront, or dead bodies lying in the guest bathtub. I sighed with relief. In fact, it didn't look like Caiyan had been home in a while. The apartment was entirely too clean. Caiyan wasn't a slob, but he abandoned socks on the floor and liked to read the *New York Times* old school style, the daily sports section left strewn across the coffee table until his cleaning lady came by on Wednesday.

I looked down the hall that lead to the bedroom and cringed.

Gertie put a hand on my shoulder. "You take the kitchen and the study. I'll get the bedrooms."

I didn't want to walk in on Caiyan and...Mahlia. In my anger, I forgot to ask him if he was sleeping with her. It should have been the first question to come to a woman's mind when her boyfriend tells her he's going to marry another woman, but the only thing I could think of at the time was why would he choose a key over me?

The study seemed untouched. His laptop wasn't on the desk, but he normally took it to work. I went through a few drawers but knew he wouldn't leave anything important in any of them.

I stood at the big window with my arms wrapped around me and stared out over Central Park. The busy lives below me rushed, and the ones who had time to enjoy strolled through the winding trails of the vast park.

Caiyan didn't leave the sword here. He wouldn't have hidden a vital piece of the puzzle at his home, but some part of me wanted to touch his things again.

I left the study and ruffled through a few papers on the coffee table in the den. There was a receipt from Bergdorfs for two thousand dollars. Was he buying her presents? I pushed the notion aside and moved on to the kitchen.

I opened the pantry in the kitchen. There wasn't any food in the pantry. No surprise there, Caiyan always ate out. The refrigerator contained enough essentials to indicate a human was living here, but not a well-nourished human.

I moved to the door next to the pantry. My hand rested on the crystal doorknob of the closet Caiyan had built for me. I wished my things were inside.

There were so many reasons why I hadn't moved in when he asked me the first time. Mainly because the Thunder key was influencing his judgment. Once he was free of the key's energy, he built the closet as a promise we would be together after he obtained his key. The closet I hadn't even been allowed to put a single shoe on the rack of because he ran off to join the Mafusos for the greater good—or so he told me. I was calling bullshit.

I turned the knob and opened the closet door. The automatic light flipped on and I blinked, then froze.

Clothes hung on every rod. The shoe racks were filled with designer shoes. Not mine. The dresses were not my size either. Nor were the colorful bottles of perfume displayed on the custom-made lingerie island, or the perfect line of designer purses.

I yanked open a drawer and rifled through piles of dainty lace panties, also not mine. I dropped to the white satin tufted footstool. My chest tightened, and I couldn't breathe.

Gertie came around the corner. "Hey, I was—" Her eyes went wide when she saw me.

She plucked the white cheeky panties from my grasp. "Just breathe." She pushed my head between my legs, and I panted for a few minutes.

"You OK?"

"I'm fine." I said, raising my head.

Instead of tears blinding my eyes, I saw red. How dare he let Satan's bitch put her slinky dresses in my closet. It was like giving the next girlfriend the same engagement ring. I wanted to rip the clothes from their hangers, toss them out the window, and watch them float down to Central Park West. Where they would lie helpless and crushed by the oncoming traffic.

"How could he let Mahlia move into my closet?"

"He's scum," Gertie said. "No, he's below scum, a real rat bastard."

Smoke and mirrors.

I envisioned Mahlia burning at the stake, surrounded by her designer undies.

"Whatever he's involved in, it has to be really important to allow this to happen." My words cleared my vision.

"You give him a lot of credit." Gertie twisted her mouth.

"You should have seen the look on his face when he told me about Mahlia. He sounded worried." I glanced up at Gertie. "When have you ever seen him worried?"

"Never. That's his problem, the guy doesn't worry."

Gertie returned the expensive underwear to the drawer and we made haste getting out of Caiyan's apartment.

Gertie and I exited through the front door. She stuck her tongue out at the doorman, and we walked back to Central Park in silence.

"I should be done with him, right?" I blinked hard to fight the tears. I didn't want Gertie to see me cry over him, again.

"Serves him right if you do. You shouldn't put up with that. Especially when he comes over, gets all frisky, then drops a bomb."

It was true he didn't tell me up front about the engagement, but part of that was my doing. I was Miss Horny Pants. He tried to stop things. I was the instigator.

My inner voice pointed out, he could have told me when I filled the pan with water, or while I was rummaging through the pantry. But instead, he told me after he ravaged me on the table.

"Shame on him," Gertie said as if reading my mind. "Besides, he has ugly silk shirts in his closet. You don't want to be seen with a guy in those clothes."

I didn't recall ever seeing Caiyan wear a silk shirt. Clothes were more of a utility to him. He tended to stay on the dark end of the color wheel. Mahlia was probably buying his clothes, too. The idea was depressing.

We passed a street vendor selling Halal food and another with a selection of pretzels. "Since we're here," Gertie said, "how about we grab a hot dog?"

"Sure." We found a park bench and watched the sun set over Central Park. Since I'd already maxed out my junk food quota for the week, and after my fiasco at Caiyan's apartment my appetite was zero, I sucked on a giant dill pickle while Gertie ate her sauerkraut-covered hot dog.

"It's hard for me to believe he's doing all of this to get his key back. There has to be another reason." Gertie wiped a smudge of mustard from the side of her mouth and demolished the remainder of the hot dog. "If not, he's a selfish prick and you'd be better off without him.

"I wish he had confided in me. I mean, what could be so important that he needs to keep me at arm's length?" My mood felt as sour as the pickle.

"We've got to find that sword. Where else would he hide it?" Gertie sucked soda through a straw.

I racked my brain to remember places Caiyan talked about, places that were important to him.

"He still owns the flat in London, but his sister lives there. I've never seen it, and he only stays there when he has business in England. He could have left it with her, but he wouldn't endanger her."

"Yeah, he would be more likely to endanger you first."

I sprang off the park bench. "Oh my gosh—Gertie that's it! I know where the sword is."

$\mathcal{W}$e arrived at our townhouse, and I hurried upstairs, Attack cat swatting at me as I flew past. Gertie followed me in hot pursuit.

I'd discovered Caiyan in my room. I had a feeling he hadn't stopped by to see me after all. In fact, he'd looked surprised I was home.

"Gertie, I think it's here, somewhere." I looked under my bed and she went through my closet. Nothing. A sword wasn't a small thing to hide.

I recalled the sliding noise from when he first arrived. It was the door to my shoe closet. I pushed the door sideways. Surely, I would have seen a sword in my shoe closet? I've opened and closed the closet several times in the past few weeks. There wasn't a sword tucked between the shoes on the floor to ceiling shoe racks or hidden next to my collection of vintage hats on the shelves to the right.

I almost shut the closet door, when a corner of a black box on the floor under the bottom shelf of shoes caught my eye. I knelt and slid the box out from under the shelf. My Tom Ford over-the-knee designer boots. Caiyan had given them to me after I went on my first official mission with the WTF. "These are exquisite, like ye are." His words echoed in my head.

I stored them flat so the soft, buttery leather wouldn't crease. I loved those boots. I removed the lid, and a giddy smile broke out on my face. The gold gilded handle of the sword peeked out from under the top of my boot. I slid the sword from its hiding place and rested the heavy weapon on my thigh.

Gertie burst into the room. "He didn't hide it in—you found it!"

The sword was weighty, the scabbard worn. "Oh, what stories you could tell." I said as I stood and removed the tarnished blade from its housing. The steel reflected the light off the crystals dangling from my vintage chandelier overhead.

"It's beautiful." Gertie reached out and ran a hand over the gilt gold handle. "I read the gold was added after the war."

I laid it onto the bed so we could examine the words engraved on the blade.

"What's it say?" Gertie asked, peering closer.

It had been years since the sword had hung above the mantle in Mr. Raney's farmhouse. Parts of the inscription were damaged, and I recalled the vandal from my trip to 1949. Caiyan had scuffed the blade before he took it from Mr. Raney. I could read the first word, FIND.

"Caiyan scratched the blade when he was at Mr. Raney's house in Purley," I explained to Gertie.

She leaned close to decipher the next word. "Why would he do that?"

"To make sure no one would ever read the sword. I don't think he expected Mortas."

"Do you think this word is key?" Gertie asked.

"The word looks longer than key. See how the letter starts here." I pointed to the letter of the first word. It was scratched beyond recognition. My heart sank when I read the rest of the words.

"At something burg." I looked at Gertie.

"Could be Vicksburg, or Williamsburg. Even Sharpsburg, but it looks longer than that one." She tucked her bottom lip under her front teeth and inspected the words.

"Could be Gettysburg," I said.

"Jen, you can't go there. Didn't you see the pictures in the book?"

"Gertie, it's my job. If that's where Caiyan goes, I need to go there, too."

"What's the rest of this? 1st something, and this here spells RW."

"Who do ya think wrote the message on the sword?"

"I don't know, but I'm going to find out."

"How?" Gertie cocked a suspicious eyebrow at me.

"I know where he's going to be, I just need the date."

"Are you crazy? You can't go to the wedding. Don't you remember what happened the last time you showed up at a Mafuso wedding?"

"Yes, I saved your life."

"Well, there was that, but you almost got killed doing it, and Marco got shot."

"Gertie, I deserve an answer. I only have to get him away from the bitch from hell for a few minutes."

"According to Brodie, there's a buzz Satan's bitch is insisting on a big wedding and reception at the house."

"Why didn't you tell me?" I asked.

"I didn't want to upset you."

I frowned at her. "I need to get the details, and I know just the guy to ask."

My first call was to Jake. I had to inform him I had the sword.

There was no way I could laterally transport the sword to Gitmo. I plopped down in the overstuffed chair in my bedroom, pulled out my phone, and thumbed through to Jake's number.

Gertie laid across my bed with a magnifying glass, trying to read the words on the blade.

I wondered how Caiyan had moved the sword to my house if his company's private jet was under surveillance from both the WTF and the Mafusos. He must have chartered a plane. I doubted he flew commercial with a sword in tow, but Caiyan never ceased to amaze me.

"McCoy," Jake answered hastily on the fourth ring.

"I found it," I said. "I found the sword. It was in my closet this entire time."

"Your closet?"

"Yep, in my boot box."

Jake paused, possibly contemplating why Caiyan would put me in danger by hiding the sword in my house. I didn't care. I was thrilled to find it before the Mafusos.

"I'm back in Dallas, but I'm a little tied up at the moment."

I heard a woman's voice in the background, and a muffled Jake responding to the woman.

When his voice came back on the line, he said, "Uhm, I'll come by in the morning. And Jen..."

"Yes?"

"For god's sake don't tell anyone else you found it."

"10-4." I disconnected.

"Jake's at his loft in Dallas. He's coming over in the morning." I told Gertie. "I think he had company."

"Jake's being very secretive about his new girlfriend," she said.

"He can't tell her about the WTF, maybe keeping her away from us is the best way to avoid the lies that come with his job."

"Huh, I can keep a secret." Gertie huffed.

"Me, too. He's being overprotective, as usual."

My second call was to Ace. If there was gossip in New York City, Ace knew about it.

"'ello doll," he answered on the second ring.

"Ace, guess what, I found the sword!"

"Brilliant!"

"You can keep a secret, my ass," Gertie mumbled under her breath.

Jake told me not to tell anyone, but he didn't mean Ace, or did he? I bit my bottom lip.

"What does the sword say?" Ace asked me.

"It's a bit hard to read. Caiyan scratched through the engraving on the blade."

"Must be important if he damaged the intel."

"Jake's coming by tomorrow to check it out."

"Another secret, down the toilet," Gertie said.

I stuck my tongue out at her. "Ace, have you heard any news about the wedding?" I couldn't bring myself to say Caiyan's wedding.

"Everything's so hush-hush. I've a friend who's a wedding planner. He's been pissin' his knickers trying to get the job. As far as I know they haven't set a date. Blimey, your Scot's probably dragging his kilt-clad bum to remain a single man."

My Scot. It was as if I viewed our relationship through a telescopic lens, moving further away from me every day until it became an unrecognizable tiny spec.

"I'm surprised they didn't go to the justice of the peace and have a quick ceremony," I said. "If the wedding was the next step in Caiyan's master plan, you'd think he'd want it over with so he could move on to…whatever."

I'd disposed of the idea this was all about his key. No way would he ditch me for his key. Or would he? My inner voice was whispering doubts in my ear.

"Gurl, no way. I heard through the grapevine, Mahlia demanded a formal wedding. She told Gian-Carlo if he forced her to marry Caiyan, she wanted the real deal."

Forced? I couldn't believe she wasn't purring like a gloating tomcat who'd captured the mouse. The thought of Mahlia becoming Mrs. Caiyan McGregor made me ill.

"Surely they would have a date if they're going to dump Caiyan in the past during the next moon cycle." A surge of relief flooded me. If they didn't tie the knot before the moon cycle, he wouldn't be dropped in the middle of a major Civil War battle.

"Can't be the July cycle if he's going to the Civil War," Ace interrupted my happy thoughts.

"Right. They don't have time to plan the wedding," I said, performing a wacky celebration dance.

"No, hon, your sexy Scot's already been there."

"Wait…What?"

"Well, yeah. He went to Gettysburg when he was on holiday from the WTF."

"Are you sure?" Caiyan had mentioned there was a time he wasn't working for the WTF, but her never told me about Gettysburg.

"One hundred percent. Caiyan left the WTF and went all maverick on us. Brodie baby and I had to chase his brigand behind all over that pigeonhole of a town. It's a wonder I didn't get me bum shot right out from under me."

"Does Jake know?"

"I'm not sure. Caiyan had his knickers twisted over something stamped confidential by our fearless leaders." Ace paused. "I remember because that was the trip your love bunny returned to us."

"What do you mean?"

"We caught him by his shorthairs and brought him in."

"You caught him?" I asked.

"Are you doubting Brodie's mad skills? I was at the tail end of the capture. I transported him back to base."

"I thought he returned on his own accord."

"Doll, your Scot doesn't do anything without a fight. As I recall, both men were pretty scuffed up, a real tantalizing testosterone smorgasbord."

Silence filled the line. I didn't know how to respond to the information Ace told me.

"Hon, you still there?"

"Yeah, just glad to hear Caiyan can't go to Gettysburg."

"If I 'ear any deets, I promise you'll be the first one I call."

"Thanks Ace."

"Sure thing, hon." We disconnected.

Smoke jumped on the bed next to Gertie and she gave him a scratch behind his ears. "Did I hear that correctly?" she asked me.

"Caiyan has already been to Gettysburg." The news that Caiyan couldn't go to Gettysburg should have been comforting, but something didn't settle right with me.

"The next major battle that lines up with the moon cycle would be Fredericksburg," Gertie said.

"When was that one?"

"December, 1862."

"At least that gives us time to prepare." And another five months without Caiyan. How long would he be married to Satan's bitch before they dropped him in the past?

"Do you think she'll keep her last name or take his?" I asked.

"Hyphenated, for sure," Gertie said. "She's not going to lose her Mafuso connection. I can't believe this is happening. It should be me walking down that aisle."

"You?"

"Yeah, I sort of envisioned we'd have a double wedding. I mean, Caiyan and Brodie are best friends. Wouldn't it be romantic to have a double wedding?"

No. Gertie and Brodie were sunflowers, red-checkered tablecloths, beer, and barbecue. I envisioned escargot, champagne, white linen, and roses.

"It doesn't matter. Caiyan, for whatever reason, has chosen Mahlia." The reason had better be life changing because if he was only after his key, he could say goodbye to white roses, champagne, and Jennifer Cloud.

\

CHAPTER 10

When morning came, I found myself in bed with the sword and my gun on the nightstand. Nothing was going to happen to my only connection to Caiyan.

Gertie left early for work. She had research she wanted to get in before her Sunday shift at the library.

Jake arrived after my second cup of coffee.

He leaned over my kitchen table, where I had placed the sword, and examined the blade with the eyes of a CIA agent, taking in every detail over the damaged area.

"Damn." His fingers traced the word ending in burg. He retrieved Gertie's magnifying glass from the table next to the sword and hovered over the scratched-out words. "I agree with you, this word looks longer than the word key, but maybe it was two words—like 'the key.'"

I placed a cup of coffee next to him and folded my right leg under me as I sat at the kitchen table. "First Texas is a regiment under Major General John Hood. It was part of Longstreet's First Army Corps. I looked it up."

Jake picked up the coffee and placed the magnifying glass on the table. He sat next to me and took a gracious sip. "You've been doing some research."

"I don't think my research will be needed anytime soon. Ace told me Caiyan's already been to Gettysburg."

"Yeah?"

"I sort of told him I found the sword."

"Jen."

"I know you told me not to tell anyone, but he would find out eventually."

"When I tell you not to do something, it's for your protection."

I sulked into the bottom of my coffee mug like a bad child.

"There aren't any records when McGregor was at Gettysburg, when he was absent from the WTF. Don't you think that's odd?" Jake asked me.

"They didn't have Pickles then, maybe someone took them." I sipped my coffee and watched Jake go over the sword again.

"Word on the streets says Mahlia is planning a formal wedding. Surely, it will take a few months to pull it together?"

"My field operative tells me the same thing. I don't know why we bother paying men to do surveillance when I have Ace's ear to the gossip ground."

"Jake, I need to speak to Caiyan before the wedding. He's got to have a good reason for marrying Mahlia."

"Maybe they deserve each other, and—"

Jake stopped when he saw my eyes fill, "Crap, Jen, I'm sorry. It's been tough not having him as an agent. I hoped he would get his key back and return to the WTF. It's been longer than I expected. Although his methods may be illicit when he goes after a brigand, his reasons are solid. He's a good agent, and I hate to admit it—I need him."

"Why hasn't he reported in?" I asked him, wiping a random tear from my face.

"I don't know what's involved this time. He refused to go in undercover, he told me it wasn't worth the risk."

"He won't get his key back if the Mafusos discover he's undercover. I can see how that's a risk." My sarcastic tone caused Jake's face to drop.

"Jen, the risk he meant was you."

"Me?"

"If they found out he was working undercover, the Mafusos might harm someone he loves. You would be a target." He finished his coffee while I digested the information. "The reason they're forcing him to marry Mahlia is to prove his loyalty to the Mafusos."

"I get that. If Caiyan was concerned about me, why did he hide the sword in my closet?"

"It's possible, by committing to the wedding, he's convinced them you're the past." Jake rubbed a day's growth of beard bristle over his chin and jawline. "I wonder how Mahlia feels about all of this?"

"What do you mean?" I'd never given her a thought. She'd been spitting mad when I started dating Caiyan. Envious. Evil in fact. She had gone to great lengths to sabotage our relationship, and now she would wear his ring on her finger.

Another tear leaked out, and it made me fume. Why was I crying over him? Caiyan still had a choice. He didn't have to marry her, no matter what it cost him.

"A few months back, my intelligence discovered information that she's seeing someone else."

"Who?"

"They can't catch the guy. He meets her at McGregor's apartment wearing different disguises. I didn't say anything to you because, at first, they pegged him as McGregor—same body type, hair, dark sunglasses.

"Finally, one of my agents got close enough and realized the man was shorter than McGregor." Jake shifted uncomfortably. "I was relieved because when he met Mahlia, they were...uhm...together."

Curious as to how they discovered the man was meeting Mahlia, I opened my mouth to ask, then it clicked. "You bugged the apartment."

Jake's face flushed a light pink.

"How long has his apartment been bugged?" I cringed.

"Whoa," Jake held his hands out in front of him. "Only since he left to join the Mafusos, and only the living area and study, but they don't exactly spend most of their time in the bedroom."

My insides tickled that Caiyan wasn't sharing a bed with Satan's bitch. "Any ideas on who it might be?"

Jake shook his head. "The last guy she dated for any length of time was Eli. We haven't seen the guy in two weeks. I don't know if he's slipping past us or if they aren't dating any longer."

"Regardless, if she's being coerced into the marriage, I deserve to know the answer. I need to speak to him." I set my empty coffee cup on the table and caught a flash of white fluff in my backyard.

"Dammit!" I bolted from my chair, rushed past Jake and out the back door.

He was on his feet, gun drawn, pushing past me onto the patio. We both stared at the white Pygmy goat eating my blue moon rose bushes.

"Stop that!" I hollered at the beast.

Jake holstered his gun and grabbed the goat's pink rhinestone collar. "She's not going to stop by your charming words."

Darryl stuck his head in through the opened back gate. "Hidee ho neighbor!" He moved into the yard and took the goat by the collar.

I introduced him to Jake.

"I see you met Lucy." Darryl looked down at the goat who was chomping her way through a planter of periwinkles.

"Lucy?" I huffed, and Darryl moved her away from the flowers.

"Lucy keeps the coyotes away."

"No coyotes in this neighborhood, Darryl." Jake said to him.

"You packin' a SIG 226?" Darryl's eyes went wide at Jake's gun.

"That's right."

"You a cop?" Darryl took a step back.

"Jake works for the CIA." I placed my hands on my hips and frowned at the half-eaten rose bush.

"CIA? I thought you smart fellas did the spy decoding; I didn't know you carried guns." Darryl eyed Jake's weapon.

"Special ops division," Jake said.

"Seen any combat?"

"I was part of the Abu Anas al-Libi Capture."

"Whoa, speak American dude." Darryl help up his hands.

"Darryl, we need to talk about your animals," I said. "They need to stay in your house and your backyard. You can't allow Lucy to run all over the neighborhood. We have an HOA and they have rules."

"She won't be no problem. She never strays too far from home. Now, Chuck, he's the troublemaker. Hard to keep him penned up, but I can't bear to part with him."

"Who's Chuck?" I asked.

"My tarantula."

Jake and I stood, mouths open. "You have a deadly spider that escapes from his cage?" Jake asked.

"He's sneaky, but he wouldn't hurt a fly."

When I didn't respond, Darryl headed toward the gate, trailing Lucy behind him. "I'm singing at the club tonight. Why don't y'all come down and I'll buy the first round of drinks for all the troubles Lucy caused."

"Maybe," I said as he slammed the gate shut behind him.

Jake and I returned inside.

"My parents bought the townhouse next door and thought Darryl should live there."

He grinned down at me. "I thought I'd met all of your crazy family."

"Darryl's a distant cousin. He didn't come around much."

I hadn't spent any down time with Jake in a while. "Are you interested in going to the club tonight to see Darryl sing?" I asked.

"Can't, I've got a date."

"With the mystery girl?"

"You'll meet her when I'm sure it's going to be a thing."

"You've never been so secretive before about the women you date."

"There's a few details I need to work out." He walked to the refrigerator and opened the door.

"What are you doing?"

"I'm looking for— Ahh…here it is." He pulled out a container of leftover chicken piccata. My mom had dropped the chicken dish by

117

on her way to my dad's store yesterday. He lifted the lid and inhaled deeply. "Guilt, conveniently packaged in Tupperware. I love your mom."

"How'd you know she'd bring food?"

"You're two peas—but *your* guilt comes in a Fendi bag."

Jeez.

"I need to head out." Jake placed his empty mug in the sink and tucked the container of leftovers under his arm. "I'll arrange for the sword to be picked up tomorrow."

"Jake, I just don't get it. Why would Caiyan come to see me and then spring the wedding on me?"

Jake bit his bottom lip, and his dimples dented inward. He thought Caiyan wanted booty.

"I don't think sex was his primary intention. He tried to tell me about the wedding before the booty call."

"He didn't try hard enough," Jake said.

"It doesn't make any sense. Why would the Mafusos force him to marry Mahlia if they don't even like each other?"

"It's a guarantee. If Caiyan marries Mahlia, they have him in the family, so to speak. They're Mafia, things run in the family with them. It's the reason Toches struggles. He's an outsider. Toches has been trying to become a part of the family for years, but acceptance by the Mafusos is rare. Gian-Carlo wants proof McGregor is loyal to them."

"I don't know why he would go through with the wedding."

"I'm sure the Scot has something up his sleeve."

"If he thinks he's going to marry Mahlia, earn his key back, get a quickie divorce, then resume our relationship, he's got another thing coming."

"If he does, the Mafusos will have him in cement shoes at the bottom of the Hudson," Jake said.

"He'll be joining quite a cast." Brodie stood at the edge of the kitchen, coffee cup in hand. His shorts hung low on his hips and his shoulder-length razor-cut hair was mussed from a busy night.

"Hey Brodie, I didn't know you were here," I said.

"Stopped by late last night. Things were going smooth at the farm." He walked toward the pot of coffee. "Boss." He nodded at Jake.

An awkward tension spiked the air. Boss Jake didn't approve of his agents mingling with people he cared about.

After Brodie filled his mug, he ambled over to view the sword.

"She's a beaut, I can see why McGregor wanted her."

"Apparently more than he wanted me," I said.

"Don't worry your pretty blond head. Caiyan's not going to marry Mahlia. He's got a plan. You'll see."

"I want to be there," I glanced at Jake. "When the wedding goes down."

"Absolutely not." Jake crossed his arms over his chest.

"He's right. It's a dangerous gig." Brodie leveled his hazel eyes at me.

"I need to see for myself. Maybe Caiyan will need my help."

Both men stared at me, speechless.

"You have to admit, I've learned a lot, I've trained hard, and I'm a decent agent."

"No way am I allowing you anywhere near the wedding. I'm sending in outside intelligence." Jake moved toward the back door.

"Don't you think we need to have a traveler inside? I'm the only one that can carry Caiyan safely away."

"There's Ace, and Tina," Jake said.

I frowned.

"I'll go undercover. I can change my look. Ace can go with me."

"Naw, I'll go. McGregor will let me help him…if he needs it," Brodie said.

"After we know the date, I'll decide who goes," Jake said.

Jake was making me insane with all his overbearing goodness.

Brodie leaned against the kitchen counter. "Mark my words, whatever Caiyan has plotted out, it will be good in the end. The guy always comes out smelling like a rose."

Dead roses smelled, too.

CHAPTER 11

*B*rodie and Gertie agreed to go with me to hear Darryl sing. I pointed my car in the direction of Terrell, a small town filled with a smattering of redneck bars, used car dealerships, run down motels, and an outlet mall.

About twenty minutes later, I exited Highway 34 and took my first right. The bar was lit up like a lighthouse directing the farmers and derelicts into the comfort of its shady shores.

I parked the car in a lot across the street from Mama's Double Wide. The bar had recently been scoured, exterminated, and reopened with a country themed venue.

A few boot clad couples straggled toward the entrance. We exited the car, and I joined Brodie, who stood staring at the bar. The words Honky Tonk flashed in neon across the front of the building.

"Wha' the hell's a honky-tonk?" Brodie asked. The Australian seemed befuddled at the southern bar.

"It's a club where a bunch of hillbillies get together, drink beer, and listen to Merle Haggard," I explained.

"And they dance, c'mon!" Gertie tugged Brodie's hand toward the tin roofed building.

The barn shaped building had whitewashed brick walls painted end to end with a depiction of the Confederate flag. I shrugged off the sensation the Civil War was trying to eek its way into my life and followed them inside.

Laughter and a loud version of the latest Toby Keith song met us as we entered. Cigarette smoke circled upwards toward the gabled roof.

Brodie stopped and stood in the foyer taking it all in. The interior consisted of bricked walls adorned with an artist's rendition of the Texas and American flags. A huge, painted corrugated metal sign emblazoned with the words Don't Mess with Texas hung from the balcony projected out from the far wall.

The lighting in the establishment was minimal, with most of the electricity centered on the rustic bar that ran the length of the right wall and the small stage positioned under the balcony across the back wall of the club.

A set of drums bookended by enormous speakers indicated a band played there on occasion. According to Darryl, his set went on at ten.

Peanut shells strewn about the floor crunched under our feet as we made our way inside. Since the live entertainment didn't start until ten, country music was piped in from speakers hidden around the room. Gertie offered to grab a table, and Brodie moseyed up to the bar for drinks.

I sought out the ladies' room to powder my nose. After I borrowed the facility and blew a kiss to the life size poster of a cowboy, shirtless and plastered on the bathroom wall, I joined Gertie at a table near the stage.

She was snapping her fingers and singing along with a familiar song when mid-snap her breath caught. Gertie frowned in the direction of the door.

"Don't look now, but here comes that beotch you went to high school with."

I turned to see Ragina Hood walking toward me.

Ragina was a year older than me. She had moved to our school in the ninth grade when her father was transferred from Los Angeles. The girls in my school went apeshit when they found out we had a

121

real live 90210 amongst us. She hung with the popular crowd in school, dated Jake for a hot minute, and disliked my friendship with him.

Ragina graduated, and I discovered Glamour Magazine, highlights, and makeup vloggers. The last time she saw me she barely recognized me. Barely.

Caiyan and I were having dinner with Brodie and Gertie at a swanky restaurant in Uptown, complete with firepits and bougie drinks, when Ragina noticed me. She was there with her boyfriend at the time, a semi-pro indoor soccer player who, turned out, played for the other team.

She plopped down at our table and told everyone about brace face Jennifer Cloud. I mentally crawled under the table and planned her demise. Caiyan thought it was cute, Gertie not so much. Her obvious animosity toward me rubbed Gertie the wrong way and she endeared Ragina a nickname.

"Hey Vagina," Gertie said as Ragina stopped by our table.

"It's Ragina," she said, teeth clenched.

"Oh, right, Ragina, my bad," Gertie said. A wicked smile made her freckles dance.

"Didn't think I'd see you out and about so soon after your breakup." Ragina flipped her long, dark hair over her shoulder and eased into the chair next to me.

According to Ragina, a guy like Caiyan was out of my league. At our last meeting, she had slipped him her number under the table. After she left, he told me she was like a Tootsie Pop. All the good stuff was on the outside. He tossed the napkin adorned with her number into the firepit, making me ecstatic. I showed him my thanks later that evening.

"Breakup?" I questioned. How did she know Caiyan and I weren't together? For cripes sake, I only found out recently.

"What are you talking about?" Gertie asked.

"You know, your breakup with the sexy Scottish guy."

I glanced over at Gertie.

"Oh, poor you. You haven't seen the latest on Gossip Gal?"

She dug in her Boite Chapeau Louis Vuitton bag and retrieved her smartphone. Holding it up for scary face recognition, she tapped the screen, careful not to damage her pointed, red, bedazzled nail.

"Here's the post." She turned the phone toward me.

I took it from her, attempting to hide my jagged cuticles. Gertie leaned over my shoulder and read along with me.

The latest feed from Gossip Gal, a celebrity stalker turned blogger, displayed on the screen. Cradled in a heart swoosh, a picture of a smiling Caiyan and Mahlia captioned *All my best to the Happy Couple! G.G. XOXO.*

The smaller print read Scottish Lord to wed Mafuso Motors princess Saturday afternoon on the second of July.

My stomach rolled. "Things didn't go as planned," I said, handing back her phone. Where was Brodie with our beers?

"I guess he figured out a southern girl wasn't his cup of tea," she said, returning her phone to her bag.

Brodie set three long-necked beer bottles down on the table. I upended mine before he took his seat. "Yer the dingo from Jen's high school," Brodie said to Ragina.

I tried to hide a smile. Ragina had no idea what the word meant. She smiled wide at Brodie's rugged Keith Urban persona.

"Why, yes I am." Ragina leaned toward him as he took the seat next to Gertie. She blinked twice when Gertie leaned over and kissed Brodie complete with lots of tongue action to ensure Ragina took the hint. This Aussie's taken.

"PDA, already..." She wrinkled her nose at the lip-locked couple.

"What are you doing here?" I asked. The dive bar was not the normal hangout for the uptight homecoming queen.

"My grandfather was a prominent photojournalist and a descendant of Civil War photographer Mathew Brady." She flipped her brown hair aside. "Anyhow, when my grandfather died, he left me all these Civil War photos and the owner of the bar wants to check them out. He might buy them from me to display in the bar."

"Shouldn't you donate them to a museum?" Gertie paused from staking a claim on Brodie to ask.

"Yes, you should donate them," I said, remembering Caiyan's promise to Mr. Raney.

"No way. The museum won't pay. The owner of the club's offering top dollar. We're discussing it over drinks tonight."

The music changed, and Gertie squealed at Brodie. "Let's go dance. I'll teach you how to do the Cotton-Eye Joe."

Brodie mouthed, "I know how," to Ragina and me as he followed Gertie to hook up with the other line dancers.

"Can I take a look at the photos?" I asked Ragina.

"You can see them hanging on the wall after I get paid." Ragina hugged her bag tightly to her middle.

"Just asking."

"How are you going to mend that broken heart of yours after your ex-hunk ties the knot with the gorgeous rich New Yorker?" She placed her hand over her heart in feigned interest.

Typical Ragina. Trying to bring me to tears over my broken relationship. If I wasn't careful, she'd snap a pic of me drowning my sorrows in beer and send it to Gossip Gal.

I lifted my chin and tried to think of some snappy remark to let her know I wasn't suffering over the news of Caiyan's impending marriage when a man encircled me from behind and kissed me my neck.

Ragina's eyes grew wide. I stiffened, ready to karate chop the frisky asshole, then relaxed as the familiar scent of Marco followed.

"There you are, gorgeous, I've been looking for you," Marco said as he grabbed the chair opposite Ragina.

I smiled at him.

"Who's this?" he asked me, nodding toward Ragina.

"Oh, sorry, this is Ragina. An old friend from high school." I turned toward Ragina. "This is Marco, my uhm…"

"Fuck buddy," he finished my sentence.

I watched Ragina lick her lips as she took in Marco's blue eyes and solid, muscular body.

The rich tone of Patsy Cline's voice came over the speakers. "This one belongs to me," he said and pointed to the dance floor.

My inner voice donned her square-dancing attire, but I held up my beer as if to protest.

He snagged the bottle from me and downed the remainder of my beer. He took my hand and led me from my chair to the dance floor.

Ragina's mouth hung open as Marco pulled me in tight to his chest. We swayed to the music.

"What are you doing here?" I asked him.

"My sister shared the latest on Gossip Gal and I decided you needed a friend. I texted Brodie and he told me your plans for tonight. Gertie just sent me an SOS. What's her story?" He cut his eyes toward Ragina.

"Ragina dated Jake in high school. She didn't like our friendship, and he dumped her."

"I take it she wasn't happy when the two of you became a couple?"

I inhaled Marco's freshly showered scent, and the cologne he wore made my toes tingle.

"Nope, and although we didn't last, she still has a vendetta against me."

"Let's give her something to be jealous of." Marco leaned in and kissed me. Long and deep. The kind of kiss seen on the big screen. The kiss where the couple's lips met perfectly, and you could tell by the tilt of the hero's head and the way he cradled the female lead, the guy was an amazing kisser.

My boy howdy lit up like a jet engine ready for takeoff. Any minute, I would turn into the Human Torch from the *Fantastic Four*. I broke the kiss and stared into his eyes.

"I think I broke a sweat," he cracked a smile and pulled me closer. The song's melody played, *I'm crazy, crazy for feeling so blue.*

When the song ended, we returned to the table, and I was thankful Brodie had ordered another round. Ragina had deserted us for a gaggle of girlfriends at a nearby table. I sat down next to Brodie and he handed me a beer.

"You're gonna need this to extinguish those flames, mate."

"That was some kiss," Gertie announced. "Reminded me of the *Top Gun* Kiss."

"No, ya wrong. I'd say it had *Gone with The Wind* quality," Brodie teased.

"Just giving the school chum something to stew over," Marco said, taking a drink of his beer then glancing over at Brodie. "You really think it was up to Rhett Butler's standards?"

"OK, stop. The kiss was merely a ruse to make Ragina go away, and it worked."

This statement got three bottles raised, and I clinked them with mine.

I gave Ragina a finger wave from our table. Ragina ignored me and joined her plastics typing on their phones.

"I swear she took a pic of you with Marco," Gertie said.

Damn, maybe Ragina wasn't the only one who'd witness the movie star kiss. Positive Caiyan didn't follow Gossip Gal, I chastised myself for worrying over what he would think about me with another man. He was engaged to Mahlia for cripes sake, and they had set a date for the wedding. The reality the marriage might happen made my heart heavy.

Distracted from my worries by the announcement for Darryl to begin his set, I set my beer down to applaud. There was a hum-ho clap from the crowd.

Darryl began strumming his guitar and sang his rendition of Chris Janson's song *Buy Me a Boat*. I wasn't sure what to expect, but to my surprise, Darryl had a good voice. The redneck crowd went crazy over the song and every song Darryl sang for the remainder of the set.

"Thanks for comin' out y'all!" Darryl announced into the microphone. "It's time for me to take a break." A few boos echoed. "But we'll have a round of karaoke while I quench my thirst." Darryl hopped off the stage and joined us at our table. A waitress came over with a glass of water for Darryl.

"How 'bought a round of beer for my cousins and their friends," Darryl signaled to the waitress.

"Thanks bloke, none for me. I'm the designated driver." I realized Brodie had only two beers after we arrived and had shifted to sipping water.

Gertie introduced Darryl to Marco and Brodie. The waitress delivered a pitcher of draft beer and four glasses. Darryl poured each of us a glass, minus Brodie, and we toasted to his first successful night on stage. We listened as a few people gave their best efforts at karaoke.

After we finished off the pitcher of beer, Darryl, overexcited about the reception he received from the crowd, ordered a round of tequila shots to celebrate.

Darryl was announced back to the stage. The rounds of beer and shots kept coming as we listened to his next set.

By the time Darryl finished his set, I was licking the salt off Marco's hand, throwing back the Jose Cuervo, and sharing a lime from between his teeth. I thanked him again for the tactical maneuver he spawned on the dance floor.

"Ragina has always been a thorn in my side," I said to Marco and emptied the last of my beer.

"That beotch needed a taste of her own medicine," Gertie said.

As Darryl took his break, he announced the mic was open for karaoke again. Gertie jumped up on the stage and gave us a rendition of *Achy Breaky Heart*. She received a standing ovation from the crowd.

"Jen you should go sing. It's liberating," Gertie said when she returned to the table.

"Nope, not gonna happen," I told her, but my words seemed slow and I couldn't help myself from smiling at everyone.

A pretty girl with purple hair sang a Carrie Underwood song and I envisioned myself carving my name into the leather seats of Caiyan's Maserati.

"Let's go, Cloud," Gertie drug me up to the stage and I blinked at the faces staring back at me. Marco and Brodie were whooping words of encouragement.

I'd had plenty of liquid courage. Gertie began with the lyrics to one of our favorite songs, Pistol Annies' *I Got My Name Changed Back*. I joined her and embodied Miranda Lambert. By the end of the song we had the entire place, including Ragina and her plastics, boppin' on the dance floor. People crowded in front of the stage wiggling in time with the music and shouting for an encore.

Darryl brought us another shot to the stage. It was followed by a song. Then it went shot, song, shot, song, until I plucked the microphone from its stand and went from the stage to the bar, leaving Gertie standing speechless at the empty microphone stand.

I sang and gyrated my way down the epoxy coated bar top turning over drinks until a pair of strong arms removed me from the limelight. Marco waved to the crowd as they applauded my performance.

"What're you doing?" I asked, my words slurring just a tad. "I'm schlinging."

"If you do another shot, I'm afraid your clothes are coming off. And I'd rather remove them in private."

Darryl began his third set, and somewhere along the way I recalled lying across the back seat of Gertie's car with my head in Marco's lap and Brodie behind the wheel.

The last thing I remembered was reaching up and touching the deep indention in Marco's chin and watching it wink as he spoke to Brodie. "Hurry up, Aussie."

CHAPTER 12

*T*he sun streamed through my window and woke me. I blinked against the light, and a sharp pain pierced my left eyeball. My French door was open, and a warm breeze came in off the balcony.

The first thing I noticed after my eyes cleared was a heaviness to my bed. I looked over and Marco lay face down in the pillow next to me. His tan skin rested on my white cotton sheets. The blanket covered his bottom half. Almost.

Oh shit. Did we have sex? I couldn't remember. I recalled the kissing, some heavy petting, I think there might have been some fondling, and tongue action on his part, but the rest of the night was a blur.

I had on a t-shirt and panties. Good sign. Maybe I didn't miss out on extraordinary sex with Marco. My head ached and my mouth tasted like cat litter. I needed water, a toothbrush, and French fries.

A muffled caw squawked in the room, and I lifted my head. At the foot of my bed sat a big red hawk with my VS pink lacy bra clasped in his beak. He perched on my footboard and raised his right talon to show me the catch of the day. A snake wiggled helplessly between the sharp talons.

I screamed and scrambled to stand on my bed. Clutching the

sheets to my body, my free hand grasped my headboard. My jostling woke Marco.

He leapt out of bed and grabbed the Confederate sword angled next to my nightstand. I ignored the brief flash from last night of him holding the sword and exclaiming he was King Arthur. Did that happen?

His upper half was naked and glorious, his bottom half clad in navy boxers currently tented by his manhood.

"What's wrong?" he shouted.

I pointed at the hawk and eyed his bottom half.

He glanced down. "It's a morning thing," he shrugged, keeping the sword pointed at the hawk.

"Where did the bird come from?" Marco asked.

"I think it belongs to Darryl."

"Your cousin from the bar last night?"

"He lives next door."

Marco sighed.

"He brought a few animal friends with him when he moved in," I explained.

The bird gave me the stink eye and then flew out the door, releasing the snake before he left. The snake slithered down the bedpost to the floor. I couldn't control the blood curdling scream that followed the snake as it shifted toward Marco, who promptly chopped off his head with the sword.

"What's the matter?" Gertie rushed into the bedroom, tying her bathrobe.

Brodie followed behind her rubbing the sleep from his eyes. His jeans were open at the top button. "What's all the ruckus?"

Gertie's eyes took in Marco. He lowered the sword to the level of his crotch.

Brodie grimaced.

"One of Darryl's pets came in through the French door," I explained. "A hawk. It had a snake in its claws."

Gertie peered around the bed at the decapitated snake. The reptile didn't faze Gertie. She yawned. "I guess we had a good time last night. I was out for the count as soon as my head hit the pillow."

"Ya, which means I didn't have such a good time," Brodie teased.

Gertie's face flushed a light shade of pink.

"Let's go make the coffee," Gertie said and left the room. Brodie followed her.

"Did we have a good time last night?" I asked, still standing on my bed.

A grin spread across Marco's face. "I had more fun than Brodie."

Before I could ask him if we did the deed, Gertie shrieked from downstairs, and Brodie hollered, "Stop tha' ya arse!"

"I'll check it out if you want to get dressed," I told Marco. Grabbing a pair of running shorts, I slid them on and snatched a headband off my dresser to hold back my unruly hair. I left him sword in hand. His tent was slowly losing its shape.

A llama stood in my kitchen chewing the tea towel my mother gave me that cleverly read, Don't go bacon my heart.

"Where'd this beast come from?" Brodie asked.

"Three guesses," Gertie said, moving around the llama to start the coffee.

I tried to pry the remnants of the tea towel from its mouth.

The sliding glass door stood open. "Did he open the door?" I asked.

Darryl entered from the backyard. A raccoon rode shotgun on his shoulder. "Sorry, I heard the screaming and I figured Baracko got loose."

"Baracko?" I asked.

"Baracko Llama," Gertie stopped, coffee in hand. "Really?"

"What can I say? I'm a hard-core Democrat." Darryl moved toward the llama. "Baracko won't hurt a fly. He's just curious about his new neighbors. Daphne, on the other hand, she's got a bit of sass to her. Best not make her mad."

"Is Daphne the hawk?" I frowned at Darryl. When he nodded, I explained, "Your hawk brought her breakfast to enjoy on the foot of my bed."

A few worry lines burrowed into Darryl's forehead. "She's a social eater. Pretty hot outside. You might want to keep your door shut in the mornin's. She likes to eat in the AC."

When my frown didn't change, Darryl handed me the piece of tea towel he'd retrieved from Baracko's mouth.

Marco entered the kitchen dressed in the jeans and white t-shirt from the prior night. "Whoa, a llama."

He carried the dead snake over the blade of the sword.

Darryl's voice caught. "What happened to Ivy?"

Everyone looked at the snake. Darryl choked back a sob. "Daphne likes to take Ivy out for a morning ride—to get some fresh air."

Now that the snake wasn't wiggling around, I saw it wore a little harness. I swallowed hard.

"Sorry man, I didn't know it was your snake." Marco apologized as Darryl removed the carcass from the blade.

"I understand. Ivy's been known to bite a time or two. Do you have her head? I'd like to get her stuffed and mounted."

The four of us stood mouth agape staring at Darryl.

"Um. There's a shop next to my brother's office. I'll be happy to take Ivy there and have them do it for you," I said. It was the least I could do. The guy was almost in tears.

"Sure, thanks," he sniffed.

I held out a plastic grocery sack and Darryl placed the snake inside.

Marco took the bag from me and went upstairs to find the head.

Darryl led Baracko outside. "I'll just take him home. You won't mention my pets to your Ma will ya?"

I shook my head. The raccoon reached over and plucked the glittery headband out of my hair.

"Sorry, Tonto likes shiny things." Darryl retrieved the headband and handed it back to me.

Darryl stroked the llama's neck. "Baracko's not much trouble."

Baracko began to chew on the honeysuckle trailing up the lattice work on the patio cover.

Darryl smiled sheepishly and they left with pieces of the flower petals stuck to Baracko's nose. The raccoon waved at me over Darryl's shoulder.

I secured the gate behind them and wondered how much a padlock would cost. When I returned to the kitchen, Marco and Brodie sat at the table. Both men stared down into their coffee cups.

Brodie's lack of witty dialog indicated he wasn't sure how he felt about me sharing a bed with Marco. I wasn't sure how I felt about that either.

Gertie stirred cream in her coffee and acknowledged the strained silence. She goaded Brodie to go upstairs and drink their coffee on the balcony.

After they left, I made a cup of coffee and sat down across from Marco. "Where did you put the snake?"

"In the freezer, next to the Popsicles." He paused. "I wasn't sure how to package it before the embalming. I used a Ziplock."

"Thanks," I said. "I'll call the taxidermy place before I leave for work tomorrow and make the arrangements."

We drank our coffee in silence.

"Did we, you know?" I finally asked him.

"You don't remember?" His blue eyes leveled with mine.

"Everything's a bit fuzzy after we left the bar."

"Wow," he leaned back in his chair. "I made a great impression."

"I'm pretty sure the answer is no, but I was really plowed last night, and if I did, I'm…well…I'm not ready to be with you in that way."

He stood, leaving his half-full cup on the table. "I think I'll head home on that note."

"Marco, wait." I stood and grabbed his forearm.

He turned and pressed his lips together before he spoke. "Just for the record, both of us had a lot to drink last night, but I wouldn't take advantage of a drunk woman. Besides, I want our first time together to be unforgettable."

Relief washed over my face, and he acknowledged my reaction with an icy stare. "Later."

After he left, Gertie bounded down the stairs as I reheated my cold cup of coffee.

"Well, was he like over the top?"

"Gertie, I didn't have sex with Marco, and I drank too much." I rubbed my temples trying to wish my headache away. "I can't remember much from last night."

"You finally had a chance for a roll in the hay with the blond god and you can't remember a thing?"

"Seems so."

"What a waste." She handed me two ibuprofen and a bottle of water.

I washed them down with the water, thanked her, and took my reheated coffee to the table.

"Brodie seemed a little put off that Marco spent the night."

"He'll get over it. Being best buds with Caiyan and all. He thinks Caiyan has joined the Mafusos for other reasons than his key." She refilled her mug and sat down next to me at the table.

"Caiyan should have confided in me, Gertie. He's engaged to Satan's bitch. Am I supposed to sit around and hope my prince charming has an ulterior motive?"

"You shouldn't have to act like Mother Theresa when he's plastered all over the cover of the National Enquirer with the twiggy witch."

I chuckled at the nickname.

She smiled. "Brodie came up with it. Fits her, right?"

Gertie was right on both accounts. Caiyan's trust issues were getting old, and I wanted more. I wasn't sure I wanted more with Marco. He had his own share of issues.

"Besides, who'd blame you if you had a taste of Marco. Did you see his shorts this morning? Lord have mercy, he's hiding something amazing in those drawers."

I couldn't control my giggle at her off-color remark. I loved living with Gertie. When she first moved in, we were so opposite I thought living together would be a disaster, but she became my best friend, my confidant, and my wing woman. We finished our coffee, and I headed upstairs to shower.

Brodie met me at the top of the stairs, dressed and freshly shaved.

"Hey, about last night," I began. "With Marco…"

"Jen, ya don't have to explain ta me, but as long as I've known McGregor, he's always had my back. He wouldn't keep intel from me unless it put me in harm's way."

He started down the stairs, stopped, and turned toward me. "Marco has always been about numero uno. When we needed him, he refused, and now that he's set his sights on you, he's free to join the gang? Think about it."

My head throbbed from all the thinking, and the effects from overindulging in booze last night amped up my pain. Brodie continued down the stairs. I headed for a shower to wash away the headache and the heartache.

The warm water relaxed my tense neck muscles. As I massaged the shampoo into my hair, I disregarded Marco's annoyance with me and Brodie's steadfast support of Caiyan. Both men would have to get over it.

I had a date. July second. The moon cycle would open at noon the day of the wedding. I heaved a sigh of relief. They wouldn't jump. The moon cycle would be well underway before they said I do. I found it interesting Mahlia planned the wedding during a moon cycle, but who knows what the Mafusos are plotting.

After I showered and dressed, I sat down on my bed to call Jake. I would inform him about the date of the wedding and politely tell him I was going to attend.

"Hey," he said after the first ring. "I was just about to call you."

"You were?"

"Yeah, the date for the wedding's been set."

"I know. I found out last night."

Jake blew out a long breath. "Sorry, I should have called sooner. I was…distracted."

"No problem. I saw Ragina at a club last night and she was happy to inform me."

"Ragina?"

"She saw it on Gossip Gal."

"Damn, Jen, I'm sorry." He paused. "You OK?"

"I'm dealing." I eased into the request. "Jake, I have to attend the wedding. I want to talk to him. He's not going to jump in the middle of his wedding."

"You don't know that. The answer is still no. We have other brigands to follow, and I need you on base. I've already got eyes on the ground at the wedding."

He was sending an undercover agent. I called bullshit. Mahlia wasn't going to honeymoon in Pennsylvania, but I left it in the wind for now.

"In case he decides to jump the following moon cycle, research the battles that take place in August. Maybe he's going somewhere I can send you that doesn't involve over fifty thousand casualties."

I was thrilled Jake considered sending me to find Caiyan, but it would be too late. He'd be a married man.

"Sure." I missed the back and forth banter Jake and I used to have. The conversations we shared over beer and wings. For the past few months he'd been all business. "So, how's the secret girlfriend?"

"Fine, and she's not a secret."

"Why haven't I met her?"

"It hasn't been the right time." He exhaled a long, slow breath into the phone. "I'm working. Can we have this conversation another time?"

"Yes, but as the adjudicator of any females I might be destined to hang out with, I would like to meet her before you get knee deep in love."

"Don't worry." He chuckled. "Have I ever dated anyone you disliked?"

Ragina came to mind, followed by Bambi, and a woman whose name I couldn't recall, but Gertie thought she had teeth like a horse.

"Never mind," he said in the absence of my answer. His cell did the blip thing when another caller wanted his attention. "I've got another call, we'll talk later."

I thumbed off the call, leaned back in my cozy chair, and stared at the ceiling trying to put together the puzzle of the sword and Caiyan's mysterious wedding. The problem was, this ten-thousand-piece puzzle had a few key pieces missing.

I raised my head and caught movement out of the corner of my eye. A brown ball of fluff carrying a flash of metal scurried down the leg of my antique dressing table and took off toward the staircase.

Skipping a few stair treads I rushed after the furball and shouted at Gertie to close the window in the den. I caught up with it trying to make a getaway out the open window. Gertie slammed the window shut and I cornered it behind the end table.

"What is it?" I asked

"I think it's the raccoon." She propped her oven mitt clad hands on her hips. "I was about to take my cake out of the oven. If it burns, Darryl's going to bake me a new one, and I'll be the proud owner of a coonskin cap."

I bent down and peered between the legs of the table. The raccoon clasped my favorite sterling silver charm bracelet.

"He's got the designer charm bracelet that Caiyan gave me."

"The one he bought you after the fight over that eighties rock star?"

I scowled at her. "Yes, that one."

"We should get that back. It could be valuable on eBay."

"I'm not selling my bracelet on eBay."

"Just saying, since Caiyan's going to marry Satan's bitch, you might want to gather up all the baubles and trade them in on a cruise to the Bahamas."

The idea of Gertie and me lying on the beach in Bimini wasn't unappealing. If Caiyan went through with the wedding, I'd reconsider, but right now I wanted the bracelet.

"How can we get my bracelet away from the little jewelry thief?"

"Stay there. I'm going to save my cake and get the broom."

"What do I do if he runs out?"

"Grab him"

"What if he bites me?"

"He's Darryl's pet, I doubt he has rabies, but put these on in case he gets feisty." She tossed me the oven mitts.

I stuck them on my hands and assumed a defensive position.

She returned a few minutes later, broom and laundry basket in hand. She handed me the basket. "When he runs out, trap him in the basket."

I held the basket upside down with my oven mitts and waited to pounce.

"Get outta there critter!" She poke-checked it with the broom, and it shot out and headed in my direction.

I tossed the basket over it and did a victory dance.

The raccoon lifted the basket off, then hissed at me. My bracelet dangled from its furry lips.

I leapt and tackled it with the oven mitts. The raccoon broke free and crawled over my head and onto my back.

"Get him off! Get him off!" I squealed.

"Quit squirmin' or I'll hit you!" Gertie shouted.

"Hit me with wha—"

She swatted at the animal with the broom. The creature "oofed" as Gertie made contact. The power of the swing caused Gertie to lose her balance. She fell on top of me and I oofed as the creature went flying across the room, landing in Darryl's arms as he entered the den.

"Tonto, what kind of mischief have you been up to?" Darryl cooed at the bandit.

The animal pointed a long accusatory finger at Gertie and me panting on the den floor.

"Your raccoon stole my bracelet," I said to Darryl.

Darryl scolded the fluff ball and retrieved my bracelet from the raccoon's tapered fingers.

I stood, and he handed me back the bracelet.

"Sorry, Tonto can't help himself when it comes to shiny things."

"Why is he wearing that harness?" Gertie asked, standing and picking up the broom from the floor.

The raccoon cowered against Darryl.

Tonto had on a harness similar to the one the snake wore before Marco beheaded it.

"It's a transportation sling. Daphne uses it to carry the other animals. Would you like to see how it works?"

"I would," Gertie said.

I shrugged. "Why not?"

"I'll get Daphne and meet y'all out front. There's plenty of room in the field across from the townhouse."

We met Darryl outside. Daphne perched on Darryl's outstretched forearm, which was covered in a protective leather glove. Her dark, beady eyes took us in. He handed me a piece of aluminum foil wadded up into a ball.

"Hang on to this until I give you the signal, and then toss it about ten feet in front of you," he said and then walked about twenty paces from us.

Tonto rode on Darryl's opposite shoulder. The raccoon's ringtail wrapped around his neck. The animal seemed almost excited about his imminent adventure.

Darryl released the hawk. Daphne spread her wings and flew upwards, then arced and glided across the air. Her graceful body coasted in the summer breeze. She circled the field.

"Throw the foil," he said to me.

I tossed the shiny metallic ball on the ground.

"Ticktock, Tonto," Darryl commanded.

Tonto jumped off Darryl's shoulder and started to run. The raccoon scooped up the ball of foil and kept running.

Darryl clicked a small plastic device he held in his hand and the hawk swooped down and picked up the raccoon, carrying him high in the sky.

Darryl clicked twice and Daphne did a 360, flew low over Darryl, and released the raccoon into Darryl's arms.

The hawk did a few more circles, stretched her wings, and glided over a clump of trees in the distance. The magnificence of the bird sent shivers up my spine.

"Darryl, that was fantastic," I said.

"Amazing," Gertie agreed.

Darryl gave a low whistle, and the hawk landed on his arm. He popped a treat into the air, and Daphne caught it in her beak.

"They make a good team," I said as Darryl walked over to us.

"Yep, back in the day, before my singing career took off, the three of us might have borrowed a few items from an outdoor flea market."

I arched an eyebrow at Gertie.

"What kind of items?" She asked him.

"Mostly jewelry, small pistols, a few switchblades, cell phones, oh, and once I was able to snag an entire collection of U.S. Quarters. I had one for every state." He dropped his head. "It was the cell phones that got me. I didn't realize one belonged to the sheriff. He used the Find A Phone app and picked me up. We didn't take nothing real expensive mind you, just a way to make a little extra income."

"Darryl, most people make extra income by delivering pizzas," Gertie said.

"I don't like pizza. I'm lactose intolerant."

"Did you go to jail?" I asked him.

"House arrest. It's the reason I had to live with my mee-maw. Let me tell you, living at the jail house would have been a lesser punishment. Mee-maw don't take kind to laying low. Every morning she had me up at the crack of dawn doing chores, made me go to church on Sunday and Wednesday nights. If it weren't for my animals, it would have been a real bummer."

"Um, being arrested is supposed to be a real bummer. It's so you don't commit the crime again," Gertie said.

"I've been clean for about a year. I'm on the straight and narrow, no more stealing."

"That's good to hear Darryl. I hope we won't have any problems with Tonto borrowing any of our things again," I said to him.

"I'll keep a sharp eye on him." Darryl scratched the raccoon's head. "He won't bother you no more. I swear."

Gertie whistled the "Ballad of Davy Crockett" as we left Darryl working with the hawk.

I gave her a jab with my elbow.

"It's only a warning."

CHAPTER 13

I did the best thing for me when I was under stress—I went shopping. Gertie was at the library working on a project, and I needed retail therapy. My day included three of my favorite men: Neiman Marcus, Hermès, and Louis Vuitton—window shopping only. I salivated over the new purses at Bottega Veneta and ended up finding a cute Kate Spade satchel at Marshalls for half off.

Lugging my bags into the house, I dropped them on the coffee table. Something was off. An eerie feeling that the air had been disturbed gave me goosebumps.

A low growl drew my attention downward. Attack cat was crouched under the table. He peeked up at me through the glass and hissed.

Had Caiyan come back? The hair on my arms stood at attention as I crept around my house. Nothing seemed out of place. There were no creaks from the floor above me, and the house felt empty. The sword.

I took the stairs two at a time, and my heart stopped as I entered my bedroom. A tornado had demolished my room. Shoes were thrown from the closet, my comfy chair was overturned, and dresser drawers were emptied onto the floor. But the worst of it was the empty Tom Ford box in the center of my bed.

The sword was gone, and so were my beloved boots. Written on the mirror in my M.A.C. Brave lipstick were the words "you can't hide love."

I retrieved my gun from the nightstand and phoned Jake. "The sword has been stolen, and creepy words are printed on my mirror."

"I'll be right there."

I sat on my bed amid the mess. At least the crook started in my room. I only had to clean up the pieces of my shitty life instead of the entire house.

Jake arrived thirty minutes later. He did a clean sweep of my house. Took pictures of the damage.

"What do you think that means?" he asked, cocking his head at my mirror.

"Maybe the Mafusos think my relationship with Caiyan isn't over."

"And since they found the sword in your possession they know for sure."

"But we aren't together."

"Jen, you can't come within five feet of the guy without sparks igniting. I knew the minute I asked you if you cared about him our time together was over."

A slight ache pinched at the mention of our past relationship.

He tucked his phone into his pants pocket. "This is my fault. I should have taken the sword somewhere else. I haven't been focused on my job. I'll do better."

"You're a great boss." I placed my hand on his arm. "You put my safety and the team first. Don't feel guilty for having a piece of life for yourself."

"I'll have security watch your house." Jake started for his phone.

"Don't bother. They have what they came for."

He hugged me. "I'll still have them do a drive by. And think about installing security cameras."

"Sure."

Cameras might be a good thing. In the last month two people and a slew of animals had broken into my house.

~

I SPENT the next two weeks researching the Civil War. Gertie and I watched documentaries and movies—good and bad. The entire episodes of *North and South* starring Patrick Swayze before he started *Dirty Dancing*. I read books, letters, and anything I could get my hands on about the war.

My focus was Gettysburg and Vicksburg. These were the two battles coming in July. Jake was wrong about the Mafusos skipping this moon cycle. I felt it in my bones.

Three nights before the wedding, I sat cross-legged on my sofa thumbing through a twelve inch by twelve inch book titled *A Photographic Remembrance of the Civil War*. The fighting at Vicksburg would be on the downward swing by the time the moon cycle opened.

The battle had begun in the middle of May and the Confederates surrendered on July fourth. I studied the town strategically located on the banks of the Mississippi River. By the time the moon cycle opened the fighting will have decreased to a minimum. General Grant starved the Rebels into surrender. I doubted the Mafusos planned to go there.

Gettysburg seemed more logical. If they dropped Caiyan there, the chances of him getting shot were greater. Flipping through the pages of the book that lay in my lap, I studied the generals. The battles. There were many that took place in the four years of the War of Northern Aggression. I reminded myself that's what the South called it. The North referred to the war as the Southern Rebellion.

Rebels versus Yankees.

Jake was right about the statistics at Gettysburg. There were over fifty thousand casualties, some seven thousand men died, and the rest were injured, missing, or taken prisoner. The chaotic upheaval of the small town completely raided of food and supplies would take years to recover. I passed quickly over the photos of dead men and slain horses left for days on the battlefields before their bodies could be moved or buried.

A cold prickle skittered my spine. Caiyan, please don't go there.

Gertie entered through the back door. Her book bag was slung over one shoulder, and her purse dangled from her forearm. She dropped her purse on the kitchen counter and grabbed an apple.

"Hey, what's up?" She moved toward me and took a giant bite of the apple.

"Not much, just going through these books again."

"If you think he's going to Gettysburg, we could zip up there and check out the battlefields." Gertie looked at me hopefully as she chewed her apple. She loved to traipse through anything of historical significance. Battlefields, castles, ancient ruins—I'd been to more museums than should be allowed in a lifetime.

"Since the wedding is on the same day the moon cycle opens, I don't think...I mean, I hope, this is not on Gian-Carlo's bucket list."

"Has Jake found anything linking a key to the Civil War?"

"No, he's coming up empty."

There was no record of any of the keys of a member of the WTF that would have been worn by an ancestor in the Civil War. My family was part Native American; we came into the show later. Tina's parents immigrated to the United States after Vietnam. I wasn't exactly sure about Gerry, and if I asked, he'd lie. The rest of my team was from across the pond.

Ace had said they arrested Caiyan in Gettysburg but had no idea why he was there. Brodie confirmed the information that when Caiyan was rogue, he tracked him to Gettysburg and apprehended him.

"All I can do is sit, wait, and hope Caiyan makes an appearance before he does something stupid."

"Yeah, like marry Satan's bitch."

"I meant, like allow the Mafusos to dump him in a past time he has already been without a word to me so I can rescue him before...you know." *He dies.*

"That's what I meant too." She wedged the apple between her teeth and upended her book bag onto the coffee table. Three stuffed files slid out.

"What are these?" I laid the book aside and picked up one of the files.

Removing the apple, she picked up a file and came to sit by me on the couch. "These are copies I made, correction, my assistant and I made."

"You have an assistant?"

"Yeah, cool huh?" she shrugged. "Anyhoo, Ragina's photos got me thinking. I have a friend that works in the American Civil War Museum. These are letters the library had on microfiche from soldiers in the Civil War. My friend mailed them to me. That one," she pointed to the folder I held, "has the ones from Gettysburg."

"There's a lot of them," I said, opening the bulging file.

"They moved them to the Internet, but it was more efficient to have them copied directly from the files."

"Thanks, Gertie." I pulled out the first letter from a soldier to his wife.

"No prob. Maybe there will be a clue in one of them."

We spent the better part of the evening reading the letters from soldiers, when I came across one that tugged at my heartstrings.

The soldier wrote to his mother about all the things he missed from home. Swimming in the pond, shooting dove, riding his favorite horse. The letter told his mother he didn't think he'd make it home, because he'd been shot in the leg and was caught in a fence. He apologized for running off and joining the war at ten and two.

Ten and two? He's only twelve. My heart thumped hard in my chest as I continued to read. He was sorry for complaining about the chores, and he wouldn't return to help care for his ma or marry the pretty neighbor girl.

The letter had a thumbprint stain at the bottom. Blood.

Tears welled up in my eyes and I glanced over at Gertie. She was wiping away the wet from her cheeks.

"I can't read any more," she said.

"This one's from a boy, he was only twelve." I handed Gertie the letter, and she read the words that still made my vision blurred.

She flipped the letter over and read the back. "The boy died at Gettysburg on the second day. That's all it says. The letter was found with him."

We sat in silence until our tears dried. I had a hollow pain in my stomach and decided if I filled it with pizza it might go away.

"I'm going to order a pizza, you in?"

"I could go for pizza." Gertie pulled open the next file.

"Gert, you're not going to read more are you?"

"Yep, I can't let you go back without me. This is a bad war, and I don't want anything to happen to you. If I study from now until the moon cycle, I'd be an asset to you."

She was right. Between her photographic memory, the papers she'd already written on the Civil War, and her knowledge of the time, she would be a treasured resource.

I wrapped my arms around her and hugged tight. "I don't know if Jake will let me go. He probably won't let you go."

"Then we need to convince him otherwise." She smiled at me after I released her. "I wouldn't mind being a southern belle. *Gone with the Wind* is a favorite book of mine." She batted her eyelashes at me. "Why Miss Cloud, I'd be much obliged if you'd add a few peppahs to that pizza."

"You got it." Gertie was a blessing; however, I didn't think we'd be sipping punch in Georgia. If the message on the sword was a clue to Caiyan's destination, I'd drop a pin on the heart of the Civil War.

CHAPTER 14

J waited in the blue room at headquarters approximately one hour before the moon cycle opened. Pickles's premonitions had my team anxiously gathering data based on premeditated destinations chosen by their brigands.

Gerry and Tina sat, heads together, studying a ninth century map of England. The Cracky Clan was splitting up this trip, and a few of them were headed to Wessex.

Brodie chewed on a coffee straw as he flipped through an iPad. Rogue targeted Philadelphia, but Pickles couldn't get the year.

Marco hadn't said boo to me since I arrived. He sat at the end of the table scrolling through his smartphone. Fine, he could ignore me, I had bigger problems. The wedding was tonight, and if Jake sent me on a mission with one of the other defenders, I couldn't stop Caiyan from marrying Satan's bitch.

"Hey Jen," Campy said as he entered the room. I stood and he encircled me in a hug. He had the same build as Caiyan, and my heart shed a small tear.

"Hi," I squeaked. His muscles bulged when he squeezed me. "You've been hitting the weights."

"Every day," he released me and blushed slightly. "A defender must have strength, integrity, and fidelity."

Marco snorted at the last word in the WTF's motto. Campy cut his eyes at Marco, then back at me. "Do you know where the Mafusos are going yet?"

"Not a clue." I gestured toward the chair next to me and we sat down. "The Mafusos are being tight minded about their plans. They probably won't jump because of the wedding."

"Blimey, me mum was mad Uncle Cai didn't want us at the wedding."

"You spoke to him?" I reined in my surprise.

"Nah, Mum told me he rang her when the news hit the telly."

"The wedding was on the news?"

"Only local, ye know he inherited the title. Mum's been on holiday at the family estate in Scotland."

I'd been there once. It was more than an estate, it was a freakin' castle. Would Mahlia be Lady McGregor after she married Caiyan? Over my dead body.

Campy continued, "'Tis time for Mum to go back to work, and she sees how the town's famous Lord McGregor is weddin' the skinny American. Mum couldn't take the time off to fly across the pond, seein' how she only just returned from 'er holiday. Called ta yell at me." Campy huffed. "Like I can control Lord McGregor, the cheeky git. She'll have his head on a pike next time he shows up on 'er stoop."

"Why aren't you going to the wedding?" Tina asked, looking up from the map.

"He told Mum he didn't want us there," Campy dropped his head.

"The guy's lost his mind, marrying that one," Gerry said. He pointed at me. "My money's always been on you."

Marco's chair scraped tile as he shot up and stomped out of the room. Everyone watched him leave in silence.

"What'd I say?" Gerry did a palms up.

My blood boiled at the mess Caiyan had gotten himself into. I had to be at that wedding and stop him from being stupid.

"I'm sure Caiyan has his reasons," I said to Campy.

Ace slumped in wearing skinny jeans and ballerina flats. "Can you believe it? General Poopy Potts has us confined to base."

"What?" I asked him.

"He's expecting this one to go AWOL and disrupt the wedding of the century." He hiked a thumb at me.

I frowned. It's exactly what I had planned but hadn't figured out a way inside—yet. I stood and grabbed a bottle of water, asking if there were any other takers in the room.

Ace took the seat Marco had vacated, and I handed him a bottle of water.

Jake entered, a handful of files in his arms. "Good afternoon, everyone. Take your seats. As soon as the cycle opens, we'll have the destinations."

I returned to my chair, but my inner voice paced the room.

Jake set the files down and rubbed his eyes. He'd already put in a full day. The other teams' marks jumped from their European locations. The moon cycle opened earlier for them.

"The Russians just left," Jake said. "Their mark jumped to Zakynthos."

"Oh, man," Campy said. "It figures. As soon as I change teams the bastard jumps to the Greek Isles. I've been freezing my ass off in Dudinka for the last six travels."

"Except for the travel when you caught the Cracky," Brodie said, giving Campy a fist bump.

"Hell yeah, I did." Campy's energy ramped up the room. "Too bad he got out of jail on a technicality."

"Ya got to wait until he actually steals the booty. You nabbed him before the take," Brodie said to Campy.

Jake pulled out his glasses. He only wore them when he couldn't use his contacts due to fatigue. I stood and made Jake a cup of coffee and returned to my seat next to him.

"Thanks, I'm beat." He clicked around on his keyboard opening windows and watching for the map Pickles would send him when he had the coordinates of the jumps. He took a generous sip of his coffee.

His cell laid face up on the table and vibrated without a ring tone.

A name flashed across the screen. He grabbed it before I could make out the name, but I thought it read Angie. The mystery girlfriend. He pocketed the phone and glanced around the room.

"Where's Marco?"

"He had to take a time out," Gerry said.

Moments later, Marco entered the room and sat down next to Tina.

"Good, we're all here," Jake said. "Almost time."

I ignored Marco's brooding and focused my energy on Jake. I only had a few minutes before he would be chin deep in his work.

"I need to talk to you about—"

"Here we go people," Jake said interrupting me. "Brodie, looks like Rogue's jumped to Philadelphia 1776." He slid a file across the table to Brodie.

"I'm on it." Brodie took the file and stood to leave for the research room.

"Ace, you're transporting for Brodie."

Ace flicked his wrist in the air. "Don't make me wait long, Brodie baby, I've got dinner plans."

"Cancel them," Jake huffed.

Brodie sauntered out of the room.

Jake turned toward Gerry. "Gerald, the Cracky Clan didn't split up as originally anticipated, but they did jump to Wessex as planned. Make sure you don't swear. Campy, you'll go with him. He'll need the help. Tina will transport."

"I've already studied our destination," Gerald said.

"Good. Bring Campy up to speed and report to the travel lab for landing coordinates."

Gerry clamped Campy on the shoulder in one of those let's be buds and exchange man cards moves. "C'mon kid, I'll fill you in on all the hotspots of ninth century moral turpitude."

Campy scooted back his chair and stood to leave with Gerry.

Marco fidgeted in his chair. He'd been silent during the assignments. His eyes stayed focused on his cell phone as Jake finished handing out the missions.

"Jen, you'll be transporting for Campy."

"But why can't Tina transport for him?" I did a mental foot stomp.

"I'll summon you if I need you," Campy said, then followed Gerry from the room.

"That's crap, you gave me this assignment to hold me here. You know I won't leave Campy without back up." I scowled at Jake.

"It's an insurance policy."

I huffed.

"Yes, I do know you, Jennifer Cloud. If I leave you to float, in case a defender needs you, you'll be tackling the bride before she walks down the aisle. If this is what McGregor wants, then you should let it go."

Marco's head lifted to observe my response.

I slammed back in my chair, crossed my arms over my chest, and huffed with a force that caused my bangs to shoot upwards.

Jake continued reading the reports scrolling across his laptop. "None of the Mafusos have jumped. Marco, stay on base in case they do." Jake shifted his gaze to Ace. "You, too. Even if Brodie doesn't need you. That's an order from the general."

Ace gave me a cocky smirk. Wise-ass, but he was right. Jake had pulled out all the stops. I wasn't going to the wedding.

We moved to the break room to wait it out. Marco sat down on the new sofa we had picketed for when the transporters were initially grounded to the base. If we were forced to wait on base, we needed a comfortable place to hang out. He clicked on the TV and found a baseball game.

Tina sat down next to him, playing solitaire on her phone.

I grabbed the most recent fashion magazine, also picketed for, and began angrily flipping through the pages, unaware of the contents.

Ace rummaged through the refrigerator.

"Dahling, never fear. Things will work out," Ace said. He pulled a tray of premade deli sandwiches out of the refrigerator. "Tuna, ham, or turkey?"

I knew a turkey I wanted to shoot, I just needed to find a way to get to the range.

An hour later my key glowed, and the strong pull of the defender summoning me vibrated through my body. Ace's key glowed as well.

"Looks like you guys are being called for duty." Marco slid his hands behind his head and kicked back on the sofa. "I'll be here if you need me."

Ace and I reported to the travel lab. Al gave us the landing coordinates. Ace and I were both summoned by Campy. I prayed no harm had come to him and cursed Caiyan for not being here to help.

Ace winked at me as we boarded our vessels. Odd, he didn't seem concerned at all.

We arrived in a clearing in the middle of what would eventually become England. Campy, dressed in the latest Robin Hood fashion, leaned nonchalantly against the trunk of a large ash tree. There wasn't a brigand tied up, and he didn't seem to be in distress. He pushed off the tree trunk when I walked toward him.

"What's going on?" I asked him.

Ace left his vessel and joined us. "It was my idea, doll. Probably going to get us grounded, but me heart breaks for you."

"We're going to the wedding?" A huge smile spread across my face, and I pulled both of them in for a group hug.

Campy grinned. "The Crackys are getting a might pissed at the tavern. Gerry's there, too. He's naugh as drunk as they are, but close. If they decide to steal something, I'll summon you, but I think Tina and I can handle tucking them in bed after they pass out."

"Those Crackys are so predictable," Ace said.

"Won't the travel lab spot us?" I asked Ace.

"They will, but Agent Sexy Buns has to monitor the other travelers, and that leaves Marco to come fetch us. He isn't welcome at the wedding since, ya know, he became a defender for the WTF."

"This is a great plan," I said, wishing I had thought of it.

"He's clever, yeah?" Campy said, giving Ace a fist bump.

"Yep, that's what I love about him."

"And all this time I thought you loved me for my fashion expertise." Ace moved toward his vessel. "Speaking of fashion, let's go, doll. We've got disguises to pick up."

I kissed Campy on the cheek. "Thanks."

"Keep Uncle Cai safe. He's in over his head this time."

"I'll do my best."

We left Campy sending us a thumbs up and a set of adorable dimples.

The last wedding I attended at the Mafuso mansion was between a teammate of Marcos and a famous singer. It was a chaotic madhouse, and I expected the same for this one.

Ace and I pulled up in our rented car. Missing was a line of tail-lights waiting to attend the wedding of the century and a band of reporters lingering in the bushes. A few cars were being handed over to the uniformed valets.

Once inside, a man in a sequined, black tuxedo approached Ace.

"'ello, Marvin, how are you?" Ace asked as the man slid up next to him.

The man whispered to Ace. "Is that you, Ace baby?"

"You recognized me," Ace sulked.

"Only because you told me you might be in disguise. Very cunning and that dress is so versatile." He kissed Ace on both cheeks.

"How are things going?" Ace asked him.

"Great, sugar. Can you believe the luck? The wedding of the century and I had to pull it off in three weeks."

The guy had done a fantastic job. Elegant and sophisticated, exactly the style I would have chosen. My hatred for Satan's bitch escalated a few notches.

Ace chatted up the wedding planner while I scoped out the venue.

Tall crystal urns shot arrangements of lilies and roses six feet tall. The house was over the top in silken draperies and white floral arrangements with just a touch of pink.

"I heard the rumors. Can it be true Mahlia has found the man of her dreams?" Ace asked Marvin.

I stiffened next to him. He interlocked his arm with mine, and I relaxed a little.

"I believe the cat has caught her canary," Marvin said. "Wait until you meet him, he's dishy."

I huffed next to Ace, and he patted my arm.

"Marvin, this is Joe. He's a friend."

Marvin sized me up. I extended my hand, and he shook it delicately.

"Go on in, I'll vouch for you and…your guest. We'll catch up later." Marvin waved at another guest and was gone.

"Did I hear a tinge of jealousy in Marvin's voice?" I asked Ace.

"Don't be silly, hon." Ace paused, considered. "Do you think he sounded jealous?"

We found seats toward the back. I estimated the crowd around a hundred people. Small for a Mafuso shindig. Noted more seats were available on the groom's side. Not many people showed for Caiyan. No family or cousins. Only a handful of clients from his art gallery, his partner, and a couple of girls from the office. People who would come in contact with Mahlia.

Ace twisted strands of his long black wig. He had arranged for the disguises and chosen full drag for himself. I must say he made a pretty girl. He had the nose for it—turned up a little on the end—and slim hips. His flawless makeup hid his five o'clock shadow.

"Your makeup looks awesome," I told him.

"Thanks, doll."

I, on the other hand, was dressed in a dark striped suit. My breasts were taped down so tight I could barely breathe, and I had a thick mustache. We looked a little like Sonny and Cher. The hair piece I wore had a built-in side part, and Ace fixed my makeup like a pro.

An elderly lady to my right nudged me. "I heard the bride is pregnant?"

"I don't think so," I said. If she was, there would be hell to pay.

"Darn, I have a bet going with the ladies at my bridge club."

Her voice singsonged with a slight Brooklyn accent. "I was Caiyan's piano teacher," she said proudly. "When he lived with his aunt in Cobble Hill. Before she moved to Florida." She said Florida out of the side of her mouth like it was a dirty word. "He had such potential. When I read he was finally tying the knot, I took the train in."

"That's so sweet of you. I didn't know he could play the piano."

"He didn't like to practice, but I saw the talent in him. How'd you know him?"

I'm in love with him. "From work."

"That's nice, dear."

"It's too bad his aunt broke her hip. I would have liked to visit with her."

Caiyan's aunt Itty fractured her hip chasing a brigand across the ice in the Swiss Alps. She was beside herself she couldn't attend the wedding. The retired agent occasionally moonlighted for the WTF and was having a passionate love affair with Al from the travel lab.

An elegant harp sat off to one side of the room and played soft Celtic music. Good choice. My inner voice held up a sign, Satan's Bitch 2, Jen 0.

I studied the crowd. "Isn't that Marco's sister, Evangeline?" I asked Ace.

He squinted at the pretty brunette sitting a few seats in front of us on the bride's side. "Blimey, I believe you're right."

"What's she doing here?"

"Since Mafuso Motors used to sponsor Marco, she would be a friend of the bride."

"Really?"

"Don't you know the Mafusos will keep a finger on Marco. If they want to pressure 'im, they'll use her. Every move Mahlia makes is calculated."

Marco was taking a huge risk joining the WTF. His ties with the Mafusos were intermingled with his family. I needed to make nice with him and sort out our friendship. After I saved my foolish, piano playing Scot from making the mistake of his life.

Once the guests were seated, a rotund priest took his place at the head of the aisle under the spectacular flowered arch constructed for the occasion.

A few moments later Caiyan entered and stood next to the priest. Black tuxedo, my heart sighed.

"Odd," Ace said. "I was certain he would wear a kilt."

A brief flutter of hope tickled my insides.

He didn't have anyone standing up for him. No best man. No Brodie, no friend from high school, or cousin he was forced into selecting. No one.

I gathered my wits. Calm down, Jen. The harpist began playing the wedding march, and my SuperJen mantra followed along in key. Deep breath. He's not going to marry her. He's not going to marry her.

The guests stood around me. My legs were frozen to the chair. Ace tucked his hand under my arm and gently helped me to my feet.

Mahlia, wide, fake smile plastered on her face, was escorted down the aisle by Gian-Carlo. Damn, she looked beautiful. Double-damn, her gown was an Ivy Isabella. It was on my list. Now I'd have to delete it off my Pinterest board.

Not only had she stolen my man, she wore my favorite wedding gown. As she passed by me, the low neckline of the gown displayed the bronzed flesh of her perfect breasts. Lace cap sleeves ran across her shoulders and connected at the neck, encircling a thin swan of elegance. I imagined my hands there instead.

"Stop plotting 'er demise and think about what she's not wearing," Ace said.

He was right. She wasn't wearing her key. The perfect diamond-shaped cutout between her neck and chest was naked.

I glanced at Caiyan. He tugged on his shirt collar and I thought the light made his face appear pale, or maybe it was pale.

Mahlia progressed toward him. She stopped in front of the priest, and Gian-Carlo gave her away.

Caiyan smiled, more at Gian-Carlo than Mahlia.

The priest greeted the guests and began his traditional sermon about love and finding the perfect someone.

Caiyan's eyes scanned the crowd. For a moment, I thought he saw me. I'm right here.

"I love weddings." Ace dabbed at his eyes.

"Ace, who's side are you on?"

"Yours, of course, doll, it's just that weddings always make me tear up."

"This isn't a real wedding."

"It certainly seems real." He patted my knee. "No worries. I'm sure the Scot's going to bail."

I didn't see how. I hoped he had a backup plan. I hoped, somehow, he'd convinced Mahlia to whisk him away, free him so she could be with her lover, but without her key she was helpless.

The priest said a prayer, and from that moment on his words sounded like "Whamp, whamp" as my head thumped. However, his voice rang clear when he announced, "If any of you has a reason why these two should not be married, speak now or forever hold your peace."

I started to rise, and Ace clamped a hand on my leg. "No can do hon. We're here to see this through. If you so much as lift a finger, the WTF will confiscate our keys. Temporary grounding I can handle, but I'll keep me key."

I slumped back into my seat, and the wedding proceeded. It was down to the vows. If Caiyan said I do, it was over.

The priest spoke harshly to Caiyan. "Caiyan James McGregor, whilst thou have this woman to thy wedded wife, to live together according to God's law in the holy estate of matrimony? Whilst thou love her, comfort her, honor and keep her, in sickness and in health, and forsaking all others, keep thee only unto her, so long as ye both shall live?"

"I weel."

I died inside.

"Repeat after me," the priest fed Caiyan the lines and he said every word.

"I, Caiyan James McGregor, take you, Mahlia Jezabella Mafuso, for my lawful wife, to have and to hold from this day forward, for better, for worse, for richer, for poorer, in sickness and health, until death do us part."

I snickered at the middle name, but my fingers white knuckled the seat of the chair. When he finished, a tear trickled down my cheek. He said his vows. He'd committed to her. She would say hers, and he would slide his grandmother's ring on her finger, and they would be married.

The priest turned to Mahlia. Before she could open her mouth, a loud crack followed by a cloud of smoke filled the air.

When the smoke cleared, Caiyan was gone, and so was the priest. Mahlia stood hands on hips, mouth scrunched up in twist.

"What the hell?" she screeched.

"Find them!" Gian-Carlo ordered.

"Where's the groom?" the lady next to me asked.

"I guess he decided she wasn't the right woman for him." I smiled down at the petite woman.

A flurry of excitement ensued. Ace and I made a beeline for the door.

As I fled the house, I saw Mortas leave through a side door.

"What should we do?" I asked Ace.

"Tuck our tails and go back to base, I'm afraid."

"Jake told me he was sending an undercover agent, maybe we won't have to give him the good news."

Ace gave me a doubtful shake of his head. "The travel lab surely picked us up. Let's go take our lumps, doll."

"They're not married, right?" I was over the moon.

Ace grabbed my shoulders and leveled his eyes with mine. "Did you 'ear him?" He gave me a firm shake. "He said his vows."

The reality hit me hard. Someone else disrupted the wedding. "Let's get the 'ell out of 'ere before the Mafusos make us."

"Yes, let's go," I agreed. I had a groom to find, and when I did, I was going to kill him. Smoke and mirrors be damned.

CHAPTER 15

*W*e arrived at headquarters. Jake's mouth dropped open when he entered the landing area.

"I have no words." His chest heaved as he expelled a long sigh. "Should I ask why you look like Sonny & Cher?"

"We didn't have time to change," Ace said.

"The wedding was a farce!" My adrenalin pumped so hard I couldn't control myself. "It seemed legit, but when Mahlia was supposed to say I do...Caiyan vanished."

Ace clapped a hand over my mouth. I shoved it aside. "For Pete's sake, he knows we were at the wedding." Or at least I assumed he would know, but the look on his face told a different story.

"Why were YOU at the wedding?" Jake's voice boomed. He shot Ace a menacing look then halted. "Vanished?"

I nodded and followed with, "It's not Ace's fault. I can be annoyingly persuasive."

"Is that so?" The air thickened with the sarcasm in Jake's tone. "Call Marco back to base. I sent him to Wessex to find you."

"Why?"

"Because you disappeared off the travel screen."

I placed my hand to my key and summoned Marco back to base. "Pickles couldn't see us in Long Island?"

"He wasn't looking for you there. He can't watch the entire world, past and present, at the same time. You shouldn't have gone, Jen."

"But, Caiyan disappeared." I was almost giddy.

"My Intel reported in before you arrived," Jake said. "I know McGregor split."

Ace shifted toward Jake.

"Not exactly. He ditched all right. Left Mahlia standing at the altar," Ace explained. "I don't believe the Scot left on his own terms."

"Sure, he did." A wide smile spread across my lips. "Smoke and mirrors, just like Caiyan told me."

"Her key jumped, or Pickles has lost his touch." Jake ran a hand through his hair.

"The priest. He had to be Toecheese in disguise." I bounced on my toes as I relayed my theory to Jake.

Ace and Jake considered for a moment.

"Toches. That little devil. I didn't recognize 'im, but now that you've pointed out the obvious, I agree. The man has bloody scary talent."

"Incoming," one of the black suits holding court at the door to the hangar reported to Jake, and everyone took a step back toward the wall.

A rumble of a 700-horsepower motor and Marco's vessel appeared on the landing pad next to mine. He hopped out and joined us.

"Holy macaroni, you guys appearing in a variety act?" Marco raised an eyebrow at our clothing. "I'd only just arrived in Wessex, where were you?"

I explained about the smoke, and how Caiyan and the priest disappeared, and Mahlia stood there looking all pissed. I was talking so fast my words were vomiting out of my mouth in a stuttering mess.

"You went to the wedding?" Marco demanded more than asked.

I bit my lower lip.

"Jesus Christ, can't you do something with her?" Marco flailed his arms at Jake.

"What do you suggest? I need her to keep our world from caving in on itself."

Yoo-hoo, stop talking like I'm not in the room.

"She's going to end up dead if you don't do something. Now she's got Campy doing her dirty work."

"Actually," Ace started then stopped when the two men gave him an angry glare.

Jake moved to face off with Marco. "I can't control her any better than you can!"

"Then for the love of God, fire her!"

Whoa. Did Marco just try to get me fired?

Jake placed a hand to his earpiece and held up a finger. His face darkened and a moment later he said, "We've got bigger fish to fry. Mortas jumped."

"Let me guess, he went back to the Civil War?" Marco said.

The thick testosterone-filled sarcasm started to suffocate me. I sidestepped toward the exit.

Ace battled back into the conversation, and the three men argued vehemently over our impending destination.

I backed out of the hangar and headed toward the travel lab. Caiyan's words "smoke and mirrors" resounded in my head and I hoped his disappearing act was part of the plan.

Al greeted me as I entered the lab. "You've changed your look."

With all the fuss, I had forgotten I wore the dark wig and mustache. "I went to the wedding."

Al's eyebrows shot up.

Pickles sat at his workstation, hands moving frantically as he watched the travelers on his screens.

I offered a greeting, and he did a double take when he glanced my way. A few more clicks and he leaned back, stretched his long arms over his head. "Das good. Everyone has settled into da pattern nah."

Al and I moved in front of the big screen centered in the room. Black and blue dots blinked back at us, signifying the brigands and the travelers.

"Where did Mahlia jump?" I asked him, praying my assumption of the jump wasn't correct.

"Gettysburg, Pennsylvania, and Mortas is on her tail." He used the remote to zoom in on the location.

Damn, I knew it! "It's not Mahlia. I saw her at the wedding after Caiyan disappeared. It's Toecheese. He was wearing her key in Salem."

"Dat makes sense."

We turned toward Pickles. "I saw a fat, dark-haired man in my vision. I thought I'd eaten too much Callaloo. We'll label as such." Pickles cocked his head in my direction. "Did the brigand put on a few pounds?"

"He dressed as a priest and wore a fat suit. He vanished with Caiyan in the middle"—yes middle, my inner voice did a happy dance —"of the wedding."

Jake, Ace, and Marco joined us as Pickles walked over to examine my getup.

"Ya look like a real man. Except, I would have put a bigger sock in da trousers. You want ta look authentic."

"Not everyone has a big sock," I said.

Pickles raised an eyebrow at Marco.

"Don't look at me, man. She's never seen my sock."

All eyes moved to Jake, and Jake huffed. "Focus people. Where's that bastard gone now?"

"Mortas is here," Al used his pointer to indicate a blinking black dot. "Gettysburg, 1863."

"Christ."

"Kishin is here," Al slapped the pointer against the map.

"Caiyan's been dumped in the past," I said. "He's got to be with Toecheese."

"I can't see him, dat boy is no wearing da key." Pickles rubbed his temples.

"It's not possible, Toches isn't a transporter," Al said.

"He can carry. Remember when we were in Berlin. He found the transporter's vessel, and I clobbered him right before he took off." Marco shifted.

162

"He brought you back," Jake said. "We didn't consider that because we were so involved in trying to save you. I thought it was a fluke."

"The Mafusos have two transporters," Ace added.

The steady whirring of the computers echoed in the room as we stared at the screen. If Toches could transport, he was more valuable to Gian-Carlo than we suspected.

Jake's cell rang and he tapped his earpiece to answer. "Yes sir, right away."

"The general wants eyes on the ground. I've got no choice. I need someone who knows the people, the battles. My gut instinct tells me McGregor's mission is not about his key, but something bigger."

"Dude, I don't know why you think the Scot isn't in this for himself." Marco stood hands on hips.

"Because I wouldn't leave the woman I love for a damn key!"

The three of us stood slack-jawed.

"I'll be fine. Look," I said. "Mortas is here, by this building, a few miles from the town. That's far away from the battlefields."

"Jen, everywhere is a battlefield in Gettysburg," Marco said.

"If I take Gertie, she can steer us away from the battlefields. She knows the area."

Jake paused for a second.

"Are you mental?" Marco shouted at Jake. "You can't let her take Gertie back to the Civil War. Let me go in alone, or with Ace."

"No can do," Ace said. "I've already been there."

Jake turned to Al. "Give them the landing coordinates. Somewhere safe. I'll get the money. Ace, pick up Gertie and meet us back here."

"Wait," I said. "What about the message on the sword?"

"We think the message on the sword read find the key at Gettysburg, First Texas, RW. First Texas is a Confederate regiment and RW possibly stands for Rose Woods, an area where the First Texas saw some action. It's much too dangerous to land there."

"But—" I started.

"No!" Jake turned and left before Marco or I could protest.

Ace shrugged and followed Jake.

163

I frowned at Marco. "Did you suggest Jake fire me?" I crossed my hands over my chest.

"I may have misspoken," Marco mumbled.

Marco and I waited in the leather chairs facing the center screen. Pickles returned to his work area and Al followed. They did their best to find a secure landing area. After a few choice words between them, they agreed. Al motioned us over.

"The North and the South alternately captured this area many times, but there's a good section of wooded flatland here." Al scratched his bearded chin. "Based on the history books, the Union Army is in control now."

"Good. We'll be on the right team," Marco said.

I scrunched my nose at him. "I'll see if I can muster up a Yankee accent."

Jake returned along with Ace and Gertie. Her prior enthusiasm to travel back to Gettysburg was knocked down a few notches, and she wrung her hands as Al explained the landing situation to her.

While Al pointed out the do's and don'ts to Gertie, Jake gave me a few of his own. "Remember, steer clear of the Peach Orchard, the round tops, the wheat field, and most of all the area in front of Cemetery Ridge. If Mortas goes toward any of the battle areas, don't follow. If the brigands kill someone, we'll deal with the ramifications here in the present. Not there."

"Aye, aye, Captain," I said.

"You studied all the research I gave you, right?" Jake asked me.

"I read most of it."

"Jen."

"I got caught up reading letters from the soldiers."

"What letters?"

"Gertie brought home letters written by the soldiers to their loved ones."

"They were heartbreaking," Gertie said.

Jake frowned at me.

"But I know the generals, and the locations of the buildings." I put an arm around Gertie's shoulders. "And Gertie knows the rest."

Jake pulled Gertie aside. "You don't have to go."

"Yes, I do," she said. "Because the Mafusos could screw up my world, and I kind of like the one I'm living in."

Jake grimaced, but agreed. "You'll need a few vaccinations, typhoid, malaria, and yellow fever."

I gave her an apologetic smile. All the WTF travelers had been vaccinated for more diseases that I cared to count.

Gertie agreed, and Ace escorted her to the infirmary.

Jake watched her go. He turned toward Marco and me. Worry lines creased his forehead.

"Jake don't stress. I'll have Marco for muscle."

"I've been practicing with a rifled musket for weeks," Marco said.

"You have?" I didn't know Marco had taken any steps toward acknowledging our possible mission.

"Haven't you?" He moved toward the travel screen, and Pickles showed him the last location Mortas landed and the dot indicating the location he now occupied. He was in a tavern on the outskirts of town, not too far from our designated landing spot.

The dot labeled as Toches blinked eerily close to the Trostle Farm, the headquarters of Union Major General Dan Sickles.

Jake handed each of us Confederate States and Union currency conveniently folded into tiny plastic packages. "Put each bill on the sides of your cheeks. In case you get captured and you need a bargaining tool, or you cross the line."

The Confederate money was useless unless we mingled with the Rebels or traveled south.

"Under no circumstances are you to land anywhere near the Trostle Farm," Jake said to me.

"Jen's got this," Gertie piped up, and I thanked her with a nod.

"Time to go." Al placed his hand on my shoulder.

I gave Pickles and Al a finger wave as we headed out. The five of us walked silently down the hall. The shuffle of feet on tile changed to cement as we entered the empty hangar.

"Jennifer drives." Jake broke the quiet.

"Awe, c'mon," Marco objected.

165

"Her vessel will blend."

"I'm going to need a drink if I have to ride in your hooptie," Marco said to me.

Ace called after us on our way to my vessel. "Doll, the next drink you'll take will be from a rusty canteen."

CHAPTER 16

*M*y outhouse landed with a weird thunk and tilted to the front. Gertie let out a breath. "Thank god!" she said. "These trips always make me nervous."

A slice of light filtered in through the gaps in the wooden planks, and our shadows danced around the outhouse. Gertie let out a giggle.

Marco's eyes grew wide. "Whoa."

"What?" I asked them.

"You're dressed as a man," Gertie said.

My hands went to my face. A short mustache and beard surrounded my mouth. Gertie reached over and tugged on my beard.

"It's not real, I believe it's stuck on with glue," I said. "Like the one I wore at the wedding."

Marco blew out a relieved sigh, then cursed. "Shit, we're on the losing team." He looked down at his filthy, faded Confederate uniform. "I thought we were landing in Union territory. We'd better find our mark and get the hell out of here before we end up on the front lines."

I eased the door open, and we exited the outhouse into a small basin tucked into a clearing of hundred-year-old oaks. The area seemed spot on. We moved under a patch of light drilled through the dense canopies of surrounding foliage for a better look at ourselves.

A gray double-breasted coat with shiny brass buttons covered the shirt and cloth flattening my breasts to teenage boy status. My vessel aped the male persona disguise I had worn from the wedding. If on purpose or accident, I had no clue. Dark gray pants and a garment at my throat completed my ensemble. A bag hung at my side next to a canteen. I removed a tall hat and inspected the red cloth wrapped around the band of the hat. The cloth was adorned with a cross. I repositioned it on my head.

"Why are you dirty?" I asked Marco after examining my uniform.

"Looks like I've seen some action. Helps me blend in."

Gertie and I wouldn't blend as easily. Our clothes didn't have the same battle scars. Gertie's burgundy full skirt and camel cotton jacket strapped with canteens and pouches had her clanging as she moved to check her gear. A red band was secured around her right bicep, and her hair twisted up into a gray bandanna.

"I'm a vivandière, I think." She pointed to the red cloth on her upper arm.

"A what?" Marco asked.

"Like a nurse. The vivandières would go out on the battlefield to help the wounded." She looked up at my hat. "And you're part of the ambulance corps. That red badge on your hat identifies you."

My clothes were cut from finer cloth than those of my teammates. The chain of a gold pocket watch hung from my vest.

"Based on your clothes, I'd guess you're a doctor. You're also a lieutenant." She tapped the insignia on my jacket.

Dang. I wasn't so good with blood.

"Maybe our mark is at the hospital," I suggested.

"Most likely your vessel outfitted us as medical corps because they move freely among the wounded and the opposing side's not supposed to shoot at us." Gertie's optimistic look gave me hope we would find Caiyan and not end up dead.

"I'm so screwed," Marco said holding his cap in his hands. "First

Texas Regiment." He showed us the top of his hat embroidered with a number one and a star. "Who'd of guessed I'd be a Texan?"

Gertie and I smiled at each other.

"Better late than never," Gertie said.

"It's also the regiment scratched on the sword," I said.

Marco shook the canteen hanging at his side. "It's full. But my cap and cartridge boxes are empty." He motioned at the leather pouches attached to his belt.

"My canteens are full too," Gertie said. "That's good because the water became unsanitary due to runoff from the dead, and the excrement deposited in such close quarters."

I shuddered and knitted my eyebrows at Gertie. "I could have lived all day without that knowledge."

"That knowledge might save your life. Conserve your water."

I stored her words away, taking note of the full canteen slapping against my side as I moved. A bag hung from my shoulder and another at my waist. I held up the sack painted black. The bag smelled like a rotten egg.

"What's this? It smells."

"I believe that's your haversack, or food bag."

I ditched the bag. "It's empty and it reeks."

"You might be sorry when you don't have anywhere to carry food." Gertie shrugged.

"I'll risk it."

The other bag contained medical supplies.

"Your vessel might have fit me in this threadbare crap colored uniform, but it forgot to give me a weapon," Marco huffed.

"Gun control?" I suggested.

He frowned at me. Gunshots sounded in the distance, and he mumbled, "We need to move out."

"Miss Scarlet…I'm good with history and maybe healing critters, but not so good with my knowledge on healing humans," Gertie said southern belle style.

Marco's eyes looked heavenward at the *Gone with the Wind* reference, then went wide. We hit the ground as the roar of cannon fire concussed the earth.

"What the fuck?" He stood and focused his attention on our landing area. We were in a tight circle of trees and brush. A tiny hole in the landscape of Gettysburg.

We moved away from my outhouse toward the edge of the clearing. Stepping over a split in the low brush, we walked a few paces down a trail for a look around. Another cannon fired in the distance and everyone flinched. We peeked through the thick brush. I bit my lower lip. We weren't in the clearing Al had designated for us.

"Where in Hell's Kitchen did you land us?" Marco asked.

A live action version of the *Call of Duty* video game LARPed in the low ground below us. Soldiers were running, cutting through the trees, firing their weapons into the thick pink dust.

Gertie's breath tickled my cheek as she leaned next to me for a better view of the situation. "Where's the tavern?"

I leaned back on my heels. Gertie gave me a concerned glance.

"Jen what the F...?" Marco pulled back from the brush and stared at me.

"I may have missed my mark." I stood unsure.

"What do you mean, you missed your mark?" Gertie's voice held a slight quiver.

"I'm not sure." I glanced around at the trees surrounding us. We stood and started in the opposite direction. A twig snapped ahead, and a rustle in the bushes had us moving closer together.

A man stepped into the clearing. He held a pistol in one hand and his hat in the other. The man seemed to be in a state of urgency. Marco snapped to a salute. Gertie stood mouth agape. I copied Marco.

"Who taught you to salute like a damn Brit?" He asked me. "Palm up soldier." I turned my palm up and held my position. The three of us were creating a stronghold in front of the outhouse I'd so carelessly forgotten to dismiss.

"At ease soldiers," the man said, then turned his attention to me. "Which corps are you from lieutenant?"

The sweat beaded up on my hairline. Jake had given us several different scenarios based on our landing location and the troops in that area, but since I had botched the landing, I went with my gut.

"First Corps, sir. We were separated from our regiment."

"Who is your division commander?"

"Hood, First Texas sir," Marco answered, adding a Texas drawl to his words.

"I do admire my Texans," he said, holstering his pistol. "You men did a good job taking these woods. Another victory in our pocket." His eyes took in the structure behind us. "I declare, I've not seen one of these so far from the farm." He removed his frockcoat, handed it to Gertie, who clasped it in her hands and gave a clumsy curtsy. His steel blue eyes sparkled as he spoke to her. "Thank you, my dear."

He moved toward the outhouse and opened the door. "Carry on, men," he said and paused, regarding Marco. "Please guard me as I use the Johnny hole."

Gertie's face screwed up in disbelief. I took a deep breath, ready to protest, but Marco jabbed me in the ribs with his elbow.

The man entered the outhouse, and we took a step back, expecting my vessel to eject the general with his pants around his ankles.

"Was that who I think it was?" I asked Gertie.

She stood speechless for a moment. "General Robert E. Lee." His name came out in a whisper.

The outhouse gave a shudder. We moved a few steps backward. The air around us began to swirl. Leaves and debris from the forest floor rose from the ground. My vessel shook and moved like a contestant in a dancing contest. A crack of thunder and it vanished. The swirling debris dropped to the ground as if it were never disturbed.

"Jesus H. Christ, what happened to the general?" Gertie held her free arm out in question as her other squeezed General Lee's coat folded over her forearm to her chest.

"Jen get it back!" Marco hollered.

I touched my key and beckoned my ride.

Nothing. The air around us stood still.

Marco grabbed me by the shoulders. "Why didn't it come back?"

"I don't know!" I yelled up at him.

Gertie moved toward the empty space my vessel had occupied. Marco released my shoulders when Gertie yelped.

"Y'all, we have another problem." She covered her mouth and pointed at the ground. A shallow grave housed the body of a man directly under the spot my outhouse had vacated.

"Did I l-l-land on that man?" My words tumbled out in a frantic slurry.

"Nice work, Dorothy." Marco brushed by me to view the dead guy.

"Is he...dead?" My voice caught as we gathered around the man.

Marco bent down and felt for a pulse. "Yeah, but you didn't do it. He's been shot."

The man had a deep scar from temple to jaw. The bullet went through his right temple above the scar and exited out the back of his skull. Blood pooled behind his head. His ripped trousers and stained jacket of a mismatched uniform made it difficult to tell which side he fought for. I had read many soldiers wore their own clothing, but nothing about this man revealed he was part of a regiment or that he had participated in a battle, except the gunshot wound that ended his life.

Relieved I hadn't killed a man, I took stock of his dark skin and husky frame. "Who do you think killed him?"

"Jen, we're in the middle of the Civil War." Marco sat back on his haunches.

"Do you think he was a traveler?" Gertie asked.

His shirt lay open and his neck bare. "If he was, his key is gone." Marco pointed to his neck.

"Based on the clothing, he might be someone's slave." Gertie said.

I winced at the idea.

A glint of steel winked at me from the side of the soldier. I knelt next to him and pushed him to his left. He laid on his unsheathed sword as if the weapon was tossed carelessly aside. The handle had the same design as the one I remembered from my bedroom. I pulled the sword away from his body.

"It looks like the sword from Caiyan's treasure room." I ran my hand across the blade. "But maybe not, there's no message on the blade."

"Who is this man?" Gertie asked.

Before we could obtain any further clues to the identity of the man, the bushes rustled again, and a young soldier stepped into the clearing. He seemed surprised by our presence and saluted me. "Doctor, what are you doin' here on the battlefield?"

"I—" clearing my throat, I returned the salute and lowered my voice. "I was summoned to help this man, but I'm afraid I was too late."

He moved in next to Marco and viewed the dead man. It wasn't the first time the young man had seen a corpse. His blue eyes held a degree of familiarity, and I saw them track to the coat Gertie still held in her hands.

"Where'd ya get that co—"

Marco gave him a right uppercut to the tip of his chin that lifted the gangly soldier off his feet. He went lights out and Marco lowered him to the ground.

Gertie and I gasped. "What did you do that for?" I asked Marco.

"If he starts yelling for help, we're in trouble."

Gertie used the general's coat and made a pillow for his head. A wisp of white hair fell across his forehead. I found his kepi hat and laid it on the ground next to him.

"Now what do we do?" Gertie asked.

I moved to the edge of an overlook. "I don't know where—" and then I saw him. The boy from the letter. His legs caught in the casualty of a battle-ridden snake-rail fence, and his left shirt sleeve soaked dark with blood. Unable to reach up and remove the heavy wood off his legs, he lifted his head and wrote on paper propped against his thigh.

"Oh no," I said.

"What?" Gertie followed my gaze to the boy.

"Oh. Jen, you didn't land us near the boy from the letter?"

"What boy?" Marco crossed his arms over his chest.

"There was a boy I read about. He was stuck on a fence and bled to death because he couldn't free his legs. He wrote a letter to his mother."

Marco frowned.

"I was concentrating on the designated landing spot, and then the words that poor soldier wrote in the letter came to mind. I'm sorry, I thought about him during the transport, and landed here um...accidentally."

"Crap on a cracker," Gertie said.

I stared at the battlefield in the setting sun. Men scattered the field, dead and dying. Medics, slowly, carefully, made their way across the open field, offering water and choosing the wounded to be carried off by stretcher. Soldiers lucky enough to walk drug their comrades by the arms away from the enemy fire.

"I'm going to save him."

"Jen, no fucking way am I going to let you go into that battlefield." Marco stomped about. "The cannon fire alone is deadly."

Gertie remained quiet.

"I know...I know, it's violating the rules, and I'll probably get in trouble, but I can't sit here and watch him die."

"Thousands of men are dying. You going to save them all?" Marco asked me.

I pondered the questions for a moment.

"For the love of God, she actually thinks she can." Marco looked helplessly at Gertie.

"Marco, you can use your gift to slow time, and Jen can free his legs," Gertie said. "If we are close to the Rose Woods, which I think we are, the fighting should be done for the day."

Another cannon blast echoed in the distance, and Marco grimaced. "It doesn't sound like it's done."

"Marco. You didn't read the letter. He's only a boy. He shouldn't be here. He lied about his age to serve his country."

"Jen's right. He enlisted as an eighteen-year-old, but he's only twelve, and well...maybe Jen is supposed to save him," Gertie said.

"Twelve?" Marco's eyes grew wide. "I'll go alone."

"No, we go together."

Marco opened his mouth to argue, but I cut him off.

"Your gift to slow time will last longer if you focus, and I'll help the boy. Gertie can stay here with…" I tipped my head toward the soldier Marco had knocked unconscious, who didn't look more than a teenager himself. "You can alert us to anything suspicious."

Gertie raised her eyebrows.

Point taken.

"Two grown men holding hands squat walking across the battle-field won't look suspicious at all." Marco pulled his forage cap down on his head. "Let's motor."

We crouch walked to the open area, and I dropped to the ground. Marco did the same next to me. My inner voice kissed her rosary and crossed herself.

"Hold my hand," he said, lacing his fingers in mine. He reached up and touched the key hidden beneath the dirty collar of his uniform. We crouch walked toward the boy. Time warped and a few sharp-shooter bullets whizzed over our heads in slow motion. I refrained from looking to my right to see if any connected with the men protecting the newly captured area.

We stopped twice so Marco could reset. His gift only lasted minutes. I did as he instructed. We passed a man face down, shot in the back of the head. Marco relieved the dead man of his gun and haversack.

"What are you doing?"

"I'm not walking around Gettysburg unarmed. He doesn't need it anymore." He gestured at the man.

Jake was right. This wasn't a smart idea. We'd save the boy, find Caiyan, and get the hell out of Dodge. Whatever Mortas was doing here, I wasn't sure I wanted to stay and find out. On our third rest stop, a group of soldiers passed us, climbed the fence, and, guns in hand, ran toward the north end of the field.

Marco jerked his head toward the boy. "Almost there."

Our last crab crawl attempt reached the boy. I released Marco's hand to examine him. Blood soaked his left pants leg and his gun rested on the other side of the fence waiting for him to make the climb over. With the letter clutched in his hand, he blinked up at us as I spoke to him.

"I'm a doctor," tiny white lie, "I'm going to move your leg off the fence." His dark hair, wet with sweat, stuck to his grimy, angelic face. When his big brown eyes focused on me, he spoke.

"Thank you, sir, but I fear I'm done for."

A bullet tore through the top stake of the fence and he winced. "It don't hurt much."

"Shut it, I'm helping you down." When I had freed his leg, he slumped to the ground. A small wound to his upper arm had stained the sleeve of his uniform.

"You're going to be fine," I told him.

"The cannister got me. I felt a piece bite my leg, my shoulder. I wrote this here letter for my momma, would you see she gits it?"

I folded the letter and tucked it into his pocket. "You're not going to die today." He smiled, the smile of an innocent boy. One that should be at home playing with his dog, dreaming about the neighbor girl, having his mother kiss him goodnight.

It would be impossible for Marco and me to carry the boy to safety. I wouldn't ask Marco to risk his life, again. A few yards behind me, medics transported an injured soldier on a makeshift stretcher off the battlefield. I looked down at the boy. "You shouldn't walk on that leg. We're going for help, stay here."

"Thank you, sir." I handed him his gun and we copied our squat walk, hand in hand, toward Gertie.

A cannon blast hit behind us, yanking us apart and knocked us off our feet.

"Marco?" I called out, but the dense smoke blinded me.

"Jennifer, keep low and make your way toward my voice."

He was in front of me. I hunkered down, moving quickly along the fence line. Men lay dead around me. Dirt, grime, and blood crusted their faces. The ground softened under my boots, and I ignored the reason why. The air, thick with smoke, forced me to cough. I covered my mouth with my hand and kept moving.

The smoke cleared momentarily. Marco waited next to Gertie in the trees, using their trunks for cover. He beckoned me toward him. Another cannon fired, and they were lost in the fog of destruction.

There was too much death. Bullets thudded as they cut through flesh, gunfire echoed in the distance like a thousand men chopping wood. The wail of the injured men and animals accompanied by the occasional boom of the cannons had me covering my ears and curling into a tight ball. My stomach clenched, and I waited for calm.

As I raised up in the dusty pink of the cannon dust, that's when I saw him, creeping through the trees toward my landing area. He was dressed in federal blues. Caiyan, a few feet from Marco. The two men I loved most were on opposite sides of the proverbial Mason-Dixon line and the battle raged on.

CHAPTER 17

arco and Gertie were waving me toward them. Another cannon blast hit close to the trees, and they disappeared in a thick cloud. I circled around behind the neck of the woods where I had last seen Caiyan. Thankfully, the shooting had stopped, and the sound of cannons rumbled further into the distance.

I took cover behind a giant spruce and peeked at my pocket watch. Seven thirty. The battle for Culp's Hill now occupied the attention of the generals—except General Lee, who, because of me, was AWOL.

The air settled into a hot, soupy haze that clung to my clothes and dampened my hair hidden under the dark wig. Keeping a lookout for the Mafusos, and my head down in case the ceasefire decided not to cease, I moved inward.

If what Ace said was true and Caiyan had been to this time before, I wasn't sure which Caiyan I was dealing with. My heart pained if the Mafusos dropped him here and I was too late. Had his young self appeared and ripped the man I loved from the fabric of time? I pushed the thought aside.

I moved stealthily through the trees. He stood, foot propped up on a boulder, transferring the weight of his pack by leaning with an elbow on his knee. He used a handkerchief to mop his brow. He pocketed the handkerchief, took a drink from his canteen. Replacing the cap, he began to move toward my landing area.

The age seemed right. Certainly, older than the man who took the sword from Mr. Raney in Purley. If the man I saw was my Caiyan, he wouldn't recognize me in this getup, dressed as a man, and that could be dangerous.

I removed my hat and wig, shaking my hair free.

Caiyan disappeared from my sight.

I hastily manscaped the beard and tucked the disguise into my hat. Securing the hat in the crook of my arm, I hurried after him. At least he'd take a second look before shooting me.

From the looks of things, he'd been busy confiscating gear after he arrived. He didn't carry the rifled musket, standard issue for a soldier, but instead holstered a handgun in the front of his belt. A far cry from the tuxedo he wore only hours earlier.

The last image of him standing at the altar with Mahlia sent the mercury climbing. When I was a few feet from him, my mouth took over, leaving my brain behind.

"You were going to marry her!" I couldn't help myself. The words came out before I could stop them.

He whipped around, drawing his Colt Remington revolver, and aimed it my way. His eyes grew wide at my disguise, then sparked with a familiar anger.

"Sunshine, I asked ye to trust me. Yet here ye are." He waved the gun horizontally in front of him. "This is not jest dangerous, 'tis suicide. These men don't care tha' yer a woman, although they willnae be able to tell." He eyed my uniform. "Is that a mustache?"

My hands flew to my mouth. I had forgotten to remove the furry upper lip. I lifted my chin and puffed out my flattened chest. "Who gives a rat's ass if I'm a woman? I can defend myself. Besides, you're the bad guy now, I'm here to arrest you."

"Arrest me?" He laughed and lowered his weapon. "Go home, Jen. I order ye to go home."

"You can't order me around. You're not my defender anymore."

His shoulders slumped and the hard muscles in his jaw tightened.

"I dinnae want ye here. Thought I took every precaution to keep ye safe."

"I found the sword."

His brow furrowed and he pressed his lips tight, pausing from his lecture.

"My shoe closet was a terrible hiding place." I wafted my hand at him nonchalantly. "It was the first place I looked." Not entirely true, but whatever.

"Go home!"

"I'm not going home without answers, and…Marco and Gertie. We got separated and I need to find them."

"Ye brought Gertie here? Has the entire bunch of ye gone mad?"

"Gertie is a competent authority on Gettysburg." I wagged a finger at him and met his glare.

"You go home now!" he shouted at me.

"I have to complete my mission and find my defender."

"I'm yer defender, and I order ye to go home!"

"Not anymore. You can't play that card." I held my ground.

"Bloody hell. Why did Agent McCoy send ye onto the battlefield?"

"He didn't. I landed here. I had business."

"Cripes."

A branch broke behind me, and Marco stepped into our hidden cluster of brush, his face flush from heavy breathing and his musket pointed in our direction. When he saw Caiyan, he lowered his gun.

"Thank God, I didn't know what happened to you and I heard you shout." Marco said, placing his hand against the tree trunk to catch his breath. "I see you found the brigand."

"Yer supposed to be watching oot fir her." Caiyan yelled at Marco.

Marco straightened and growled at Caiyan. "I'm keeping her bed warm, isn't that what you did?"

Caiyan's face dropped for a moment, then anger replaced the shock.

My mouth hung open. I couldn't find the words to explain.

Caiyan's face flushed a savage red. He waved his gun in the air. "Ye take her home now!"

"I can't—" Marco started, but Caiyan cut him off.

"Ye weel," he pointed his revolver at Marco and shot him in the leg. Marco fell to the ground, holding his thigh.

"You crazy sonofabitch! You shot me!"

I rushed to Marco's side.

He held pressure on his thigh with one hand and scrambled for his rifle with the other. I pushed it out of his reach as Gertie stepped into the area.

She gasped when she saw the blood oozing from between Marco's fingers.

"What happened?" she asked me.

"Caiyan shot Marco," I answered.

"Why would you do that?" she hollered at Caiyan. She bent down over the two of us.

While I applied pressure to his bleeding leg, Gertie fumbled through the pack Marco had stolen and came up with a tourniquet. "Here, let me use this." I moved aside, and she knelt to apply the contraption.

"These guns don't have good aim. You could have killed me," Marco shouted at Caiyan, following up with a string of profanities.

Caiyan walked over. He tapped Marco with the edge of his boot, "'Tis only a flesh wound. Now she must take ye home. And dinnae come back! I willnae be here much longer."

"I can't!" Tears threatened as my anger spewed. "I can't summon my vessel."

"Dinnae mess wit' me, Sunshine."

"General Lee went inside my outhouse and it left. I tried calling it back, but it won't come."

His gaze fixated on me, and for the first time, I noticed his weary, bloodshot eyes.

"She's telling the truth," Gertie said.

He pinched the bridge of his nose like he was trying to control his internal beast from strangling me. Removing his hand, he glared at Marco. "For fuck's sake, don't die."

"Now he's worried about me, or should I say he's worried about himself. You sack of shit." Marco scowled at me. "Why can't you see him for what he really is."

Gunshots sounded in the distance. The second wave of attack was commencing on Little Round Top.

Caiyan walked away from us, cut through the brush.

I left Marco in Gertie's care and followed him.

He stood at the edge of the small hill and scanned the trees for soldiers.

My back ached from my gear. I set my hat down, removed the heavy medical bag. The sword dangled at my side, free from the weight of the gear that hung on top of it. I walked up behind him.

"Why are you here?" I asked him.

He spoke without turning around. "The Mafusos have a seer, but no key. I know of a seer, but she doesnae have her key here. The Mafusos think she does."

"A seer? Like Pickles?"

"Aye, my plan was to get my key and warn the seer the Mafusos will take her. I didnae expect them to force me into marriage, 'twas their safety net."

"You didn't have to marry her."

He turned toward me. His eyes softened when they met mine.

"Hurting you was the hardest part, but my intentions were for the greater good. Unfortunately, Gian-Carlo refused to return my key until after I proved my loyalty to him."

"Proved your loyalty by marrying Mahlia," I huffed.

"Toches knows of the seer. He's using his information of her to win the respect of Gian-Carlo and bargain his way into the Mafuso family. The Mafusos have been trying to find her since I dangled the sword under their noses."

"You were driven by the Thunder key, you didn't know it was possessed," I moved closer wanting to wrap my arms around him but chose to keep my distance.

His shoulders slumped. "Toches found her last cycle, almost snagged her."

"The girl," I said. My mind clicked the pieces together. "In Salem."

"Ye were there?" His eyes widened.

"Yep. My assignment."

"Gian-Carlo locked me up last moon cycle. Toches said he tried fir her but failed. He dinnae tell me ye were there."

"He's sneaky that way."

"Aye, dinnae go as planned. Gian-Carlo was naugh happy with Toches. The old man realized he wouldn't find the sword withoot me, and…" He stopped mid-sentence. "Where did ye get that?" He pointed to the sword I had taken off the fallen soldier. The sheathed weapon angled at my side.

"I accidentally landed on a guy," His brows tightened together, and I cleared up the confusion. "But he was already dead. I thought it was your sword, but there's no engraving on the blade."

"Bloody hell, ye shoudnae be here." His anger flared again.

"You should quit keeping secrets and let me help you," I said, matching his tone.

"Was the man ye killed—"

"Correction, landed on."

He moved close to me. So close I wanted to brush a kiss across his lips. I reminded myself not an hour ago this guy was standing at the altar with Satan's bitch spouting I weel.

"Did he have a scar alongside his cheek like so?" Caiyan ran his finger down my cheek.

"Yes." My stomach knotted. The direction of our conversation wasn't sounding good.

"I'm too late." He dropped his arms to his sides and stepped away from me.

"Too late?"

"The man's name was Boon. He traveled with the seer I'm looking fir. He was my contact. I believe he scratched the message into the blade and gave Sam Raney the sword."

I bit my bottom lip. "But I have it."

"Jest as weel, this trip has gone to shite."

"What do you mean?"

183

"Mahlia didnae want to marry me." He almost looked upset. "At least that's what I thought."

"Why didn't she want to marry you?"

"Sunshine, ye didnae accept my proposal either."

"You were under the influence of the Thunder key."

"Ye dinnae know that at the time." His green eyes cut through me like laser beams.

"You're changing the subject."

He shook his head at me in surrender. "The wedding was naugh supposed to go as far as it did."

"What are you talking about?"

"When Gian-Carlo ordered me to marry Mahlia and find the seer before he would return my key, she offered to help me."

I arched an eyebrow at him. "Seriously?"

Ignoring my sarcasm, he continued. "Mahlia told me she had no interest in marrying me and promised to transport me before we said I do." He spread his hands and wiggled his fingers. "Smoke and mirrors."

"I guess you were surprised when she walked down the aisle without her key."

He paused for a moment, taking in the fact I was at the wedding. He chuckled. "I shouldae known ye wouldn't miss it."

"And you didn't think she would double-cross you?"

"I dinnae know what to think. I went along with the wedding until I could figure oot a plan. After I said my vows, that's when Toches dropped a smoke bomb and signaled for me to follow him from the house. He transported me here."

"We should have known he could transport."

Caiyan thought about my words for a moment, assembling the puzzle pieces. "Toches can transport, but only if he's wearing a trans-porter's key."

"Like Ace," I said.

"Aye, I suspected such, but didnae know for certain." He paused. "They conspired together, Mahlia and Toches."

And a piece of the puzzle clicked into place. The colorful silk shirts in Caiyan's apartment, the jealousy I felt when I read Toches in the jail cell at Gitmo, and Mahlia's panties in my closet. Mahlia and Toches were an item.

"My guess is they've been doing more than conspiring."

Caiyan paused as he connected the dots. "Wouldnae have pegged her to go for the likes of him."

"And not the likes of you?"

He frowned. "I told Toches the seer doesnae have the key. He said I have three days, and once he has the seer, he'd take me back to our time. I ditched him so I could warn Boon; he's out there searching for me."

"He won't take you back." I knew if Toches was having an affair with Mahlia, Caiyan stood in the way to his happily ever after. "They've been living together in your apartment. She has her things in my closet!"

His face clouded. "I thought it wouldae a good idea for Mahlia to be seen at the apartment, to convince everyone the wedding was the real deal. I dinnae know she moved in, and I dinnae know aboot Toches. I've been staying at the Mafusos' house in Amagansett."

"Toches was wrong about the three days. You can't stay, you've already been here." When he raised a questioning eyebrow, I answered. "Jake has your travel dates, and Ace and Brodie confirmed. Why didn't you tell Toecheese?"

"I hoped to find Boon before he died, save him, and warn the seer. Maybe she would have had a better life." He released a long, slow breath. "I thought I still had time, but the wedding didnae go as planned, and I guess I've arrived too late."

A silence settled between us over the reality of our situation.

"I didnae know how Toches figured oot it was Gettysburg."

"Someone stole the sword from my closet. I think it was Toches."

He paused for a moment. "He knew I wasnae going to bring him the key. He's using me to gain Gian-Carlo's respect."

Gertie exploded through the trees. A branch whipped her across the face, and she stood stupefied. Shaking off the surprise attack, she focused on us. "They're taking him."

185

"Who?"

"The medics. They're loading Marco on a stretcher."

"They cannae see us together. They'll think yer a spy." Caiyan drew his gun.

I held up a hand at him and nudged Gertie toward the medics. "Go with Marco. You're a nurse, sort of. Act like you should be there. I'll come find you when I figure out a way to get us out of here."

Gertie's face paled. "I'm not really a nurse."

I grabbed her by the shoulders and looked firmly into her worried blue eyes. "Gertie you're a strong woman. Keep Marco safe, and I'll find you. I promise."

She gave a shaky nod and headed off in the direction of the medics.

"Don't let them cut off his leg," I hollered after her.

Caiyan took off his cap and ran a hand through his hair. When his eyes met mine, they grew glassy. Either due to dust or dignity, I couldn't be certain. He tossed the hat aside and walked further away from me, collecting his thoughts, then turned back toward me.

"Jen, I'm sorry. I love you and that shouldae been enough fir me. I thought I could fix the problem I created when I was under the influence of the Thunder key and get my key back at the same time." He dropped his head. "'Tis my fault yer stuck here in this deathtrap."

"What's your escape plan?" I asked him. "How are you planning to get home without your key?"

"Now that I know Toches is against me, I've no way home."

"What do you mean, no way home?"

I'd never seen Caiyan without a plan B. He always had a backup plan, a way out.

"Caiyan, you can't be serious. I'm going to watch you die?"

"I'm not sure what happens, 'tis been told when a traveler rips the thread of time, they no longer exist."

"Caiyan, there has to be another way." My palms began to sweat. "How do we find the seer?"

"There's no time. In the past, after I arrived and found Boon dead, I met Sam Raney and went to Longstreet's camp. We found the seer.

She traveled with Pickett's division. They havenae arrived yet. She willnae be there now."

General George Pickett. He led the attack on the center of the Union line in what was referred to as Pickett's charge. It was the worst of all the battles at Gettysburg.

"We have to find the seer."

"Jen, there's soldiers camped throughout these woods. I willnae be able to find her withoot being shot, or captured, and there's no time." He placed a hand on my arm. "If ye interact wit' the young me, it could change things." His eyes held steady with mine. "But I'll be keepin' my memories of us as they stand." He pulled me in, and I breathed in the heady scent of earth and the familiar pinch of cinnamon. He lowered his lips and kissed me.

With my anger at him forgotten, I clung to him, unable to remove my arms. A tear spilled down my cheek.

He chuckled. "You're mustache tickles. I've never been hugged by a man in such a way. If the Rebels find us like this, weel...it wouldnae be good."

Releasing him, I stepped back. There had to be another solution. "You damaged the sword in Purley. What did it say?"

He turned toward me. The sun low on the horizon silhouetted his solid frame. My pocket watch ticked. Minutes, an hour at the most.

"When I was younger, and not working for the WTF, I found the sword at the museum. I saw the message and knew it was from Boon. 'Twas code to meet him. Ye see, the seer, she's a bit of a crusader. Often finds herself into wee troubles." A small smile tugged at the corner of his mouth. "When I saw the markings on the sword, I traveled back to the original owner to find out how he came aboot it. Next moon cycle, I came here. Dinnae realize until I was at the Raney house that I was the one who put it in the museum."

The loop made my head spin.

"If ye wait oot the moon cycle, Ace can come get ye next cycle."

I nodded and brushed away the tears.

"That's if Mortas doesn't find us first."

"Mortas?"

"Yeah, he's the reason we jumped here. Pickles saw him on the travel screen. Mortas and Toches. Two brigands in one place, General Potts ordered Jake to send us."

"I wasnae sure, but this is it."

"This is what?"

"Toches takes the seer back to our time. I wasnae sure which time he was from, but it makes sense."

It didn't make sense to me.

"You need to find the seer, warn her Mortas is here. She must leave this place."

"You said the seer doesn't have a key."

"She doesnae have one, naugh exactly." His voice ratcheted up a notch.

When I looked confused, he drug his hand through his hair at an agitated rate.

"I don't have much time to explain the details. I arrive there by the giant oak at sundown. After I discover Boon, follow me. I weel locate her."

Could this be happening? I refused to believe it. Caiyan moved toward the edge of the woods, looked out over the field of dead and wounded.

My brain worked overtime trying to figure out a safe way home, for all of us. I tried to summon my outhouse. Again, a futile attempt and the ground only rumbled with the madness beyond the woods.

"I can't leave you," I said and gathered my things. I reapplied the beard and tucked my hair under the wig. Good enough. I slung the medical bag on my shoulder and looped the haversack over my head. Plopping my medical corps hat on my head, I walked over and stood behind him. "Let's go soldier, we have a mission."

He turned toward me, and his eyes widened. "You're the doc—"

A gunshot sounded behind Caiyan and he jerked forward. I caught him as he stumbled, and we fell to the ground, his body on top of mine.

"What—" I lifted my head and saw the boy I had saved from the fence. He had hobbled to the edge of the battlefield, swayed from his injury, but stood proudly as he lowered his musket.

"I got him. I killed a damn Yankee!" As the words left his mouth, a bullet pierced the side of his head, and he fell to the ground. The boy lay still fifty feet from me. His mother would get the letter after all.

A bullet tore bark off a nearby tree, and I flinched. A division of Union sharpshooters were stationed on the small hill above the battlefield and were steadily picking off any stray Confederates that dared leave the open field.

My pack and Caiyan's weight pinned me to the ground, but he was breathing. Good.

Obscured from the sharpshooters by the undergrowth and brush, I surveyed the damage. Running my hand over his back, blood dampened the back of his jacket. I ran my fingers under the wet material and across his back to find the entry point. Right lower flank.

When I jostled him, he moaned, and his eyes fluttered open. We had lain in each other's arms like this many times before. His green eyes searched deep into my soul, finding my secrets, and keeping a lock on his.

"What happened?" he asked me.

"You were shot."

"Who?"

"A mistake."

"It doesnae matter, Sunshine."

I cursed the air around me. I saved the boy and changed history, and now the past was setting things right.

He started to close his eyes.

"Stay with me," I tucked a finger under his chin. "Can you move?"

He gave an effort, then collapsed.

"I'm pretty sure the bullet went straight through, that's good right?"

"Naugh so good when yer the one it went through." He ran a hand over my cheek. "Dinnae let them take the seer."

"Caiyan, I—"

He covered my mouth with his and kissed me long, deep. A kiss I would remember forever.

He fumbled in the pack on his side. "Show her this." He pressed a small box into my hand.

"What is it?"

"A way home, but dinnae try to break it open, 'tis booby trapped." He gave a lopsided grin. "The maker was wickedly wise."

His face changed from a quirky smile to a hard grimace as he fought against a wave of pain. Closing his eyes, he passed out.

I secured the box in my pocket and tried to shake him awake.

His breathing labored. The warm spreading over my front as the blood leaked from his body confirmed there was an exit wound. He was losing too much blood, too fast.

"Please let him live." I placed my hand on my key and begged for my outhouse to return. When nothing happened, I wished for any of the transporters to come. Hadn't anyone returned to Gitmo?

Tears stained my face as the leaves began to swirl in the stifling heat, and a flash of lightning blinded me.

Ace's vessel appeared twenty feet from me, in a sparse patch of brush. He peeked out from the purple velvet drape. When he gained the coast was clear, he moved out into the clearing.

"Ace," I shouted from my hidden spot under Caiyan, and waved my free arm frantically at him.

"What in the Queen's name have you done, calling me 'ere?" he stomped from his vessel dressed in the short open-fronted jacket and baggy trousers of the Zouave uniform I'd seen pictures of in the books I studied. His plumed hat bobbed as he scolded me.

"You're cutting things pretty close 'ere, sister. I told you, I've already been to Gettysburg," he griped steadily as he moved toward me.

"Caiyan's been shot. Can you help me get him in your vessel?"

His face ashened when he saw Caiyan on the ground. "Damn gurl, you could have given him a piece of your mind. You didn't have to shoot 'im?"

"I didn't shoot him. He's hurt bad, please, hurry." Ace helped me lift

Caiyan. I slid out from under him and stood. His blood soaked dark into my trousers. I dropped my packs on the ground.

"Holy Mother Theresa, you're not supposed to be here. You're on the battlefield." Ace's voice raised a few octaves when he realized my location. "And you're dressed like a Confederate soldier."

"Ace! Focus! Help me move him!"

Ace sprang into action and together we pulled an unconscious Caiyan toward the photo booth.

"I can't believe you came." Another tear leaked and dropped into my mustache.

"Of course, doll. You summoned me, and I don't get to this hell hole until tomorrow morning. Remember, I don't travel with my defender."

The benefit of the transporters waiting at base slapped me in the face.

"Ace, if we don't get him back to base, he's going to bleed to death."

"Where's your outhouse, hon?"

"It's a long story, but General Lee accidentally went inside my vessel, and then it vanished. I can't get it to return."

"THE General Lee?"

"Yes. I can't leave until he comes back with my vessel and I find Marco and Gertie."

Ace glanced around, and I answered his unasked question. "They're not here. Marco was shot in the leg. He was taken to a field hospital and Gertie went with him."

"Oh, my heavens, the boss is going to flip his lid. How do you get yourself into these situations?"

I frowned at Ace as we heaved Caiyan closer to the photo booth.

"Al is tracking Mortas on the travel screen. He's somewhere near the Confederate headquarters and that can't be good news."

Caiyan groaned. "Come on, lover, Ace has you."

Ace's words caused Caiyan to groan louder, but he didn't regain consciousness.

"Agent Hot Buns isn't going to like me leaving you."

"Give me some time. Caiyan told me about a seer. That's who the Mafusos are searching for."

"A seer?" he paused. "There was a girl, way back. Got herself in trouble with the boss. Didn't see 'er after that."

Jeez. That wasn't reassuring at all.

"I'm going to find her. Where did you arrest Caiyan?"

Ace thought for a moment. "I believe it was close to the Thompson farm near General Lee's headquarters, end of the third day, after the big battle."

I had time.

We hauled Caiyan into the photo booth. His six-three frame of solid muscle had both of us breathing heavy after we placed him in the vessel. A trail of blood dripped onto Ace's fuzzy velvet cushion.

"Bloody 'ell, that's going to leave a stain."

I huffed at Ace. "See if you can locate my outhouse."

"Will do. Good luck, doll. But remember, at sunrise even I can't come back."

"If I don't find a way home, I'll summon you next moon cycle."

Ace gave a visible shiver. "That's a long time to be stuck 'ere."

"Promise me, when you get back to base, if the doctors can't help Caiyan, you'll get Eli."

"You want me to transport the chiropractor to headquarters?" Ace's eyebrows rose.

"Just promise me, OK?"

"Cross my heart," Ace said.

I laid my hand against Caiyan's cheek, and kissed him lightly on the lips, hoping it wasn't the last time.

He moaned again, and I stepped away from the vessel, allowing Ace to enter.

Ace left in a cloud of dust and a crack of lightning I barely heard over the cannon fire. The battle in the Peach Orchard was over, but the battle for Culp's Hill was only beginning.

A rustle in the brush started me, and I caught a movement of gray out of the corner of my eye. The young soldier Marco had knocked unconscious stood slack-jawed in the mouth of the clearing. He clutched General Lee's uniform like a safety blanket.

I moved toward him and he took a step backward.

"What was that?"

"What?

"I saw a box and it took that wounded Federal soldier away."

"You fell earlier and hit your head. You're hallucinating."

"The tall man hit me."

"No, he reached to grab you when you fainted."

The boy cursed, then looked guilty that he had. "I never fainted."

He was shrewd. It would be hard to convince him otherwise.

"I could use your help,"

"I have to find the general. He was under my protection."

I raised an eyebrow at him.

"Well, he sent…" he stuttered. "He sent his scouts to deliver orders, and I was all that was left. Did you put him in the box?"

"No. Are you one of the general's aide-de-camp?"

"Yes, sir."

Even faced with the possibility that I might be the enemy, he was polite.

"Look, I promise I didn't hurt General Lee." Using Ace's oath, I began, "Cross my heart and…" Maybe not that one. I switched tactics. "How about if you help me find my friends, I'll help you find the general."

The boy paused, considered, then accepted. He held his hand out to me. "Sam Raney."

I hoped my face didn't reveal the shock over the recognition of his name.

I shook his hand and said the first name that came to mind.

"Dr. Seuss."

CHAPTER 18

On the heels of Ace's exit, voices moved toward the thicket of trees we occupied. Sam hastily shoved General Lee's coat in the knapsack Marco had left behind.

I picked up the discarded musket.

"They're Rebels." Sam shook his head and laid a hand across the barrel of the gun, causing me to lower the weapon.

When the men entered the thicket, they didn't see us at first, hidden in the shadows of the trees. Five men, part of a company patrolling the woods. Two of the men favored each other, dark hair, sharp chins, and hawk noses. Brothers or cousins, I surmised.

"Did ye see that light?" One of them asked. "It's them damn Yankees playin' tricks on us."

"Damn Yankees think we're dumb as rocks, but we showed 'em," one of the hawk-nosed soldiers said.

"We'll show them again t'morrow." The burly one spat a wad of chew.

"We're goin' to whip their tails as soon as Old Granny gives the orders."

When they spotted me, they slapped a salute.

I returned the gesture, and they relaxed. "Sorry, Doc, didn't see ya there," one of the hawk nose said to me.

I cleared my throat. "Carry on, men," I echoed the orders General Lee had issued to me earlier.

"Doc, you lost?" Burly guy asked.

"Uhm…naw, just waiting for sunset to tend the wounded. I'll make my way safely back to camp after I've done all I can do here."

"God bless you," the other hawk nose said.

The men saluted again. I stared for a moment, realized I was to return the gesture in approval of their exit.

The men proceeded on their way, leaving me with the setting sun illuminating a crop of lifeless bodies among what used to be a golden field of wheat.

Gunfire boomed in the distance, and the sun's final rays turned the sky a smoldering purple haze.

"What should I do about the general's horse?" Sam asked me.

"Horse?"

"Well, yeah, General Lee always rides Traveller when he goes out in the field. He's tied up yonder tree." Sam pointed in the direction the good general had left his mount.

I needed to find Gertie, but I also needed to wait for young Caiyan to appear and follow him.

"I'll watch over General Lee's horse while I wait for—uhm, the general to return. Can you find the man that was with me earlier?"

"The soldier who hit me?"

"Uhm, yes, that one, and the woman who was with him. It's important I know their whereabouts to ah…find General Lee."

Sam, used to taking orders, straightened his shoulders and saluted. "I'll return as soon as I have located the soldier, sir." He waited.

I waved a salute, and he disappeared, leaving me alone for the first time since I had arrived in Gettysburg. Moans from the wounded echoed across the battlefield, and it gave me chills. There wasn't a book I had read or a movie I had watched that truly captured the horrific reality of the Civil War.

As I waited in the shadows for the young Caiyan to appear, I settled myself. My mind rotated through the happenings of the past few hours. I had landed in the wrong spot at the tail end of a violent battle on top of a dead man, lost General Lee, saved a boy whom I shouldn't have, and played a hand in Marco and Caiyan getting shot. My day had not been a productive one.

When I thought about Caiyan, my heart skipped a beat. I had faith in our doctors and in Eli. My brother wouldn't be happy with me for telling the WTF he had skills and a key, but I hoped he would forgive me.

I only had twenty-four hours to find the seer. Caiyan didn't leave me much to go on. First order of business was to prioritize my mission. One. Find Marco and Gertie. Two. Find a way home. Three. Find the seer. Four. Prevent Mortas from gaining the seer's key.

This wasn't the order in which a good WTF agent worked. Caiyan would find the seer first and prevent Mortas from harming her and taking her key. Friends would come last, no, scratch that, he wouldn't have brought any friends with him.

Caiyan told me the seer didn't exactly have her key, whatever that meant. Maybe another traveler was coming, and maybe that would be my ride home, or at least the traveler could take me to another time where I could summon Ace. There were a lot of maybes in my plan.

How was I going to find the seer in time? And there was the whole missing general problem. What would happen if General Lee wasn't giving orders?

I needed to find Gertie. She was the only hope to keep this battle from becoming more of an unorganized mess without the leader of the Army of Northern Virginia.

Gertie knew every move of every officer in the entire battle. She could give the orders that Lee would have given.

One thing at a time, Jen. My inner voice hid her head under a blanket. I yanked it off. Not this time. I was on my own, and nothing would prevent me from keeping Mortas away from his prize.

I unlatched the key around my neck and tucked it inside a spare sock I'd found in my knapsack. I secured the key in an area not likely checked in a pat down.

For the moment, the key would offer some protection against dying of a gunshot wound, but the protection to prevent Caiyan from identifying me as a traveler, I feared, would be greater.

I'd need to keep my distance from him. Hopefully, he would lead me to the seer, and I wouldn't mess up our lives together by interacting with him.

I hunkered down as the last light disappeared from the horizon and the symphony of cannons and guns played in the distance.

A haunting darkness crept through the hazy smoke. The full moonlight offered a ghostly illumination of the woods.

Occasionally, I would see soldiers patrolling them and medics retrieving the wounded. The spooky hallows and the smell of earth turned with the metallic scent of blood had my creep-o-meter off the charts. I rubbed my arms and hugged them around me, worried my goosebumps might be permanent.

After the haze settled, Caiyan had not appeared.

"Where are you?" I asked out loud. "You should have arrived by now." I looked down at the blank sword. The words Caiyan damaged in Purley were missing. Then it hit me. It was me. I wrote the words on the sword.

I searched my medical bag. Inside I found a small kit containing a bottle of laudanum, scissors, gauze, needles—I shuddered—and a small scalpel.

Choosing the scalpel, I scratched the words into the steel blade. Find Victory at Gettysburg 1st TX RW. I returned the unsheathed sword and scabbard next to Boon, made the sign of the cross, and retreated to my hidey-hole.

Leaning back against the hard rock, I waited and I prayed.

Shortly after I added my graffiti to the sword, a subtle flash followed by a sharp pop and a swift breeze filled the area around me with static electricity. Caiyan's red phone booth appeared between two giant white oaks.

My heart sighed. It had been years since I had seen his vessel. After he traded his key to save me, he had been traveling in the Thunder key's vessel, and then nothing. A wayward warrior lost without his armor and valiant steed.

Caiyan strode from the phone booth, this time dressed in Confederate grays. A confident gait to his step. He relaxed when he thought he was alone and sent his vessel away with the snap of his fingers.

I sat stone still in the shadows, half hidden by the thick vines from a nearby gooseberry bush.

He walked to the clearing where Boon lay dead.

I swallowed hard as he bent at one knee and surveyed the man. He reached in and checked his pulse. Then the surprising happened, a tear leaked down his cheek and he swiped it away with the sleeve of his jacket.

I had never seen him cry. Never. His concern over this man broke me, and I wiped away a tear of my own.

Caiyan's head jerked up at my careless movement and he scanned the area. When his gaze passed over me, I let out a breath.

He sheathed the sword, stood, and attached it to his belt. He turned and left in the opposite direction. I moved to follow him.

Keeping to the shadows, I entered the path he took and watched my footing in the darkness as I moved slowly after him.

Not too far down the path, he pounced on me from behind. I gave a startled shriek, and he covered my mouth. His arms wrapped around me pressing me to his body. His other hand a deadly grasp on my throat. A flashback of the first time we met gave my heart a tug.

Thankful I had taken off my key and the heat between us could be blamed on the humid July weather and not our gift, I controlled my emotions and the heat lessened.

"Who are you?" he asked. A perfectly mastered southern drawl, husky and infectious, demanded more than asked in my ear. His scent made my lady parts tingle and I mentally counted to five.

"Answer me," his grip around my throat tightened.

"I'm...I'm a doctor." I said into his hand.

He removed his hand from my mouth.

"I'm a doctor."

"Did you kill the man back yonder in the woods?"

"I did not. Now take your hands off me, Sergeant." I'd seen his stripes, and I outranked him.

He released his grip, but not before he ran a hand across my collarbone, searching for a key. When he satisfied himself I didn't wear the coveted jewelry, he stepped away from me.

I turned to face him, adjusting my coat in a display of feigned irritation. "How dare you assault an officer."

"I apologize. Thought you might be the enemy."

"Well, you can see for yourself I am not!"

"What do you know about the dead man in the clearing?"

"I know nothing. He was dead when I arrived, like the hundreds of other men scattered about."

We stood staring at each other. Him deciding if I was legit, me avoiding his gaze, and grateful the moon provided shadows of anonymity.

A twig snapped and we turned toward the sound. Sam stepped into our space, lantern in hand.

"Doc, there you are," he said, breathless. He saluted and started to speak, stopped when he saw Caiyan.

"Sam, this here's," I caught myself, and turned toward Caiyan. "What did you say your name was, soldier?"

"I didn't." Caiyan offered his hand to Sam. "Cal McGregor."

Sam grabbed his hand and shook wholeheartedly. "Sam Raney." Caiyan's eyebrows shot upwards, unnoticed by the excited aid.

Sam turned toward me, "Dr. Seuss, I have retrieved the information you wanted."

Damn.

Caiyan eyed me suspiciously.

"Call me Jeb, we're all in this together." I tipped my hat instead of offering my hand. Clearing my throat, "Good reconnaissance work, Sam. Important to know the locations of the wounded we'll need to attend."

"You came a long way today." Sam directed the conversation toward Caiyan, acknowledging a patch on Caiyan's sleeve. "I heard your division arrived only recently."

"Rode in with a cavalry company, lost my horse. Skittish beast was frightened by the cannonade. Saw him come this direction and thought I'd pursue." His accent was spot on, but Caiyan lowered his eyes. The tell of a liar, and a mistake the Caiyan I knew would never allow himself to make.

"Proud to meet you," Sam said.

"Seem to be a bit turned around in these here parts." Caiyan thickened his accent.

Do not roll your eyes. I commanded myself.

"Can you fellas point me toward the camp?"

Sam indicated the direction to the base camp.

"Will you be joining me there, after..." he paused and shifted toward the battlefield."

"Yes," I said. "We'll make camp there tonight."

"My pleasure meeting you, Doctor," he dipped his chin toward Sam. "Private." He flattened his hand over his right eyebrow and waited.

At my salute, he disappeared down the path Sam had indicated.

Stranded at a crossroads, I swallowed hard as I watched him walk away. I could follow Caiyan, warn him about the shooter who might have taken his life, and risk changing our destiny together. I could follow stealthily, and hope he led me to the seer, possibly save the key. Or, I could let him leave and find Gertie and Marco.

Superagent Jennifer Cloud should have followed Caiyan, but my friends' safety meant more to me than the key, and I had Sam to consider. I made my choice, and my inner voice sobbed uncontrollably as I held my face steady and turned to hear the information Sam waited to share.

Sam led the way to the barn-turned-hospital where he'd found Gertie. Men lay in rows waiting to be seen by the handful of medical staff. Vivandières and temporary medics gave them water and offered comfort by way of threadbare blankets—some of which covered men completely, indicating they had lost their last battle.

The stench of death permeated the air and I stopped by a nearby tree to dry heave, until my nose became accustomed to the foul smell.

"Are you unwell, sir?" Sam handed me a handkerchief, oblivious to the wretched scent of war. He eyed me curiously.

I thanked him and mopped the drops of perspiration from my upper lip and brow.

"It's funny how when you're around an awful smell long enough, the foul odor becomes a normal fragrance to the air," I said to him, recalling a particularly odoriferous patient who came into the chiropractic clinic. After being in the room with the patient for a time, the smell lessened, and the treatment proceeded like any other. The stench became air. It was only when I returned home, I noticed the smell lingering on my clothing.

"I suppose stepping into the woods, away for a moment, my senses forgot." I hoped my philosophical ranting masked the peaked pallor I was sure my face reflected.

Sam seemed to agree with my sentiment.

I resumed my pace toward the barn. We walked past the rows of men. Empty, hopeless eyes watched us pass. Others called out for help. It was the reason I didn't summon Eli to me. He would have come, and he wouldn't have been able to turn his back on all the men he could save with his knowledge and power. Men meant to die.

Sam was called over by a wounded friend from his corps, and I took the opportunity to find Gertie.

I discovered her sitting on a rotten log catty-corner to the barn. Her body bent over her legs and her forehead rested on her arms crossed over her thighs.

An alarm pealed in my head. Did something happen to Marco?

"Gertie?" I asked as I approached her.

Her head flew up. "Jen, thank God!" She rose and embraced me.

"Jeb, remember?" I whispered in her ear as I hugged her.

"Right, Jeb," she said, releasing me.

"Are you all right?"

She bobbed her head in an uncomfortable tempo.

"Where's Marco?"

"He's inside." She jerked her thumb toward the barn. "On a filthy blanket, on the floor. I cleaned and bandaged his wound the best I could. The bossy-pants nurse made me come outside. He's mean as a snake."

"Why did he send you outside?" My concern for Marco escalated a notch. If they practiced nineteenth century medicine on Marco, he'd never forgive me for waiting on Caiyan instead of rescuing him.

Gertie fidgeted. "I passed out when they started to cut off the foot of an injured soldier. When I came to, they sent me outside. Said I didn't have the fortitude for surgery."

I encircled her shoulders with my arms and squeezed.

"It's OK. You aren't really a nurse you know."

"I'd like to think I could play the part, but they're whacking legs off without any pain medicine. A little whiskey is all the injured get—that, and a strip of leather to bite on."

"Better than dying of gangrene," I offered.

"I thank my lucky stars we live in the time of modern medicine." She paused. "Did you find the general? Did Caiyan find the key? Can we go home now?"

I held up a hand to stop her onslaught of questions. "No, we haven't found the key, and…" I couldn't get the words out.

"And what?"

"Caiyan was shot…by the boy I saved."

Gertie stood speechless. "Is he…?"

I shook my head, but my eyes shone, and I hoped the darkness masked them. "But he's hurt bad. I summoned Ace. I didn't think he could come, but he did, and he took Caiyan back to headquarters." I explained to her about the seer, and what would happen to the WTF if the Mafusos got their hands on that key.

"Thank the lord. Caiyan will be…" She stopped midsentence and I turned to see who caught her eye.

Sam walked toward us. His gangly legs ate up the ground.

Gertie's eyes grew wide. "Here comes the soldier Marco knocked out."

"He's been helping me. Follow my lead."

"Dr. Seuss, will you be staying here or moving to the Lady Farm field hospital? Got plenty more men there needs tending."

Gertie bit her bottom lip at the name I'd chosen.

"Sure thing," I said, but my mind was working on how to remove Marco without anyone asking questions.

Lanterns hung haphazardly from the trees as people shuffled between the men. A rather large gentleman laid toes up a few feet from me. His scraggly hair and long gray beard gave me an idea.

"Sam, how far is General Lee's horse?"

"Through them trees. I should probably git him. I don't know where the general's gotten off to." He shot me an inquisitive gaze.

"I'm going to need a favor."

Sam nodded.

"Get the general's horse and meet us there, at the edge of the woods."

Sam left to find the horse, no questions asked.

I dug in my medical pouch and located the pair of scissors. I walked to the large, dead man, bent, and clipped off his beard.

"What are you doing?" Gertie asked.

I knotted the ends together. "I think I can stick this to Marco's little scruff of a beard and if we put him on the horse, with the darkness, I can pass him off as General Lee."

"Are you batshit crazy?"

"Gertie, if we don't call the shots, the outcome of this war may change. Men may die—"

"Or not die," she cut me off.

"Gertie please. You know the orders, the moves General Lee made."

"Damned if I don't." She shrugged.

"C'mon. We need to get the general on his horse."

Gertie followed me inside the barn. The two-story structure reeked of the metallic scent of iron, tobacco, and uncleanliness. Men lay in heaps on the ground, each carving out a small space for themselves.

Marco was huddled in a corner, asleep.

"Marco," I said. He didn't budge.

I raised a concerned eyebrow at Gertie.

"Sorry, when the medics started to take him away, I swiped the bottle of Dover's powder from your medical pouch."

"Why?"

"He threatened to use his key to go home and get someone to take us home. I told him you had a plan, and if he'd stop acting like a titty baby, I'd give him some medicine to help with the pain. I wasn't too sure about the dosage. You have a plan, right?"

I nodded and hoped one would develop soon.

All the transporters had traveled except for Ace, and it was risky for him to travel so close to his arrival.

"Ace is working to find my vessel."

"Good," Gertie said and glanced down at Marco. "After we got here, he was really doped up. Told nurse pain-in-the-ass he was calling his racecar and going back to his home in the twenty-first century. The nurse confiscated the medicine."

I kneeled and gave his shoulder a shake. "Marco."

His eyes opened and he blinked a few times. "Hey, Jen." His lips pulled into a crooked grin. "You have a caterpillar on your lip."

He reached out and petted my mustache.

"Lordy, he's high as a kite," Gertie said.

"Let's go, big boy." I helped him stand and he looped an arm around Gertie and me, using us like a pair of crutches.

Gertie grabbed the blanket he used.

I pushed aside the image of lice and maggots and took the blanket from her. We headed toward the exit.

"Uh-oh, here comes nurse crotchety," Gertie bobbed her head in the direction of a slim, heavily mustached man marching toward us.

"Where do you think you're going with that soldier?" He blocked our path, hands on hips.

"He's the nephew of a colonel. I have orders to take him to the base hospital," I said.

"Which colonel?"

"Colonel Sanders," Marco slurred, and then laughed at his own joke.

"Sanders, never heard of him." The man flipped his delicate wrist at us. "He's merely a leg wound. Soon as the drug wears off, he can report back to duty. He should stay here, close to his regiment."

The man stood his ground and I decided to pull rank. "Out of our way, Sergeant."

His chin raised as he noted my insignia. Refusing to salute, he turned on his heel and left.

We moved outside. Gertie helped Marco drink water from the canteen.

I attached the confiscated beard to Marco's little scruff of chin hairs, batting away his hand when he tried to touch it.

"No touching, I'm making you look sexy."

Marco gave me a toothy grin.

I inspected the rest of him. His pant leg, torn and stained where the bullet ripped through, might be a problem. A bandage poked through the hole in the fabric, but there wasn't any sign of blood. At least the bleeding had stopped, and with the cover of darkness, maybe my idea had a chance to fly.

We moved toward the trees where Sam waited in the shadows with General Lee's horse.

"Can I have General Lee's frock coat?" I asked Sam.

Sam tightened his hold on the knapsack.

Marco focused on Sam. "Hey, it's the guy I decked earlier. Welcome back, dude." He stumbled over the words.

"What's wrong with him?" Sam held his lantern up to have a better view of Marco.

"He's had some medication. Can I please have the coat?"

Sam didn't budge.

"How about if I hold Marco and you can punch him in the jaw?" I didn't think the kid could do much damage, and the pain medication would numb the effect.

Gertie glanced at me, then at Sam. "Give him your best shot."

Marco tilted his chin upwards and tapped his dimple. "Right here." He was a good sport.

Sam considered and then yanked the coat from his knapsack. "Forget it."

205

"I know you don't understand what we're doing, but know it's for the greater good of the Confederacy."

"I can't say why, but I trust ya. My ma always said people had a way about 'em if'n they was up to no good. You don't have that way, Doc."

I smiled at Sam and took the coat from him. Shaking it out, I tried to put it on Marco. He frowned at me and kept his arms glued to his sides.

"Be a good soldier, and I'll give you a present later."

"A soldier?" Marco asked, eyes wide and innocent like a child. "I have little green ones at home."

"You do?" Gertie smiled up at Marco.

"Gah! Focus!" I held the coat for Marco. "You're going to pretend to be General Robert E. Lee. Won't that be fun?"

"Fun," Marco repeated, and slid his arms into the coat.

Marco winced when he moved his weight to his injured leg. An incapacitated defender wasn't good for apprehending the bad guys. Remorse for refusing Marco a trip home made me swallow hard. I needed Marco and pushed the guilt aside.

After I secured the buttons on the coat and confirmed it covered the wound.

Gertie took the blanket from me and draped it over Marco's head. His hat provided a hooded effect, shadowing his face.

"Hey, that's not bad," she said.

"Alley oop," I pointed toward the horse. Marco put his injured leg in the stirrup, and we gave him a push onto the horse. His face twisted in a painful scowl at the effort, but he stayed in the saddle.

Sam held the sturdy gray stallion steady. I met his curious gaze. "If we can pull this off, you won't get in trouble for losing the general. We'll say he's sick, and you need to convince the guards to let us inside the general's headquarters."

"Yer not spies, I think, and I didn't lose the general. I'm not sure what you've done with him, but I know it has somethin' to do with the disappearing box. I'll stick close to you until I've found my answers."

The kid was a good soldier. I'd need to be careful not to screw up his life.

Gertie raised her eyebrows at me.

"He saw Ace."

"Uh-oh." Gertie's eyes held the same worry as mine. If Sam learned too much about us, it could change his path. He may not become the man who lives to be one hundred and three, has six children, twelve grandchildren, and a mess of great-grandchildren.

"It's a deal. If you help us, I'll explain the box. And here," I said, handing him my pocket watch. "You can keep this. Consider it payment for services rendered."

Sam admired the watch briefly, then slid it into his pants pocket, patted Traveller's muzzle, and led him out of the woods.

We moved slowly, keeping to the edge of the trees but using the moonlight as our guide. Gertie carried Sam's small lantern and we followed the trails carved into the terrain by the cows that once graced the farmland of Gettysburg.

CHAPTER 19

arco remained quiet during our journey across the Confederate-controlled land of Gettysburg. My Spidey sense told me he was gaining control of his faculties. As Sam walked in front, leading the horse, I capitalized on the opportunity to develop a game plan with Gertie.

"Do you recall what the history books say the general is doing for dinner this evening?"

"He's monitoring the battle of Culp's Hill," Gertie rolled it over in her mind. "I believe he was suffering from a bout of the shats and he stayed close to his headquarters tonight. Longstreet was a bit pissed at him because he wanted to lead a defensive battle and General Lee refused."

"Where is Longstreet?" I asked.

"Longstreet stayed at his camp. A few other generals met with Lee and members of his staff, that's recorded anyway. Information got lost, burned, and stolen. I'm not entirely sure who was where, but one thing's for sure, at three a.m. General Longstreet receives an order to move Pickett's division forward."

"Pickett's charge. It's tomorrow afternoon, right?"

"Yes," Gertie said. She twisted her hands together. "I don't know if I can issue the order for Pickett's charge. So many lives were lost."

"When the time comes, I know you'll do your best to save history."

"Is that what we're doing?"

"It's what we do."

We walked in silence for a while. Cannons hissed in the distance; the earth moaned under our feet.

"After we secure you and Marco, I'm taking Sam to find Caiyan and the seer."

"Shouldn't Sam stay and keep the curious away from the general?" Gertie nodded her head toward Marco.

"He's familiar with the area; I'll need him to help me stay away from the line of fire."

"Marco's taller, more muscular, and younger than General Lee, you know."

"Hopefully, he'll be lying in a bed, and with the beard, dim lighting, and the blanket over his face, they won't realize the general's about thirty years younger."

"Let's hope so, for all our sakes."

"If they discover you, have Marco summon me, then find an escape."

"You're not wearing your key," Gertie tapped my bare neck."

"I hid it so Caiyan can't make me. If I don't come back, I'll meet you at the Black Horse Tavern before midnight tomorrow. And for God's sake, don't let Marco use his key and take the first flight out of here."

"He talks a good game, but he would never leave us stranded here."

Sam slowed the horse as we arrived at a camp south of the Chambersburg Pike.

"Isn't General Lee's headquarters at the house owned by the Thompson widow?" I asked Sam upon entering the base camp.

"His personal tent is there," he indicated a wall tent in the center of the camp under a cluster of strapping oaks. "The general has his runners at the house. Not so good for a commander to have his whereabouts known to all. He takes his meals at the widow's house."

The area around the tent allocated for General Lee's headquarters was heavily guarded. An officer's tent, taller than those issued to a lower rank, it had four walls and a canopy across the front. In the light from lanterns hung in the trees, the tent cast a dark shadow.

"Tie up the horse over there, in that dark area to the left of the tent, and move him inside quickly," I told Sam.

Soldiers saluted as we passed. Marco, keeping his head down, returned them. As we neared the tent, Gertie's back stiffened. On the opposite side, a group of generals clustered around a wooden door they used as a makeshift table. They were playing cards, and one nudged the other as Sam brought the horse to a halt.

A short, stocky man with ear to jowl sideburns rose from his seat on a decayed stump and headed toward us. His sword clanged against the gun at his side.

"General Lee, I would like a word."

I moved toward him, blocked his path to the fake general.

"Back away," I ordered, holding my hands up to stop his progression. "General Lee has acquired a contagious affliction."

The man froze. Worry lines creased his brow.

I stalled the lieutenant colonel long enough for Sam and Gertie to help Marco off the horse and into the tent.

The men gathered around me.

"Sir, is it bad, sir?" a scout to my right asked me.

"General Lee will be under the weather for twenty-four hours." I figured if that's all the time I had, then that's all the general needed, too.

"What does he have?" A lean, balding general with a bandage across his forehead demanded.

Realizing my error, my eyes cut toward the tent. Gertie was inside. We hadn't discussed the ailment from which the general suffered. I couldn't remember which one was fatal. If the general happened to reappear, I wasn't sure which disease he would recover from rapidly. I couldn't choose dysentery because practically all the men suffered from it, and a bad case of diarrhea wouldn't keep them at bay. I needed something contagious, but not so dreadful the subordinates would question the general's decision-making ability.

"What has the general ill?" A general with kind eyes and a nicely groomed beard asked.

I stepped back and spread my arms wide.

"The general suffers from—germs."

"Germs? Never heard of it." The lieutenant colonel balked at my improvised illness.

"Very contagious. He'll need complete isolation." Gertie appeared next to me.

"What are his symptoms?" the balding general asked me.

"Diarrhea, vomiting and...enlargement of the genitalia. Extremely contagious."

The general winced.

"Dr. Seuss has offered to care for General Lee as he's been exposed to the germs," Gertie told the skeptical group.

"Yes, yes. I've been exposed to it and lived to see another day, therefore I have an immunity. Only affects the men. My vivandière will assist me in the care of the general."

"A vivandière?" one of the general's huffed. "Why? Where is Dr. Guild? He's the best in the entire corps."

Another general puffed his chest out. "I beg your pardon, Doc McGuire'd do a better job tendin' the commander."

As the men began to rabble-rouse, I stepped between them.

"I assure you, generals, I am the only doctor present who understands the exposure to germs." I paused for effect. "General Lee won't be pleased y'all are questioning his orders."

The thin man's back straightened. "Please give the general my regards, and I wish him a most speedy recovery. I'll wait for his command."

"The general will issue orders via his aide." I indicated Sam, who stepped from the tent.

"I'm supposed to take orders from a junior aide-de-camp?" The squat general bellowed, a cigar clamped between his teeth.

"Doctor, you're needed in the uhm, tent," Sam said.

211

"Private Raney has volunteered to expose himself to germs to support this war and General Lee."

The men's eyes dropped to the level of Sam's crotch. I fought the smile twisting at my lips. Occasionally, a man's concern for his privates outweighed his valor.

"The general has sent orders for General Ewell to attack at first light," Sam said, his eyes glued on a general who had remained sitting at the table.

Upon hearing his name, Ewell rose bent in a painful stoop. Using crutches, he limped toward us. He stopped in front of Sam and scowled.

"These are my orders?"

Sam nodded. "And I'm to take an order to General Longstreet, attack the enemy at its center."

The men stood in silence. No one addressing the order. Gertie had done her job by telling Sam to take the order. I was proud of her.

An amused soldier with an English accent sidled up to the discussion. "I've heard of this germs. Can be deadly if not left for the poor chap to recover. I suggest you mind the good doctor and plan your moves accordingly."

General Ewell saluted and limped off toward a group of horses corralled toward the rear of the camp.

I gave the Englishman a nod and followed Sam toward the tent. Before entering, I spoke to the soldiers stationed on either side of the tent flap.

"No one enters this tent. The general has a highly contagious illness that could wipe out an entire corps in days."

The soldiers took a step back from the tent, and I saluted them.

Once inside, I took note of the provisions. A small desk and chair, possibly confiscated from some poor banker or lawyer in town, sat against the wall to the right. The desk held a large lantern, maps, a bible, and a pair of spectacles.

Marco laid on a makeshift bed built from timbers. An upgrade from the cots provided to the colonels, and a world away from the cold, wet ground the lower ranks slept on in the open fields. It was the

reason many generals headquartered in the homes they commandeered from the locals.

"What are you up to?" Marco asked me.

"You're feeling better." I sat on the travel trunk next to the bed.

"I'm not hallucinating any longer if that's what you mean. My leg
still hurts like a mother, thanks to the asshole you worship like a
Greek god."

My eyes fell, but not in time for Marco to miss the shine in them,
and the anguish on my face.

"Jen?" He placed a hand on my arm.

"Caiyan was shot in the back by a Rebel soldier," Gertie explained,
handing Marco a cup of water she poured from a canteen.

A glint of concern showed on Marco's face. He stared down into
his cup. "Is he—"

"No," I said. "He was still alive when I summoned Ace, but the
gunshot could have been fatal.

"You summoned Ace?"

"I didn't know it was possible. He doesn't arrive until the morning,
so he came and took Caiyan back to base."

"What about me? I could get an infection in this god forsaken
place. To hell with the Mafusos, I'm summoning my vessel and getting
the hell out of here." He placed his fingers on his key.

I covered his hand with mine.

"Marco, I need you to be General Lee until I can figure out why
my vessel won't return, and until I can find the seer and Mortas."

His blue eyes pierced mine with an icy glare, but he lowered his
hand.

"For fuck's sake. How long do you think Lee's staff is going to let
me sit in here before they come inside?"

"I told them you have a contagious illness and need a day of rest to
recover."

"What, Malaria? Yellow fever? Pneumonia? What have I got that's
not carried by half the army? Your lie won't keep the generals at bay."
Marco's voice escalated to how do I get myself into these situations
level.

"You have germs," I explained.

"Germs?"

"Pasteur's germ theory hasn't been accepted yet. That was quick thinking, Jen. I mean Jeb." Gertie winked at me and moved to stand next to Marco. She held a bottle of whiskey in her hand.

Marco rolled his eyes, but a small smile tugged at his mouth. "Great, I need a drink."

"It's not for you to drink." Gertie smiled down at him. "This is medicinal whiskey. Now, take your pants off!"

While Gertie changed Marco's bandages, I spoke with Sam about the best place to find Sergeant McGregor.

"If'n he's at General Longstreet's camp. I heard Major General Pickett is restin' his men at his bivouac near the Cashtown road. I'd say the Sargent we met in the woods is a scout sent ahead to retrieve the general's orders. Don't make no sense him being so far ahead of his regiment."

I hoped it made perfect sense.

I sent Sam to secure horses for our reconnaissance trip. While he was away, I informed Marco and Gertie of my plans to infiltrate Longstreet's camp, each giving me their take on how completely insane I am.

I snuck out the back of the tent with my childhood mantra playing in my head. I'm spunky and I'm fierce and I'm smarter than most men, bad guys run and hide 'cuz here comes SuperJen.

WE RODE SOUTH KEEPING Seminary Ridge to our left. Confederate patrols stopped us along the way demanding to know our destination. Sam's story of escorting the doctor to Longstreet's camp by General Lee's command was never doubted and papers never demanded. The soldiers knew Sam and they trusted him.

He swatted at a mosquito. "Damn gallnippers! They're fierce in these woods."

I mentally thanked Jake for the bug repellent he made me lather on before our journey.

"How did you come about being General Lee's aide?" I asked him.

"My uncle served under him in the war against Mexico. He asked as a favor to select me from my regiment, the Seventh Tennessee, and serve as his aid." Sam's voice shifted and I caught a touch of anger. "I'm sure my ma had made the request."

"I see. Can't blame her, kept you away from the front lines of the battles."

"I'm a good shot. Better than most of my friends serving in the Seventh." Sam was obviously upset by his lack of active participation in the fight.

"You'd rather be getting shot at?"

"I'd rather be serving my country alongside my friends." His words held the resentment of a boy wanting to do more than deliver messages. A man breaking free of a boy's shell by proving his worth to his peers.

"The war can't survive without communication, and I'm sure your friends recognize the danger you encounter taking messages to the generals."

"My friends have tales of battles, and wounds to show for their bravery."

I wondered how many of his "friends" would be able to share their tales after tomorrow. I took another tactic and changed the subject.

"What will you do after the war?"

"I don't know, probably go back to my family's farm in Tennessee, if there's anything left of it. My ma wrote she's gone south to stay with her sister in Texas because the Federals have confiscated our homestead. The livestock and the finery were taken."

"Sorry to hear that," I said, but actually I was thrilled. If he ended up in Texas, I hadn't screwed up his life, yet.

"I'm sure we'll get it back. General Lee will win this battle here and we'll march down the Baltimore Pike toward Washington. Lincoln'll mess his britches when he hears the rebel yell coming for him."

Jeez. I was grateful the last patrol stopped us, and Sam knocked his reverence for the Rebels down a few notches.

Arriving at the base camp was like entering a small town. Hundreds of tents were erected west of Seminary Ridge.

"We need to find a place to rest, maybe find your soldier in the morning. He'll be difficult to locate this time of night."

We passed wagons and wooden structures thrown up to provide the things a soldier might need on the road. There was a photographer, post office, women doing wash. Food tents, clothing tents, and places to worship. A small army had traveled to support the larger one, and like fans at a football game, this was the tailgating party.

A black man came to secure the horses, and it dawned on me that the soldiers had also brought their servants with them to the battlefield. Was that who Boon was? A slave to one of the soldiers? Was the seer a slave? My mind whirled. How would I find her in the hundreds of encampments around Gettysburg?

I dismounted, and Sam handed me a lantern.

"Wait here," he said, and moved toward a group of men.

Men gathered in circles around campfires discussing the fighting from the day. I didn't have time to waste resting, but the effects of the time travel were wearing thin on me.

Sam spoke with one of the privates lingering around a nearby campfire. He and the man looked over at me. The man scratched his beard and then pointed down an aisle of tents. Sam shook hands with the man and walked toward me.

"This way." Sam motioned for me to follow him. "General Longstreet has a tent that'a way. His aid told me he's not there, gone to speak with his staff. Should return in a few hours."

I breathed out a sigh of relief. I still had a few hours before I had to meet with Longstreet and issue the message of Pickett's move.

"There's a tent not in use anymore we can use for the night," Sam said.

I was afraid to ask why the accommodations were available. As we turned down a row of neatly aligned tents, I saw a figure move across the path. The swagger I recognized. The man stopped at a tent and spoke with a soldier.

As we passed, I held my lantern up as if lighting my path and caught a full glimpse of Brodie's face. He glanced at me but didn't break from his conversation with the soldier shaking his head in response to Brodie's questions.

He was searching for Caiyan, and I needed to find him first. I considered it a positive sign. If Brodie was here, then Caiyan had to be close.

Sam found the tent, and I explained I was going to use the privy, wherever that was. I had no clue.

Sam eyed me skeptically and stretched out on a bedroll.

I made haste going from campfire to campfire in search of Caiyan, avoiding Brodie, and making small talk with the soldiers.

When the soldiers asked why I wasn't in the hospital tending to their friends, I simply stated I had been assigned to tend the wounded from tomorrow's battle and ordered to rest.

I wandered back to the tent and met Sam on the way.

"I thought you might like some food. There were rations in the tent, and I found the chuck wagon, but it don't have much."

He was holding two cups of hot coffee. I took the cup from him and the warm liquid calmed my empty stomach. It was a far cry from Starbucks, but it would do.

He smiled wide. "I found your soldier."

I almost spat coffee on him. "What? Where?"

"He's over yonder by our tent. I found him at the supply wagon. He needed a place to rest, seems he couldn't find his regiment or his horse."

I brushed off Sam's curious stare and made a beeline for our tent. Caiyan sat leaning against a supply pack outside the small tent, legs stretched out in front of him, drinking coffee.

"We meet again, soldier," I said as I joined him.

"Good to see you unharmed, doc," Caiyan said. His slow, sexy drawl made my lady parts tingle.

Sam distributed hardtack and jerky to us. I gobbled down the jerky. It was the best I'd ever tasted, and I was a tried and true Slim Jim fan.

The men dipped their hardtack into the coffee. I copied them, but the small brick of a biscuit broke apart like a cake of chalk when I took a bite. Bits stuck to my mustache. Being a nineteenth century man was hard.

"Doc, you havin' a time with the tack?" Sam chortled.

When I made a sour face at him, he threw back his head and gave a deep, hearty laugh. A contagious guffaw that made everyone chuckle.

Moments later a young soldier stopped to whump Sam on the back.

"Thought that was you. I'd recognize that laugh anywhere. Haven't seen you since Murfreesboro."

Sam stood and clasped arms with the young man. He had a few years on Sam, but barely enough to reach the age of enlistment.

"I received a reassignment after my furlough. How's James?"

The man shook his mop of dark curls. "Lost him in the fight the first night."

Sam put a strong hand on the man's shoulder, and the man clasped Sam's forearm. "He was a good friend."

"Sure to speak." The men held a moment of silence for their lost friend.

I glanced over at Caiyan. He stared down into the cup of coffee resting on his lap.

Sam turned toward us, moving into the light of our camp. The man's eyes widened when he saw our ranks and slapped to a salute.

"At ease private," Caiyan said. I frowned at him because I outranked him. I should have given the command.

"This here's Dr. Seuss, I'm travelin' with him to meet up with General Longstreet, and Sergeant McGregor has been separated from his company." Sam patted the man on the back. "My good friend, Will. He's from my hometown in Tennessee."

We stood and the soldier greeted us.

"Have you word about the battle tomorrow?" The young soldier asked me. "I've heard tale we're going to take them on their right flank."

"No," I said to him, but Sam looked my way.

Caiyan didn't miss the concerned look Sam sent me, and I fidgeted as I averted my eyes from Caiyan.

"Is the regiment bivouacked here?" Sam asked the soldier.

Will eyed Caiyan and me, then pulled Sam aside.

"No, we're a few miles south. Since tonight might be my last night," the soldier blushed, "I visited the tent of the Soiled Doves."

Sam's mouth dropped open. "You didn't?"

I glanced over at Caiyan and his head was lowered, but I caught the corner of a smile.

"Yep. If'n it's God's will I'm gonna be dead tomorrow, I wanted to lay with a woman just once. She was beautiful, smelled like oranges. You should go, Sam."

Sam's face paled under the moonlight.

"It don't cost too much, and I feel better about the battle tomorrow. She said I did real good for my first time, and now that I was an experienced man, I'd be stronger on the battlefield."

"What about your sweetheart back home?" Sam asked Will.

"Miss Maggie, that's the Madam's name, I asked her if'n I was being unfaithful in God's eyes. She told me war was different. Ida Belle, that's my girl back home, shouldn't have to know the hardships a man endures during wartime. We're to be married when I get my next leave."

"Married, landsakes Will! I'm proud for you." Sam clapped his friend on the back.

Will beamed the crooked smile of man in love who had recently been laid. Even though it wasn't with the same woman. Technicalities. Will showed Sam the heart adorned to his jacket.

"I had a rip in my sleeve and her darkie fixed it for me. Did a real good job too. Even sewed on a red heart for luck tomorrow."

Caiyan's head shot up. "Where can I find this Soiled Dove's tent?" he asked Will.

"That's the spirit," the soldier grinned wide, showing a few missing teeth. "Yonder them wagons." He pointed toward a group of supply wagons.

He shook hands with each of us and wished Sam the best, then left us whistling a happy tune.

Caiyan set his tin cup down and pulled a flask from his jacket, unscrewing the cap.

"Whatta ya say we go check out the ladies?" He took a pull from the flask, offered it to Sam.

Sam hesitated. "I don't drink much."

He angled it my direction.

I grabbed the flask and took a mouthful of the moonshine, let it burn down the back of my throat. A calm followed, and I was grateful. I lowered the flask, and Caiyan watched me with cool, curious eyes. I handed the flask to him, and he turned his attention toward Sam.

"You ever felt the smooth skin of a woman's breast?" He asked Sam.

Even in the darkness I could see Sam's face turn pink.

"What about you, Doc. What kind of woman do you like?"

I coughed into my hand. "Not sure."

Sam's eyes grew wide. "You never been with a woman neither, Doc?"

I can honestly say, "Never."

"Men have needs. Let's go get you two some experience." Caiyan started to walk in the direction Will had indicated.

"I don't need any experience," I said to him.

"You got a woman back home?" Caiyan asked.

"No."

"What about you?" he asked Sam. Sam shook his head.

"Well then, Will had a point. What if you get shot dead without ever feeling a woman underneath you?"

"I'd go to heaven?" I said more than asked.

Caiyan's sense of urgency had me guessing this was not about the women, and I should follow his lead and see where it took me. I hoped directly to the seer.

"Crimany!" He tugged on the sleeve of my jacket, and I followed him with Sam slinking alongside me.

CHAPTER 20

I carried the lantern to light our path to the Soiled Doves. We passed tents with groups of men biding their time by cleaning guns, gambling at cards, and playing music. The sweet, bluesy sound of a harmonica played an upbeat version of a tune I recognized as Dixie. Gertie was right. It would be hard to give Longstreet the order to move more of these men to the front lines.

As we approached a cluster of wall tents, a sturdy woman dressed in satin and lace sat in a high-back chair outside the first tent. I didn't miss the pistol holstered on her belt, or the knife secured to her right leg that peeked out from the ruffle along the hem of her dress as she uncrossed her legs.

Grunting and moaning came from the tents around us and I felt Sam cringe beside me.

"You men looking for a go with a few of my doves tonight?" the woman asked.

"Yes ma'am," Caiyan responded. "Are you Miss Maggie?"

"The one and only. Show me your money."

Caiyan retrieved a small roll of Confederate dollars, and the woman licked her lips.

"They're busy. Wait over there by the tree and I'll call you when one's available."

We moved to the location she indicated. I overheard the woman holler into the tent. "Make it quick, we've other customers."

Sam opened a pocketknife and began to whittle at a limb he'd picked up nearby.

Caiyan took another pull from the flask and handed it to me. As I tipped back the flask, out of the corner of my eye I saw him rip the pocket from his coat.

A few minutes later, a small man stumbled from the tent. It was Gerry, my irritating teammate. Caiyan saw him and moved under the shadows of the tree.

He was much younger, and his hard lines hadn't reached their full potential. He buttoned his trousers and the girl who followed him from the tent giggled.

"You git that Billy Yank tomorrow, ya hear," she hollered after Gerry.

I watched Gerry waltz down the row of tents. Some agent he was, getting his rocks off instead of searching for his mark. Caiyan was practically gift wrapped and wearing a bow.

My future teammates were scattered throughout Gettysburg searching for Caiyan. I'd have to keep close quarters to protect him until I was ready for him to be arrested. The idea of Caiyan carted back to the WTF against his will made me smile, a Soiled Dove indeed.

"Let me have a go at him, Miss Maggie," the girl said running her gaze up and down Caiyan's sexy body. Her gown dipped low exposing the ample cleavage of her milky white breast.

Miss Maggie waved us over. "Sugar's ready for ya, she's my best girl, a real professional."

Caiyan kept his gaze focused on the girl's ample bosom.

At first, I was appalled at the behavior of these soldiers on the night before a major battle. Where was their focus? Hadn't they ever heard of being prepared mentally?

And what was with Caiyan's ogling of the Soiled Dove? Then I caught that glint in his eyes. The one he gets when he's searching for a mark.

"Change the bedding," Caiyan said, adding another bill to Miss Maggie's chubby, outstretched hand.

"Victory!" The woman bellowed.

I stood speechless as a beautiful girl with milky brown skin rounded the corner. She carried a basket full of clean linens. The message on the sword wasn't the key. It was Victory. And Victory wasn't a key, but the name of the seer. I felt her presence the minute she came into the light. Unrestrained power.

She dropped her basket when she saw Caiyan.

He gave a slight nod at her.

Those amber eyes I recognized from Salem lit up, and then darkened. She was angry with him, and she was older than the woman in Salem. I hid my excitement as my mission unfolded in front of me.

"Clumsy girl. Change the bedding," Miss Maggie ordered. "I don't like keeping paying customers waiting."

Victory gathered her basket and ducked inside the tent, returning moments later with a basket full of dirty blankets.

"I don't think I wanna go inside," Sam whispered to me.

"Ready for a go?" the young prostitute coaxed Sam.

"I'll wait my turn," Caiyan said. The Soiled Dove frowned, then shrugged.

Miss Maggie pointed to Sam and me to enter the tent.

"Together?" I asked her.

"My girls ain't got all night," Miss Maggie said. "One of you can go first, then you swap and the other can watch. It's an easy way to get things going, if ya git my meaning." She threw her head back and cackled, showing sparse, yellowed teeth.

I frowned and Caiyan gave a low chuckle.

"Be brave, soldier," I said to Sam. I, on the other hand, was going to find a way out.

The prostitute huffed as if dragging us into the tent spent too much effort. She took him by the hand and towed him inside. I followed, holding my lantern with white knuckles.

On the way, I overheard Caiyan ask Miss Maggie if she had someone who could repair his torn pocket while he waited.

I ducked through the flap, allowing it to drop behind me. That was my cue. Caiyan was going after Victory, and I needed to be there.

Sam and I sucked in air as we stood taking in the stale scent of sweat and sex. The aroma wasn't masked by the heavy French perfume the dove sprayed from a glass perfume bottle.

She spritzed the cot and Sam tensed beside me. I took the chair in the corner of the room and set the lantern down next to me. An orange glow cast shadows over the walls of the tent.

"I'll sit here," I said. "And snuff the light. Some things are better in the dark."

"Suit yourself," she said.

While Sugar removed her gown, Sam's eyes grew wide and the scared shitless look on his face told me I should move quickly, because this might be over sooner than later.

When Sugar started to fuss with his clothing, I extinguished the lantern, and slipped out the back of the tent.

Tiptoeing past the watchful eyes of Miss Maggie, who was attempting to persuade a flirtatious Brodie into tasting her wares in exchange for information.

Not good. He was getting close.

A sharp slap of skin to flesh had me pause; around the corner from the prostitute's tent, a lean-to provided shelter for washing and sewing. I hunkered down at the side and peeked through the branches of a squatty bush.

Victory stood in front of Caiyan; a red handprint burned his left cheek. I was sorry I missed the show.

"Where have you been? You told me you'd return months ago."

"Aye, ye were no in Baton Rouge, where they left ye. I didnae know where to look."

"How did you find me?"

"Boon sent word."

It wasn't Boon, it was me.

"Boon," she huffed. "I haven't seen that no good man in days. He's a sorry soul. I sent him to deliver a message and he hasn't returned."

"Vic," Caiyan placed a hand on her arm. "I'm sorry to tell ye, Boon's dead."

"Dead?" Tears pricked at her eyes. "It can't be, how?"

"Dinnae kin. I found him in the woods. Shot."

She lost control of her tears and Caiyan pulled her to him. She sobbed and he held her. I was watching two people who had history. My inner voice turned green and I told her to slow her roll. Maybe Caiyan was a good friend to this woman.

She pulled away from him. "Do you think the Federation was involved?"

"No," he ran a thumb across her tear stained face, lifted her chin and kissed her."

My inner voice screeched Nooo!

"Stop it. You can't be coming on to me now."

"Why are ye always turning me oot?"

Because she just lost someone important to her, you horny bastard.

"'Tis too dangerous for ye to stay, ye need to come with me, away from here. I must find a way to transport ye to safety."

"I can't leave."

"Why the hell naugh?"

"Because of this." She lifted her apron to reveal a round belly.

Caiyan's eyes grew wide. Mine did too.

"Is it—?" Caiyan couldn't finish the question, but I could. The child was his. He was a father, and he never told me. My heart did a swan dive. Somewhere in the eighteen hundreds, Caiyan and Victory had a baby together. Is that why he needed to come back here?

"I wanted to tell ya, but you didn't return the next moon cycle, and then they sold me. I thought you'd be upset.

"I could never be mad at you." He embraced her and kissed her on the mouth, again.

Suddenly the hazy battle smoke cleared. Mortas was here to kill her and their child. The child must have incredible powers, or was the child a parent to one who endangered the Mafusos' existence? I had so many questions, and the two people who could answer them, I couldn't ask. The worst part was Caiyan hadn't trusted me enough to share this part of his life with me. I held back the tears of anger that threatened to spill out.

"So ya prefer the darkies, do ya?" Miss Maggie's bulk moved in front of the lean-to.

Caiyan froze, his hand went to his revolver. Fumbling in my medical pouch, I extracted a bottle and a piece of cloth and poured the bottle's contents into the cloth. I stood from my crouched position behind the bush and rushed around to where Miss Maggie stood, hands on hips.

"Excuse me, I've got an issue with your girl."

Miss Maggie turned and moved away from the couple. "What problem you got with my Sugar?"

"She bit my hand."

As Miss Maggie bent her head down to view the damage, I clasped my hand over her mouth and wrapped my body tight to her. She struggled for a few minutes.

"Go down, go down!" I said. I wrapped my legs around her and held on cowboy style until she went lights out.

Caiyan and Victory stared wide eyed watching the show.

I asked for Caiyan's help to drag her under the shadows of the canopy.

Victory, eyes like saucers, reached out for me.

No, you don't. I avoided her contact, wiping my hands on a dry cloth. I wasn't sure if she could read me or if she only saw visions of the future, but I knew our contact would spark.

"Who are you?" she asked.

"Seemed like Sergeant McGregor needed a hand. We'd better get Private Raney and skedaddle before the chloroform wears off and Miss Maggie regains consciousness."

I removed my cravat so both could see I wasn't wearing a key. Dabbed my face with it. My ruse needed to continue as long as possible, or until I could get a grip.

"Wait, I need to gather my uhm, things." Victory began stuffing pieces of cloth into a knapsack.

One dropped to the ground, and I saw the map of Gettysburg sewn on it. The placement of Lee's army, and the red heart she had cut to sew into the jackets of the soldiers. She glanced my way as Caiyan bent and picked it up, studied it. She yanked it from his grasp and stuffed it alongside the rest of them.

Miss Maggie made a low growl, and I chloroformed her once more.

We retreated toward the tent where I had left Sam and found him leaning against the tree.

"C'mon, we need to leave, quick like."

Sam's gaze stopped on Victory.

"She's coming with us. Miss Maggie didn't treat her well," I explained.

"You'll get in trouble taking someone's property, Doc."

"I'm no one's property," Victory said.

"She's my property," Caiyan said. "I've been searching for her. We can discuss this later, right now we need to hide." He glanced behind him, and I saw what he did—Mortas spoke with Sugar, at the entrance to the Soiled Dove's tent.

We detoured three rows over and walked at a brisk pace toward out tent. When Caiyan was positive we weren't being followed, he slowed his pace for Victory.

Sam was quiet. Possibly in shock from his first sexual encounter. Say something manly, I told myself.

"Did ya ride her like a hog?" I slapped him on the shoulder, then immediately regretted my redneck banter. What was wrong with me? The anxiety of this mission combined with Caiyan's secret past caused me to act like a jerk.

Sam's eyebrows raised. "Never ridden no hog, but I told her I wasn't ready to have relations. Just didn't feel right, besides, my mamma would tan my hide if'n she found out." He glanced sheepishly toward Caiyan. "I hope you're not mad, Sergeant, 'cuz she kept the money. I can pay you back."

"Not necessary," Caiyan said.

"You're lucky you didn't have relations with that one, she's got syphilis," Victory said to Sam.

Huh, maybe that's why Gerry is such a pain in the ass.

"We need to find Lee's Old War Horse; I've got a message for him." I used the nickname the soldiers gave General Longstreet. Keeping my identity safe just became more difficult. My inner voice slapped on a pair of black rimmed glasses and gave me a thumbs up. I reminded her Superman was a comic book. Batman, now he was the real deal.

CHAPTER 21

$\mathcal{W}$e arrived back at our campsite. Caiyan helped Victory into the small two-man tent. Better for her to hide inside. Here I was with my future lover, the mother of his child, and a hundred and three-year-old man. How did I manage to get myself into these messes?

A scout rushed toward us. He stopped short and saluted me. I saluted him. The entire process was exhausting.

"I have a message for General Lee's scout."

Sam stepped forward. "I'm his aide-de-camp."

"General Longstreet declines his offer to meet at headquarters. He feels his duties are required here with his corps. Here is the message to give to him."

The scout handed Sam a sealed paper.

"I have orders from General Lee," Sam said, as I had instructed.

"Give them to me and I will deliver them to the general." The scout held out his hand.

"They are to be delivered in person. The general has taken ill. I have brought the doctor treating him to relay the information of his illness."

The soldier seemed apprehensive at the request but relented. "I'll report to General Longstreet straight away and return with his response." Another salute and he departed double-time in the direction of Longstreet's headquarters.

Gertie was right. This was like playing an intense game of telephone. No wonder half the orders were misconstrued.

I glanced over at Caiyan. After the scout left, Caiyan ducked inside the small tent. Choosing a thin branch to whittle like I saw Sam doing earlier, I sat as close as I could manage without being obvious to eavesdrop on their conversation.

"What do you make of the good doctor?" Victory asked.

"He's no wearing a key."

"If he were a brigand, he would have made his move I imagine."

"'Tis true. We need to leave here. Find a safe place for you to have the baby."

"I can't leave here, there's still work to be done."

"For the love of God, you're pregnant. You cannae go traipsing around the battlefield in your condition." Caiyan's voice escalated. I was familiar with the Scot's temper and was curious to see how Victory handled it.

Glancing over at Sam, he raised his eyebrows toward the tent, and shook his head. "Ma always told me you never argue with a woman when she has her mind set. Do you find this to be true, Doc?"

"Smart woman, your ma." I smiled at him. "In my experience, it's always wonderful to get to know women, with the mystery and the joy and the depth. If you can make a woman laugh, you're seeing the most beautiful thing on God's Earth."

Sam's mouth hung open. I wished I could take credit for the quote, but I had read the profound words from the actor Keanu Reeves in Rolling Stone magazine and it had stuck with me.

"Those are words to live by," Caiyan moved to the side of the tent and sat listening to my advice. The brogue he used when speaking to Victory had been replaced with the southern drawl I'd become accustomed to on this trip.

"Women deserve the same respect as men demand, I suppose." I added the last words to sound speculative in relation to this time when men ruled the roost. I thanked my lucky stars the quote wouldn't be published until later in Caiyan's life.

"Why don't you take this off my hands," Caiyan said to Sam, handing him the sword. "It belonged to a good friend of mine, and I won't be needing it anymore."

Sam's eyes grew wide. "It's finely made."

"Yes, it is." Caiyan leaned forward on his knees and watched Sam strap on the sword.

Sam stood, drew the blade, and practiced sparring like a Jedi knight using his light saber.

"Any more thoughts on women, doctor?" Caiyan asked me.

"Don't drag your feet when you find the one."

He glanced at the tent, and my heart ached.

I needed to get back to Marco and Gertie. Would Caiyan be here when I returned? Most likely not. He'd take Victory to a safe location and stay with her until the baby arrived. How long could that be? Four months maybe. It was hard to tell. Did he leave her here or have them transported back to my time?

I needed to tell Caiyan about the shooting. I had to tell him I know him in the future. If he has a child, he can't die because of my screwup. What were the chances Victory lived in our time? I thought about all the trips overseas, the business trips when I couldn't get him on the phone. It all made sense. He was seeing someone else. A woman he chose to hide from the WTF the same way I kept Eli's key a secret. A woman he hid from me.

Before I could dwell on the matter for so long that it made me crazy, the snort of horse and hooves on ground interrupted me. The scout appeared, riding next to a bearded man astride a dark horse. His deep-set eyes took in our campsite and we stood and saluted. General Longstreet commanded the area. It was much like being in the presence of the rich and famous, and reminded me of the time I met Rocksanna, an eighties diva and vocal music legend. The smell of importance and fame preceded him.

The general saluted. The scout was quick to dismount before his commander and take control of the horses.

"You have information from General Lee?"

"I'm Dr. Seuss." I offered my hand, and Longstreet shook it, albeit hesitantly. "General Lee has come down with a case of germs."

"Germs?"

"Very contagious but should only last another day."

"Soldier, I don't have another day. I need orders."

"Yes, sir." Sam stepped forward. "I have brought you orders to move General Pickett's division of fresh troops to the front and attack the enemy at its center."

"The center? Is the General…" his words trailed off, and I knew he stopped himself from committing an act of insubordination. It was a fool's order, and many men would die, but Sam delivered the words Gertie told him to say.

"It's General Lee's command to move the troops forward, sir. You will have support from Hill's Third Corps. He wishes you to organize an attacking force composed of Pickett's division, the four of Heth's divisions, two of Anderson's and two of Pender's divisions. Colonel Alexander has been ordered to move his artillery to the high ground and prepare to support the forward attack."

Sam paused, waited for Longstreet to accept his delivery of the orders.

I prayed Gertie had instructed Sam correctly, and she had done her part and issued the orders to the Corps in support of Longstreet.

His eyes searched mine and I held firm, not breaking eye contact. A trick Jake forced me to practice until I could lie without lowering my gaze. A feat that could save your life. Jake's words rang true, as I stared forcibly at the general.

Longstreet averted his eyes, frowned, and—finally—saluted. "Give the general my regards." He snagged the reins from his scout and addressed him directly. "Take the orders to General Pickett. As soon as he makes ready, move his corps into position under the ridge of trees west of the Emmitsburg road." Longstreet pointed into the direction of the ridge, and my inner voice gave me a high five for keeping history intact.

As the general and his scout departed, Victory, wide eyed and flustered, exited the tent.

"The Rebels are attacking tomorrow in the center?"

"That's right," I said.

"I...I must leave, I have mending needs tending." Her eyes darted between us. Caiyan pulled her aside. "'Tis better if ye stayed here."

Sam and I stared at them.

"I have work to do. I need to leave immediately," she insisted.

"What work do ye have at this wee hour?" He had slipped back into his Scottish accent, and I wondered if Sam caught the mistake.

"You're not going anywhere."

I turned to find Sam pointing the sword at Victory. Nope, he didn't miss a thing.

"She's a spy. She's going to warn the Feds," he said.

Caiyan stepped in front of Victory. A man protecting his own. His hand reached for the revolver strapped to his belt.

"Hold on," I said, but Sam's aim of the sword didn't falter.

"Doc, I believe both of them is Yanks."

"Sam, put the sword down," I ordered.

"Tell me how you warn them. Are you bedding the soldiers like the Soiled Doves?" He swished the sword at her bulge. "Is that a Yank in your belly?"

I wasn't close enough to try and take the sword away, and if he stabbed Victory, there would be two lives lost.

She lifted her chin and stepped away from Caiyan's outstretched arm. "That's right. It is a Yank." She cut her eyes at Caiyan. "The child of a brave man. A man who would never treat people like animals, caged, and whipped when they don't obey their masters."

Sam's face screwed up in anger. "We never treated our slaves as such. They're like family to us."

Victory threw her head back and laughed. "Family? Does your family empty your chamber pots, rise in the wee hours to make your breakfast? Clean the shit from your animals' stalls?"

When Sam didn't answer, Victory continued. "I sew the maps of your old Bobby Lee's plans into the Rebel coats. Even give the Northern soldiers a lovely red target to aim for."

Sam's face drained white. "Will. The red heart." He turned and hightailed it into the darkness.

Damn. "Sam!" I jerked around to chase him. The cock of the hammer on a revolver made me stop in my tracks.

"Yer no going anywhere, Dr. Seuss." The condescending way he rolled the name off his tongue told me he thought I might be a brigand.

Turning around slowly, I froze. My inner voice cautioned me to be careful. He was a known killer, and I was walking on thin ice. If he chose, he could break the fragile layer out from under me and end his life in the process. I had to tell him.

Caiyan leveled his revolver at me, but his eyes held questions. I knew the look of uncertainty. He'd used it on me often enough when discussing our relationship. He wasn't convinced I didn't have the gift. If he killed me, he might die, too. My layer thickened.

"Where's yer key?"

"My what?" I used the lie fueled by my anger from Caiyan's deceit. My eyes locked on his. Victory came forward and patted down my clothes. I'd secured the key in a knit of woolen sock and placed it in a position where a man should have a little something. She ran her hands down the outside of my pockets, across my crotch, but didn't grope my bogus male member. Checked the inside of my frock coat and came out with the handkerchief and the bottle of chloroform I had used on Miss Maggie.

"He's clean." She waggled the bottle in front of Caiyan.

Good! "I need to retrieve my scout. You should be ashamed of yourself," I said to Victory, then turned toward Caiyan. "And you, you should be court-martialed." Was that the correct term? I wasn't sure, but it sounded right. I flailed my arms making a big show of my disappointment in him.

"I've got to warn Mead. I've sent word the attack will be on the right flank. If he doesn't know about the change, the south could win this battle," Victory said. "I'm going to speak with him."

Caiyan kept his gun on me, his eyes wide. "Let's take care of the good doctor first."

Not good! I turned toward Victory to plead my case. It was time to come clean. "Wait! I have to tell you—"

The last thing I remembered were his familiar arms wrapped around me and the scent of earth and cinnamon as Caiyan covered my mouth with a handkerchief. I tried holding my breath, considered fighting, but if he discovered my identity, our memories together would change. The first time we met in the barn in Scotland, and the first time he took me in his arms and made love to me.

My heart's pace quickened, anxiety, but not mine. The surprise of reading him without wearing my key. Tenacity, bravado, insecurity, swirled inside me, twisting me into his tornado of emotions. Confusing emotions from the man I thought I loved.

It was his fear that forced me to give in. Fear that he wouldn't be enough. I didn't want to lose him. I wasn't ready to forget the memories we made together. Inhaling deeply, I tasted the sweet of the solvent and allowed Caiyan to escape with his pregnant lover.

When I regained consciousness, my head pounded like a thousand cannons firing simultaneously. I forced my eyes open and blinked against the light filtered in through the opening in the tent. It wasn't my head that concussed like cannons, it was cannons firing in the distance. Many of them.

I cursed Caiyan. He had gagged me with the chloroformed handkerchief, tied my hands in front of me, and hauled me inside the tent. How long was I out? My guess was that with the lack of sleep and the fatigue from the time travel, I'd been out for a while. Colonel Alexander had already started his cannon attack. I surveyed my prison. The small tents were open in the front. They didn't have the flap like the wall tents, and the opening was held up by hardy tree branches.

I lifted my head, the camp felt deserted. Of course it would. The main attraction was about to take place on the battlefield. There would be injured on the far side of the camp in the field hospitals, but I was far away from them. I dropped my head to the ground and a sharp pain shot into my left eye, causing me to cry out. My stomach churned, and I fought against the desire to throw up. Side effects of the chloroform. I took a deep breath through my nose, inhaling as much oxygen as possible. Staring up at the worn material, I sighed. Who was going to find me here?

Marco. If I could get my bound hands inside my pants, retrieve my key and somehow place it around my neck, I'd be able to summon him to me.

I worked the buttons. Damn button fly. These people are going to flip out over the invention of the zipper. As I fumbled with the second button and forced my hand inside my pants a deep guffaw rebounded in the tent.

"Looky who I found, and takin' care of business his-self. My girls could a done that for ya, but instead you used your potions on me." Miss Maggie taunted me as her bulky frame leaned inside the tent.

She drug me out by my Brogans and hovered over me. I spoke into the gag. "Your slave's a spy."

"What are you sayin'?" She ripped the cloth from my mouth.

"Ouch!" The way she tore the gag from my face smarted and displaced my fake mustache. Covering my top lip, I repeated myself, "Your slave girl is a spy."

"That's ridiculous, she ain't got the smarts to be a spy."

"I was supposed to take her to General Lee, he'd give a mighty fine reward if you help me catch her."

"Too late. There's another fella that's offered me a fair price for the girl." The silhouette of a man stepped into my line of vision. Mortas. Perfect timing.

"Here's one of them no gooders. Says my darkie's a spy."

Mortas assessed me with his cold, menacing eyes. My bare throat was dry and scratchy. I pushed hard to secure my mustache in place and swallowed hard. Two minutes later and they would have found me with my pants down and my key around my neck.

"Found him in the tent pleasin' his-self."

Mortas twisted his face and raised a disgusted upper lip at me.

As if. I recounted my lie. "Your slave girl ran off with a man."

"What did this man look like?" Mortas asked.

He didn't act like he identified me. We hadn't had much interaction over the years. I had dealt more with his younger siblings.

"Dark hair, green eyes, spoke funny like a Brit. I'm just trying to help these soldiers."

Toches sidled up to Mortas. When he looked down at me, instant recognition gleaned in his eyes.

I was busted and there was nothing I could do about it. My tale of the helpful doctor just went south. They would probably feed me to Miss Maggie.

"We should leave him," Toches said. "He'll be a burden, and he's going to have a mess of injured to handle shortly."

Toches didn't blow my cover. What the heck?

"Which way did they go?" Mortas asked me.

"Toward the town." I wasn't sure which way they went, but it would keep the brigands on a search away from the places I intended to go.

Toches squatted down beside me. "Better work those knots doctor, in a few hours you're going to be very busy." The three of them stepped away from me, leaving me spread eagle on the ground, my pants undone, and relief flooding my bones. Toecheese didn't give me away? The first battle of the day was a victory.

"Well if it ain't that wanker from York town and his sidekick."

I huffed. Dammit, not now. Mortas stopped and turned toward the voice.

I lifted my head to see Brodie standing hands on hips. "Look at ya, old git. You didn't age well. And check out Kishin Toches, ya hairs all tidied up, like the boy Robin to evil Batman. The Mr. Smee to his Captain Hook, the—"

"You Aussie asshole," Toches snarled, "We eliminated your friend."

Brodie's face dropped. "If you're referring to the Scot, we aren't friends."

"Not yet," Toches said.

"Ah, since you've finished my job for me, I'll be taking my arse home."

Mortas gave Toches a sideways glare. It was never good to inform about the future. They may not be friends yet, but Brodie would warn Caiyan about his impending doom.

"What Kishin means is young McGregor has used this doctor to locate the key and has chosen to take his prize into an area of imminent danger." Mortas waved a hand over me.

Brodie dropped his gaze downward, took me in. "Who are you?"

"I'm General Lee's private doctor, and I'd appreciate it if you'd untie me."

Miss Maggie decided to chime in. "He's the one used his medicines on me, knocked me plum out, then stole my girl."

"I was ordered to do so by the man in question. He had a gun, and I didn't know your slave girl was a spy." My lie sounded like truth even to me.

"She ain't no spy." Miss Maggie stumbled over her words.

"This meeting has been well…ordinary," Mortas said to Brodie.

"Thank you, Miss Maggie, you've been a tremendous help. He peeled off a few dollars and gave them to her, then turned toward Brodie.

"We shall confiscate the key shortly, and by the by, you didn't age so well yourself."

Brodie reached a hand up and ran it over his glorious hair.

Mortas chuckled, "See you in ten years." Toches followed him accompanied by an overzealous Miss Maggie offering more of her tremendous services.

Brodie bent down and frisked me. Avoiding my crotch. When he didn't come up with anything, he pulled out a bowie knife and cut my ropes.

I rubbed my wrists. "Thank you. These ropes were cutting into my flesh."

"Don't think about running," Brodie waved his knife at me. "You're going to take me to the Scot."

My mind gathered the data and made a list of reasons for and against the request. I needed to find Sam. He was on the battlefield because of Victory. In order to find Sam, I needed to speak with

238

Gertie for the location of Will's regiment. I couldn't take Brodie to Lee's headquarters because he might see Gertie, and I wouldn't risk screwing up Gertie's happily ever after.

If I led Brodie where I thought Caiyan went, I'd at least put him on the right track to catch his brigand, but I'd leave Gertie alone for more time than I had intended.

Brodie placed his hand to his key and a soft glow lit under the bandanna he wore around his neck. "Let's get going, Doc." He held out his hand to me and I allowed him to pull me up. Confidence and determination shot up my arm. Same old Brodie. His passion gave me hope.

A few minutes later, Ace met us standing on the trail to hell.

"Who is this?" Ace wasn't all glam and avant-garde like the man I had become accustomed to and loved like a brother. In fact, he seemed repressed.

"A doctor who's seen our mark," Brodie said.

Ace stared at me for a long moment. "Have you checked 'im?"

"Ya, I did. This ain't my first rodeo."

"Bloody 'ell. Just askin', don't get your knickers in a twist."

Ah, there he is. I smiled. "Nice accent."

Ace's eyes widened. "Brilliant, we're out of character, and you started it, hon." He pointed a finger at Brodie.

Brodie huffed. These two were acting like a clip of the Three Stooges, and as the show developed the third stooge came to the front line. Two guns strapped to his belt.

"Who are you supposed to be? Clint Eastwood?" Ace asked Gerry.

"In your dreams." Gerry shot a glance my way, "Who's he?"

"The doctor," Brodie said.

"He knows which way our crafty Scot has gone," Ace added.

"Yeah? So do I. Saw the mark riding north on the Emmitsburg road. Got a girl with him."

I bit my bottom lip. They were riding toward Mead's camp.

"Why didn't you follow them?" Brodie asked Gerry.

"They're heading toward the battle. I'm not going anywhere near

Cemetery Ridge this time of day. Getting shot is not in my contract. I'm the intel guy."

Gerry hadn't changed much.

"Guess who else is here?" Ace asked Gerry as if they were guests at a cocktail party.

"Your momma?"

Ace rolled his eyes. "Mortas, sporting an adult vibe and looking very devilish with his salt and pepper hair."

"And he's towing Toches with him," Brodie added.

"What should we do with 'im?" Ace asked, nodding a head in my direction.

"I'm taking him with us. He's seen the Scot and he might be of use if one of us catches a bullet," Brodie said.

"It won't be me. I'll be at the tavern." Gerry gave a wave as he walked away. "Let me know when you've apprehended the nasty Scotsman."

"What are the chances of 'im getting shot today?" Ace watched Gerry walk away.

"Chances are good," I said. "Of it actually happening…we couldn't be so lucky."

"Hey, I like this wanker," Brodie chuckled. "Let's ride."

CHAPTER 22

$\mathcal{B}$rodie sent Ace to follow Mortas. Discreetly. The Ace I knew didn't do discreet, and I wished him luck as he left us.

As Brodie and I rode toward Lee's camp, we passed hordes of men making ready for battle. Some dozed in the warm sunshine, others sewed their names inside their jackets.

The machine gun cannonade ceased fire, and the calm before the storm settled among the men. Some of the men watched curiously as we passed, their weary faces touched with a tint of pink from the prior days' march in the summer sun.

I scrutinized each soldier in search of Sam. His lanky frame and tuft of white hair didn't present itself. As we left the soldiers and cut across to Lee's camp, I made small talk with Brodie.

"I take it you're some sort of bounty hunter?"

"Sure."

Brodie wasn't much on small talk.

"The man you're after, is he a spy?"

"No, he's a criminal."

"Like the two men earlier?" I wanted him to peg me as a nosy doctor. "Seemed like Yankee spies to me."

"They're Yankees all right. Make their living stealing things that don't belong to them and controlling people."

"Like the key everyone's looking for?"

Brodie gave an uncommitted grunt.

"That key must open something valuable."

"The criminals think it opens an ancient treasure."

"What do you think?"

"I think ya ask too many questions."

"If it's valuable, I can help you find it."

"Thanks, Doc, but I have a feelin' you're going to be in high demand in a few hours."

I agreed and kicked up the pace on my mount. Brodie followed suit. I had to hurry—in less than an hour these men would be lined up and marched forward.

As we entered Lee's camp, things seemed to be disorganized. A group gathered around his tent. I dismounted and explained to Brodie I needed to check on the general.

"There's the doctor," one of the men hollered and pointed a thick finger my direction.

"I demand to see the general!" A bulbous nosed, bearded man shouted into my face.

I gave him the hand, and he halted, flustered by my abrupt motion.

"I'll see him before the likes of any of you. If he's free of germs, then you can be permitted a short audience."

The crowd bucked and hissed. Brodie helped me push my way through the throng of men.

He was unsure about the germs, and took precautions by standing guard, arms across his chest, daring one of Lee's staff to breach his position.

Thankful Gertie wasn't outside and Brodie didn't want to come inside, I ducked under the flap.

My gaze swept across the room. Marco sat with a blanket over his head and a gun across his lap, and Gertie stood at a table stirring a foul-smelling substance in a chamber pot.

She startled when I entered the tent.

"Where in the hell have you been?" Marco peered from under the blanket. His blue eyes flooded with relief, but his words singed me like a branding iron.

I placed a finger to my lips and spoke in a soft tone.

"Good to see you too. How are you feeling?"

"I'm peachy keen, what do you think?"

"He's grouchy. Did you find the Victory key or the seer?" Gertie whispered to me.

"Victory is the seer. Caiyan is with her. She's pregnant."

Gertie's eyes went wide. I turned toward Marco. "Caiyan seems to know her quite well. Do you know of her?"

Marco shook his head, and I had to assume he didn't, or the clue on the sword would have been obvious to him. There was no way he'd protect a secret of Caiyan's, especially if it involved a woman.

"If Caiyan is rogue, it's during the time I wasn't working for the WTF."

"It doesn't matter, I need to find Sam."

"Where's Sam?" Marco asked.

"I don't know. Victory is a spy for the Union." I explained the situation about the maps. "She identifies the carriers with a red heart sewn into their coats. Sam took off after a friend. He—."

"His friend had a heart sewn on his jacket." Gertie finished my sentence.

"Yes, I need to figure out what regiment the friend is in. If Sam gets killed our entire mission goes awry."

"Sam won't have the sword for Caiyan to discover," Gertie said.

"Sam won't be alive and living in Texas." Marco moved to sit on the side of the cot. "I see your point."

"Sam's friend was...is named Will. He's from the same regiment as Sam, the Seventh Tennessee. He told Sam he was under the command of Major General Heth." I walked over to the map General Lee had spread across the desk. Using a pencil, I drew the patch I recalled from Will's jacket.

"That would be the third brigade." Gertie placed a marker on the map. "They're part of Pickett's charge."

"Pickett's charge!" My DEFCON level shot to a one.

"Jen, this brigade along with General Armistead's brigade made it to the high-water mark."

"The furthest in the battle of Gettysburg." I grabbed Gertie's shoulder. "He's going to the front line. I've got to stop him!"

"Jen, you can't."

I reached for my pocket watch to check the time and realized I gave it to Sam. "I still have time. Where do they enter the battlefield?"

"Here," she pointed to a spot on the map. "They line up along Seminary Ridge. Archer's brigade is the fourth regiment down from our direction."

"What's General Archer look like?"

Gertie shook her head. "He won't be there. He was captured on the first day of the battle. I believe Colonel Fry oversees that brigade, but I've no idea how to identify him."

I surveyed the letters on the table. Requests from other generals, letters from loved ones. An incomplete letter written by General Lee to his wife lay aside from the other papers. "I'll need an order. Can you copy his handwriting?"

Gertie set to work providing me an authentic order to retrieve Lee's aide and his good friend.

Marco limped over to view the map. "As your defender, I forbid you to go."

I raised an eyebrow at him.

He cleared his throat. "What I meant was, I don't like you going alone. I should go with you."

"I'm riding over there and pulling Will and Sam off the front lines, General Lee's orders." Gertie handed me the letter and I stamped it with the seal on Lee's desk. "I'll be back before the battle begins."

I started to leave and stopped short. Turning around to speak to them, "I have another problem. Brodie thinks I know where Caiyan is, he's outside."

"My Brodie?" Gertie's eyes twinkled.

"No, not yet, and I don't want you to talk to him because it could ruin your meet cute in the future."

The scary thing about time travel is there's always a chance when I return, my life will be different. People I love would be gone because I messed up history, or they won't have any recollection of me. If I tell Caiyan who I am and how we met, he wouldn't take advantage of me in the barn. Our relationship wouldn't exist. My first love affair would be sucked down the toilet in one revelation, and I feared the same for Gertie.

"You'd better hurry. I don't know how I'm going to keep Lee's staff at bay much longer. The natives are getting restless." She hiked a thumb toward the front of the tent.

"How are you keeping them out?"

"The concoction I have in the bowl is part cow manure, part tobacco, and part gunpowder. I call it sewer manure."

"Imagine smelling that for the last twenty-four hours." Marco wrinkled his nose.

"It's the sulfur you smell. Every so often I carry it outside and announce how painful it was for the general to pass such foulness. I dump it in the waste, tell the onlookers General Lee's germs is starting to show signs of improvement. Seems to keep them at a distance."

"You're brilliant." I draped an arm across her shoulders.

"How are we going to get General Lee back from the abyss?" Marco asked.

"I don't know. What I do know is I've got to concentrate on what matters most, and that's saving Sam."

"I can help with Brodie," Gertie said. "He's always up for a good game of cards. I saw some of the men playing cards on that old door they've got set up as a table."

I remembered seeing the men gathered around the table when I arrived.

"You can take this," she pointed to the bowl of ick. "The waste is on the other side of the table. Brodie will follow you and get his mind on the game, then you can sneak away."

Marco chewed on his lower lip. His need to keep me safe fought against the injured leg and knowing he had to keep up the ruse as

General Lee until we figured out why my vessel wouldn't return. "Be careful."

"Awe, you care about me." I smiled at him.

"Sure I do." I stood on my toes to give him a peck on the cheek, and he turned his head. "I can't kiss you dressed like a dude. You don't look like you."

"That's a good thing because there's lots of people we know here, and I can't afford to be identified."

"Who else is here?" Marco looked alarmed.

"Mortas for starters. He didn't make me, but Toecheese saw me, and I'm sure he recognized me, but he didn't call me out."

"Huh, you can be assured, that weasel has a reason." Marco waved his hand in front of his nose as Gertie added another ingredient to the bowl of sewer manure "Man, that shit stinks."

"I'll be back before you know it." I picked up the bowl and the aroma made me gag. I held it at arm's length and exited the tent.

Gertie was right—it worked like magic. The sea of men parted, giving me a broad path. Brodie held his nose and followed me but detoured at the cards. I dumped the bowl into the sump hole the camp used to contain waste and scurried around the backside of the camp.

Escaping from Brodie wasn't difficult. When he saw the card table he was drawn in like flies to a cesspool. He joined in the game with members of Lee's staff and generals who had already seen time on the battlefield.

My only problem—the horse I had commandeered on the way here was tied up behind Brodie. There was no way I'd make the distance on foot in time to save Sam. General Lee's gray stallion grazed in the pen at the edge of the camp.

After securing my transportation, I rode in the direction Gertie had shown me on the map. Cutting back along Seminary Ridge, I passed men from the Second Corps. Their eyes grew wide at the sight of a man on General Lee's horse. A brazen colonel stopped me. I held my breath and I showed him the sealed paper. He waved me on.

I moved deeper into the woods, away from the mass of men readying for battle. This would never work. I'd be stopped and questioned at every checkpoint. A cardinal chirped anxiously on what was left of a burned-out tree. My mom told me cardinals brought good luck with them.

The bird chortled and flew away, hopefully not taking the luck with him. I needed a set of wings for a bird's eye view, or a lookout tower. I stopped in front of a giant oak. Its trunk forked halfway up the base, making for an excellent climbing tree. A small orchard of peach trees surrounded the base of the giant oak. It was nothing in comparison to the orchard trampled flat from the prior day's fight, but the pink blooms still clung to the branches as if defending their part of the battlefield.

I dismounted and secured the horse to one of the peach trees. I climbed as high as I could manage, and the view stole my breath. Thousands of men had stepped from the woods, still out of the view of the Union Army hunkered down behind the stone wall thirteen football fields away.

Bands played as if the regiments were passing in review. Onlookers cheered their support from the sidelines. My stomach went queasy as I scoured the men for Sam.

Division colonels rode their mounts, shouting their battle cries. The captains paced back and forth in front of the lines, dressing their men. I counted as each one met the end of his responsibility and guesstimated Sam's place amongst them.

I lowered myself from the tree and about halfway down I stepped on a branch damaged from a cannon. The old tree had seen its share of the fight. The branch snapped, gave way, and I fell. My back struck hard against bark and limbs on the way down. One of the peach trees broke my fall and I landed on the ground with a huff.

I stayed still for a long minute and noted my injuries. I wiggled my feet, Ok, not broken. My back hurt the worst, but I could move my arms. Not paralyzed. I touched my face. The beard was gone, lost on the way down. I blinked at the tree above me. Something furry hung in its branches. Too big for a squirrel. A raccoon? A possum? I moved slowly not to frighten the animal and a soft gust of wind blew a strand of my blond hair in front of my face.

I sighed, stood on tiptoe, and snagged my wig from the branches. I hastily tucked my hair under the wig and found my cap a few feet from my landing spot. The beard was history, but at least I still wore the fuzzy mustache.

Planting the cap on my head, I removed my key from its hiding place, and dumped it from the woolen sock into my palm. I needed it now. If I found Caiyan, I'd tell him. I would show him my key and warn him not to come here.

Securing the key around my neck, a warm hug enveloped me followed by a soft glow. My key was happy to be connected once again to its owner.

A sharp crack of thunder and my outhouse appeared a short distance from me.

"Now you decide to appear?" I yelled at my vessel.

The door banged open and General Lee stumbled out.

I rushed to his side. "General Lee."

He blinked rapidly. "What happened?"

My mouth flew open. He smelled of Mamma Bea's moonshine lemonade. Where would my vessel have taken him? Then the obvious hit me. My outhouse went home. Like a scared rabbit, it hid in the safety of its rabbit hole, my backyard. General Lee had spent the night drinking moonshine with my cousin Darryl.

Lordy, how was I going to explain? I waved my outhouse away and prayed it would return at my summons.

"Where am I?" His words slurred slightly.

General Lee was a little tipsy—I'd use it to my advantage. "General, we're riding to the most important battle of your life. General Pickett's leading a charge toward the enemy's center."

"Pickett?" he removed his hat and scratched his head of gray hair.

"Yes sir. General Longstreet has followed your orders to attack the Federals at the copse of trees on Cemetery Ridge."

"I can't remember."

"You've had a spell of germs and you've been recovering. You might be having a relapse."

"Germs?"

"Yes, sir, do you remember who I am?"

He shook his head. "I'm the doctor who's been taking care of you."

"I recall the most interesting of dreams, but I do not recall riding out here."

"You wanted to give the troops support, sir. Maybe it's too soon."

I spoke the magic words. Never suggest to a general that he's weak.

General Lee squinted his eyes, determined. "I must ride to my men and give them my support."

I remembered reading the historians believed General Lee watched the battle from Seminary Ridge. "General it would be safer for you to watch from the ridge there." I pointed at a high area of ground.

"I should do that, yes. Where's Traveller?" He scanned the area, stopping when he saw his trusted stallion.

The horse lifted his head high, an intelligent look in his eyes. A loyal friend to the general.

General Lee mounted Traveller. I wished him luck and raised my hand, palm up, to salute.

"I bid you thanks, Doctor. I'll request President Jefferson to reward your valiant efforts." He returned my salute, gathered his reins, and rode toward the thousands of men about to die fighting a losing battle.

I watched him from the woods. The soldiers cheered when they saw him. The men not yet in formation touched his boot for good luck. One of his aides rode toward him. "General, glad to see you've recovered."

"Yes, it was germs that had me under."

I smiled after him as he rode away to command his men.

A bugle played, and the men gave one last whoop. Different versions of the rebel yell echoed down the mile of soldiers, and then quiet fell over the troops as they moved forward.

I ran behind the lines of men in the direction I thought Sam would be marching. I searched, but there were so many. I wanted to shout, don't go, but the hands of liberty covered my mouth, and the words of the Gettysburg Address kept me from it. All men are created equal.

This charge must happen in order for one of the greatest leaders of our country to write the most profound speech ever spoken.

A hand clasped my shoulder. "In line soldier."

I tried to protest but the stubborn captain ordered me forward. When I turned to run away, the soldiers behind me gave a scowl. I marched forward. The only weapon I had was the revolver tucked into my waistband.

I marched with the men, my heart pounding hard in my chest. Please let me make it long enough to find Sam. We stopped as the captains addressed their troops, giving words of encouragement. I leaned forward and looked down the line. I spotted Will. His tall frame stood above the other men. He had removed his jacket. Sam had found him. Now, I had to find Sam.

The order was given to march forward, and we moved, going only a short distance until the opposing cannons began to fire. Long rows of men jerked off their feet, writhing on the ground. The men continued to march, and more men were ordered to fill in the gaps. I marched and sidestepped until I was an arm's length away from Will.

"Will!" I marched next to him.

"Doc, what are you doing here?"

"I'm searching for Sam. I have orders," I tried to catch my breath. "The general is requesting both of you to his headquarters."

"What?" Will held a hand to his ear as he continued to walk. He couldn't hear me over the steady roar of the cannons.

We had to stop and climb over a stake and rider fence. Gunshot struck the fence and we dropped to the ground. Will pulled me up. As I turned to holler again, Will pointed to a group of men to his right. Sam tore the paper on his gunpowder and poured it into his musket, ramming the ball down deep as he prepared to shoot.

A cannon blast knocked me off my feet, and something stung my leg. Will was face down in the dirt ten feet from me. I crawled over to him and pushed him face to the sky. He blinked at me.

"I'm hit."

I looked down at his right ankle. There wasn't one. Blood leaked onto the dry earth. "Your leg and foot are injured."

"Doc," he grabbed my jacket. "Can you save my leg?"

I searched in my medial pouch for my tourniquet and tightened it around his left leg, just under the knee. "Stay on the ground, the medics will help you to the hospital."

"Doc, you got to save Sam. He's—"

"Stay down. I'll find Sam." Hunched over, I moved toward Sam, then decided hunching wouldn't spare me—I was still an enemy target. The pain in my leg ached, but I didn't have time to see what bit me. I could run, and that was all that mattered. I ran as fast as I could across the field.

As I closed in on Sam, he kicked backward, falling to the ground.

"NO!" My words were lost in a barrage of cannonade. My hat was shot off my head as I wove my way through the men to him.

I dropped to his side.

A bullet had grazed his temple and blood ran into his eyes.

"Are you an angel?" He wiped at his eyes.

A strand of blond hair covered my face. I pushed it aside. Damn. My wig went with the hat. Long, blond tresses of my hair whipped in the summer breeze with the sun beating down behind me. My shadow fell across Sam's face. I guessed I did look a bit angelic to him.

"I'm going to help you." As I leaned over him, a pink flower petal from the peach tree floated down from my hair and landed on his cheek. He smiled. "I was brave."

Blood seeped through his shirt over his left abdominal area. I untucked his shirt from his waistband and found the remnants of the pocket watch I had given him. A small round ball stuck to its mechanical guts. The impact of the bullet against the shattered gold metal had cut into his side. I patched him up with cloth from my medical kit.

"My vision is blurry," he said. "Did them Yankees get me in the head?"

"Your head's rock hard." By the way his head hit hard against the ground, he had a concussion and shock, most likely. "C'mon soldier. We're getting the hell out of Dodge."

He stood and we made our way in the opposite direction.

"I wanted to reach the wall."

I looked out across the battlefield. Hundreds of men lay dead and wounded. "You got farther than most, I reckon."

I deposited Sam under an oak tree far away from the battle. I gave him a drink from my canteen, and I instructed two men with a stretcher to carry Will from the battlefield. General Lee's orders, I spoke harshly to the men, but there were so many wounded who needed tending.

Sam shut his eyes. I waited until the men had Will securely on the stretcher and watched them double step toward the closest hospital. They might take his leg, but Ida Belle would get her wedding.

"Are you going to be OK?" I asked Sam. "No more fighting."

His light eyelashes fluttered open and he gazed at me with his serene blue eyes. "You're a good angel, but I ain't ready to go with you, yet."

Yep, not for almost ninety years. His eyes shut for a minute and a pretty vivandière knelt next to us and wiped the blood from his face.

"You take care, Sam." I rose to leave and he grabbed my wrist.

"Doc, the box?"

I wasn't sure if he realized I was the angel or if he thought I'd arrived later. Mamma Bea's voice reciting the bible verse the truth shall set you free rang loud above the deafening sounds of battle.

"Sam. I'm from the future. General Lee is back in the saddle, running the show. I was sent here to make sure you have a long and happy life."

He smiled. "Will I get to know a woman, and see the most beautiful thing on Earth?"

The vivandière blushed beside me.

"Yes, Sam, you will," I said, mentally apologizing to Keanu Reeves for hijacking his words.

"Thanks, Doc."

I left Sam in the hands of a the pretty vivandière, who assured me she would see him to a medic. I had to get back to Lee's headquarters before they figured out Lee was in two places at the same time.

A riderless horse ran past me, skittish from the roar of the cannons. I limped toward it. My leg ached, but only a trickle of blood stained my shoe. The horse calmed when it reached a thicket. I commandeered the horse and rode toward the Thompson farm.

Lee would return to his camp on the farm grounds immediately following the battle. I had to get Marco and Gertie, and we had to find the seer. Ace told me he arrested Caiyan near the Thompson farm, maybe they were close.

My time was running thin and when I returned home and saw Caiyan again, I was going to kill him. My heart took a jump at my thoughts. He might already be dead.

Nope, not going to think about it. I pushed my ride harder.

My wig was in the dust, and my mustache hung on by a sticky hair. I yanked it off and tossed it in the breeze. No more hiding. If the brigands wanted a battle, they'd have to fight Jennifer Cloud.

CHAPTER 23

*B*roken men straggled off the battlefield. The Thompson house was flooded with the injured.

When I arrived at General Lee's headquarters, the mass of staff was missing. Probably packing their things to flee the area. A group of men stood outside a tent, an injured man laid across a table probably confiscated from someone's dining room.

I tried not to look at the men as I hurried toward General Lee's tent. The guards were absent from their position in front of the tent, and a knot squeezed my stomach. I peeked through the tent flap and entered when I found the room empty.

Marco and Gertie were gone. The desk didn't have a note that read hey, stepped out for some hardtack and coffee so I moved carefully out of the tent. Was Marco discovered impersonating an officer? Where would they have been taken?

As I stood in the shadows of the canopy outside the tent contemplating my options, I saw Victory cut across the campsite toward a densely wooded area. She paused and looked over her shoulder. Checking for a tail. Where was Caiyan? She disappeared into the thicket. And then I saw him. Moving stealthily behind her, at a distance. Odd. Why weren't they together? His eyes swept across the campsite. I froze, hoping the dancing shadows caused by the sun cutting through the canopy of trees hid me from his view.

He smoked into the woods. The guy really did have a talent for stealthily stalking his prey. I followed him at a respectable distance. I heard their argument before I saw them.

"Victory, where do ye think yer going?"

"I found another way home."

"What are ye talking aboot?"

"I've done all I can do here. I can't stay any longer. I want to go home."

"Ye cannae travel in yer condition."

"I saw it in a vision. I make it, and the baby too."

"Vic, yer visions are no always correct withoot yer key."

"I'm willing to risk it."

As I drew closer, I bumped into Toches coming in from the opposite direction.

"What are you doing here?" I asked keeping my voice low.

"I'm here for the key. You should have left when I let you go the first time."

"Where's Mortas?"

A wicked smile crawled over his face. "He's got your buddies about a mile up the road. He can't do much with big, dumb, and blond, but he's taking a little catnap. I imagine he'll have a nice bump on the head, but since you're a doctor, you should be able to fix him right up." He poked the patch on my uniform jacket indicating I was with the medical corps. "I wouldn't waste any time getting to your cousin. I'm not responsible for what Mortas might do to her."

"There's WTF all over this area," I said, hoping Brodie might show.

"Oh, we took care of them. The chloroform came in real handy. You're all alone now, princess. Better get a move on if you want to save your friends."

"Why are you working for the Mafusos?" I stared him down. "They don't care about you."

"The heart wants what the heart wants." He grinned.

Toecheese quoting Emily Dickinson. He was full of surprises. I started to make a witty remark, and the quote's meaning snapped another piece of the puzzle together.

"You're Mahlia's plus one, aren't you? Those were your clothes in Caiyan's apartment."

"Your Scot's got a nice place—or had one. I didn't know he had already been here. Once I found out, it was too late. Mortas made me stay. Sorry for your loss." His face dropped, and I almost thought he was sincere.

"You're going to be disappointed when they screw you, Toecheese."

He frowned at the name. "When I bring the seer and her key to Gian-Carlo, he's going to cream his pants."

Gross.

"He'll have to let us get married."

My face screwed up trying to imagine what Mahlia saw in this guy.

Toches huffed. "Don't look so shocked. I've got talents not even I knew about. I'll send you a wedding invitation." He took a step toward the clearing.

I grabbed his arm.

"Go ahead, try and stop me. I'll tell the Scot everything about you. The life you had together will be ruined."

I released his arm.

"Time to break up the happy couple, or not so happy from the sound of it." He rubbed his palms together and moved through the trees.

My brain told me to help Caiyan, but my heart cemented my legs to the ground.

The rumble of a motor vibrated the ground under me. I pushed my feelings aside and hurried down the path Toches had taken.

I entered at a high point behind the cover of overgrown brush. Toches sat straddling Mahlia's Harley-Davidson Sportster.

"Stop!" Caiyan yelled over the noise of the motorcycle, his back to me.

Victory ran toward Toches and climbed into the sidecar of the motorcycle.

Toches throttled up the engine.

"Tell Elma she can go to hell and take her toy with her!" Victory threw a small brown box at Caiyan. He ducked and it sailed over his head, landing a few feet from me. The girl had good aim. Toches's face contorted into a disturbed look and he shouted "Nooo!"

Caiyan rushed toward them. They vanished with a loud crack, knocking him backward. He landed flat on his back.

Gaelic curses spewed from him as he got to his feet and retrieved the box. He turned and stared at the empty space where the Harley stood moments before. Placing his hand on his key, he dropped to his knees.

I expected him to call his vessel. It was my last chance to save his life—I had to warn him now.

With his back to me, he dropped his head to his chest as he leaned back on his brogans and looked down at the box he held.

I had never seen him like this. Defeated. I read his ache from across the clearing, and my heart shed a tear. I would miss our rocky relationship, and the way he held me in his arms when his secrets were tucked way down deep and I was the only one he cared about. What would my life be like when I returned to the WTF?

I moved from my hidey hole toward him. A loud crack and my vessel appeared across from us. Did he call my vessel?

The door opened and a familiar face with white hair pulled back into a tidy bun stepped from the outhouse wearing her best Annie Oakley gear.

She started forward, saw me, and cut her eyes toward the large tree next to me. When I scurried for cover, she winked at me. Caiyan didn't raise his head as Elma approached.

"You summoned me, boy?"

"I lost her."

Elma placed an aged hand on his head of dark curls. "You didn't lose her. She chose. Like she always does."

He raised his head and looked up at her. "She's pregnant."

Elma's eyes widened. "Now, there's a twist I didn't see coming."

"Toches took her on a vessel I've never seen before. He was older. I'm afraid he tried to take her forward."

"If he's capable, you'll find her."

"I didnae kin 'twas possible."

"There's so much we don't know about our gift." Elma searched Caiyan's face. "Why don't you quit this gypsy lifestyle, and come home?"

He shook his head, dropping his gaze to the ground again. "'Tis naugh my destiny."

"Oh, I think it is." She glanced in my direction and our eyes met and held.

"I'm naugh a good man."

"Now don't go gettin' all righteous with me, boy. John's death wasn't your fault."

"I know otherwise." He stood, towering above my petite aunt. I held my breath and stayed hidden.

"John's death was meant to happen exactly as it had. Believe me, I've tried to change the past and nothin' good ever come of it."

"The suits would never grant me safety. They'd take my key for what I've done."

"My God, boy, you're too hard on yourself. You've got talent. I'd see to it the new boss knows of it. They could use a man like you, a good man, and besides, Brodie misses you."

"Brodie," he chuckled.

"Well there's no convincing you otherwise. Like Victory, you'll make your own choice. The crow only flies where the meat is good, but the eagle, they build their nests to last."

He held her gaze for a long, mindful moment, then lifted his hand.

"What should I do with this?" The small puzzle box balanced on his open palm.

She closed his fingers around it with her own. "When you find her, you can return it to her."

"I dinnae kin if I'll ever see her again?"

When Elma didn't answer, Caiyan frowned at her. "Why didnae ye jest give her the key back?"

"She has to learn what's important, then she can claim the key for herself."

"Riddles. Puzzles. Why cannae ye jest speak clearly. Tell her what she needs to do?"

"She won't grow that way. I could say the same for you." Her head lifted like a deer hearing the footsteps of an approaching hunter. "They're coming. You need to decide if you're going to be like the eagle or live like the crow."

With that she walked away and vanished into the landscape.

Caiyan pocketed the puzzle box but stood his ground.

"I saw him come this way," Brodie said as he and Ace stepped into the clearing.

Ace swatted at a mosquito. "The bugs here are awful, and my tummy feels woozy from the chloroform. When can when we leave?"

"As soon as I kick his arse." Brodie halted as he came face to face with Caiyan.

Ace glanced around and frowned. "What are you doing here?"

"Screwing up my life," Caiyan said.

"Tired of being such a sneaky git?" Ace asked and moved to flank Caiyan.

"All right mate, we're here ta stop ya, but first, I'm giving ya what's due." Brodie pushed up his sleeves and dropped into a crouched position, fists at the ready.

Caiyan gave a long, low sigh and held his fists up as if agreeing for the sake of it.

Brodie lunged for Caiyan. Caiyan dodged and gave him a good punch in the kidney. Brodie came back with a right hook that caught Caiyan square on the jaw. Round and round they went until they were on the ground punching, kicking, and roughhousing like two pubescent brothers.

Ace sat on a nearby log and examined his manicure. After several minutes, both men lay spent on the ground. The brush parted and Gerry stepped into the ring. "Are you guys finished dicking around? The moon cycle's about done and I'm out of whiskey."

The moon cycle—I'd almost forgotten I was on a schedule.

Caiyan stood, used his sleeve and wiped away a trail of blood leaking from his nose, offered Brodie a hand. Brodie clasped his hand, and Caiyan hauled him up.

"Sorry mate, we're gonna take ya in."

Gerry secured Caiyan's hands behind his back. "Can't have you making a run for it."

"If I wanted to run, ye wouldnae be able to stop me."

His eye had a deep cut above the brow. I remembered kissing that scar. The memory twinged my lady parts. I couldn't leave until they did, without being noticed.

"Let's go, McGregor."

The leaves swirled on the trees and Ace's photo booth appeared. They loaded Caiyan inside and Ace joined him. Poof! Caiyan had been arrested. The story of the way he returned to the WTF was complete. I hoped I hadn't made the mistake of my life.

"Did ya really drink all the whiskey?" Brodie asked Gerry.

"Yep. Shall we make a pit stop before we head back to base?"

"Not on your life. I've been waiting a long time to bring that wanker in. I want to have a front row seat." A flurry of wind shook the leaves on the trees. The men boarded their vessels and were gone.

I stepped from the bushes and fumbled in my haversack, retrieving the small wooden box Caiyan had given to me. I had a feeling I knew what was inside. The only thing that could travel through time, not secured inside a host.

I tucked the box back inside my jacket and ran as fast as I could toward the area Toches indicated Mortas held court. My leg was on fire by the time I found Gertie standing on the rails of a post oak fence.

"Jen," she waved. "You lost your man parts."

"Are you all right?" I asked her. "Toches told me Mortas was holding you and Marco prisoner?"

"He did, the creep, but Great Aint Elma stopped by for a visit. It was surreal."

"I saw her in the woods. Caiyan summoned her."

"Good thing he did. Mortas got all nervous when Aint Elma showed up. She kicked his bottom and told him if he didn't behave hisself she'd make a steer out of him. His key did that glowy thing and he took off."

"Where's Marco?"

"Yonder trees," she thumbed toward the trees behind her.

I smiled at her usage of Sam's words.

"He's recovering from the knock on the head Mortas gave him. Elma told me to wait right here and you'd be along." She scrunched up her face. "Did you find Sam?"

"Yes, and Will. They're both safe."

"Praise Jesus!" Gertie said. The troubled expression on my face triggered more questions.

"Did Caiyan, you know, stay with Victory?"

"No, Toecheese took her."

"Toecheese?"

"Yeah, I think he can carry people forward."

Gertie tilted her head, considering my notion.

"She'll skip a few years," Gertie finally said, recalling the brief rundown I gave her about Victory. "So, she'll still be young, pregnant, and beautiful?"

"We'll find out when we get home," I shrugged.

"Caiyan's got some splainin' to do."

"We changed his path; he'll have a lot more than explaining to do." I prayed he would be alive to explain, to raise his family. We headed into the woods to find Marco. Gertie interlocked her fingers with mine. It was time to take my family home.

Marco insisted on driving himself back to base. As Gertie and I exited my vessel, a suit came forward and welcomed us home.

"Agent McCoy will meet you here shortly," he said, turning to join the other two suits blocking the exit. His jacket stretched tight across his muscular back, and his twinzies stood at parade rest.

Odd. Jake always met me when I returned from a travel. A strange vibe hung in the air. I glanced behind me. Marco's racecar bounced the overhead lights off his hood on the platform next to mine. How did he always beat me back? Ace's photo booth and Brodie's tub book-ended us. Gerry's confessional towered on the platform behind mine.

That's when I noticed all the platforms were loaded. Everyone had returned from their assignments but remained on base. It reminded me of a…wake.

Gertie threaded her arm through mine and ushered me forward. My legs grew heavier with each step. I didn't want to know the answer. I wanted to hold on to my memories.

Please let Caiyan be alive.

"If it's not good news, we can fix it, right? You're a time traveler," Gertie reassured me.

The problem was when I tried to fix things, it led to disaster.

Jake met us at the entrance to the hangar. I tried to read his face, but he revealed nothing.

"We're back," I said. A bead of sweat formed on my upper lip as my heart raced from anxious to full on panic mode.

When Jake didn't speak right away, Gertie clasped me tighter and I prepared myself for the bad news.

He glanced down at me and grimaced. "Jen, why didn't you tell me Eli had a key?"

I exhaled, and my mood changed from panic to irritated. Before I could say anything, Gertie stepped in.

"Can't you see she's worried sick about Caiyan, and she's got her leg hurt. You have some nerve scolding her about a key." Gertie unlatched herself from me and pointed a finger in Jake's face. "Shame on you!"

The suit stepped forward. Jake shook his head and held up a hand.

"McGregor's in medical. The doctors tell me he'll recover, but his injuries are serious. He lost too much blood; he would have died if Ace hadn't brought Eli to base."

I released a long, slow breath. "I'm sorry. I promised Eli I wouldn't drag him into this world, but something told me Caiyan wouldn't make it if I didn't."

"Don't apologize to him." Gertie crossed her arms over her chest and huffed.

"I love you, Gertie." Jake broke into a grin. He slung an arm around her shoulders. "C'mon, momma hen, let's go see the troops while Jen has a short visit with McGregor and pays a visit to the infirmary. Everyone's been waiting to hear about the Battle of Gettysburg."

I followed them from the landing zone and detoured left toward the infirmary. The WTF kept medical staff on base. They worked with the prison in the four-story hospital attached to our unit via a secret passage through the basement. I still wore the Sonny Bono suit, but the wig didn't make the trip home. It seemed like a lifetime since the wedding I attended with Ace.

A matronly nurse with ample curves and short kinky hair led me into Caiyan's room. Monitors bleeped a steady, pulsating, thank god he's alive, beep. Bags of fluids and medicines pumped through plastic tubing into his arms, and lines connected him to the monitors and the machines.

The nurse checked the readings on the screens while I moved next to his bed. A bristly stubble roughened his jaw, and those menacing green eyes hid from me behind pale, closed lids. I watched him sleep for a few minutes while the nurse did her thing.

"Still keeping secrets from me, huh?" I reached over and tucked one of his dark curls cast loose across his forehead back into place. His monitor did a blip instead of a beep and I looked anxiously at the nurse.

"It's OK, just a flutter in the heartbeat, but he's not out of the woods, yet. He's sedated so he comes in and out of consciousness." She smiled at me and placed a gentle hand on my arm. "I'm sorry but you can only stay a few minutes."

I nodded.

She picked up her electronic notepad, tapped a few times on the screen, and turned to leave. She paused on her way out. "I've had him in here many times before, but he sure did some damage this time."

"He didn't do the damage, I did," I whispered as she left the room.

I leaned against the railing on his hospital bed and wondered what kind of father he would be. Would Victory stay with the Mafusos or seek him out? The Caiyan she knew was younger, a rebel. This Caiyan, still the rebel, but owned a company, ran a business, had worked for what Victory referred to as the enemy. Would Caiyan still love her? Did he still love me?

I sat down in the chair next to his bed and pulled the puzzle box from my jacket pocket. It hummed in my hands.

"I know you're in there." I tapped the box lightly with my nail. Flipping the box around, its contents shifted. The hand-carved wood reminded me of my uncle Durr's envious collection of wooden games. His favorite hobby was woodworking, and he had made me a jewelry box out of similar wood for my sixteenth birthday.

Examining the end of the intricately carved piece, it wouldn't be easy to cut through, and the owner risked damaging the contents. The box had letters that slid around Kryptex style until they formed a word across the center of the box. If the letters were placed in the correct order the box would open. Victory had the box for three years and couldn't figure it out. Maybe Al would know how to open it.

I slid the letters around. Caiyan told Aint Elma to stop with all the puzzles. If Aint Elma made the puzzle, what would she want Victory to learn? Loyalty. The box stayed shut.

I slid the letters around again. They moved easily in the wooden grooves. I thought about my feisty old aunt and how Gertie had more of her spunk than I did. What was most important to my great aunt?

I moved the letters in place. The box clicked open at the end. A wide smile spread across my face. I tilted the box and slid its glittery contents into my hand. The key was smaller than the key I wore. Raindrops splashed across the surface of the moonstone in the form of blue diamonds.

"You opened the box."

His scratchy voice made me jump. Caiyan stared at me from his bed, his green eyes soulful and sad.

"Yeah, I guess I did."

"What was the word?"

"Family."

He raised his eyes to the ceiling, then turned them back on me. "Should have known Elma would choose her greatest love."

I stood and moved next to him. Held the key up for him to see. "It's pretty, like it's owner."

"You found her?"

"Yes, and I found you."

He began to cough, and his face drew up in a painful scowl.

"You want some water?"

He nodded. I laid the key and the box down and held the plastic jug of water up for him to sip through the straw.

"Thanks." He dropped his head down on the pillow and closed his eyes. "You were there." His eyes popped open. "The doctor."

"Dr. Seuss at your service." I sat the water jug down on the bedside table and bowed.

He smiled. "Clever, I should have picked up on it, but I had other things on my mind." His eyes searched mine and I looked away.

"I'm sorry I got you shot."

"I shouldnae have kept secrets from ye."

Our eyes held for a moment.

"Speaking of secrets, I'm going to tell Jake that Victory threw the puzzle box down before she left with Toecheese. And I found it." It was a tiny white lie. She did throw the box...at Caiyan's head. If the WTF knew Caiyan had the puzzle box all these years, and he had information about a seer, it couldn't turn out good for him.

He gnawed on his bottom lip, then agreed. "Toecheese would have brought her to our time."

"Most likely, I haven't been to the debriefing, yet."

"'Tis good. I thought I'd never see her again. I dinnae kin what weel happen now."

My head bobbed, but I wanted to ask him why he didn't tell me he had a kid somewhere, past or present. The reality was that he didn't have a kid, not yet. I didn't want to have that talk with him hooked up to machines. My query could wait.

He muttered something in Gaelic, closed his eyes again, and drifted off.

I scooped up the box and the key, and left him, stopping by medical to have the doctor look at my leg.

265

I'd caught a piece of grapeshot. The round ball had left a perfect indention in my leg. My first bullet wound. The doctor bandaged my leg and gave me an antibiotic, no questions asked.

On the way out of the infirmary, I passed Marco cursing at the nurses as they redressed his leg. I pitied them, but, like Caiyan, he'd been in the infirmary many times.

"Mr. Ferrari, that sassy attitude is gonna cost you. Don't be sending us no Snickers either. We want the ones from Belgium with the delicious centers," a rather sturdy nurse told him as she held down his leg so the doctor could stitch his wound closed.

I chuckled as I left the hospital. Tomorrow, the nurses would receive flowers and chocolates to make up for his bad behavior. They knew him well.

CHAPTER 24

I picked up my things from my locker before I headed to the blue room. I wanted to text Eli and make amends.

I'm back, I texted. *Gertie and I are fine. Sorry, I outed you. Can we talk later?*

He replied immediately. *Glad you came back in better shape than your boyfriend. I didn't know I had that kind of power. Let me know when you get home. The pizza and beers are on you.*

I smiled. He wasn't mad at me.

Ace met me in the hallway. I launched myself at him, throwing my arms around his neck and embracing him tightly.

"Thanks, Ace," I said. "It was a risk for you to come."

He squeezed me back, then released me.

"Did things work out with the general?" he twisted his lips in an I've got a story demeanor.

"You found him?" I asked. "I wasn't sure how he made it back to Gettysburg."

"He fancied himself drinks with your cousin."

"You met Darryl?"

Ace grinned ear to ear. "The bloke has stories. He could make a few quid selling them. Thankfully, Darryl agreed to let me tuck the

267

general in bed. By the amount of moonshine left in the bottle, I'll be surprised if either one of them remembers what happened."

"The general arrived at exactly the right moment in time."

"Brilliant. It was a bloody battle forcing the man to sit in the outhouse. I chased 'im around your garden a few times, finally had to knock 'im on his bum."

I snorted at the image Ace conjured.

"I'm glad you're home safe and sound." He glanced at the bandage on my leg. "What's that?"

"My first gunshot wound, or in this case grapeshot."

"Gurl, you need to think about what you fight for. Staying on base has its perks. I don't have any of those wounds. Just sayin'."

"I'm fighting for freedom, to be considered an equal."

"Didn't Gettysburg teach you anything?"

"Yes, to be strong, brave, and fight for what you believe in."

"Bloody 'ell, you've been drinking the Civil War Kool-Aid. You'll have the transporters assigned to our own missions before you're done."

"You think that's a possibility?" I asked, hopeful.

"Gurl." He looped an arm around my shoulders, and we headed for the debriefing.

All the teams were present in the blue room, making it standing room only.

The Russian team leaned against the wall. Fredericka scrolled through her phone as I passed. Her glittering black fingernails tapped against her screen. She paused and gave me a thumbs up.

The other teams gathered around the conference table. General Potts sat at the head like the stoic Queen Bee waiting for the hive to bring news of the world. He hadn't visited the blue room often since I joined the WTF. Gettysburg was a big deal.

I took the open seat next to Gertie, who was in the middle of describing the horrible conditions the soldiers dealt with in the field hospitals.

General Potts turned a light shade of green when she gave a

detailed account of the way grapeshot from a canister artillery took a man's privates clean off.

Jake asked a few questions, and Gertie and I took turns answering.

I explained my part, describing Victory and revealing to them she was pregnant, but leaving out the part about Caiyan being the father.

General Potts coughed into his hand. "As you know, Agent McGregor received a serious wound in Gettysburg. He's returned to our team, but for the sake of rescuing the seer from the Mafusos, I am pronouncing him dead."

"He's always been dead to me," Gerry spouted off.

It took a minute for General Potts's words to sink in. Wait? what? We are supposed to fake Caiyan's death? And the seer doesn't need to be rescued. She agreed to go with them.

Jake noticed my uneasiness with General Potts's statement and shook his head. My instincts told me to keep my mouth shut.

I retold the scene I witnessed between Caiyan and Victory, hitting heavy on the part where Victory left of her own free will, and with only a few minor changes.

I replaced the part where Caiyan recovered the box with me picking up the box after Caiyan had left the area and explained how since the box made it back to headquarters, I assumed there was a key inside.

Everyone shifted closer when I produced the key. No one refuted my story or claimed to have seen this key before. I finished my recollection of the events in Gettysburg,

General Potts, satisfied with the outcome, left the Victory key, which it was now called, in Jake's care and excused himself from the room.

The interrogation was deemed officially over, and the other teams dispersed. My team remained at the table.

Campy stood. "I'm going to check on Uncle Cai." He squeezed my shoulder as he passed me on the way out.

"I can't believe that was you. We rode together across Seminary Ridge," Brodie said. "I asked ya medical advice." My team was astonished that I was Dr. Seuss.

Were their lives different than before I had left for Gettysburg? Had an alternate universe now become their reality? Another life, like the one they had lived, but with the good Dr. Seuss present to help General Lee with his germs, had replaced the previous one. The unfortunate result of time travel.

Jake told me technically, it was a loop. I had always been there to save Sam Raney. My brain ached trying to make sense of it.

Gertie had done an amazing job calling the exact orders Lee had given to his corps commanders. I told her so as she finished flipping through a history book on the battle of Gettysburg and reported there were no changes.

"Except this one," she said and pushed the book toward me. The book was opened to a chapter on the medical doctors in the Civil War.

A paragraph read General Lee suffered from what one doctor labeled as germs. Most likely it was a type of influenza, but the doctor used the word germ almost a decade before Robert Koch and Louis Pasteur contributed to the Germ Theory of Disease. The unnamed surgeon, who most likely died in battle, was ahead of his time.

"Huh, I'm a little upset they didn't remember my name."

It went on to read General Lee gave credit to his speedy recovery from the germs to something the unnamed doctor gave him called Mamma Bea's lemonade.

"At least he didn't mention the outhouse took him to another time," Gertie said.

Heads bobbed in agreement.

"Well, mates," Brodie stood. "I, for one, am glad to be back home. He scooped Gertie up in a long, tongue-filled kiss.

"Get a room," Gerry catcalled.

"As fast as I can," Brodie replied.

Marco limped in and stopped short at Brodie's PDA.

"Whoa, are we celebrating?"

"Some people can't control their urges." Gerry threw shade Brodie's direction.

Tina lifted a dark eyebrow at Gerry, then turned her attention to me.

"I wish I had already joined the team when Gerry and Brodie were younger, but I was still a babe in my homeland."

"Nah you don't, because I wasn't here to make things exciting." Marco sat down at the table.

"How's the leg?" Jake asked him.

"Better, after the torture session. Sixteen stitches, but I made a date with one of the nurses, so it's all good." He cut a quick glance my way.

"Jen found the Victory key," Ace told Marco.

"You did?" He raised his eyebrows at me.

"It was in the puzzle box Victory threw away before she left with Toecheese."

He held my gaze for a long, intense moment. Drumming a few taps with his fingers on the table, he turned toward Jake. "Since McGregor is on the road to recovery, and we have the key, can we get on with my debriefing so I can head out?"

"Hey, does your nurse have a sister?" Gerry asked.

"You're disgusting," Tina said to Gerry. "So did General Potts approve the transporters to travel alongside their defenders?" she asked Jake.

Tina didn't like being left behind either.

"He's giving me an answer based on this travel," Jake said.

Tina looked hopeful; Ace did, too. I couldn't decide which situation General Potts would deem accountable. Me saving Caiyan because I was there, or the fact Ace was available to save him because he didn't travel with his defender. The outlook wasn't good in my opinion.

Jake's phone pinged, and he frowned at the screen.

"What is it?" Ace asked. "Problems with the new girlfriend?"

"The Mafusos want a trade."

Brodie and Gertie returned to their seats, and we waited for the details.

"The Victory key in exchange for the seer."

"Why would we give up a key?" I asked. "She chose to go with them."

"She may be in danger," Brodie said. "When the Mafusos figured out she didn't have the key, she was of no use to them."

"I agree with Brodie," Jake said, "They would have had her killed if she had kept the key, so it was good she tossed it at Caiyan."

"Maybe she did it on purpose," Gerry said.

I huffed, and Gertie cleared her throat at me.

"How do we know she's not working with them?" Tina asked.

"Yeah," I said.

"What if she reveals our location to the Mafusos?" Ace chimed in. "I mean, she did leave with them on her own accord."

Yes, Ace. Make Jake see it's a dangerous move. I couldn't bear to watch Caiyan and Victory work with my team, not to mention baby McGregor's impending arrival. My inner voice held up a pair of knitted booties, and I cursed out loud.

Jake's phone pinged again. Saved by the bell.

"They want Jennifer to meet them, with the puzzle box."

"Me?"

"They think you're the weak link, cupcake." Gerry said.

Jake texted back.

"What did you say?" I asked him.

"I told them, I'm not sending you alone. We will match our defenders to whatever muscle Gian-Carlo brings."

We sat in silence, everyone waiting for the next ping. When it arrived, Jake read aloud.

"She can bring three people. Only WTF, no goons, no guns, and if Marco is present, he's not allowed to wear his key."

"Why the fuck not?" Marco fussed.

"You know why," Ace waved a hand at him. "The Mafusos don't want you pulling any of your Jedi mind tricks when they snatch the key from us."

"You think they're going to take the key and keep the seer?" Tina asked.

"Ya bet your sweet arse they are." Brodie crossed his arms over his chest.

"Tell him we agree, but only if we pick the meeting place," I said.

Jake paused, considered, then typed my words.

"They agreed." He squinted his eyes at me. "I told them no goons or guns. Now, you want to tell me what's going on upstairs?" He tapped the side of his head.

"They said I can only bring three people. They didn't say anything about animals."

A wide smile spread across Gertie's face. "Mama's Double Wide?"

I grinned back at her. "Oh, yeah."

Twenty-four hours later, I arrived at Mama's Double Wide. Jake had secured a meeting during the day when the club was closed. It didn't take much to persuade Darryl to assist Jake on a top secret mission.

Once inside, Jake greeted us.

"I'm not usually on this side of the law." Darryl grinned ear to ear. He had Daphne secured in her travel cage and Tonto riding shotgun in my backpack.

Jake cut an uncertain look my way.

Daphne gave a squawk. Darryl opened a Tupperware container and chose a treat that resembled slimy chicken gizzards. He passed it between the wire grid. Daphne took it in her claw and tore off a piece with her sharp beak.

Intel reported the Mafusos had flown to Texas by private jet. Mahlia could have transported the keyless, but one day wasn't much time to acquire goons in the area. My money was on Gian-Carlo brought his own. If he was abiding by the terms of our agreement, no goons, no guns, the hired hands would stay away from the bar but circle the perimeter like starved hyenas.

I peeked in at Tonto. He was curled up in a ball asleep. The cuddly quarters of my backpack provided a cocooned haven for the burglar.

I escorted Darryl upstairs to the second story loft inside Mama's

Double Wide to wait for the Mafusos' arrival. Marco, Jake, and Brodie waited downstairs. A breeze blew in from the large, open pitching window across the loft. The air smelled of Texas summer, hot and humid. I pulled my hair back into a messy bun, securing the bun with a hair tie I wore around my wrist.

Darryl placed Daphne's cage on a table near the balcony and removed his cowboy hat, taking in the scenery.

I joined him looking out through the giant window at the parking lot below. The loft provided a bird's eye view for the manager of the club to observe the bar, tables, and shenanigans below, and offered an area for VIP guests. A picture of the actor Jamie Foxx, a native of the area, hung on the wall above a cozy lounge area.

Marco turned and looked up at me from his position by the door. I gave him a finger wave. He gave me nothing.

The high vaulted barn roof was perfect for what I had in store for the Mafusos. Daphne gave another objection to being confined in her cage.

"Do you think Daphne will be able to do her thing in here?" I motioned toward the thick beams running parallel to the ceiling. Jake had originally objected to my plan; it took some convincing before he agreed.

"No problemo," Darryl said. He replaced his hat and pushed another treat through the cage. "Daphne's a professional."

We moved a large, potted plant in front of the table to provide Darryl a screen from the Mafusos. He could watch the goings on below without being seen.

"Incoming," Gerry's voice broadcasted across everyone's in-ear communication devices. The Mafusos weren't stupid. They knew we would have people on the outside, too. Tina and Gerry blocked the exit to the highway in case the Mafusos thwarted my plan and got by us. But my plan didn't allow them to have the key.

"Aboot time. I'm sweating my bloody balls off out here." Campy reported from the roof of the Taco House next door.

A black Lincoln pulled up at the entrance to Mama's Double Wide. A hired hand exited the Lincoln and scoped out the place.

When he was satisfied we didn't have a militia waiting in the wings, he opened the car door. Gian-Carlo stepped out, followed by Mahlia.

"That the bad guys?" Darryl asked me.

"Yep, the Big Kahuna and his granddaughter."

The hired gun got in the Lincoln and the car drove away.

"Looks like Gian-Carlo is complying with the agreement." Jake alerted us of the situation. "Brodie is checking the old man and his twiggy witch."

He had picked up Brodie's nickname for Mahlia. I suppressed a smile.

"Where's the seer?" Ace asked from his position at the Grab-N-Gas across the street.

"Good question." Jake responded into the microphone attached to his earpiece.

Where *was* Victory?

"Jen, let's go," Jake said to me. It was time for this barn dance to begin.

"Wait for my signal," I said to Darryl, then cut my eyes at Daphne.

He acknowledged my request with a quirky grin. He was having too much fun. "Your uncle told me outthinking the enemy was the key to a successful victory."

"My uncle?" I arched an eyebrow at him.

"Yeah, the one who thinks he's General Lee and likes to sit in your outhouse. We had a good talk. He enjoyed Mamma Bea's moonshine."

"Um…my uncle likes to live in the past."

"Yeah, he seemed to be stuck on Gettysburg. I told him it was too bad we lost, but it worked out for the best."

Crap on a cracker.

"He insisted the fight wasn't over, and if he could get inside the head of his enemy, things would turn around."

I mulled over General Lee's words. "Wait for my signal."

Darryl saluted and pulled on the protective glove he wore for Daphne.

I took the flight of stairs down to join the others.

"Gertie, get ready," I spoke to her through my communication device on the way down.

"Roger that," came her response.

GIAN-CARLO SAT at one of the cocktail tables wearing a dark suit, black silk shirt, and stony poker face. He was old school. Used to the way things were done in a mafia family. There were no earbuds dangling from his ear, or communication devices to call his goons. Every order handled by him.

Mahlia leaned against the bar. Her key returned and present in the open neck of her Alexis Virginia Lace white button-down. I swear the bitch was stalking my Pinterest boards. Where were Gian-Carlo's other slaves? I expected Mortas and Toches, or at the very least Mitchell to be here.

Gian-Carlo shifted in his chair when he saw me, and Caiyan's key gleamed in the V-neck of his silk dress shirt.

"Ah, there you are Jennifer Cloud." Gian-Carlo's words rolled off his tongue when I entered the room. His tone reflected years of practice grooming his grandchildren into the perfect pawns.

"OK, you have us here. Where is Victory?" Jake asked.

"Interesting choice of locations." Gian-Carlo waved his hand in the air. "Makes me curious as to why you chose this place."

"Cut the crap." Marco stepped forward. "Where's Victory?"

"How nice of you to join us, Marco." A wicked smile creased Gian-Carlo's face. "I can't tell you how pleased I am to see you. Don't worry. The seer will arrive momentarily. I had to make sure you came with the box. You know...you show me yours and I'll..." he didn't finish the sentence.

I looked over at Jake, and he nodded. This was my show. I reached into the pocket of my backpack, retrieved the Victory key, and held it up for everyone to see. The key sparkled as it rotated on the titanium chain suspended from my hand.

"She has the seer's key," Mahlia gasped. Probably disappointed she couldn't march over on her stilettos and snag the key out of my hand.

"You figured out the puzzle of Elma's box. She always liked to make the simple things difficult." Gian-Carlo pressed his lips together. "Make the call," he said to Mahlia.

She tapped out a text on her phone, and we waited. For what, I wasn't sure.

"A white SUV is headed your direction," Tina's voice buzzed in my ear.

We stood three across from Gian-Carlo. Marco was to my right, and Jake on my left. Brodie was positioned by the door.

Mahlia pushed off the bar and paced in front of us. Her heels clicked on the concrete floor. She cut her eyes at me. "Mortas found your defender in Gettysburg and your little sidekick, too. I don't believe you just sat by and allowed Caiyan to die in Gettysburg."

She planned on me rescuing Caiyan. She knew we'd track her key, and by loaning it to Toches, she wouldn't be blamed for helping Caiyan. Maybe she did have some feelings for Caiyan's well-being.

"Did she call me a sidekick?" Gertie's irritated voice grumbled in my ear.

"She's needling you for information. Trying to figure out if you saved the bastard," Gerry said in my ear. "Can you at least shed a tear and look like you're suffering miserably from Caiyan's death? I can feel you steaming from way out here."

I dropped my eyes. Maybe having everyone connected via in-ear communication devices wasn't such a good idea.

"Think about those abused animal commercials," Campy suggested.

Jake moved in between me and Mahlia. "The loss of Agent McGregor was a travesty," he said. "But he made his decision to leave us months ago."

"Yes, a huge loss for Mahlia as well." Gian-Carlo clicked his tongue. "A mistake on Kishin's part, I'm afraid. He'll pay the price for his defiance."

I wiped a fake tear from my cheek and lifted my head, expecting to meet Mahlia's judgmental brown eyes. I caught a glimpse of something, fear maybe. Was it possible Mahlia didn't want to lose Toches the same way she thought I had lost Caiyan?

"My sidekick told me Aint Elma showed up and taught Mortas a thing or two." I stared directly at Gian-Carlo.

Gian-Carlo sighed. "Even long after she's been dead, Elma still intervenes."

The SUV rolled up outside.

"Mortas and a pregnant girl are getting out of the car. Two goons are flanking," Campy announced.

Mortas led Victory into the bar. The goons stayed outside. Her hands were tied behind her back. A knife was at her throat.

"You said no weapons." I did a palms up at Gian-Carlo.

"You misunderstood; I said no guns."

He had us on a technicality. The creep.

Mortas relinquished Victory to Mahlia, then returned outside. What was he up to?

"Where's Mortas going?" Jake asked Gian-Carlo.

"We agreed on equal terms, did we not? I need something in the car, and I cannot have one of my boys entering the premises, correct?"

Gian-Carlo remained seated at the table and seemed not to have a care in the world. The vibe was wrong. An electricity I couldn't put my finger on floated in the air.

General Lee's words *get inside your enemy's head* forced me to focus. I tried to read Gian-Carlo from across the room. A gift my aint Elma mastered, but I had to make contact to execute.

Focus. Arrogance consumed me and I envisioned myself standing on a battlefield raising the Victory key high above my head in triumph.

That's it. Confidence. Gian-Carlo was entirely too confident he would get the key. My inner voice gave me a thumbs up for the evolution of my gift.

Victory stood next to Mahlia. Not a lot of contact for a hostage. Mahlia barely pointed the knife Mortas gave her toward Victory. It was a setup. Victory assumed I would trade the puzzle box to save her. She wasn't being held hostage. She was in on the deal. I'd bet money that she didn't know about Gian-Carlo's grandson, the seer, the reason the Mafusos sought the key.

I dangled the key in my hand, and Victory's eyes bugged. "She solved the puzzle?"

"Yes, I did."

"Who is this woman?" Victory asked.

"Jennifer Cloud is Elma's niece. She seems to have performed a task you could not." Gian-Carlo said to Victory.

She cast her eyes downward and wrapped her arms protectively under her belly.

This wouldn't be too hard. When we made the trade, I could put my plan into action, but I had to make Victory understand she was on the wrong side. I couldn't tell her Caiyan was alive and waiting for her and the baby. General Potts would have my key if I disobeyed a direct order. Caiyan was dead to them. I had to get her away from the Mafusos.

"All right Gian-Carlo, let's get down to business," Jake said.

Gian-Carlo held up his hand. "Oh, I almost forgot, just to have a little insurance."

A resounding, "Bullocks," from Campy came through my earbuds.

Mortas entered the bar tugging a gagged, bound, and struggling Evangeline-Marco's sister-with him. He held a knife to her throat. Her eyes grew wide when she saw us.

"Angel!" Jake and Marco cried out.

Marco looked at Jake, and Gian-Carlo chuckled.

"You asshole," Marco yelled at Gian-Carlo. "She's not part of this."

"I know, that's why I can kill her." Gian-Carlo stood, smiled. "We agreed on three extra people at this meeting, no guns, no hired men. I've kept my side of the bargain."

"Let her go," Jake growled.

"Which one are you referring to?" Gian-Carlo waved a hand at the girls. "The seer, or the woman you've been seeing?"

Marco's eyes widened. *Jake's secret girlfriend.*

Everyone looked at Jake.

"You see, Marco, your boss has been spending a lot of time with your little sister." Gian-Carlo lifted his chin at Marco.

"You son of a bitch!" Marco grabbed Jake by the shirt.

"Not here." Jake kicked Marco's injured leg out from under him. Marco rolled around on the ground in pain, then recovered and stood. The two men squared up against each other.

Mortas snickered.

"Stop it, both of you." I shouted at them.

Marco dropped his fists, and Jake followed suit.

"That was amusing, but I haven't got all day," Gian-Carlo stood, adjusted his jacket, and turned toward me. "Now, you give me the key, and I'll let you choose which one lives."

Victory's head snapped up, and her eyes narrowed at Gian-Carlo. "What do you mean?"

Mahlia held Victory and placed the knife against her pregnant belly.

"They have a seer," I told her. "They don't need you, only your key."

"You can't kill me," Victory said to Mahlia.

"She can bleed you, and who's to say your unborn child will survive a blood bath?" Mortas said to Victory.

"Ya wankers are scum!" Brodie called out.

Jake raised a hand to subdue him.

A wiggle in my backpack reminded me of my plan. I'd have to make a few modifications now there were more cards on the table. Get inside his head, my inner voice reminded me. I prayed Mahlia wouldn't hurt Victory until I could put my plan into action.

"Did you know Caiyan works for the WTF and went back to warn you?" I glared at Victory.

"He couldn't, he's already been..." her words trailed off when the shock of Caiyan's devotion brought tears to her eyes.

"Jennifer Cloud, bring me the seer's key and I will free the woman of your choosing." Gian-Carlo was done talking, and so was I.

I glanced over at Marco and mouthed, "I'm sorry."

"Jen, no." Marco dropped his hands to his side.

"Gian-Carlo, send Angel forward, and I'll give up the key."

I saw Victory stiffen next to Mahlia.

Gian-Carlo nodded at Mortas.

Mortas walked Angel to the center of the room. I met them. He unbound her hands and I hugged her tightly, transferring the Victory key in the process.

"You can't kill Angel or Victory." I moved toward Gian-Carlo. Closer, I needed to get closer. "You see, you're wrong about Angel, she does have the gift."

Gian-Carlo's eyes jerked toward Angel, who was now wrapped in Jake's arms, the Victory key securely fastened around her neck.

Marco eased toward Mahlia.

"I don't believe you!" Gian-Caro seethed. "Marco's grandfather would never have neglected one with the gift."

"You're right. He didn't," Marco said. "You had him killed before she came into her power."

"Kill him!" Gian-Carlo pointed at Jake. He shouted at Mortas, who stood alone and dumbstruck in the middle of the room. "He's the only one that can die here."

"No!" Angel cried out, clinging to Jake.

I rushed toward Gian-Carlo as Mortas rushed toward Jake. Out of the corner of my eye I saw Marco take the knife away from Mahlia. The two goons who were waiting outside burst through the front door. Brodie slowed their assistance to the Mafusos with an attack on their flank.

I jerked to a stop in front of Gian-Carlo.

"What are you going to do to me little girl?" His sharp, cynical eyes almost laughing at me.

"I'm going to hit you where it hurts the most." I lunged at him, grabbed Caiyan's key from around his neck and yanked.

The key came off, dangling between my fingers, my secret talent exposed.

Gian-Carlo's hands flew to his empty neck, and his smug, calculating eyes changed to those of a surprised child. "Impossible."

I drew the necklace close to my chest, hugging the key like I was holding the last piece of the puzzle. The piece that made Caiyan complete. I stepped away from Gian-Carlo.

"Give me the key!" He came for me.

"Tick-Tock!"

Tonto scrambled from my backpack, peeked his head over my shoulder, and I slid the key over his head. He raced up the post next to me.

"Get that animal! It has my key!" Gian-Carlo shook his fist at Tonto.

"Correction, he has Caiyan's key." I clenched my fist and socked the old man right in the kisser. He reeled backward.

One of Gian-Carlo's goons turned and jumped at the raccoon, but Tonto moved higher and hissed at him.

I gave Darryl the signal and he released Daphne. She opened her wings, swooped down, and scooped up Tonto, carrying him safely out the pitching window toward the clickety-click of Darryl's clicker Gertie manipulated in the parking lot of the Grab-N-Gas.

"I've got the key," Gertie sang into our ears. We'd meet her back at the townhouse later.

Victory and Angel were huddled together behind Jake, who had just broken a chair over Mortas.

Marco grabbed Mortas from behind. "He's mine, boss man!"

Jake turned his attention toward Gian-Carlo.

"Gian-Carlo, you're under arrest for extortion and kidnapping a non-traveler." Jake moved toward the old man.

Gian-Carlo backed up a few paces toward Mahlia. He signaled one of his goons.

The burley Italian tossed a canister at Jake. It rolled across the floor and exploded, releasing billows of smoke. Caiyan wasn't the only one using smoke and mirrors.

Brodie tackled the burley henchman as the smoke shrouded the room, allowing Gian-Carlo and Mahlia to exit the building.

"The old man and the twiggy witch are leaving," Ace said.

"Try to stop them." Jake coughed the order to Ace.

"What do you want me to do, hon, throw myself in front of their moving vehicle?"

Four simultaneous yeses blasted into my ear.

"Rude," Ace replied.

"We'll block their exit," Gerry said.

"Scratch that," Ace said. "They didn't get into the car, Mahlia called her vessel. She's taking Gian-Carlo with her."

"Bullocks, they were gone before I could get to them," Campy reported in.

The smoke was so thick I barely discerned Mortas and Marco trading punches. A payback for the goose egg Mortas left him in Gettysburg.

"You about done, Rocky Balboa?" I hollered at Marco.

He dropped a bleeding Mortas on the ground. "You want to take him in?" Marco asked Jake.

Jake pulled a pair of cuffs from his pocket and put them on Mortas. "Your grandfather left you to pay for his crime, again."

Mortas threw a disgusted curse at the three of us.

Marco massaged his knuckles and left us, asking Campy to bring a car for Victory and Angel.

As the smoke lifted, I surveyed the damage to Mama's Double Wide. A few overturned and broken chairs, a cracked window, and a broken bottle of Nue Vodka that Marco had smashed over his combatant's head. Not bad for one of our brawls. Brodie had the two goons unconscious and cuffed by the door. They would spend some time in the local lockup, then be released.

Marco herded the girls out of the bar toward Campy, who swung in driving a bright yellow Hummer.

My work here was done. I looked up at the loft.

Darryl leaned against the railing nodding his head approvingly. He tipped his cowboy hat my direction. "God bless America!"

CHAPTER 25

I entered Caiyan's hospital room. The blinking lights on the bank of monitors and machines to the right of his bed reminded me his injuries were still considered life threatening.

"How's he doing?" I asked the nurse checking his vitals.

"We can't seem to stabilize his blood pressure. He drops so low I expect him to go into cardiac arrest, but then he recovers. His CT scans are normal, and his organs haven't shut down, so we're still hopeful he'll improve. He joins us occasionally, checks the room like he's searching for someone, then goes right back under."

"Maybe this will help." I held his key in my hand. "It's his good luck charm."

The nurse smiled. "It's pretty." She turned to replace the empty bag of saline solution hanging from the IV pole.

I agreed. Clasping it around his neck, the moonstone glowed softly. A brilliant sun sketched into the stone like one a child would color on a drawing from school. Tiny blue diamonds extended in the sun's rays and shimmered against the pallor of Caiyan's skin.

A tuft of chest hair peeked out from the neck of his hospital gown and I remembered how much I loved to run my fingers through the fine curls on his chest, and the way his muscles clenched when I ran my hands over the cut of his sculpted abs, then down to things I may never hold again.

I cursed myself for taking that stroll down memory lane. I had to think of him like Paulina referred to my brother, "in an unavailable way."

The morphine drip attached to his IV pole lay unhooked and powered off.

"Why isn't the morphine running?" I asked the nurse. "Doesn't he need that for pain?"

"He came around long enough to tell the doctor if he didn't remove it, he'd kill him." She laughed softly. "He's still got a lot of fight in there." She tapped her own temple.

The medical staff wasn't in the know about our time travel abilities. They knew we were agents, didn't know for who or what, but they knew keeping us alive was a top secret priority. To the nurse I was Caiyan's concerned partner.

I assumed one day someone would identify the strand of DNA that held our genetic mutation for time travel and create an army of little mercenaries, or Amazon would sell it like eye cream and put the airlines out of business.

The nurse left us alone. I sat with him for a while. The silence made me sad, so I told him what happened at Mama's Double Wide and how Gian-Carlo got away. Smoke and mirrors. The guy was a pro.

I wished he would open his eyes and scold me for getting too close to Gian-Carlo. But he didn't.

"You need to wake up, big guy. There's going to be a little guy or gal soon that's going to need you around."

I didn't know how I fit anymore. I was the odd-shaped puzzle piece that had somehow found its way into the wrong box.

After twenty minutes, the nurse came and ushered me away.

I met Campy coming down the hall toward Caiyan's room.

"How's Uncle Cai?"

"He didn't wake up this time."

Campy's face went from dimpled to alarmed.

"I'm sure it's just the recovery. The doctor said it would take time for his body to repair."

"Thought I'd stop by and see how he's doing. Me mum's worried. I know General Potts wants us to pretend Uncle Cai is dead, but it's going to kill me to lie to me Mum. I mean, are we going to have a funeral and everything?"

Welcome to the WTF, I thought but didn't say out loud. Campy was in enough distress over Caiyan's fake death.

"We still have some time before the WTF decides if an official announcement will be made." Waiting to see if it would be the real deal.

"I dinnae see why he can't work for the WTF, be a defender again."

"I'm sure when he recovers, things will return to normal. The WTF needs him." I gave his arm a comforting squeeze. I doubted things would return to normal but agreed that the WTF needed him. I needed him. Strike that. I wanted him. Victory would need him.

"Is Jake back?" I cringed. When Jake found out I had returned Caiyan's key, he wasn't going to be happy.

Gertie slipped me the key while Jake was handling the fallout from the confrontation with the Mafusos, Angel's questions about her gift, Victory, and Marco. Jake secretly dating Evangeline wouldn't rank high on Marco's list of tolerable things.

I assumed the WTF would hold the key over Caiyan's head if—no when—he recovered. Possibly grounding him until he swore allegiance to the cause. By placing the key around his neck, I allowed him to make the choice.

Campy shifted. "Last I heard, Agent McCoy was at yer house. Something about finding a safe place for Victory to stay until he could figure oot where to place her."

Jeez. Of course he would want her to stay with us. One of her kind. She wasn't used to this time. Things had changed since Aint Elma plopped her down in the past.

I had an extra bedroom, and Jake needed a safe house until the Mafusos calmed down and decided to play fair. They'd use Mortas as a pawn to keep Gian-Carlo from blowing a gasket, and in the mean-time, I'd live with the mother of Caiyan's child.

My mantra started to play.

"Jen." Campy's voice scratched the record.

"Sorry, what did you say?"

"I said, ye should get some rest." Campy's subtle brogue made my heart ache for Caiyan. "Uncle Cai will be up and aroond in no time. He's tough."

I hoped so, because raising a child might be his most difficult chal-lenge to date.

I said my good-byes to Campy and headed home to face my own challenges.

287

CHAPTER 26

$\mathcal{I}$ slid the glass door open and met the chaos in my house head on.

Marco leaned against the living room wall, arms across his chest, listening to a lecture from Angel. She had the right to be mad. When I first met her, I guessed she had the gift. When we found the Sleigh key in Berlin that belonged to Marco's family, it confirmed my suspicion, but it was Marco's choice to keep it from her. I didn't want to rock the boat.

Jake was on the phone pacing in my kitchen. He saw me and held up a finger.

I couldn't gage his mood. I couldn't tell if someone at base had called him and ratted me out. Was he on the phone with headquarters discovering I had returned Caiyan's key? Time would tell.

Victory, Brodie, and Gertie sat in the den. Victory's eyes were wide and curious, and I knew they were filling her in on all the things she'd missed in the last ten years. She'd been dropped into a fast world filled with technology even I didn't understand.

I walked over and sat down in the chair next to her, extended my hand. "Hi, I'm Jennifer Cloud, Elma's great-niece. We didn't formally meet after the um…Mafuso thing."

Her amber eyes held an intelligent sparkle, and she wore a hand stitched summer maternity dress that I assumed Mahlia had found for her. Her dark hair was piled on top of her head with a matching scarf to hold it in place. She was beautiful.

She took my hand and held it. A soft tingle fluttered up my arm like the wings of a butterfly tickling my skin.

"So, you're the one." She smiled at me with perfect pink lips.

"Yeah, I'm the one who opened the box and found your key." I unlatched my hand from hers and the butterfly massage stopped.

Gertie slapped her palms together and interlocked her fingers. "Wait until you hear this!" My cousin was almost giddy.

"Hear what?"

Victory clasped hands over her large belly and gazed into my eyes. "You're the one who ends this."

"Ends what?" I lifted an eyebrow at her. Pretty but a little cuckoo.

"I had a vision when I was in Gettysburg. A woman with blond hair and Elma's eyes would save me from the war and return my key. I didn't understand the raccoon at first, but I do now." She reached over and I realized Tonto was sitting next to her in the chair.

She scratched him behind the ears, and he looked up at her adoringly.

"I've seen you in many visions, and now that I have my key back, you're as clear as ever. You end us."

"Can you believe it?" Gertie continued before I could answer her question. "You're the one who finds the King's key."

"Say what?"

Victory threw her head back and gave a throaty laugh. "You end this, the gift, this genetic monstrosity that we have."

"Hey, I kinda like zipping over to see Gertie," Brodie said, taking a sip from the bottle of beer he held. The amber liquid made my mouth water, and after the seer's visions, I wished I had one, too.

"How do I do that?" I finally asked her.

"I'm only a seer, but I see you with many keys, and I see the king's vessel." She waved her hand in the air. "Maybe with time and normal hormones, I'll be able to see more."

"Maybe you shouldn't tell me." I bit into my lower lip.

Jake ended his call and joined us in the den. He gave Angel a stern look. "You shouldn't have given Victory the key, but now that you have…" he turned his attention to Victory. "General Potts requests you to be inducted into the WTF as soon as possible."

Victory seemed taken aback. I didn't blame her—with a baby on the way, why would she want to risk her life? Besides, when Caiyan wore the Thunder key he was all aboot the woman should stay at home and raise the bairns.

Toches told me the Thunder key enhances your desires. Maybe I wasn't supposed to be with him. Maybe this was how it ended for us.

"Jen, I need to speak with you." Jake tilted his head toward the back yard.

I followed him outside. He turned and stared at me, hands on hips.

Yep, he knew.

"Seems like Angel's not the only one returning keys to their owners. You returned the key to McGregor." It was more of a statement than a question.

"Did headquarters call you?" The tattletales.

"No, when Gertie told me she gave you the key, I knew where you were headed." His big brown eyes held an understanding I hadn't seen in a long time.

"It belongs to him," I said. "He put his life in danger to save Victory. She's an important piece to our puzzle."

"I agree; she sees things that will help us. General Potts is going to have my ass, and probably ground you for returning McGregor's key. He wanted a carrot to dangle."

"Do you believe Victory's vision that I unlock the secret to the King's key?"

"I don't know what to think. I've got an agent who was shot over one hundred and fifty years ago, the Mafuso attorney breathing down my neck, my girlfriend's brother threatening bodily harm, and a traveler who just skipped ten years of her life. My system's on overload."

"Can I help?" I knew the answer, but thought offering sounded nice.

"Are you OK with Victory staying here for a few months?"

"A few months?"

"I need to find a safe place for her to live until we get things worked out. She'll need someone to help her acclimate to this time."

By things, was he referring to Caiyan's recovery? If she stayed a few months, the baby would be here. I wasn't sure I could hang.

"I guess so." Did I say that?

"You're great! Have I told you that lately?"

"No, you've been keeping secrets." I frowned up at him.

His dimples winked out at me. "No more secrets. Angel and I have been dating for about six months."

"Did you know she had the gift?"

"Not a clue." He grinned wide. "But that explains a few unanswered questions."

Jeez. Was I ready to hear about Jake in love with another woman? It was all over his face.

"I didn't tell you or anyone else because I wasn't sure how to handle Marco's wrath, and I felt like a hypocrite. I was always on everyone's case about dating a coworker. I even gave Gertie grief for hooking up with Brodie. I was a real piece of shit."

"Don't be so hard on yourself. We ignored you."

Jake dimpled at me.

Angel slid the door open. "Can I come out?"

Jake motioned for her to join us, and his face softened when he looked her way.

She walked toward us. Her dark hair rippled down her back in a mass of glorious waves. A playful smile spread her cute button nose that resembled her mother's, but the rest of her appearance screamed her Italian father. She was the dark to Marco's light; however, based on her perky attitude, he got the quick temperament of the Italian side.

Her dark lashes fluttered at Jake. This girl had it bad, and I was a little envious of the secret love affair these two shared.

She wrapped her arms around Jake's middle, stood on her toes to accept a kiss from him. They made a cute couple. I hoped Marco would accept his sister dating the boss.

"Did you talk Marco out of murdering me in my sleep?" Jake asked Angel.

"He's agreed for a trial run, as long as I stay away from the WTF."

Jake chewed on his lip. It was his nervous tell. He didn't want her there either. Another woman he cared for under the command of the gift.

"Did you agree?" he asked her.

"I told him I'd think about it. I mean, a girl has got to make her own decisions."

I smiled. Angel was going to keep my best friend and her brother on their toes.

After Jake and Angel left, I cornered Marco in the kitchen.

"This was a crazy moon cycle." I chose a coveted beer from the fridge and offered him one.

He accepted and twisted off the cap. "Yeah, I thank the stars it's closed and over."

"Jake's a good guy," I said, opening my beer and glancing at him for his reaction.

"I know." He took a long pull from his beer.

"Are you going to give Angel her key?"

"Not if I can help it," he sighed. "I probably won't be able to keep her from it."

"You've been protecting her for a long time."

"Maybe it's time I stopped keeping secrets from her. She deserves to know about her grandfather. The good and the bad."

I clinked bottles with him. We leaned against the kitchen counters and drank in silence for a few minutes.

"How's McGregor?" he asked.

"The nurse told me he's not doing so good. She said his blood pressure keeps dropping, and he hasn't been awake for more than ten minutes."

"That was a pretty bad hit he took in Gettysburg."

I forced the swig of beer down my throat. "I was mad at his desertion, but I understand why he had to stay close to the Mafusos. If they knew Victory had visions of the King's key, Gian-Carlo never would have let her go." And there was the kid thing.

"Sometimes we can't see the forest for the trees."

"Amen." I looked up into his crystal blue eyes and wished my heart did the trippy thing for Marco that it did when I was within a hundred feet of Caiyan.

Marco finished the beer and tossed it in the recycle bin.

"Do you want to stay for dinner?" I asked him. "We're going to introduce Victory to Chipotle."

"No, I've got to bolt."

"Because you have a date?"

"Yeah, jealous?"

"A little."

"Good." He pulled me in and hugged me tight, kissing the top of my head.

My inner voice reminded me about Caiyan's little secret growing in the other room and encouraged me to take Marco upstairs and relieve him of his t-shirt and jeans.

Another time, I told her. I needed Caiyan to share his secrets before I could move on and open my heart to someone else.

I INVITED Darryl over for Chipotle.

Since the club had been the scene of a CIA shakedown involving a notorious crime family and needed repairs, he had the night off.

Darryl didn't know Victory missed the last decade, but he entertained her with stories about things he'd come across in his business as a picker.

I called the hospital at Gitmo to check on Caiyan while we waited for the food. The nurse told me his blood pressure had stabilized and he was doing much better. She thought his lucky charm was the real deal. I knew it was.

We sat around the coffee table eating burrito bowls and listened to how Darryl manipulates steel remnants into funky art animals. Ragina breezed in through the front door.

"Thanks for knocking," I said. With the Mafusos on the mad, I needed to remind Gertie to lock the door.

"Whoa," Darryl said.

Ragina hovered over us in designer pink cowboy boots and matching sequined cowboy hat. 90210 had gone all out sparkly cowgirl.

"I don't know how you did it." Ragina tossed her photos on the table and scowled in my direction.

"Did what?" I asked her.

Brodie picked up one of the photos and his face lit up.

"The owner of Mama's Double Wide rejected my photos. Thanks for doctoring them up with your Photoshop," Ragina said.

"What are you talking about?" Gertie leaned in toward Brodie to examine the photo. Her mouth formed a giant O.

Ragina plucked a photo off the table and shoved it into my hands. The black and white reproduction of a vintage photo showed a group of doctors standing next to an amputation table. Dr. Seuss minus the wig and mustache stood in the background.

"That man sort of looks like me," I chuckled. I vaguely recalled a group of men gathered in front of the medical tent where I had stopped to watch Caiyan disappear into the woods. I didn't realize they were posing for a picture.

Brodie flipped his photo over to show us. A bleary-eyed Gertie stood with Marco in front of General Lee's tent.

"How do you explain that one?" Ragina asked.

"Coincidence?" I shrugged.

"The owner of Mama's Double Wide told me he couldn't pay me for photos of the karaoke queen and her bar-dancing sidekick."

"Look who's the sidekick now." Gertie beamed at me.

"I'll be your sidekick anytime," I said to Gertie.

"You bet your sweet ass." Everyone laughed, causing Ragina to storm out of the house.

"I'd better go after her. She'll need to release all that pent-up hostility, and I know just the guy to help her." Darryl stood, a determined grin across his face.

"Good luck, mate." Brodie gave Darryl a fist bump.

Darryl thanked us for the dinner and excitement, then followed Ragina's trail.

"I don't suppose ya have any pent-up hostility you'd like to set free?" Brodie asked Gertie.

"There might be a strong agitation I need to get off my chest after you help me clean up the kitchen."

Gertie stood and gathered our empty plates.

Brodie flashed his million-dollar smile and followed Gertie into the kitchen, leaving me alone with Victory."

"I like him," Victory said, waving a hand at Brodie as he disappeared into the kitchen. "I can see why Caiyan is friends with him."

"Yeah, Brodie's a sweetheart."

"I can also see why Caiyan has a thing for you, too."

My eyebrows shot upwards.

"Angel told me." Victory adjusted herself in the chair, so she sat facing me. "She also told me her brother has it bad for you, but you've always been with Caiyan."

"We broke up before he joined the Mafusos. He never told me about you."

"I was the WTF's shameful secret. Elma tried to help, but in the end, she sided with the politics instead of the cause, and dumped me in the past."

"It's hard for me to believe my aint Elma would do that."

"I messed up in Salem. Almost got myself hung. Kishin saved me, but Elma saw the whole thing."

"Elma was there, I saw her." I bolted upright. "I didn't realize it was her until now."

"You were there, too?" Victory looked surprised. "I guess you saw. I was only trying to scare the idiots so they wouldn't hang all those innocent people, but I went too far. Got myself arrested."

"You would have changed history."

"Yeah, for the better."

"Sometimes changing the past causes more problems than you'd think." I pictured the boy I saved, and Caiyan hovering near death.

"When the WTF found out I was traveling without their permission and saving people in the past, they banished me."

"How did they get your key?"

"The boss man at the time held a gun to Caiyan's head and threatened to kill him. It's the reason a non-traveler is in charge. I didn't think they would kill him, but it wasn't a chance I was going to take. Actually," she thought for a minute, "when Caiyan had that gun to his head was the first time I saw the vision. The one where you find the King's key. I told Elma about the vision and she dumped me in the past."

"Aint Elma hid you to save you," I said. She was talking smack about my family. "If the Mafusos or the WTF gets their hands on the King's key, it could be a game changer."

"She told me it was for my own safety. She didn't realize I'd run away from the family she had left me with and get captured by a bastard of a man. He made me a slave on his cotton plantation. Now there's some back breaking work. Dawn to dusk with overseers eyeing me like I was some kind of mule."

"How did Caiyan find you?"

"He found Boon." She smiled and rubbed her belly. "Boon was a freed slave. See, your aint Elma left me with a family in Texas, thought she'd fix things back home then come get me before the war broke out. Boon worked for them. They didn't believe in owning slaves."

She took a drink of her water. "I was stupid. I thought, since I'm here, why not go help the Underground Railroad? Be a part of something that has meaning. That would show the WTF I could still fight for my cause even without my key." She sighed. "That's how I got captured."

"Caiyan spent every moon cycle meeting up with Boon and they'd search the plantations from Texas to Georgia looking for me. They became close friends."

"I'm sorry he was killed."

"Me too. They found me in Louisiana about six month ago. Caiyan told me he'd be back for me the next moon cycle, but he never came."

"I guess you'll have to adjust to living in this time," I said to Victory.

"From what I've seen so far, it looks pretty good. You've got phones that fit in your pockets, cars that practically drive themselves, great takeout, and thousands of movies on the TV. I think I'll adjust fine."

"Can I ask you something?" I didn't want to be nosy, but I had to know. The secret was picking at a scab. "Why did you leave with Toches and break Caiyan's heart?"

"I doubt I broke Caiyan's heart. He doesn't seem to let anyone or anything near his heart. It's shatterproof."

She made a good point, but I disagreed. "Don't you want him to see the baby?"

She looked at me funny. "He can if he wants. He's not good with kids, you know?"

I'd never seen him with kids. We never talked about it.

She rubbed her expansive belly. "This girl's sure going to miss her daddy."

"It doesn't have to be that way. I'd never break up a family."

"Are you okay?" She cocked an eyebrow at me.

"Yeah, I just wanted you to know that I won't get in the way. After Caiyan recovers, y'all can see how things work out. I'm not sure he's marriage material." That might have been more my fault. I was the one who didn't want to move in with him. Both of us had commitment issues.

"Oh, he'll be mad at me for ditching him, but I knew Toches could take me home. I saw it in a vision. I wasn't sure about the time or place, but I knew Caiyan would be here. And I knew you would rescue me from the Mafusos. It's the reason I led them to believe I was on their side. When I saw you at the club, I knew my vision was correct. When this baby comes, I want you to be her godmother."

"Uhm. I can't do that. I mean. I'm going to give y'all some space so you and Caiyan can...you know. Be together."

Victory threw her head back and laughed. "Do you think Caiyan is the father of this baby?"

I nodded slowly. Did I miss something?

"The guy has a heart of gold, but we've been friends too long for me to go down that road with him. Thomas is this baby's daddy."

"Thomas?" I asked with raised eyebrows.

"Yeah, Thomas Boon." She placed her hand over her heart. "God, I loved that man. We didn't always get on so well, but I loved him."

"The man who died at Gettysburg."

"Yeah. It's Caiyan's fault we got married."

"Caiyan's fault?"

"When Caiyan and Thomas finally found me, he..." she paused, by the look on her face she was deciding if she would offend me. "Let's just say he had a good time with the plantation owner's daughter."

I rolled my eyes. "It was before me."

She blew out a short breath. "The moon cycle closed, and Caiyan promised he'd return the next cycle with a transporter to bring me home. Left Boon there to work the farm. The next thing I know, the owner's daughter's accusing me of sleeping with Caiyan and that was punishable by a real beating."

Her eyes went misty and I handed her a tissue from the box on the table. "Sorry, the hormones make me so emotional. Thomas gave up his freedom and took the beating in my place. I married him the next day, in a small grove of apple trees. Then the war broke out and the owner sold me to Miss Maggie. That's how I ended up in Gettysburg."

"Did Boon find you in Gettysburg?"

"Yes," she wiped at her eyes. "Boon ran away from the plantation and found me. After that, we fought together to make sure the Underground Railroad helped as many men, women and children make it to freedom as we could. When I got pregnant, Thomas wanted to stop and use the Railroad to gain our freedom. But I had work to do at Gettysburg to make sure the South didn't win that war."

"But you knew the North won, right?"

"Did they?" she cocked an inquisitive eyebrow at me.

Had the South won the war in another timeline? I paused, considered. "They won because you gave the Union Army General Lee's plans sewn into the lining of the Rebel coats, and because you warned Mead about the final attack on the center. It's a loop."

"Yes, I believe the North won not only because of me, because of Boon and all the brave men and women who fought. You can't look at it any other way. Boon was killed fighting a noble cause. And I'll make sure his daughter knows him well."

A tear slipped down her cheek.

Her eyes shined and I placed my hand over hers.

"I'm sorry he died."

"I am too, but we fought for a good cause, together."

If her visions were correct, maybe she was supposed to be here.

"You and Caiyan have known each other a long time?" I asked her.

"Since we were kids. The three of us, me, Caiyan, and Kishin sort of grew up together. Our grandparents were, let's say, in the business." She dropped her gaze to her hands resting on her stomach.

"Kishin knew the WTF banished you?" I asked her.

"He did, but he didn't know where. I imagine it drove him nuts." She stifled a yawn.

"Let me show you to Eli's old room."

She pushed up from the chair, and I showed her the room and adjoining bathroom.

"Thanks for letting me stay," she said.

"No problem." I handed her a set of clean towels. "Stay as long as you need."

"Gian-Carlo was pretty mad when he found out I didn't have the key." She turned to move into the room then paused and turned back around toward me. "Who'd have thought Elma would put it in the box. It was the only thing I couldn't see. I hope nothing bad happens to Kishin."

"Me, too." And I meant it.

CHAPTER 27

*A*fter getting Victory situated in Eli's old room, I drug myself upstairs. My legs and eyelids were equally heavy. Part of me wanted to lateral travel to Gitmo and sit with Caiyan, but I needed a shower and sleep. Figuring out that man's secrets wore me to the bone.

I took a long, hot shower and felt better. I sent Eli a text letting him know my work for the WTF had concluded, I was home, but I would need one more day before I returned to work. There was one more duck that needed tending. Caiyan.

Eli offered plans to meet for dinner tomorrow night.

I replied, *Pizza, my treat.*

He responded back with *I'm there, glad you're home safe.*

I sent him a tired emoji, plugged my phone into the cable on my nightstand, and slipped between my sheets.

A gentle breeze blew in from my open window, ruffling the curtains. I thought about Daphne and her early morning breakfast routine, considered closing the window, but the fresh air smelled nice with the hint of summer rain looming.

Temperatures in the Texas summer rarely dropped into the open window category, so I'd risk having breakfast with Daphne.

I stared at the ceiling, scrolling through the events during the moon cycle and ending with the Mafuso mayhem. Between losing the general, conniving my way through Gettysburg, almost losing Caiyan, keeping Sam on the right path, saving Victory, and faking out Gian-Carlo to snag Caiyan's key, I felt like I had lived a year in five days. This transporter was exhausted.

Jake got the green light from General Potts to approve travelers on a case by case basis, with the defenders and the transporters allowed to have input on who travels for each jump. I'd won a huge victory for the transporters, and Ace would still be my friend.

He was on a date with Marvin, wedding planner extraordinaire. I hoped it went well. He deserved to find love.

What about my love? My gut told me Caiyan still had secrets he hadn't shared. Did I want to continue a relationship filled with lies and secrets? At least he wasn't going to be a father. My inner voice reminded me that was my bad. I assumed he was the baby's daddy.

He didn't marry Mahlia, although he would have married her to gain his key. Maybe.

Where did that leave me? Alone eating the cake. We still had a lot to work out. I'd go see him tomorrow, and hopefully he'd be sitting up in bed flirting with the nurses.

I yawned and pulled my new, ruffled duvet from Anthropologie under my chin. I liked the soft, girly texture of the bed cover. It was comfortable, like this part of my life.

Being a chiropractic assistant and a secret agent wasn't so bad. My life was filled with good friends I considered family, and family I considered good friends.

Aint Elma knew the most important thing in life is to surround yourself with loved ones. People you could count on, people who loved you, people a girl could share secrets with. I had to agree that the woman was wickedly wise.

A light rain began a tap dance against the glass on my French door. Lightning flashed outside. I did the count thing and waited for the thunder, but it didn't come. The Texas weather, summer storms in particular, were so unpredictable, exactly like the men in my life.

I cuddled deeper into my burrow and drifted to sleep.

A buzzing noise woke me. My phone. Jake's name flashed across my screen along with the time. It was after five in the morning.

"Everything OK?" I managed to mumble into the phone.

"Good morning." Jake's voice sounded husky on the other end of the line.

"It's still dark outside, technically it's still night."

"It's after five, and I have some news you're going to want to hear."

"What news?" I propped up on an elbow.

"McGregor's gone."

My heart stopped for a full minute. I bolted upright in bed and sat rigid, preparing myself.

"Jen, did you hear me?"

"What do you mean he's…g-g-gone?" My voice quivered.

"Shit Jen, I didn't mean dead gone, I meant, he skated the hospital." He sighed. "I'm sorry, I'm tired and I didn't think."

"But the nurse told me he wasn't stable."

The pause meant he ran a hand through his hair before he continued. "He just got up and left. Took out his IVs and vanished in his vessel. I imagine the key played a big part. The moon cycle is closed, so Pickles can't track him. I wanted to let you know in case he comes your way."

A shadow crossed my balcony.

"Thanks, I'll let you know if he shows."

"See you soon."

I disconnected and slipped from my bed.

"Holy shite!" The sound of shoes skittered across the tile on my balcony.

I flung open the French door and flipped on the overhead light. Caiyan stood outside, his face flush with surprise.

"What are you doing?" I crossed my arms over my chest and leaned against the door hinge.

"I need to see ye, but the biggest fucking spider I've ever seen was guarding yer door." I looked down and a furry black spider sprinted across my bare feet and into my bedroom.

I jumped into Caiyan's arms, then squinted at the spider. It wore a little vest.

"I think that's Chuck."

"Who's Chuck?"

"Darryl's pet spider."

"Who's Darryl?" Caiyan's jaw clenched.

"My cousin. He moved in next door."

His body relaxed and he pulled me in tight.

"I missed ye, Sunshine." He snuggled his face in my hair and inhaled.

I wiggled away from his intoxicating scent and shushed the spider out the door. It made a quick scurry over the balcony railing and disappeared into Darryl's backyard.

"Can I come inside?"

I waved my hand, and he walked past me. His hair and clothes were damp from the rain. He'd stolen a pair of scrubs with a doctor's name embroidered on the right chest pocket.

"How long have you been out there, Doctor Goldberg?" I cocked an eyebrow at him.

"A few hours. I called up to ye, like Romeo, but ye didnae answer. So, I came up. When I gained my nerve to wake ye, I noticed the spider."

Jeez. How could I be mad at the guy?

"Aren't you supposed to be in the hospital recovering from a gunshot wound?"

"Aye, when I woke and had my key, I knew you were the one who returned it to me."

"So, you just yanked out the IVs and vanished in the night. I bet the nurses were beside themselves trying to find you."

"'Twas a bit dodgy. I had to find clothes. I couldnae show up at yer doorstep with my bare bum flapping in the breeze."

I laughed at the image.

"Weel, I couldnae keep lying in the hospital bed wondering if Marco was here keeping yer sheets warm, as he put it."

303

His eyes held questions, and I thought maybe he deserved to suffer, a little.

"You're right about the key. I was the one who returned it to you," I said.

"How did ye get it?"

I explained the situation with the Mafusos. A grin tugged at his lips. "Ye did all that?"

"I did."

"I dinnae like ye being so close to Gian-Carlo. He may be an old man, but he's naugh a nice one. He'll play by the rules in the present, but he willnae be nice when we travel back in time. And now that he knows aboot yer gift, he'll be ruthless to turn ye to the dark side."

"Does that mean you're going to stay with the WTF?"

"If that's where ye are."

He started toward me, and I put a hand up.

He stopped.

"I dinnae handle this situation weel, Sunshine, but I'd like to explain things, shed some light on my actions."

I gestured to my comfy chair.

He shook his head. "I'm better if I stand."

I crossed my arms over my chest and sat down on the edge of my bed.

"When I was a wee lad, I had the worst crush on Victory. I thought she would've been the one I married. You know, young love."

I raised my eyebrows at him. Not the words I wanted to hear, but I understood. I had felt the same way about Jake.

"I beg ye to jest hear me oot."

Him begging, I liked. "Continue."

"She told me she had a vision of me opening the gate to the King's key. My gift. The one ye dinnae know of, is that I'm the gatekeeper."

"What's that?"

"I've no idea. She also told me a woman with blond hair would drive me crazy, steal my heart, and end me from time traveling."

"You didn't want to give up your gift," I said.

"Rattled me to my very core. I was afraid. If a blond woman came near me, I ran."

"You didn't run from me."

"Naugh exactly, but I've been keeping a lid on my feelings for ye."

"How did you meet Victory?"

"My grandfather raised Victory since she was a wee lassie. Her parents died early in her young life. When he died, we were taken to the WTF. I met Elma, and I thought she was the one who would end me. And then Victory was taken away, and I was lost. That day in Gettysburg, Elma saved me.

"Maybe it's not me who ends you."

"Oh 'tis you." He moved closer, standing an inch away, his spicy scent causing my toes to curl inside my fuzzy socks. He tucked his index finger under my chin and lifted it to meet his eyes. "You drive me completely insane. Yer all I thought aboot while I lay in the hospital, helpless. If I lost ye in Gettysburg, it wouldae ended me. I don't care if I never travel again, as long as I have you."

I turned away. "If you want me, then I want to know everything. No more secrets."

"I'll tell ye whatever ye want to know."

"What did Aint Elma mean by you're responsible for my grandfather's death?'

"When I was first brought to the WTF, she sent me back on a mission. An unauthorized travel." He lowered his eyes. "'Twas a time in the past when her brother John." He paused, then lifted his eyes and they met mine. "Yer grandfather, died. She wanted me to change history, to warn him."

"She was trying to change the past."

He confirmed with a soft nod. "My grandfather was also there. He was stealing a key, and John was the agent assigned to stop him. It hadnae been long since my grandfather's death. I couldnae find the nerve to go against my grandfather, so I didnae warn John. I failed on purpose, and he died."

"Elma was right," I said. "His wasn't your life to save. You can't change the past because the past bites back."

"Aye, I feel it in my gut, literally."

"Why did you almost marry Mahlia?"

"'Twas naugh legal. I knew Toches was the priest, but she didnae. Besides…" He paused, lifting his gaze and held mine as if he wanted to pour all his thoughts into my soul.

A strong sense of hope, respect, and love whooshed through me. I'd read him without making contact.

"She's naugh the one I want to marry."

My insides clenched. Was I ready? Did I want to marry Caiyan?

"Sunshine, I want to marry you, but considering ye jest looked at the balcony like ye might jump off, I'm no asking ye now." He pulled me into his arms. "But know one day, when the time is right." He glanced at the clock on my nightstand. "And it's not five in the morning, I'm going to ask, and I hope ye weel say yes."

I encircled his neck with my arms.

"Maybe one day, when the time is right." I arched a playful eyebrow at him. "And by the way, it's After 5."

"Yeah?" He tucked a loose hair behind my ear. Pulled me in close and kissed me. "Maybe I should remind ye why I'm the one to be warmin' yer sheets."

"You can try."

He scooped me up. A grimace shot across his face.

"Should you be lifting me in your condition?" I asked, alarmed.

"I'm going to do more than that to ye, lassie. Thanks to ye, I've the rest of my life to spend time with the woman I love."

The End

If you loved reading about Jennifer Cloud, it would mean the world to me if you would leave a review at https://www.amazon.com/After-5-Janet-Leigh-ebook/dp/B0836GPMYQ

ACKNOWLEDGMENTS

- Thank you to The Gettysburg Campaign by Edwin B. Coddington.
- The Gettysburg National Military Park Rangers.

For more information about Gettysburg or if you would like to donate to help preserve our national parks and historic battlefields, check out the links below.

https://www.battlefields.org/give
https://www.nationalparks.org/

~Yours in health and history,
Janet

ABOUT THE AUTHOR

 Janet Leigh, a B.R.A.G. Medallion Honoree, was born in Garland, Texas, and has remained a loyal Texas native her entire life. She combined her love of storytelling and her archive of crazy family stories and wrote the Jennifer Cloud series. Today, she is a full-time chiropractor and acupuncturist who splits her time between seeing patients and working on her next Jennifer Cloud novel.

Visit JanetLeighbooks.com for updates, excerpts and all that extra stuff!

Find her at:

f facebook.com/janetleighbooks

🐦 twitter.com/@janetleighbooks

📷 instagram.com/Janetleighbooks

ALSO BY JANET LEIGH

THE JENNIFER CLOUD NOVELS

The Shoes Come First

Dress 2 Impress

3 Ways to Wear Red

In Style 4 Now

Made in the USA
Monee, IL
16 February 2020

21874607R00185